VM

PRAISE FOR *SOME DAYS THERE'S PIE*

"A remarkable tale of a special friendship . . . told here with a refreshing new voice. . . . [Ruth] could be a distant family relation of Huck Finn, who went looking for the meaning of life."
—*The Atlanta Journal-Constitution*

"The Dixie equivalent of Sherwood Anderson's *Winesburg, Ohio* . . . Whether you're home or abroad, the warmth and charm of these women's lives will transform your beach grass into kudzu and expand that horizon stretching out in front of you."
—*Newsday* (A Summer's Best Read)

"Catherine Landis subtly develops the relationship between these women at different stages of life. Ruth and Rose do the best they can amid disappointment, failed dreams, and acts of forgiveness."
—*Southern Living*

"Extraordinarily engaging . . . A new voice for Southern America that will most likely find a ready market at the beginning of the twenty-first century."
—*Tampa Tribune*

"Catherine Landis's sweet Southern tale, about a young woman's unlikely friendship with the town eccentric, is the perfect beach read."
—*Marie Claire* (10 Best Summer Reads)

"Uplifting."
—*Woman's Day*

"Chock full of colorful characters . . . This is an outstanding first novel full of insight, pathos, and what Rose might call 'hard sayings.' Like her character Rose, Landis is digging for the truth, and she nails it time and time again. She writes with confidence and with the rhythm of springtime breezes off the coastal sounds. Someone has called Landis the next major Southern female writer.' Move over, Lee Smith, Gail Godwin, and Fannie Flagg; you've got company."
—*The Roanoke Times*

"Vivid . . . The author [writes with an] admirably individual style."
—*Dallas Morning News*

"Catherine Landis fills her book with wryly sympathetic views of small-town life, its little charms and its little evils."
—*Augusta Magazine*

"Both Ruth and Rose are stunning characters, drawing on the traditions of genre mavens Lee Smith and Jill McCorkle. Landis's Rose brings dignity to a class of older Southern woman usually depicted as porch-dwelling gossips. . . . A treat. One can only hope that there's more of this talent waiting to be served."　　—*Macon Telegraph*

"Landis's writing is deft, and often the book surprises with its insight and wisdom. This is a solid debut novel."
—*The Winston-Salem Journal*

"Witty and charming . . . Ruth, Rose, and their menagerie don't escape life's harsh realities . . . but they do manage to offset them, with connection, with defiance, and sometimes with quiet acceptance. . . . Redeeming."　　—*The Hippo Press*

"Catherine Landis's debut novel is a sweet, sassy, and tart story. . . . The narrative voice is warm, gentle, and funny, with just enough bite to keep the story's sadness at bay. . . . A memorable novel of friendship based on love, yet free from expectation, obligation, or a shared history."　　—*Bookpage*

"Alternately wise, poignant, droll, and sassy . . . Landis does a fine job of rendering these memorable characters. . . . [Landis] could take off as a voice of the modern but eternally quirky South."
—*Publishers Weekly*

HARVEST

ALSO BY CATHERINE LANDIS

Some Days There's Pie

HARVEST

CATHERINE LANDIS

THOMAS DUNNE BOOKS / ST. MARTIN'S PRESS ♏ NEW YORK

THOMAS DUNNE BOOKS.
An imprint of St. Martin's Press.

Grateful acknowledgment is made for permission to reprint the following:

Excerpt from *The Wild Birds*. Copyright © 1985, 1986 Wendell Berry.
Excerpt from "First Snow," from *American Primitive* by Mary Oliver. Copyright © 1978, 1979, 1980, 1981, 1982, 1983 by Mary Oliver. By permission of Little, Brown and Company, Inc.

www.stmartins.com

Book design by Jonathan Bennett

ISBN 0-312-28723-2
EAN 978-0312-28723-8

First Edition: October 2004

10 9 8 7 6 5 4 3 2 1

For Bruce

I even thought once that the way things ought to be was pretty much the way they were. I thought things would go on here always the way they had been. The old ones would die when their time came, and the young ones would learn and come on. And the crops would be put out and got in, and the stock looked after, and things took care of. I thought, even, that the longer it went on the better it would get. People would learn; they would see what had been done wrong, and they would make it right.

—from *The Wild Birds*
by Wendell Berry

and though the questions
that have assailed us all day
remain—not a single
answer has been found—
walking out now
into the silence and the light
under the trees,
and through the fields,
feels like one.

—from the poem "First Snow"
by Mary Oliver

FLOOD

ONE

ARLISS

The story of the farm on Bearpen Lane, how it was won then lost, begins not there, but twenty-seven miles away on another farm in the community of New Hope, where Arliss was born. He remembered one morning in particular when he woke to the sound of a skillet scraping across the top of the woodstove, mad at himself for not waking earlier, even though it was still dark outside. A mockingbird was singing in the walnut tree, and, he told himself, he should have heard that bird. He crawled over his sister Rosemary, who would take her time waking up, and pulled on his pants and tied them together and climbed down the ladder and walked toward the front door as quietly as he knew how. He had wanted to get outside before his mother started breakfast, but the best he could do now was keep from catching her eye. If she stopped him, she would tell him to sit down and eat a corn cake, then she would make him help Rosemary bring up water or else hunt for mouse nests, which she stored in a basket and used for tinder. Arliss did not mind the work. Already at six years old he was a harder worker than Rosemary, because he did not lose himself in daydreams, and Rosemary did, so it was not the work he minded, but the likelihood that he would not do it right and be rewarded with a willow switch that carved thin, straight lines of blood across the backs of his legs. Later, when he went to school, his teacher would turn him over a desk and paddle him and the other boys when they fought or cussed or carved their names into their desks, but she never used a switch because, she said, "A switch'll draw blood, and a paddle won't." Arliss took from this that his teacher was afraid of blood.

So Arliss kept his eyes on the floor as he crossed the room and slipped out the front door to the porch, where he waited for his father. There were mornings when his father would come out and put his hand on top of Arliss's head, and say, *You stay here with your mother,* but more and more he did not say it, and that was what Arliss waited for. If his father did not say anything, Arliss would be free to follow him down the road with nothing worse than a Bible verse from his mother shouted at his back, most often Proverbs: *Foolishness is bound in the heart of a child; but the rod of correction shall drive it far from him.*

Arliss was the only living son of Joseph and Marion Greene. His two sisters were much older than he was, Rosemary by ten years, and Virginia by twelve. There had been three other children born in the years between Rosemary and Arliss, but Arliss did not find out about them until the TVA men came to dig up their graves.

Arliss's father, Joseph, grew corn with his brothers, Luke and Roy, on land both their father and grandfather had farmed, but the land was so leached out and rutted now, they were lucky to get twenty-five bushels an acre when once it had yielded ninety (or so the old stories claimed). Luke, also called "Rooster Man" because of his red face and a cowlick that stood his hair up in the middle of his forehead, was the oldest of the Greene brothers and lived with his wife Belle in the original farmhouse. Arliss could not see it from where he stood on the porch, because his daddy's place was farther up the mountain from there, but he could see his uncle Roy's cabin, which was next door. He remembered when it was built, soon after Roy came back from Detroit saying there was no work anywhere, and he was not born to spend his days standing in a line for food. The cabin was one small room with four walls and a tin roof, but it suited Roy, who was the youngest of the three Greene brothers and did not have a family yet.

Standing on the porch, waiting for his father, Arliss could tell that Roy had left already for the barn. He listened to the mockingbird in the top of the walnut tree and watched the sun come up over Spinner Ridge. His father did not say anything when he came out of the house but handed Arliss a corn cake and walked off the porch. Arliss followed, and this morning the only voice he heard behind him was Rosemary singing as she walked to the spring. The barn was behind Luke's house, and they headed there.

Arliss could not keep up with his father. On the road down the mountain, Joseph tended to walk ahead, sometimes disappearing completely around a curve, and Arliss would find himself alone. He imagined his father forgot he was there, because he never stopped or turned around to say, *Come on, Arliss,* or *Hurry up, son.* Joseph kept his own pace, and Arliss figured he was free to follow or not; his father was too deep in his own thoughts to know the difference. Arliss did not mind. He liked being alone. On that day, he was looking forward to making squirrel traps while his father and uncles hoed corn. He had only just learned how from his father, who, when he handed him the knife, told him about the time Ricky Cantrell's son cut his finger off with just such a knife, and the blood poisoning set in, and his hand swelled to twice its size before he died. Joseph hardly ever told Arliss something simple like, *Be careful.* He told stories, and Arliss got from them what he could.

It was not much past dawn but already a hot and a windless morning. A cloud of gnats followed him, and now and then he waved them away from his eyes. He made a game out of jumping over ditches in the road while humming the song he had heard Rosemary singing, and he found a piece of flint and stuffed it in his pocket. He had his head down, looking for another, when he came around the last curve and nearly walked into his father, who was standing in the middle of the road, staring at Aunt Belle. Arliss stopped and stared, too. His Aunt Belle was sitting on the porch in a chair doing nothing. Arliss wished they could just go on to the barn, but Belle sitting on the porch doing nothing meant something was wrong.

Belle was related to Arliss both by marriage and by birth, because she was his uncle Luke's wife and his own mother's sister, but, unlike his mother who spewed bad news like breath held too long, Belle would wait. She just sat there. Arliss noticed it was a rocking chair she was sitting in, and she wasn't even rocking; that's how still she was. Arliss was afraid of Belle because Rosemary said she could hex you, and all you had to do to think it might be true was remember Lettie Thurman, who died from a copperhead bite two days after Belle said she would. His own mother, Marion, was known to be a dowser, although Arliss had never seen her find any water, but he knew she could stop blood, because he had been there the night Millie Reid drove up with her husband, Charley, who had cut his heel string with a broadax. It would not stop bleeding, and Millie was running around the room, yelling about how he was going to bleed to death, until Marion put her hands on him and said the verses from Ezekiel three times, and it stopped. She was also a wart charmer and could cure the thrush in a baby's mouth, but she could not draw fire out of a burn. Belle could. Marion told people, if you catch yourself on fire, go to Belle, but Rosemary said, if they did, they'd be sorry. Rosemary said there was such a thing as a gift and such a thing as a curse, and you better know which is which.

"Where's Luke?" Joseph asked Belle.

Unlike his mother, who wore her hair up, Belle let hers hang around her shoulders like a horse's mane. Her eyes were cloudy, while Marion's glittered like the flint Arliss liked to pick up and stuff in his pocket. Belle turned her dull and terrifying eyes toward Joseph, then looked away again. "You tell me," she said.

Roy came out of the house, shaking his head. "He ain't in the barn neither, and you know what that means." He stepped off the porch and stood next to Joseph in the yard. Like all three Greene brothers and now Arliss, too, Roy had hair a shade of yellow like cornsilk and pale blue eyes. It was what the Greenes were known for, that yellow hair and those blue eyes, although Joseph's hair was a darker shade than the others, and "Rooster Man" Luke had the complexion that earned him his nickname. None of them were especially tall men, but Roy was the tallest of the three, and he was scrawny, so that parts of him, his feet and knees and elbows, looked too big for the rest of him. He had lost all but an inch of one of his fingers in the car factory in Detroit, and, whenever he saw Arliss staring, he liked to put the stump in his nose and make it look as if the rest was sticking up behind his eyes. Joseph and Roy had already turned and were heading toward the woods when they heard the ax. They stopped and looked at each other. "Told you," Roy said.

They followed the intermittent bursts of ax-chopping, until they reached the clearing in the woods where Luke was trying to build a barn. It's not like they did not need a new barn; they did, but now that the TVA was building the Cove Creek Dam and making everybody move, there was no need. Besides, Luke's barn was a fool idea even if there were no Cove Creek Dam, no TVA, no relocation workers driving people to ragged land all over east Tennessee, pleading, *How about this one? Won't this do?* Because it made no sense to build a new barn in the middle of the woods. It was the kind of thing Luke did, though, to get it in his mind to build a barn, then not see clear to build it in the right place. There didn't have to be any Cove Creek Dam to make Luke think crooked.

Arliss was used to hearing his parents talk about Luke this way, and he knew the problem. The problem was that Luke walked in an unchristian-like manner. He knew because he had been at the New Hope Primitive Baptist Church all three times Luke had been called up for it. He had been there all three times Luke had apologized, and all three times Pastor Stiles had forgiven him in front of everybody, but now the question was, how many more times could it happen before they kicked him out for good? None, if Arliss's mother had anything to do with it. Marion was an Old Testament Christian, and when it was her turn to sit at the table with God, she was going to tell him exactly what she thought about this forgiveness business. She was going to ask him, at least, to reconsider. Arliss did not know what it meant to walk in an unchristian-like manner.

Luke was chopping a felled tulip poplar into logs, and when Joseph and Roy got there, he leaned his ax against the tree and picked up a jar of stump juice off the ground and drank.

"It ain't going to do any good," Joseph said to Luke.

"You don't know that."

"I don't have to know. That feller done told you."

"He don't know."

Luke took another drink and wiped his mouth on his sleeve. "If he thinks I'm leaving, he's got another think coming." He picked up the ax and heaved it over his shoulder and brought it down on the tree.

Joseph and Roy looked at each other. They had been over this before, and it always came down to the same thing. Luke believed if he built a new barn, he would not have to move, and it was a horrible thing, like watching a cripple try to walk, watching Luke try to figure out what he could do to keep from leaving New Hope. A new barn would not do it. A new barn would not even force the TVA to offer them more money; the relocation worker had told them that much. The relocation worker had driven them to farms in four counties, listening to Luke say "No, sir" to this one, and "No sirree" to that one, sometimes not even getting out of the car, until they found the one in Knox County, and Joseph said that was enough. They would take it. The land was not the best they had seen. It was hilly and rocky and had lain fallow for years, but besides a barn, there were two ramshackle houses. Joseph figured he could patch up one for his family and the other for Luke and Belle. Also, there was a small graveyard already in place on the property.

Luke and Belle had a son still living, but he would not be going with them. Eli was his name, and he was headed for Bristol, where he sometimes ran moonshine for a man named Tiny, although, if anybody tried to tell Belle he was going to do anything but haul watermelon, she would tell them, there's a special place in hell for liars. She swore her boy wouldn't know moonshine from creek water. Marion would just shake her head, and mutter, "My foot."

Roy was not going either. He planned to hire on at the dam and tried to talk his brothers into going with him, but they said they were too old to give up on farming. The relocation worker from the TVA, a young man named Mr. Fielding, explained to Joseph and Luke that they would be wise switching from corn to cattle, and he claimed there'd be a man from the state sent out to show them how. "It's going to be a new day for farming in the Tennessee Valley," he kept saying. Mr. Fielding had the kind of face that you could tell every single thing he knew he had learned from a book. Standing on the rocky hill with Mr. Fielding, squinting at the forest of cedar trees that would have to be cleared, Luke had nodded, and said, "I reckon we can make it work." But when Mr. Fielding, in his white shirt and striped necktie, got into his Ford and drove away, Luke turned to Joseph and spit. "If he thinks I'm going to fool with cattle, he's got another think coming."

Luke was not chopping the poplar tree right. He was hacking at it, and wood chips flew like spittle. Arliss kept out of the way. He sat down on a stump in the woods a few feet from the edge of the clearing. He felt his father's knife in his pocket and took it out and held it. It was heavy in his hand. He opened it and picked up a stick and began carving away from himself the way his father had taught him, the wood yielding under the blade as if it were made of lard. A dull knife is more dangerous than a sharp one, his father always said. Arliss had whittled the end down to a point when Luke missed the tree. He stumbled forward on the downswing, and the ax landed on the other side of the trunk in an awkward angle, which nearly pulled him headfirst over the top. He swore. It was embarrassing to miss like that, and Arliss looked away to spare his uncle the idea that everyone had seen, but Arliss knew that, had Luke stepped backwards and missed on the opposite side of the log, he would have cut off his leg. Luke let go of the ax, picked up the jar, and took another drink.

Arliss was the first to see Eli. He was standing near the edge of a rhododendron thicket about twenty yards from where Arliss sat, a whiskey bottle tucked into the waistband of his pants, a rifle resting on his shoulder. Arliss did not know how long he had been standing there. He was supposed to be in Knoxville, but he must have come back, just like Uncle Roy and all the other people from New Hope and down the road in Loyston, who were always going off somewhere and coming back, because of the Depression. Arliss did not know what the Depression was, but it had to be bad to chase so many people away. Eli was a small, misshapen man with one leg shorter than the other and the skin of his face drawn tight over his bones. He always had the kind of look on his face like he took offense at everything. Almost twenty now, he had been running away from home since he was eleven and had spent time in jail for running moonshine, although it was said he had killed a man, and he never went to jail for that. The last time he'd been home, he had almost burned down the barn by tying a paper sack to the tail of a cat and setting it on fire to see how fast it would run. The answer was, fast, only it headed toward the barn and up the ladder to the loft. It had taken everything they had, Joseph and Luke and Roy together, to put out the fire, and Joseph still talked as if he would never forgive Eli.

Arliss watched Eli in the rhododendron thicket for several minutes before Eli caught him looking. Slowly he took the rifle from his shoulder and aimed it at Arliss and acted as if he might pull the trigger. Or he might not. Arliss had seen him barely aim at a bird or a squirrel or a rabbit and drop it dead for no reason, leaving it there for somebody else to pick up. Or not. Arliss felt the warm wash of urine running down his legs. What made Eli put down the gun, Arliss did not know, because he did not smile or laugh or wink as if it were a joke. He did not say anything, which made Arliss believe he had been saved by chance.

Neither his father nor his uncles had seen Eli yet. Luke finished drinking from the jar of stump juice, placed it back on the ground, wiped his mouth on his sleeve, then grabbed the ax handle. He braced one foot against the tree and worked the ax back and forth between his hands. Joseph walked over to help. He spied Eli, who stepped out of the thicket and met his gaze. Then everybody looked. Nobody moved. Finally, Joseph broke the silence. "You could be of some help here," he said.

Eli grinned some kind of a grin he had not learned from his father nor from his mother, and he took the bottle of whiskey and placed it on the ground in front of him. Then he switched the gun to his other shoulder and walked back into the woods. Luke sank to the ground like a scarecrow robbed of its stake.

Roy got him back up but had to hold him there, because Luke kept his head bowed low and his arms hanging down like willow branches. "What's wrong with him?" Arliss asked his father.

"He's just wore-out," he said.

"Because of Eli?"

"Because of a lot of things."

They got Luke to go with them through the woods to the creek, stopping near the waterfall that gave the creek its name, Stickpin Branch, a short, wide waterfall that pitched four shoots of water straight as stickpins down to a large pool. The Greene brothers had gotten into the habit of throwing rocks into the shoots. If you aimed right and threw hard enough, you could send a rock through all four to the other side. Arliss could not do it yet, but he liked to watch his father and uncles. Above the waterfall was a small island that split the creek in two, with the main channel on one side and a narrow off-shoot on the other. Joseph stepped over to the island, squatted, and began picking rocks out of the mud and stacking them on top of each other in the narrow stream. Roy rolled cigarettes and handed them out. Luke took one, but Joseph shook his head and kept piling up rocks. For a while they did not talk but listened to the rocks knocking against each other, the sound echoing up the creek.

Finally, Roy spoke. "Y'all should come with me to Norris. You don't have to know nothing about building a dam. We can dig a ditch, can't we? Haul rocks? They're building a new town up there, and the preacher swears they're building houses for them that works for them."

Joseph fished a long skinny rock from the bottom of the creek. "They're not going to give you no house just for working on their dam."

"You don't know."

"I know they're not going to give nobody no house."

"You get your pay regular; that's what I know."

"It'll be hard work."

"Not any worse than this here."

"You won't be your own man; that's the part I don't like," Joseph said. "At least when you've got land, you're the one to say what's what."

Roy nodded. "There's good and bad in that."

"*This* is our land," Luke said.

Joseph looked at him. "There's other land," he said.

"If they think I'm moving, they got another think coming," Luke muttered.

Joseph asked Roy for a cigarette. He held it between his lips while he scooped handfuls of mud from the creek bank onto his wall of rocks. The stream was managing still to find a way around the wall, but Joseph kept piling rocks, slapping mud, and smoking. When he was done, he took the cigarette out of his mouth and stuck it upright in the mud on the bank of the island. Smoke rose from the end, curling upward. Then the stream began to back up.

Arliss watched it back up. It hit his daddy's wall and spread out, taking inches from the muddy bank, rising higher, but the rocks held, and in no time, the water flooded the shore. The cigarette vanished. There was no trace of it at all. Joseph looked at Luke. "You don't have no choice."

Arliss did not know for a long time that it did not happen that way. The dam did not instantly flood New Hope, although it did happen fast. Heavy rainfall in the spring and summer of 1934 filled the reservoir behind the dam (no longer called Cove Creek, but Norris, named for a senator from Nebraska) in just three months. By then, Arliss's family had been gone a year, but on the day they left, Arliss listened for the sound of rushing water and did not understand why his parents moved so slowly, or why his father kept taking things off the wagon and putting them back on. *Pile it on, and let's get out of here,* was Arliss's philosophy, especially since he knew that, even when they finished, they would not be finished. They still had Luke and Belle to get, and ever since the day Joseph drowned the cigarette, nobody knew what Luke would do.

Arliss had stayed with him beside the creek that day. His father had stood up, saying it was time to get some work done, and Roy stood up with him, but Luke had stayed seated with his knees bent, his arms resting on his knees, his head buried in his arms. "You coming or staying?" his father had asked Arliss.

"Staying, I guess."

When they left, Luke drank from the bottle Eli had left him, and he offered Arliss a sip. Arliss shook his head but peered into it, wanting to see what a shortcut-to-hell looked like. Sometimes Luke cried. It wasn't the kind of crying Virginia did the day she found out Jimmy Badgett had run off to Chicago. It wasn't even like when Rosemary fell and broke her arm. Luke's crying was silent, just tears running down his face. Arliss began sharpening another stick with his daddy's knife, and, after a time, Luke showed him how to make a little boat. When they finished, they set it in the pool above Joseph's rock dam and watched it float. Luke said. "You ain't never been nowhere else but New Hope, have you?"

"No, sir."

"I have."

"Are you going to stay here and get drowned?"

From this question, Arliss got told things he already knew about New Hope, along with some things he had not known, but he never got an answer to the question. Luke talked about how his grandfather had come over from North Carolina to clear this land for farming and had run a gristmill on the creek, but Arliss already knew that. He knew where the ruins were, because he had gone with his daddy to raid them for old boards. They had closed the mill when the flu came through in 1918, killing people Arliss had never heard about. Luke talked about his two sons who had died, one in a sawmill accident, the other from a breathing sickness. Arliss's pants were still damp from where he'd wet them. He shifted so he was out of the shade. He carved on his stick to keep from feeling drowsy from the sound of Luke's voice and the sun coming through the trees, but he roused when Luke remembered seeing the ghost on the road up to Spinner Ridge. Oh yes, Luke had seen it with his own eyes, crossing the road near Alvin's Bluff with a sack in its hands.

Then Luke put the toe of his boot on the top of the rock dam and pushed. It crumbled, and the water poured over the top. It took only a few minutes for the rest of the wall to collapse, and the stream to get back to the way it was.

"I'll stay here with you," Arliss said.

Luke looked at him. Then he reached out his hand and touched Arliss's face. Arliss almost jerked his head back from the shock, but just that quickly, felt how good it was to have his uncle's hand on his face and kept still.

On the day of the move, Arliss hurled his six-year-old body into hauling frying pans and overalls and quilts and dinner plates and baskets to the wagon until, finally, they finished, and the house stood empty. Joseph rigged chairs for Arliss and the girls to sit in, and it was in this way that Arliss left the place where he was born, riding backwards on top of a loaded wagon. He had to peek between his sisters, who sat side by side in front of him, Virginia, stiff-backed like his mother, who was behind him on the wagon seat facing forward. His mother was not looking back, not saying a word, not thinking one sentimental thought that he could tell, but how many times had he seen her slapping cornmeal off her hands, and wasn't this the same thing? One sorry farm was as good as the next in her eyes. Arliss noticed his father was also not looking back, but that was altogether different. Joseph slumped forward over the reins, urging the mules to walk as slowly as they wanted. Arliss watched the farm receding in front of him and understood in a way that had not seemed real until that moment that he would never see it again.

"Wait!" he called.

But he did not know what to say next. Joseph stopped the mules. His mother and Virginia both whipped their heads around from their opposite directions to look at him. It was like being in the middle of a stare sandwich, and he felt his face turn red. Rosemary reached back and helped him crawl into her lap, where he buried his head, but when the mules resumed their trudging, he sat back up and, within the folds of her arms, memorized what he could. There was the house with its peeling clapboards, bare windows, and slanted porch, standing like a pillar in the wasteland, one lone walnut tree beside it. In every direction, from the house outward to the ring of woods around them, stretched the sun-scorched, leached, and barren earth. There was the hog pen, the chicken house, Roy's tiny cabin, and the broken fence that, this year, nobody bothered to fix. He imagined fish swimming in and out of the gaping windows of the house, between the crooked fence rails, through the tangled woods. He pictured tree limbs bending to river currents instead of the wind. In the sky, he could almost see the bottoms of boats where clouds floated now. Around the first curve, they lost sight of the house, and Arliss scrambled to memorize the trees, gullies in the road, and rocks, because each inch they traveled was another inch gone. Then Rosemary began to sing.

I fell in love with a Knoxville girl with dark and rolling eyes.

She got Arliss to sing with her. The song was about a boy who falls in love with a girl, kills her, then can't hide his guilty face and goes to jail. Arliss hated the song and did not understand it and searched for clues to explain why, if the boy loved that girl so much, what in the world made him want to hit her over the head, but he never found one. *Why'd he kill her?* he asked Rosemary every time she sang it, but Rosemary did not know, either. He asked her if that's how they acted over there in Knoxville, but she laughed, and said, "It's just a song, sweetie."

Rosemary had learned the song, and all the songs she sang, from listening to the battery-operated radio owned by her friend Maggie Tredwell, whose daddy ran the mill in Loyston. She and Maggie were the only ones happy to be leaving New Hope because, how many pie suppers did they have to endure to know, and know again, that there were no boys around there anywhere close to what they were looking for? They were not like Virginia, who would have settled for any one of the Badgett boys. Rosemary and Maggie listened to the radio and talked about moving to Nashville, where they hoped to meet boys who sang on *The Grand Ole Opry*. Or maybe they would end up singing on the radio themselves. Arliss believed it could happen. He did not know anybody to have a voice better than Rosemary's, even on songs about boys who kill people for no reason.

Arliss loved Rosemary. From his position of youngest and smallest in the family, he often watched Rosemary sing, oblivious to the disapproving stares of their mother, and he would be amazed, because he could not escape those stares unless he left the house, and even then he could see them in his mind. He decided that Rosemary took after their father, whose affection for her may have explained why she got away with so much. Arliss knew, for instance, that the fiddle that had hung by two nails on the wall of the house in New Hope belonged to his father, although he did not remember how he knew, nor did he ever once see the fiddle in his father's hands. But somehow he knew, and it stuck in his mind that his father, like Rosemary, was a musical sort of person. At the time, Arliss was forming a great many ideas about his father; some of them were true and some were not.

It made an impression on him, for instance, that Joseph could read (he was the only one of the Greene brothers who had gone down to Loyston to school) and was the only grown-up Arliss knew who owned a book other than the Bible. The book, which was spine-broken and smudged with red clay, told a history of the War of Northern Aggression, and Joseph kept it hidden so Marion would not yank out the pages each winter to stuff between the cracks in the walls. Lying awake at night, Arliss would see light from the lantern through the holes in the floor and know his father was up reading that book, even though his mother warned they did not have the oil to spare.

Rosemary, with Arliss's help, reached the end of "Knoxville Girl," at which point the boy in the song is securely in jail, and Arliss was glad for it. She had just started up another song when they rounded the last curve on the road through the woods and caught sight of Belle hanging a cat from the limb of a dogwood tree.

"Stay here," Joseph said.

The cat was howling and clawing Belle's arms to red ribbons as she shoved its head through the noose. Even after she let go, it jerked and twitched as if it might find a foothold in midair and get out of there. It's hard to kill a cat; anybody can tell you that, but by the time Joseph got there, calling, "Stop it, Belle, stop that," the cat was still. Two more cats hung from different limbs, and there was more rope lying on the ground.

"Where's Luke?" Joseph yelled. This time Belle did not act ignorant, but pointed behind her to the barn.

Maybe Joseph would have told Arliss not to follow had he taken time to think, but he was walking fast, then he was running, and Arliss slipped in behind him, but not too close. He did not want to be sent back to the wagon. His mother and sisters were hovering around Belle and would not notice him gone. Joseph ran until he reached the barn, then stopped at the door. Arliss stopped a few yards behind.

What he saw, or at least *how* he saw it, resembled a photograph. At least that was the way he would remember the moment, like a single, static image. The angle at which the afternoon sun shone from behind the barn put Joseph in shadow, so both men appeared dark and featureless, his father standing in the doorway staring at Luke in the barn. Both were perfectly still, his father rooted to the ground, his uncle by the rope around his neck. Later he would think of a stalagmite and a stalactite, one sticking up, the other hanging down.

Here's what else Arliss saw; his father was not surprised. Joseph stood there in the threshold of the barn, seeing what he seemed to know he was going to see. He never looked back at Arliss, but after a while, he said, "You still got that knife?"

Arliss reached into his pocket and felt it there.

"See if you can't climb up there and cut him down."

Which he did, and when Luke fell, Joseph caught him, letting himself be knocked to the ground as if there might be something wrong in allowing the body to fall to the floor by itself. Joseph situated the body over his shoulder and walked out of the barn.

Virginia rang the bell, fifty-three times to mark his age, but there was hardly anybody left in New Hope to hear it. Marion and Virginia agreed to lay Luke out, and they sent Rosemary and Arliss for water to bathe the body. Arliss kept his eyes on the ground and held on to Rosemary's skirt all the way to the spring, where she placed a bucket under the pipe and sat back to watch it fill. Arliss crouched beside her. His heart was pounding. He did not have enough breath in him to speak louder than a whisper. "His face," he gasped, "was almost turned black."

"Oh, sweetie, I'm sorry," she whispered back, hugging him to her.

He settled into her arms and closed his eyes and felt her heart beating against his cheek until it was time to change buckets. "Why'd she hang the cats?" he asked.

"She's sure the Devil's got into one; she just don't know which one. She thinks that's why Luke done what he done."

"Is it true?"

Rosemary lifted the second bucket full of water and put a third in its place. "No. But don't go telling Mama I said that neither."

"I won't."

"You better not."

"I promise."

She put her arms around him again, and said, "This weren't nobody's fault, Arliss."

After Luke's body was bathed and dressed, Joseph laid him on the front door, which he had taken off its hinges and propped up on chairs, and he folded his hands across his chest and tied his feet together. Marion handed him two stones, and Joseph looked at them. He told Arliss, "Fetch me two from Stickpin Branch," and with only the moon to light his way, Arliss ran clear to the creek and selected the smoothest, flattest stones he could find, but before he ran back, he picked up another stone and threw it as hard and as straight as he could through the four shoots of the waterfall. It was too dark to see if it made it. Then he ran all the way back and handed the stones to his father, who placed one on each of Luke's eyelids.

Roy came down from Norris to help Joseph build the casket, but there was no sign of Eli. They left with still no word, but Belle made Joseph write him a note, which she nailed to the porch in case he came back before the house was underwater. They rode out of New

Hope with one milk cow tied behind Joseph's wagon, and Virginia driving a second wagon, which they had loaded with Luke's casket. They planned to bury it in the graveyard on their new farm, where Arliss's long-dead brothers and sisters were waiting. Arliss could not say he liked the idea of all these dead people coming with them. He could not swear he would not have left them to lie under the lake.

TWO

ARLISS

You cannot cut down a cedar tree and expect it to stay gone. Even a sprig as thin as a pencil will grow back if you don't get rid of the roots, and to do that, you have to dig them up or burn them out or else tie them to a mule and pull them out, but whichever way you choose, the roots have to go, or you'll be starting all over again. This was the task that faced the six members of the Greene family who made it from New Hope to the farm on Bearpen Lane in north Knox County in the summer of 1933. Before them were some ninety acres of cedar trees, wild cherry, hackberry bushes, and blackberry cane that had grown up in the decade or so that the land had lain fallow, ninety acres that they were going to have to remake if they were going to survive. It was Arliss's job to pick up rocks with his mother, which they tossed into a mule-drawn sledge. When it was full, they dragged it off and emptied it onto a pile near the house to be used later to fix chimneys and build rock walls. At first, Arliss did not mind the stooping over and picking up rocks, and he rather liked tossing them into the sledge, but he hated the fact that they never seemed to get anywhere. Each time they emptied the sledge and came back, there seemed to be just as many rocks on the ground as before they started. While he worked alongside his mother, his father and sisters and Aunt Belle cut down trees with a two-man saw. They saved out and stacked six-foot cedar logs to be used later as fence posts, but the dug-up roots, stumps, branches, briars, and other brush they dragged to expectant bonfires. On days when the wind was down, Joseph would light the fires, and the smoke would blacken the sky.

Joseph had bought the land, not from the farmer who had worn it out in corn, then abandoned it, but from the man's nephew, who did not live in Tennessee but somewhere in Ohio. From Bearpen Lane, the land rose sharply before leveling off. The house where Arliss and his family moved was situated on the side of the hill near the road. At the top of the hill was the barn, and about seventy-five yards to the left was the second house, which Joseph planned to fix up for Belle. The graveyard sat on a small rise behind it. A small creek followed the southern boundary line, crossed Bearpen Lane under a rickety plank bridge, and emptied into a larger creek behind another man's farm. Toward the back corner of the property, the land rose steeply again to a ridge along the north and west boundaries of the farm.

Arliss would have complained that the farmer before them never grew corn, only rocks, if he were allowed to complain, which he was not. Summer turned to fall, and his hands and arms stayed cut and swollen, his back ached, and he felt banished to a world where there was only picking up rocks, and tossing them, and hearing them scrape and smash against each other, and no longer thinking it was fun, and not even wincing at the sound anymore, and no longer distinguishing between pain in his hands or pain in his back or pain in the cuts on his legs, and no longer wondering when it would end, because it wouldn't. Forever was all there was.

The girls, too, were scratched and cut and blistered and dirty from chopping trees and digging up roots and dragging logs and brush. As she worked, Rosemary sang the songs she remembered from Maggie Tredwell's radio, but they failed to cheer anybody up. There was no garden yet, and all they had to eat was boiled-down greens they found in the woods and along the side of the road, which they washed down with the little bit of milk they could get from the cow. Sometimes Joseph would shoot a rabbit or a squirrel. Mr. Fielding from the TVA pulled up in a truck one day, saying he had heard the news about Luke and had brought a hog. Joseph made a ramp out of a couple of planks, and it took both of them, Mr. Fielding pulling on a rope and Joseph pushing from behind, to get the hog down to the ground. They had to wait until the weather turned cold to butcher it, or the meat would spoil, but with no corn to eat, it did not put on much weight anyway. Joseph was the only one who had any energy at the end of the day, and he used it standing and looking out the door at the hill covered with cedars, and more cedars beyond that, and swearing it was impossible. What they had to do, they could not do. No one could. Not in a million years. Arliss fell asleep most nights listening to the droning list of things that could not be done, but by morning Joseph would have forgotten all that and would plunge into the day with the impatience of a person just inches away of getting what he wants.

He grew more impatient every day. When Mr. Fielding brought the hog, he had explained again about the money to be made raising beef cattle, and Joseph was ready to get started. He was *owed* this. Joseph, who had never once fooled himself into thinking anybody owed him a single thing, did not mind saying now that, for the loss of his brother and the loss of his home, he was due. For such pride, Marion warned, God would punish him, but Joseph only snapped at her. "He already has." Marion said it was a sin to say so, and Joseph said he never claimed to be no sinner.

But no matter how frenetically he cut down trees and hacked out briars and pulled up roots to drag to the piles, he never got so impatient that he could not wait for a windless day to burn the brush, which was why Arliss was surprised to see smoke the same evening he smelled rain. There was not much wind yet, but there was also no mistaking the heavy scent of water somewhere not far off and wind right on top of it. He would have thought his father would have known that much, but there was the smoke and there, at the edge of the clearing was a brush pile afire. Arliss would have said the flames were bigger than usual right from the start.

In his memory, it happened all at once. The wind picked up; Joseph was yelling, and Rosemary's dress was billowing in the wind.

No, first there was the sound of her voice. Clearly above the wind, Rosemary was singing, *then* the wind picked up and carried off her voice so Arliss could not hear it anymore. Joseph was yelling, and Rosemary was singing, but Arliss could not hear anything but the wind, although he could see everything. The hem of the dress and the flames flicking at each other. Joseph waving his arms. Then the flames caught the dress, and Rosemary was on fire.

Then she was running, and Joseph was running after her, both of them across the clearing toward the house, Rosemary surrounded by fire, Joseph screaming one word over and over, "Stop, stop, stop, stop!" Virginia and Belle followed Joseph running, but Arliss did not know what to do and ran back and forth like a dog on a leash, skittering toward his flaming sister, then back to his mother, who stood next to the sledge, then forward again, and back, carving a line in the dirt with his indecision. His mother was still. There was a sense that if he ran into her, it would be like running into a stone wall. Then Rosemary changed direction and stumbled, but Joseph stumbled, too, then fell, or else he would have caught her. He would say it for the rest of his life; he would have caught her, but he fell.

When, finally, he did catch up, it was too late. She slowed, then sank to the ground. He took off his shirt and beat at the flames, and here came Belle, whom everybody said could draw fire, but not this time, and not this fire. Behind her was Virginia with a bucket of water. Arliss did not know where she got the bucket or where she got the water. She poured the water over Rosemary, soaking Joseph and Belle, who knelt helplessly on the ground beside her.

Arliss, skittering back and forth, began to whimper, his tear-streaked face stained with soot and dirt. Suddenly his mother grabbed him by the shoulders and stopped him still and looked into his eyes. "God is bigger than you are," she hissed. "Don't you never forget it, neither." Then she turned and walked back to the house.

THREE

· ARLISS

Arliss had a way with cows. It was what people said about him and what he knew for himself to be true, although he would not boast. But he understood the animals, unlike his father, who never even liked them, who never tried. That was the part that got to Arliss; that his father never tried. It was the reason Joseph was trampled to death when he fell and, because he refused to appreciate the nature of cows, rolled around on the ground, cussing and waving his arms in the air. Arliss was fourteen years old and saw it happen. It wasn't the cows' fault.

A cow's eyes are located on the side of its head, making it hard to see anything directly in front, which means if you find yourself head-on with a cow, you need to be careful. Any strange or sudden movement, like a person rolling around on the ground, cussing and waving his arms in the air, will scare a cow, which only made sense to Arliss. Sneak up behind anybody, and he'll startle, and so it was with cows, only cows don't stop to ask, *what is it?* That split second a human being gets to stop himself from doing something stupid; cows don't have it. This was what Arliss wished he could have made his father understand, because Joseph alternated between expecting his animals to think like humans or not at all, both flaws of arrogance if you asked Arliss, who hated arrogance. Joseph tried, mostly unsuccessfully, to raise beef cattle for eight years before he died, and in that time, Arliss saw him yell at his animals, and he saw him hit them. It became like a litany between them for Joseph to shake his head and say, *Them cows are too stupid to breathe.*

To which Arliss would say, *No, sir.*

Then Joseph. *Them cows'll be the death of me.*

Then Arliss. *Yes, sir, if you don't watch it.*

But Arliss did not actually believe it would happen. Arliss guessed his father sprained his ankle, which was why he did not get up. It was winter, and the cows were in the barn eating hay from the troughs along the walls. Arliss was in the loft with the pitchfork dropping hay and did not see what made his father fall. Joseph was carrying an armload of buckets he had left outside, so maybe he could not see where he was going, and because he could not see, slipped on the patch of ice in front of the barn door, the buckets crashing to the floor all around him. The first to charge was a cow Arliss called Pepper because she was high-strung anyway. When Pepper ran at the loud and wiggling object in front of her, the others followed, some nine hundred crushing pounds with every cow, and there were twelve of them.

He should have seen it coming and gotten out of the way. Anyone would have. That is why Arliss believed there was something else going on, a sprained or broken ankle, a hurt knee, something that kept his father from standing up, but if Arliss let himself consider what his father did wrong, he could not stop there at the barn door. He had to go all the way back to the buckets that should not have been left outside to collect rain, which freezes in winter and breeds mosquitoes in summer, and not only that. A good farmer does not leave buckets, or anything else for that matter, *out,* if for no better reason than pride. You keep your farm up, that's all. But allowing for the fact that everybody makes mistakes, and the buckets were out for some reason, legitimate or otherwise, what fool would blunder into a barn filled with cows trying to carry all the buckets at once? Ice or no ice, around cows, you have to be aware of your body in space, how much room you take up, your shape and movement, because even if you aren't paying attention, the cows are.

Arliss did not let himself go that far back. He preferred to think, not that his father had been stubborn or ignorant, but that he had been hurt, which was why Arliss stood so long in the hospital corridor where he felt small and strange and out of place. Fourteen years old, his hat in his hands, mud on his shoes, blood on his overalls, he waited for the doctor, a busy man, to walk back down the hall.

"Excuse me. Sir? I was wondering if you might be able to tell me, were either of my daddy's ankles sprained?"

The busy doctor stopped and peered at him. "Young man, your father was trampled by a dozen cows. I can't tell you how many bones were broken, because I never finished counting, and you are asking about a sprained ankle?"

Joseph had not wanted Arliss to grow up to be a farmer, and he said so all the time. *You oughta learn to be one of them engineers like work at the TVA,* was the kind of thing he told him, and he saved money in a jar to send him to college, but when Joseph died, he had no choice. His sister Virginia had moved to Norris shortly after Rosemary died to marry a man their uncle Roy knew, who planned to open a marina on Norris Lake. Roy was covered up with work on his own farm, which he had bought on the western end of Anderson County once the dam was finished. The first thing Arliss did after his father died was quit school. He had no desire to be an engineer and would have done anything before working for the TVA, but, mostly, he never cared for school.

It was not that he was dumb; in fact, just the opposite. He caught on to his lessons faster than most of the other boys and girls in the classroom, but that, combined with the fact that he refused to speak to his teacher any more than he had to, was part of the problem. His teacher thought he acted too big for his britches, and she told his mother, who whipped him for it. So he had never liked school and had spent his first years there getting paddled for fighting.

The schoolhouse was in a small wooden building on Raccoon Road, about a mile and a half from where he lived on Bearpen Lane.

The first day his daddy made him go was only a few weeks after Rosemary's death, and he had nothing to say to the other children, especially the boys, whom he regarded as strange creatures who seemed to want something from him, although he did not know what it was. They beat him up for it. They called him a mountain boy and beat him up for that. He was small for his age, and they beat him up for that, too. Arliss learned to fight back, and because he was quick and stronger than he looked, and because he did not care if he got hurt, he managed to inflict enough pain to make the boys think hard before they fought him, but even with their respect, they could not get his attention.

Most days, he never made it to school. He would start off walking in that direction but end up in the woods, picking up rocks along the way to use in his slingshot. He shot anything—birds, rabbits, lizards, squirrels, and snakes; he especially liked killing snakes. He felt a kinship with his cousin Eli, which he never would have guessed possible only a year earlier, and he daydreamed of running away to Bristol to find him. It felt good to be mean, he thought to himself, but better if you could do it around somebody who was good at it. He often speculated about what Eli would have done if he had been the one to cut Luke down in the barn, or if he had had to stand by and watch Rosemary burn up. He concluded that Eli would have marched down to whatever fancy building those TVA people worked in and killed somebody.

Sometimes he did not shoot anything but dragged himself to the woods on the top of the ridge and cried. The hurt he felt missing Rosemary was physical, as if he were being squeezed to death, and it was worse than any beating from his classmates or his teacher or his mother. It made him cry when he did not want to cry, and even if he might want to head over to school, he could not show up there with tear stains on his face. He practiced breathing hard and stuffing the tears back down until he got good at it. He did not know what was happening to him, but he swore this: He would never let it happen again.

He was eight when his father sold twenty acres to buy a couple of heifer calves, which he bred with a borrowed bull. By that time Arliss was expected to help out on the farm for two or three hours before breakfast, then after school until dark, except in the spring, when there was no time to spare for school. Now with his father gone, there was not even that much time to spare. So he quit school, buried his father, shot Pepper between the eyes, and buried her in the field. Then he took the money in the jar and bought another heifer and kept his daddy's farm going with his aunt Belle and his mother, who had never wanted her son to be anything but a farmer.

Before he died, Joseph had managed to clear thirty-five acres for pasture, but Arliss knew he could not keep that much up by himself and let ten grow back. It about killed him to do it. It was not just that their hard work had been for nothing; it was knowing that he would have to clear it all over again when time came to expand. And the time would come. He was too young to take it on now, and with the war on, there were no spare men to hire on as hands, but Arliss could see that both conditions were temporary. For now they were down to twenty-five acres of cleared pasture, twelve cows, and a mule, although the mule did not last long. Arliss was the only one who would go near it anyway, because it would kick if you walked behind it, but even if you did not, it could swing around so fast you'd swear it was a miracle if you got out of the way. Arliss was not afraid of the mule, and he did not take the kicking personally. He knew to put his hand on its flank and walk close in behind so it could not get a leg out, but his mother's solution was to arm herself with a pitchfork. One day the mule kicked, and a pitchfork tine went right through the hoof and into the leg, crippling it for good. Arliss shot it, too.

For the next several years, Arliss's world consisted of his mother, his aunt Belle, and the cattle, and of the three, he was partial to the cattle. Belle was already living in the house near the barn, which Joseph had fixed up for her and which was forever after called Belle's House. Just as she had done for Joseph, she helped Arliss with the hay and the small crop of corn, but she was afraid of the cattle. She insisted their air-shattering bellows, a sound Arliss had come to think of as natural as the wind, were Satan-inspired and would say so when she came down the hill for her meals, which she did every night, although she picked at the food and once accused Marion of trying to poison her. She grew skinnier and complained of ailments in her stomach, and more and more she spent her days in the woods gathering medicinal plants or cooking them up in her house. Then one day she went inside and never came back out.

It took Marion several days to figure it out; then she began taking food. She carried it up the hill in a basket twice a day, grumbling, *If she wants to be so much trouble, she ought to move down here and save me a trip,* but Belle never did, and Arliss was thankful for it.

He had not seen Belle in two months when his mother went to bed with a fever and asked him to take the basket of food. It was dusk, and Belle's House was dark, but he did not think about it until later, when he wondered when he had last seen even a lantern light from there. He knocked on the door and waited, then knocked again. He could hear no sound from inside the house. His mother had told him to put the basket on the kitchen table, so he tried the door and found it open and walked inside. The smell stopped him, a sickly-sweet stench of overripe food. He could not see a thing. The curtains were drawn against even the faintest light from outside. He walked slowly in the direction of the table until he found it, set the basket down, then groped in the air for a string to pull. Electricity had come in the form of a line down Bearpen Lane several years back, and Joseph had made sure both houses had a single lightbulb hanging from the ceiling of every room. He found the string and pulled, but nothing happened. Then from a corner of the room he heard Belle's voice. "It ran out."

"Aunt Belle?" His eyes were adjusting to the darkness now, and as he made out the form of her coming toward him, it registered what she was saying. "The electricity?" he asked.

"I done told you, already, it's gone."

When she got closer, he could tell her hair was completely white and cut off close to the skull. She wore a nightdress that smelled like sweat. She took the basket and carried it to the Frigidaire and began stuffing the food inside. Arliss could see that it was full of other foods his mother had brought. Belle was jamming them in, trying to make them fit, but when she shut the door it did not close all the way. He reached up and unscrewed the lightbulb. "It's probably just burned out," he said, but she did not answer. Already she was shuffling out of the room. He took the lightbulb back to his house.

It was possible, when he told his mother what Belle said, that there was the tiniest trace of a smile on his face; he did not remember, but from her bed, where she lay covered with blankets up to her chin, Marion flung her most potent of Proverbs. "Every one that is proud in heart is an abomination to the Lord."

Belle died a few weeks later. Marion found her already stiffened to the point where her arms would not straighten. At the time Arliss had no idea why or how Belle died, but one day, many years later when he was married and talking to his wife, Merle, he happened to wonder out loud.

Merle did not hesitate. "Cancer," she said.

He looked surprised.

She nodded. "Mark my words."

For several summers Arliss made extra money helping neighboring farmers harvest tobacco, before he got older and leased a couple of acres from the man across the street and set out his own plants. He got good at trading cattle. He would go down to the stockyard and buy, as cheaply as possible, a group of five or six heifer calves, some of which he would keep to breed, others to trade. He saved his money and, when he was twenty-four, bought his first Black Angus. Over the years, and with the help of men he occasionally hired to work on the farm, he cleared the ten acres he had let grow up, then twenty more, and planted half in fescue, which required fertilizer and lime and the equipment to spread it. The cost was considerable, even though he bought only used equipment, but it did not scare Arliss. He knew what he was doing. From the start he was the kind of farmer who kept the grass around his fence rows short and neat, his barn spotless, his machinery clean and running, his cows healthy, but he was never good at keeping farmhands. None of the teenagers he hired ever did a good enough job to suit him, and older men chafed under the demands of this youngster who had to have things just so. Arliss found himself secretly relieved each time one of them quit. He did not seek human companionship. He never had, and he did not need it now. He accepted the fact that there were things a farmer cannot control, such as weather, illness, and the price of beef, but Arliss believed there was one thing no one could take from him, and that was his own hard and careful work. He did not expect anything else, nor did he want it, so he was surprised the day he walked into the house at dinnertime, and there was Merle, sitting on the sofa with his mother.

In that instant, Arliss had to travel in his mind from, *I wonder what's for dinner,* to *Who is Merle,* to *Why is Merle,* knowing that his mother would not help him. If he wasn't smart enough to figure it out, that was his problem, but he did figure it out and tried not to stare.

Merle was a big girl, taller than he was by two inches and heavier by fifty pounds, although a good portion of that weight was in her bones. She was older than him by four years, and if ever there was a flicker of flirtation in her body or her face, she had squashed it. Her hair was dark and thick and stiff, her skin, pale and flecked with tiny moles, and if her figure brought to mind anything, it was the trunk of a large and sturdy tree. Arliss never asked himself if she were the right girl for him. Having assumed he would not marry, this change of fortune left him no room to be picky.

He understood his mother's thinking, that this big strong girl could be of some help on the farm and, in time, bear them big, strong sons, but Merle turned out to be loud and clumsy, her movements jerky and unpredictable, and the animals worked themselves into a state of agitation whenever she was around. That left Merle with only one redeeming feature in Marion's eyes, the fact that she was, at least, a Baptist. But unlike Marion, who was a Primitive Baptist, Merle was a Missionary Baptist. Some people might not think there is such a big difference, but then, some people do not think.

So Merle was a disappointment to Marion, and after the first child was born, Marion moved up to Belle's old house, where she lived until she died.

As for Merle, she knew what she was getting in this little man who left the house before sunrise, and came back in the evening smelling like cow manure, and sat slouch-shouldered at the table shoving his supper in his mouth, and stayed there when the plates were cleared to read his newspaper, and went to bed, all without saying more than a few sentences, and those were short. As she liked to say, if she wanted intimacy, she'd get a dog. One time he woke her up in the middle of the night because of some dream and started to tell her a story about when he was a boy, but she put an end to that nonsense. Merle prided herself on being as uncomplicated a person as you were going to find, and the past was complicated. You can dredge it up if you want; you can beat yourself over the head with it, but leave her out. As for what went on in their bed on those nights Arliss did not fall dead asleep but rutted around her ample body, Merle barely felt it.

But it gave them two children and fairly quickly. The first they named Robert, called Bob, after Merle's father, who ran a wholesale produce warehouse downtown. Two years later they had Daniel, named because Merle was set on something biblical. Bob would have been known back in New Hope as "pure Greene," because he looked like all those Greene brothers, with their light hair and pale blue eyes. Daniel had his mother's brown eyes and dark curly hair, and, like his mother, he was stocky, but while Merle appeared lumpish and slow, Daniel was athletic and always moving and, more than that, always talking. Arliss ignored him, but three or four times every day, out of Merle's mouth would come the same words:

Daniel would you sit down and hush!

To the customers at Carr's Big Orange Grocery, she said, *That boy's going to drive me to an early grave.*

Carr's Big Orange was named in tribute to the University of Tennessee's football team, the Vols, whose players wore orange and white and whose fans called their part of the world Big Orange Country.

No one in Merle's family had ever gone to the University of Tennessee or even to a football game there, but she had grown up in a house where there were two main topics of discussion: God and how the Vols were doing, and often both were featured in the same conversation. It was the variety of Big Orange paraphernalia sold along with the grocery items that got Merle shopping there and led to her friendship with Lydia Carr. She only started working the cash register as a favor to Lydia when her husband Bill got sick, but the reason she stayed depended on whom she was talking to. She told friends it was the neighborly thing to do. She reminded her mother-in-law that it might be helpful if *somebody* in the family had a steady income. But she told Arliss she had been chased off by his mother. "There's room for only one woman on this farm," she had said. That was the day she had knocked over a bucket of tomatoes Marion had just picked and received her own dose of Proverbs. "As smoke to the eyes, so is the sluggard," Marion hissed.

Merle had faced her right back. "He that is without sin, let him cast the first stone." Later she told Arliss his mother was crazy.

"She's just strong in her religion."

"Shitfire and a cat's ass, Arliss, I know the difference between strong and crazy."

Merle did not say it, but anyone who bothered to walk into Carr's Big Orange could tell she loved that job more than anything. Everybody who came in there talked to Merle. They told her things, and she in turn had things to tell. The way Merle saw it, there was no better place to be, unless you just happened to like cows.

Bob was in school already by the time she started working, but she had to bring Daniel with her. She let him build a fort out of empty boxes in the corner of the store next to the soft drinks, where he hid with his toys and his books and talked to himself. Anybody paying attention would have noticed he talked about himself in third person. . . . *And he went to the Martian commander and demanded the release of the hostages.* . . . He was so loud, customers would go over there to see what was going on.

"I can't understand nothing he says," Lydia said to Merle one time.

"He's just wanting attention," Merle said. "He'll learn."

She started him in the first grade when he was only five years old because he could read, but she did not think of that as any accomplishment. She was just glad not to have to worry about him anymore.

The elementary school was in the same location on Raccoon Road where Arliss had gone to school, but it was in a brand-new building big enough to hold two classrooms each for all six grades. As their father had done years earlier, Bob and Daniel walked to and from school every day. They had chores, but they did not work on the farm with their father the way Arliss had worked at their age. Their mother said they did not have to. But there were other reasons, and one was that Arliss found they were, simply, in his way. He suspected there was something wrong with this, but he did not have time to change it. When he was a boy, he had wanted to tag along with his dad, and what choice had there been? If you wanted to eat, you worked, but now there was money for groceries, and Merle brought them home and cooked them, and there was always something tying the boys up at school. Used to be, everybody missed school to work, but these days nobody missed school for anything. This was something else Arliss noticed but did not know how to fix.

It was also during this time, when the boys were at an age to learn from their father, that Arliss happened to hire the best hand he ever had. No one knew the man's real name, but he was called Freight Train, because he came through the door making train noises with his mouth like whistles and chug-chug-chuggings, and a sound like wheels slipping on tracks. When he left, he would back himself out the barn door, then steam off. Freight Train was as strong as his name indicated and tireless. He could fix fences and pull cedars and bale hay faster than anybody. Faster and better than Arliss. His only weakness was that twice a year he would buy a supply of Red Rocket, port wine so raw it could clean rust off an iron pipe, and he would stay on a drunk for a week or two, showing back up with at least one new scrape or cut wrapped in a rag. Arliss did not care; that's how good Freight Train was.

But one day, Freight Train and his cousin Ronnie got into an argument over whose car was stronger, Freight Train's 1955 Ford Galaxy, four-in-the-floor, or Ronnie's brand-new 1960 Oldsmobile with automatic transmission. The next Sunday afternoon they drove to the end of Bearpen Lane and chained their rear bumpers together. At first, both cars went into motion with their wheels spinning and dirt scattering, but, finally, Freight Train's car started gaining and began dragging the Oldsmobile. Faster and faster down the road they went, the Ford pulling the Olds, Ronnie facing forward but going backwards and screaming. Finally, Ronnie took his hands off the wheel, pulled out a pistol, and started shooting at Freight Train's car. Bullets flew every which way, and though Ronnie said he did not mean to hurt anybody, one caught Freight Train's shoulder, and that's when they stopped. Arliss heard the shots and offered to drive them to the hospital, but Freight Train would not let him. Eventually he came back to work, but his arm was not as strong, and after a couple of months, he left and never came back.

Arliss tried to put the boys to work then. Bob was thirteen and Daniel, eleven, so they were big enough and strong enough to be of some real help, but it was too late to make them love it. Bob was the better worker and did not complain, even telling people he was going to be a farmer when he grew up, but as soon as he was through with his chores, he hurried back inside to work on his model train set. All Daniel ever wanted to do was play baseball.

Marion called them shiftless. Arliss went to see her every afternoon after lunch, because she had quit going down the hill to see him. She was not a recluse, not in the sense that Belle had become at the end of her life; she simply had no use for Merle. "That woman talks too much, and her cooking'll kill you," she told Arliss. Arliss would find her sitting in her kitchen in a straight-backed chair reading the Bible, or she might be on the back porch facing the hill where the graveyard sat, shucking corn or stringing beans. If the boys went, too, she would reach up, quick as a snake's tongue, and grab them with her bony hands by their shoulders or the backs of their heads. If they were quicker than she was, she would make do with their shirt-sleeves and tug until their faces got up close to hers and whisper, *A foolish son is a grief to his father and bitterness to her that bore him.* She had only a few brown teeth left, and Arliss once heard Daniel tell Bob that her eyes could look right through to the back of your head and tell what you were thinking. Bob quit going up there. Daniel never figured it out, but Bob always managed to be in the middle of working, and not just at any work, but farm work, stacking hay bales for instance, whenever it was time to visit their grandmother. Daniel never thought fast enough to pull off something like that, but he rarely protested. He seemed to believe that if he went over there often enough, he might see her die, and sometimes he dared his best friend Brian to go with him.

But more often Arliss went by himself. Sometimes Arliss and his mother passed the entire time without a word between them. Sometimes she would give him some beans or a handful of okra, although the gifts felt more like accusations, as if to say that Merle's garden did not measure up.

She died when the truck she was driving ran off Bearpen Lane into a tree. No one knew where she was going, and no one saw it happen, so it was hard to tell if she swerved out of the way of an oncoming vehicle, or if she drove off the road on her own. Marion had learned to drive on a tractor and never got the hang of sharing the road. It was a head injury, and the doctor said it was likely she died instantly. Merle never had a problem saying right out loud to anyone who would listen that, overall, it was a blessing.

FOUR

ARLISS

Arliss walked out of the barn and stopped. Most of the herd had wandered over to the big maple tree that shaded the middle of the back pasture, but four were next to the south fence, and, looking again, he saw that one of them was on the other side. He called over his shoulder to Bob and said he'd be back in a minute, then started down the dirt path, watching the fence for breaks. The path, like all the paths on the farm, was not the result of intentional clearing but of years of walking the same way every day.

He did not hurry. When he reached the cows, he did not go around but walked through them slowly, touching the ones who would let him on their necks or their backs. This particular cow had escaped before. She was a small heifer with markings so neat and defined they looked fussed-over, which was why Merle called her Prissy. Arliss was not in the habit of naming his cows, but had he known this one was going to be so adventurous, he might have called her Rascal instead. He crossed the creek over a plank. He was in the process of burying drain tiles along the bank to clean up the muddy mess the cows had made of it, although his plan was to put in a pond like the one that Lloyd Pitt, his neighbor across the road, had dug for his cattle. The fence was on the other side of the creek, and beyond the fence, the land fell away down a rocky slope. The rocks were large, not like boulders that had tumbled down from the ridge; rather, they rose jagged from the earth like spikes on the tail of a hidden serpent. Prissy was in the middle of them, belly deep in brambles.

The gate was closed, and Arliss breathed easier when he saw it, because he had been afraid that Daniel had left it open again. Not Bob. Arliss knew Bob would never leave a gate open, and not because he was thirteen and Daniel only eleven. Age had nothing to do with the fact that Bob was careful, and Daniel was not, but this time the gate was fine, and Arliss saw what the problem was. About fifteen feet away, a post was down. He had brought with him a fence stapler, a hammer, a coil of rope, and a bucket of loose corn. He lifted the sagging wires and tied the post back temporarily with rope, then went to get Prissy. She followed him back through the gate easily as soon as he showed her the bucket. Once she was through, he let her eat from it.

He was watching her walk back toward the rest of the herd, or he might not have seen Daniel running across the top of the northwest ridge, heading for the woods. Arliss never wore a watch, but he knew what time it was, too early for Daniel to have finished weeding the beans. It was the only chore he had been given: Weed the beans, *then* you can go to Brian's; Arliss could not have been more clear, but with Merle at Carr's Big Orange all the time, no one was around to see that Daniel did what he was told. Daniel's friend Brian lived in the new subdivision where James Rudder's farm used to be. To get there, you had to drive out Bearpen Lane to Raccoon Road, then south to Glen Pike, then several miles back north on Quail Road to what used to be hardly more than a dirt path. Now it was paved and called Barrington Road and went right up through the subdivision called Barrington Heights. By car, the drive was a good ten minutes, but taking a short-cut through the woods behind the farm, Brian's house was only a half mile away, and the two boys had built a series of trails so they could get back and forth without ever getting out on a road. Back and forth was not exactly how it went. As far as Arliss could tell, Brian never came to Daniel's house. Daniel always went to Brian's. It was like he lived there.

Nobody had to tell Arliss what had happened; he could guess.

Daniel had pulled up a few weeds, mashing some into the dirt, flinging others without thinking where they might fall, but enough so when Arliss confronted him about not weeding the beans, he could whine, "But I *did.*" Arliss could hear him just by thinking about it. *But I did!* It was enough to make your stomach turn, he thought. Slipshod was the way Daniel did everything, while there was Bob, unwilling to say a job was finished until it was done right, although most of his attention and energy went into his model trains, which Arliss considered a waste of time. Still, Bob did not worry Arliss the way Daniel did, because Bob was not the one who reminded him of his father. He felt flanked by carelessness; first his father, now his son, and he did not know what he had done to deserve it.

With Bob's help, he fixed the fence by lunchtime, but it put him late going up to Clinton to pick up the salt blocks from Ted Minton's Feed and Seed. He had planned to be back home by midafternoon, and he still could, but not if he hung around Ted's place. Ted collected old engines from cars and tractors and boats, and in a shed behind the shop, he was restoring a Model A. He kept a jar of toffee on the counter, and you could take a couple of pieces and chew on them and listen to Ted tell about the latest trouble he had working on that old car. Ordinarily Arliss did not think much of people standing around talking, but Ted was different. Ted had grown up in Loyston, down the road from New Hope, and his people had been moved out by the TVA, just like Arliss. He had written a booklet called *A Mountain Boy's Life on the Farm,* which he had taken down to Knoxville and run off some copies, which he kept stacked next to the cash register and sold for two bucks. Sometimes he just gave them away. Arliss had bought one. Because Ted lived not five miles from the dam itself, he still kept up with some of the old families, the Hatmakers, the Bledsoes, the Stokeses, people like that. Ted was older than Arliss and remembered meeting his father once and also his uncle Luke. There were feed stores closer than Clinton, but Arliss made a point of going up there to trade whenever he felt he could spare the time.

He had assumed Bob would go to Ted's with him that afternoon, but Bob said no. A friend had offered to take him swimming instead. Arliss did not understand that. If he'd had the opportunity to go to a place like Ted's when he was a boy, he would not have passed it up, but when Arliss drove up, Ted wasn't even there. A girl he did not know was minding the counter. He tried to remember if Ted had ever mentioned a daughter or, wait a minute, could be a granddaughter. He noticed the toffee jar was down to three or four pieces left. The girl had one hand spread flat on the counter, and she was painting her fingernails white, an odd color for fingernails, and Arliss speculated that it might be some sort of medicine. He turned sideways to keep from staring. A back door was open, and he could see through it to the shed out back, which was closed and padlocked. He took off his hat and stuffed it into the back pocket of his overalls and told her what he wanted. She nodded to the side yard, where the salt blocks were stacked under a shed. Arliss took out his wallet and asked after Ted.

"He went down to Knoxville."

"I see."

The girl must have picked up on his disappointment because she stopped painting her nails and looked at him. "He'll be back by four."

Arliss was embarrassed that this girl had guessed his feelings. He had no intention of attracting sympathy from anybody for anything. He straightened his back and took his hat out of his pocket and held it.

"You should call ahead if you're wanting to see Ted."

Arliss noticed the girl was chewing gum. He nodded to her and put his hat on and started walking toward the door.

"Anymore, that's the only way to catch him."

She was still trying to talk to him! He threw his hand up in a backhanded wave, opened the door, and stepped outside, where he stood for a minute and wiped his face. The day was overcast and steamy, and the sky looked like rain. It would not rain, but it was the kind of day when your hair stood on end waiting for it. He backed the truck up to the shed and loaded four blocks of salt into the bed, then pulled out of the parking lot and headed for home. On the way he passed the road to Norris Dam, marked with a small brown sign. He slowed down but did not stop. He had never made that turn.

When he arrived home it was not too late to put the salt blocks out in the pastures, or to bush hog the brush along the roadside after supper, or for Bob to cut the lawn around the porch with the small mower, and it was not too late for Daniel to finish weeding the beans. He turned off Bearpen Lane into his driveway, which climbed straight up the hill before curving around the back of the house, where you could pull in and park or keep going up to the barn at the top of the hill. Arliss swung around the house and just missed running into a new 1967 powder blue Cadillac. He knew the car. It belonged to Mr. McMillan, Brian's father, and he had parked it in the spot where Arliss usually parked. Arliss pulled his truck around beside it and got out. Mr. McMillan was sitting behind the wheel of the Cadillac, and he cut the engine and rolled down the window. "You're just in time, Arliss."

Arliss stood by his truck. He took off his hat and held it with both his hands.

"Why don't you come on with us tonight and watch the game. Daniel's pitching."

"I've got work to do."

Daniel came out of the house, wearing white baseball pants and a red shirt. He carried a bat under one arm, his glove hooked over the end of the bat, and he smiled and waved to Brian, who was waiting for him in the backseat of the Cadillac. He did not acknowledge his father, but as he trotted toward the car, Arliss put his hand up. "You aren't going anywhere until you finish weeding the beans."

"But I *did*."

"You didn't do it right."

"I'll finish tomorrow, Dad. I promise."

"You'll do it now."

"But you don't *understand*. We're playing the Tigers tonight." He looked frantically at Mr. McMillan, who was already getting out of the car. Mr. McMillan shut the car door behind him, but instead of the expected *thwack,* there was a quieter, solid *click,* and this measured, restrained closing of an expensive door by a wealthy man was more threatening to someone like Arliss than any loud or angry slam. He turned his attention toward his son, and on the chance that Mr. McMillan would not hear him, whispered. "It was the only thing I asked you to do today."

Mr. McMillan managed to step in between him and Daniel and placed his hand on Daniel's shoulder. "Daniel's right, Arliss. This is an important game we're looking at tonight. If we win, see, we'll be number one in the league, which means home-field advantage next weekend at the county tournament, and I guess I don't have to tell you what that can mean for us." Mr. McMillan's voice was as measured and quiet as his car door. Arliss did not know exactly what Mr. McMillan did for a living, other than that he was in some sort of land development business. Real estate, possibly, or was it insurance? He wore light gray slacks and the white dress shirt he had most certainly worn to work, and tasseled leather loafers but no socks. Arliss stared at the man's feet. Did he come home from work, slip off his shoes, take off his socks, then put his shoes back on? "We could use home-field advantage," Mr. McMillan was saying, "because, don't get me wrong; I mean to win that tournament. But the simple truth is, we're not going to beat the Tigers tonight if Daniel doesn't pitch. The way I look at it, Arliss, he made a commitment to the team, and I need him."

"His commitment is to do what I tell him to do."

Mr. McMillan took Arliss's elbow and led him a few steps away so the boys could not hear. Arliss balked, jerking his arm away, but found himself following anyway. Mr. McMillan spoke confidingly, man-to-man, but Arliss saw how he did not have a say in this, that talking to Mr. McMillan was like trying to hold on to a handful of sand. "I see what you're trying to do here, Arliss, and I'm behind you one hundred percent. You've got to teach kids responsibility these days; I don't care what anybody says. I run into parents every day who don't bother, and you can see it in their kids, so don't get me wrong. I'm on your side, but here's the deal. If your beans get weeded first thing tomorrow morning, nothing will happen. Same result, see, whether they're weeded now or twelve hours from now. But if Daniel does not pitch this game, we're going to lose. Different result, see? That's why it looks to me like Daniel ought to be able to do both: honor his commitment to you first thing in the morning, honor his commitment to me tonight, and everybody wins."

Arliss turned away and started walking toward the house.

"Daniel's a good boy, Arliss. I'll see to it he doesn't let you down."

Daniel was already in the backseat of the Cadillac with Brian, but Arliss did not look at him as he walked past the car and stepped onto the porch.

"I meant that about coming to a game," Mr. McMillan called after him. "If not tonight, sometime. You ought to see this boy pitch, Arliss. You won't believe it."

Merle had supper waiting. Meat loaf, mashed potatoes, green peas. Daniel's plate was at his place at the table, a few bites of meat loaf gone, the peas pushed around.

"You let him eat early?" Arliss asked.

"He had a ball game," Merle said.

Arliss hung his hat on a hook beside the back door. It was a peculiar fact about this house that it had no front door. It faced backwards, away from the street, but then, when it was built, Bearpen Lane was only a wagon track. The house was set into the side of the slope, with the downhill side propped up on stone pillars. It had been only recently that Arliss had closed up the space between the pillars to make a bedroom for the boys, but he did not think to add a door down there. A real estate agent might find it, at least, a strange arrangement, and at most, a crying shame, that the only porch was out back, with a view of the old barn at the top of a straggly hill instead of the other way, toward the Great Smoky Mountains in the distance, but nobody living there seemed to notice. The door opened from the small, concrete porch into a room that contained a kitchen to the right and a living area to the left, divided by floor coverings, green linoleum in the kitchen, brown carpet in the living room. Arliss and Merle's bedroom and the only bathroom were to the right of the kitchen. Directly across the room from the door was a narrow staircase leading down to the boys' bedroom. Also down there was an unfinished room, with a concrete floor and exposed insulation, where Bob was building his model train. The train took up only one corner, leaving plenty of room for Daniel to play, but he considered it cold and dirty in there and preferred to stick to his bedroom, where he could read or listen to the radio all he wanted without anyone bothering him.

At the table next to Daniel's dirty dishes, Bob had placed the lid of a shoe box, where he kept the plastic pieces of a tiny general store he was building for his train set. He was bent over it, gluing two sides together. Arliss watched him for a minute, then said, "Get that mess off the table and help your mother."

Bob looked up from his work but did not say anything. With one hand he held the glued pieces together; with the other, he picked up the lid and carried it to the coffee table in the living room.

"Not in there," Arliss said.

Bob did not even stop. He veered toward the stairs and went down to his room.

Arliss washed his hands in the sink and dried his hands on a paper towel and reached up to the windowsill to flip off the radio.

"That's the *Gospel Hour*," Merle said.

"It's always the *Gospel Hour*."

Arliss sat down at the table. Merle set his supper in front of him, then sat down, and said, "Barb Robinson went into that Red Food and came back saying it's one big store of nothing. She went just so she could come back and report, but I told her, don't bother. Lydia is not a bit worried, and neither am I. There's no Red Food that can compete with Carr's Big Orange. They don't sell guns."

Arliss looked down at his food getting cold, but he would not begin eating until Bob got back to the table. He said, "You ever seen him pitch?"

"Who, Daniel?"

He nodded.

"No."

Bob came back upstairs and sat down. "You ever seen your brother pitch?" Arliss asked.

He shrugged. "Baseball is stupid."

"But you might have seen him."

"Who hasn't? He's the biggest show-off there is, but I don't see what's so great about it."

Merle said, "Barb says there's bins of hothouse tomatoes you wouldn't eat on a bet, and get this: The meat's already ground up. How're you supposed to know what's in it; that's what I want to know."

Arliss turned to Bob, whose hair was thin and stringy like his own, except he kept his cut short, while Bob's over there was falling in his face. "I fixed the mower. See if you can't cut the grass around the porch after supper."

"Can't I do it tomorrow?"

"Sure you can," Merle said, then turned to Arliss. "He doesn't have anything else to do tomorrow."

"He ought to be getting a haircut."

"You wouldn't grind up meat unless you had something to hide," Merle said. "Barb said she'd ask them about it the next time she's in there, but I got a made-up mind not to care. Anybody with any sense is going to know where to buy meat, and we can't help the rest."

Bob cleaned his plate, took his dishes to the sink, then went back downstairs to work on his train. He would not come back up for the rest of the night. Merle washed the dishes, then turned on the TV. Arliss put his hat back on and walked out to inspect the fence that he and Bob had fixed that morning. When he saw that it would hold, he walked among the herd, counting, not because he had to—he knew in the sweep of an eye they were all there—but from habit. When he got to the heifer called Prissy he patted her neck and whispered in her ear, "Don't you try nothing."

The overcast sky made it seem later than it was, and it occurred to Arliss to wonder how Daniel was going to play baseball once it got dark, then he remembered the new lights on the ball field. Did Merle tell him, or did he read it in the newspaper? It was Mr. McMillan again and others from the new subdivision, who had gotten lights put in at the park after they got the new school built. There were streetlights, too, on Glen Pike all the way to Quail Road and lights in the parking lots of the new school and the new Red Food Store. He could see the glow they sent skyward, making it possible to walk from the barn to the pasture without a flashlight even under a new moon. Used to be you could not do that. Used to be nights were so black you could not see your hand in front of your face.

There was still time to clean up some cedars he had found trying to push up near the broken fence, and he took a mattock out there and dug them up and threw them into the wagon to haul away later. Then he cut the grass around the porch. When he finished, he put the lawn mower away and returned to the porch. He took off his hat and hooked it on his knee and listened to the wind and the chorus of tree frogs that had started up while the mower was running. He was waiting to hear the sound of tires on the gravel driveway, but it did not come. After a while, he went inside.

Merle had gone to bed with the TV still on. He turned it off and got the radio from the windowsill above the kitchen sink and took it back outside. There were three metal chairs on the porch and a small metal table, and he set the radio on the table and turned it on. It took him a few minutes to find the station. He was not used to working the dials anyway, the radio being the province of Merle with her gospel shows and Daniel with his baseball. Arliss had never found a use for it, but wait a minute; there it was. WNOX with the game out of Cincinnati. The Reds were playing Chicago.

The game was in the bottom of the sixth inning before he heard the Cadillac, and he shielded his face as the headlights came around the corner. Daniel jumped out even before the car stopped, slamming the door behind him. Mr. McMillan's hand shot out the window in a wave, and Arliss heard him shout, "We won!" Daniel stood in the driveway with his bat and his glove, waving back as the car turned around and drove away.

Arliss stood up, dug his hands in his pockets, and watched his son. There was something in the way he stood, the way he held his head, the way he grinned when it seemed like nothing was funny, that made Arliss remember what Lydia down at Carr's Big Orange once told Merle. If ever there was a lady-killer, she had said, Daniel's it. Arliss did not understand that. But seeing him in the half-light of the driveway, his uniform covered with dirt, his dark curly hair around his face, his broad shoulders, his muscular legs, Arliss sensed there might be something here. When Daniel turned to walk toward the house, Arliss saw that he was limping. "You okay?"

"I'm great," he said.

"I thought you'd be home sooner."

"The game went into extra innings, but we pulled it out, nine to eight. I got seven strike-outs, two in the last inning to win the game. We stopped at the Krystal on the way home." He stopped talking for a minute and looked down at the radio on the table. "What's the score?"

"Five to three, Chicago."

"What inning?"

"I don't know."

Daniel stepped up onto the porch.

"Sixth, I think."

Daniel nodded. "I ate ten Krystals, but Brian ate twelve." He put his hand on the doorknob to go inside.

"Which Krystal?"

"The new one. Next to the Red Food."

"You going to listen to the game?"

"I guess."

"I could keep it on out here."

Daniel stopped in the doorway, half-inside, half-out, holding his bat with one hand, the doorknob with the other. He appeared to be giving it some thought. "That's okay, Dad," he said, then closed the door behind him.

Arliss heard him in the kitchen filling a glass with water. Then he heard him go downstairs, where he knew Daniel would turn on his own transistor radio. If Bob were still awake, he might snap at him, *turn it down,* and he would. He would take it with him under the covers if he had to. Arliss turned off his radio and listened to the frogs.

FIVE

DANIEL

When Daniel and his friend Brian were in high school, they took English from a teacher named Mr. Jameson, who stalked back and forth across the front of the classroom, clapping his hands together and yelling, "Great stuff!" as students read out loud passages from books he had assigned. Daniel and Brian tended to agree with Mr. Jameson. They thought *Catcher in the Rye* was great stuff. Also, *A Farewell to Arms, To Kill a Mockingbird, Hamlet, Walden, The Great Gatsby,* and dozens of other books, some of which he suggested they read on their own, which they did. Mr. Jameson, whose personal hero was Ernest Hemingway, spent weekends camping in the Smoky Mountains, and sometimes he took Daniel and Brian with him. He taught them the names of trees, and how to spot poisonous mushrooms and to cook the ones that weren't, and how to fly fish. He taught them how to use a knife and build a fire without a match, and quote lines from William Butler Yeats, Wilfred Owen, T. S. Eliot, and Robert Frost, and as they sat beside the Little River, carving sticks and shouting, *Two roads diverged in a wood, and I—I took the one less traveled by,* Daniel believed there was no better way to be a man. The Woodsman Poet, that's how Daniel saw himself.

When they were old enough to drive themselves, Daniel and Brian went to the mountains without Mr. Jameson, once surviving for a week in the summer without anything but their knives, a book of matches, their sleeping bags, and a package of water purification tablets. At least that was their story. They discovered they could not catch fish with their bare hands; squirrels were out of the question, and mushrooms, no matter how harmless they might look, were too risky without Mr. Jameson there to tell them if they were right. Besides, they had brought nothing to cook with, no pot, no skillet, so they hiked out to a store and bought fifty sticks of beef jerky and four packages of M&Ms and lived on those plus some blueberries they happened to find.

That same summer they ran their own lawn-mowing service, spending their days cutting lawns in Brian's neighborhood, their nights playing guitars in Brian's room, drinking vodka they stole from Brian's parents' liquor cabinet. Daniel's parents they dismissed as hopelessly provincial, but they scorned equally the upper-class life of Brian's parents, which they considered empty, even ludicrous, and they swore to each other they would live their own lives with more imagination. Secretly, though, Daniel sometimes stood in front of the liquor cabinet in Brian's house, staring at the exotic shapes and rich colors of the bottles, the weighty highball glasses etched with the country club seal, and wondered what it took to get yourself a liquor cabinet like that.

With Mr. Jameson's help, Daniel got a scholarship to a college in North Carolina, but he almost did not find out about it because his mother hid the letter. The day it arrived in the mail, he came home from school and found her in the kitchen, frying chicken. She told him to take his dirty baseball practice clothes straight to the washing machine downstairs, just like she did every day, but then she said, "Lydia Carr has a niece who moved to North Carolina, and the next thing they knew, she'd gotten herself involved in them drugs, then she tried to kill herself, and now they say her mind's half-gone. They've had to put her in a home."

"Did it come?"

"Slit her wrists, is how she done it."

"It came, didn't it?"

"What?"

"You know what, Mother. The *letter*. The one I've been waiting on for three months; did it come?"

"UT's been good enough for Bob, I don't see why it ain't good enough for you."

"Where is it?" But Daniel did not wait for an answer. He raced around the house and found it lying opened on his parents' bed, where a blind man could have found it; he was just glad his mother was not smart enough to hide it well. It was all there, the acceptance and the offer of scholarship money. It was enough. He was on his way out of there.

"I can't believe you opened my mail," he said, rereading the letter as he walked back into the kitchen, but again he did not wait for her answer. He blocked out of his hearing whatever his mother was saying about opening anything she pleased while he picked up the phone and called, first Brian, then Mr. Jameson, to tell them his great news. By the time he hung up, his father had come in and was sitting at the kitchen table.

"She doesn't have the right to read my mail," Daniel said to him.

Arliss's hands were small, but the knuckles appeared disproportionately large, swollen, certainly misshapen, and Daniel thought they made his father's hands look like those of a much older man. He had once asked if they hurt, and Arliss had looked at them as if he had never seen his own hands before. "I don't hardly feel them," he had said. Now he placed them on the table in front of him and clasped them together. "I already told you; I can't afford to send you to that fancy school," he said.

At the time, Daniel still wanted to interpret his father's great silences as having roots in wisdom, and he was willing to assume that, if Arliss was a closet deep-thinker, it meant he could be reasoned with, unlike his mother, who, he believed, never shut up long enough to have a thought deeper than a loaf pan. So he sat down at the table across from his father and explained all over again about the scholarship, which should have been unnecessary, given the fact that Bob was at UT on a scholarship, and Arliss had not expressed any difficulty understanding why he never got a bill. Daniel had gone over it all before, but this time he tried a simpler version. "It's like they're going to pay me to play baseball for them," he said.

"You can play baseball at UT," Merle said. "Down at Carr's, we sell Big Orange baseball pennants right alongside the football ones. Not as many, but we got them. Pennants, hats, seat cushions, pompoms, ashtrays, cup holders. Shitfire and a cat's ass, Daniel; you play baseball for UT, maybe you'd have half a chance of being on a winning team."

"You know what, Mother? They ought to pay you a recruiting fee."

"What is that supposed to mean?"

"Nothing."

"I don't know what he's trying to get at, Arliss, but don't you let him talk to me that way."

"Don't talk to your mother like that."

"I'm just saying," Merle continued, "UT's been fine for Bob. I don't see what's so special about you."

For Daniel, it was like a gift to hear his mother bring up this particular point, because for weeks he had been listening to her blame this same exalted university for corrupting Bob's mind, driving him to switch his major from agriculture to business without asking a single solitary soul. So it was with some pleasure that he reminded his mother of that. She stood in front of him, hands on her hips, nodding vigorously, yes, and yes again, but when he finished, she said, only, "You have to admit; Bob always had a mind for business."

"Okay. Fine. But I happen to have a mind for literature."

And when he said it, he knew it was true, and for a few seconds his heart quickened to know something like that about himself. Really, it made him temporarily breathless. He had a mind for literature. How could anything his parents say hurt him if he had that? Just the other day, he and Mr. Jameson were discussing how much more they could learn about human nature by reading Shakespeare, for instance, than any textbook on psychology. Fiction, they had concluded, was the path to a deeper truth in the same way that music can make you feel things you cannot explain. Brian, of course, had

argued, like Eliot, that music was better, while Daniel had maintained it was all the same thing. Mr. Jameson had not taken sides; he
never did, preferring instead to throw out the questions, then let the
boys go wherever they wanted with the answers. It did not matter.
Mr. Jameson had convinced Daniel that his was a unique gift, the
ability to extract truth from fiction, and now he realized it was going
to take him away from any dreamless life his parents were likely to
cook up for him.

But his mother looked at him as if he needed to have his mouth
washed out with soap. Not that she had ever attempted such a thing,
either to him or to Bob, although she and Lydia talked about it all
the time. It was understood that Lydia Carr had certainly washed her
own children's mouths out with soap, and for good reason, and both
women could list dozens of children whose mouths needed a good
cleansing. It was Daniel's contention that his mother never listened
close enough to him or Bob to know what they might or might not
have said, so her soaping opportunities always passed her by. But
now, she looked as if she were the one with soap in her mouth, or
something that made her screw up her lips when she said the word.
"Literature? How do you aim to make a living out of that? Bob's at
least getting out of this with a job. I never heard such nonsense in
my life."

Daniel considered the enormity of the task ahead of him, explaining to his mother the difference between getting an education
and getting a job, and he had not yet decided whether it was worth
it, when, suddenly, and quietly, Arliss spoke up. "Nobody's going to
work on the farm, then."

Merle and Daniel both stared at him as if he had just said something shocking, a curse word, for instance, out of a person who never
cursed. He was sitting stiffly in the chair, his hands still clasped in
front of him.

"I guess not, Dad."

Over glasses of celebratory ginger ale (which Brian spiked with
bourbon under the winking eye of Mr. Jameson), Daniel later re-
layed this conversation to Brian and Mr. Jameson, and he also told

them about his mother's attempts to sabotage his plans, although it was Mr. Jameson's contention that, if Merle had really wanted to keep Daniel from seeing the acceptance letter, she would have thrown it away. Or burned it. Daniel got in his head the odd idea that Mr. Jameson would be the one who took him to college, or maybe it was not so odd, given his teacher's involvement in the process, so it surprised him when autumn came and Mr. Jameson refused. Mr. Jameson was always careful (Daniel called it hypersensitive) about getting between a student and his parents, which was why he encouraged Daniel to go ahead and let his mother take him. Daniel packed light, despite the things his mother piled on his bed. Here were a few:

Pots and pans. *(There's a cafeteria, Mother. Honest to God, I won't need to cook.)*

A three-foot stack of bath towels. (He took two.)

A year's supply of laundry detergent. *(I'm not going to the damn wilderness. There are stores there. I'll be able to buy stuff.)*

A Bible, King James Version. (This he stuck in his bag, because anybody who knows anything about English literature knows you can't get away from the Bible.)

He managed to keep his load down to an easy-to-carry two suitcases and his guitar, because his plan was to park as far away from his dorm as possible, so nobody would see that he had come in a truck. Worrying over whether he would be able to execute this plan occupied his thoughts for the first half of the trip, as he drove over the mountains from Tennessee to North Carolina, tuning out his mother's babbling about not getting mixed up with drugs, and how to do laundry, and what to wear when the weather turned cold, and sticking with his own kind. The latter was code for the fact that he better not get over to that school and try to marry a black girl or an Asian girl or a Jewish girl, particularly one from the north, or, come to think of it, a northern girl of any kind, or what she called a Spanish girl, which included Italian or anyone who looked foreign. He appeased her with an occasional *Uh-huh,* while keeping his mind on the road and the possible excuses he might use for parking across campus, but the farther they got from Knoxville, the more anxious he became. *Let's go,* he repeated to himself; *let's just go,* which led him to the opening lines of Prufrock's song, and before he knew it, he had arrived at the question; *Do I dare?* All of a sudden he was scared. Because, at the end of the road, he believed he would be joining people who did dare, easily, without even knowing it, people to whom daring was as much a part of living as breathing and eating, who woke up every morning and ate dare for breakfast. He was the one forced to think first, to understand exactly what he was doing, stepping out of his parents' world to make his own life, and he knew what that meant. It meant he could fail.

When they arrived, he found there was only one place he was allowed to park anyway, right next to the dorm. He worked to get away from the truck as quickly as possible, but while he was scrambling to untie the ropes holding his suitcases in the truck bed, two guys carrying a small refrigerator passed by. "Cool truck," one of them said. It stopped Daniel. He stood there, staring, as the guys reached the end of the parking lot and walked into the dorm. He took another look at his mother's bright red truck. His mother was still sitting in there, blessedly silent for what seemed like the first time all day. She was staring at something, what, he could not be sure, but in front of her were impeccably groomed lawns, neat rows of holly bushes, perfect beds of pansies, swept sidewalks, old brick buildings. He took his time with the ropes, and when a pretty girl passed by and smiled at him, he smiled back.

He let his mother help him unpack his suitcases. When it was time for her to leave, they stood in the hall, surrounded by the other guys in his dorm, his future friends, all sons of worldly, educated men (he could tell). She looked each one in the eye, and said, "Don't none of you give him them drugs, hear?"

When Daniel went east to North Carolina, Brian headed south to the University of Georgia, but never having been the student Daniel was anyway, all he wanted to do when he got down there was play his guitar and drink, so he formed a band that played for fraternity parties and managed to make it work for a couple of years before flunking out. His father, using money that (as he repeated often) was intended for graduate school, set him up with a small pizza restaurant with the understanding that, this was it, and he better not blow it. To everyone's surprise, he didn't. Brian turned out to have a knack for the restaurant business and, over the years, became known for serving not only the best pizzas in town but other specialties such as spinach quiche and iced carrot muffins. He called his restaurant the Flying Dog, named in homage to the Flying Burrito Brothers and his dog, a Labrador retriever he called Chicken because it was afraid of thunder.

The summer before he flunked out of school, Brian got jobs for both himself and Daniel working as cooks in the mess hall of a girls' camp in North Carolina, which happened to be owned by one of his father's old fraternity brothers. The night he called to tell Daniel, it was three in the morning, and Daniel was asleep. "What's the matter, man?" Daniel whispered into the phone. His roommate was sleeping somewhere down the hall, but wedged into the bed beside him was a girl he hardly knew, and he did not want to wake her.

"Nothing. I'm fine."

It was possible he was fine, but Daniel could tell he was also drunk, and sometimes, although not always, that meant that he was not fine. When Brian woke him up like this in the middle of the night, it usually had something to do with Susan, his girlfriend since ninth grade, who had stayed in Knoxville to study art and landscape design. Daniel had already lost one bet, that Brian would not make it six months down in Georgia without Susan. (Now they were on their second bet, which gave him two years.) So Daniel made a guess. "Is it Susan?" he asked, but Brian said no and explained about the jobs while Daniel half dozed, knowing Brian would call him back the next day, anyway, because he would not remember making this call. "You got to go up there with me, man," Brian was saying. "This camp is in the middle of fucking nowhere. I can't do this alone."

Roused by an urgency in Brian's voice, Daniel sat up. "Don't do it, then," he said, then listened while Brian took a sip of whatever he was drinking. "Shit," he heard Brian mumble to himself, as if there were something else going on the other end of the line, Brian spilling the drink, falling off a chair, getting caught in the phone cord, tripping over something, looking in his wallet and finding it empty, catching a glimpse of himself in a mirror, discovering the potato chips gone, breaking a guitar string, choking on a Cheeto, confronting a burglar, having a heart attack, something, anything, that had taken him away from the phone. Daniel waited. He never knew when this sort of thing happened if he should get alarmed. But Brian came back and, as if he had never left, said, "Dad's making me get a real job, and you know what he means by real. He means anything but playing music. Come on, man, I can think of worse than spending the summer in the mountains."

"Sure. It'll save me from a summer in Knoxville."

"Then you'll do it?"

"I just said I would."

But the night before they were scheduled to drive up there, Susan called Daniel and told him Brian was not going to make it after all.

Daniel went anyway and found he was not sorry about the way things had turned out. He was housed in an old log cabin behind the mess hall, but there were only three other men besides himself at camp that summer, two cooks and the hiking counselor, and because Daniel claimed the only bed in the small upstairs loft, he ended up having more privacy than the others. It was a bunk bed, and if Brian had come, mostly likely he would have slept in the other half, and their every night would have been a party, which might have been fun, but partying with Brian brought with it a certain number of headaches and not just the literal ones. There were always messes to be taken care of in Brian's wake. Daniel liked living in the woods. He found himself profoundly relieved to be there after a year at college, where he had discovered that there were a great many people who had minds for literature and who suggested he might not be as unique as Mr. Jameson had led him to believe.

And it was fortunate that he enjoyed the solitude, because he had started out the summer badly, attempting to date two counselors at the same time, and his reputation did not recover. After that, he spoke politely to people but did not get close to any of them, and to his surprise it felt good. He limited his contacts to his fellow cooks and the small group of older campers whose job it was to set the tables for meals. Of these, he especially liked a girl named Leda whom he nicknamed *Tennessee* because, like him, she came from there. She was not what he would normally call attractive, her body slightly on the chunky side, and her face merely ordinary, but he was often surprised by her eyes, which seemed more than usually alive and on the verge of saying something clever. Or interesting. Or kind. More than once he had handed her a stack of napkins or a pair of salt and pepper shakers and, when she smiled at him, found himself asking, *"What?"*

"I don't know," was what she always said back to him. *"What?"*

Once he had overheard the girls teasing each other about boyfriends, and when they got to Leda they would not let up. She had told them she did not have one, but they insisted she at least give them a name of someone she liked. So she crossed her arms, and said, "Sammy Davis Jr." That shut them up. He was impressed by the easy way she kept herself apart and did not seem to care what anybody thought of her. As for a girlfriend, though, he was not looking at her that way. He spent most of his time by himself in his loft, reading and writing poetry. It made him feel monastic and clearheaded, and each night, as he reread *Walden* by the light of a flashlight, he began to think, if he ever found his way to a solitary life, he would build himself a simple cabin in the woods.

"Count me out," Brian said. Brian had come for a weekend visit, and the two of them were sitting on a hill, admiring the bodies of the adolescent girls below while sneaking sips from Brian's flask of Jack Daniel's and talking about what they wanted to do with their lives. "If we're building anything, I'm voting for a sailboat. I don't see why we couldn't sail around the world."

"We don't know how to sail."

"Since when did you learn how to build a log cabin?"

"We could hike the Appalachian Trail."

"Holy shit, they're flexible," Brian said, nodding to a group of girls by the lake. "Daniel! Stud man! What have you been doing with yourself?"

Daniel shrugged. Just then he spied Leda and pointed her out. "She's an interesting girl."

"Aw, man; she's a dog."

"Cut it out, Brian; she's a nice kid, and she's from Tennessee. That's what I call her."

"Tennessee Stud."

"Just Tennessee."

"What's her real name?"

"I forgot."

On the last night of the camp session, Daniel was in charge of the bonfire, which he had started with a half a dozen gasoline-soaked tampons. It was a secret method the camp director had taught him, warning, if the girls ever found out, they would squeal and yell *gross* and run away. He had stayed out of sight, far back from the fire circle, while the girls sang their songs and shed their tears of farewell (he had never seen so many girls crying at one time), but when they went back to their cabins, he moved closer. He was looking forward to staying there by himself until the fire went out but soon realized he was not alone. There, on the other side of the fire with her back against a tree, sat Leda.

FIRE

SIX

LEDA

Daniel was not the first one Leda fell in love with. The first was Dave, the hiking counselor, who had long, sun-streaked hair that looked as if it would feel silky if you touched it, although Leda never got that close. On hikes led by Dave, she separated herself from the other giggling girls, rock-hopping, for instance, to the middle of a stream to sit on a boulder in the sun and study the water, demonstrating that she was more mature than others her age. Deeper, more soulful, worthy of some attention.

Over here. Hey, are you paying attention?

She imagined Dave watching her and thinking, here was someone he could talk to, someone who could understand the complicated workings of his heart, but in fact she was not sure he even noticed her out there alone on those rocks, and nothing in the words he spoke to her, which ranged from, *Hand me that rope,* to *Did anybody remember to pack the raisins?* ever gave her a clue.

The pimpled and oddly angled boys her own age bored her, but the truth was, none of them were interested in her either. Leda knew she was not pretty, not in the same way other girls, with their flat tummies and cooperative hair, were pretty. She felt like a hodge-podge of body parts put together as an experiment, then forgotten: thick legs, full bottom, but tiny breasts! Around other girls she felt clumsy, because her feet were bigger, and her hands were bigger, and her hair was not curly or straight but something thick and in between that frizzed when it rained. People said she had nice eyes and a pretty face, but people also said she looked like her father, which to Leda meant she looked like a man, possibly handsome, but never pretty. She reasoned that only a grown man, mature enough to see further than skin-deep, would be able to appreciate someone like her. A man, for heaven's sake, like Dave.

Leda had been coming to camp for nine summers, starting when she was seven years old, even though the minimum age was supposed to be eight. Her father, or possibly it was her grandmother, had talked someone into letting Leda start early. This summer she was sixteen and had made it finally to the level of CIT, which stood for Counselor-in-Training, girls who were not campers and not counselors but a little of both. They set the tables for meals and were expected to assist the real counselors with activities such as archery, swimming, canoeing, crafts, horseback riding, hiking, and tennis, but they got to live in a cabin to themselves on the hill behind the infirmary, and, when they were not working, they were free to do what they wanted. Their own counselor was a University of South Carolina student named Paulette who was thin and tan and had straight black hair braided in one long strand down her back like an Indian princess, which meant that when it came time for the campfire skit, there was no contest over who should play Pocahontas. Paulette looked exactly like what Pocahontas should have looked like, the Pocahontas of your dreams. She was a swimming counselor and strode around in tank suits the way other people wore clothes, reminding Leda of the girls who sat cross-legged under the blue-striped tent at the country club pool, playing cards and eating orange slices before sauntering off to win the hundred-meter freestyle. Paulette's boyfriend happened to be Dave, who also went to the University of South Carolina, although Leda did not hold this against her. She loved Paulette almost as much as she loved Dave, but so did all the other CITs, who were young enough to believe there was still time to grow up and *be* Paulette someday.

At rest hour each day, Paulette and the other CITs wrote letters or traded magazines or played cards or fixed one another's hair, but Leda liked to hike to the top of the hill behind the cabin. The trail passed the outdoor chapel with its pine-filtered view of the lake, stone pulpit, and wooden benches, before heading straight up to a rock ledge called Crows Nest. No one else ever went up there during rest hour, which was one of the reasons she did, the other being the hope that she would earn the reputation as the girl who really, no kidding, liked to hike. A perfect companion for, say, the hiking counselor.

One afternoon she came down from Crows Nest and found Paulette sitting on a chapel bench talking to a girl named Bitsy, who was considered the funniest girl in the cabin by everyone but Leda. Leda suspected Bitsy knew this. Just the other day, when Leda was singing "Old Man" and got to the part that goes *I'm a lot like you were,* Bitsy had jumped in and said, "I'm a lot like you *are.* It's *are,* not *were.* If you're going to massacre Neil Young, at least get the words right." Then all the other girls had laughed and agreed with Bitsy. What difference did it make, really, but the way Bitsy had looked at her, she felt stupid and did not know how to defend herself.

Bitsy and Paulette did not look up from their conversation on the bench, so Leda left them alone, and she might have forgotten about it, except the next day she came upon the same thing, only this time it was Paulette and Katie. Then the next day it was Jill, and by the fourth day, Leda figured out that her friends were confiding their problems to Paulette. In some cases their problems were serious, such as parents who were divorcing or alcoholic. Leda did not know all the problems, but she wasn't deaf. Word got around. One girl was flunking out of her prestigious Atlanta private school, although Leda happened to know she was doing it on purpose so she would not have to go there anymore. Several girls had boyfriend problems, and one could not absolutely swear, for sure, she was not pregnant. (Paulette ended up driving her to the Planned Parenthood in Asheville to find out, for sure, that she was not.) Paulette had become the bearer of problems, and with the girls who shared them she developed a special relationship, which involved sympathetic looks, like secret bond rays, shooting across the mess hall. Having a special bond with Paulette turned out to impart more status than being known as a genuine, no-kidding, hiking fanatic.

So Leda wanted to sit on the chapel benches and tell Paulette her problems, only she did not have any. Pregnancy, for instance, was not going to be a question for someone whose only kiss so far had been a surprise, lip-mashing ordeal with a blind date. In truth, she did have one very large problem, the fact that her mother had died in a car accident when she was six years old, but she did not care to talk about that. Plenty of people wished she would. There were girls who longed to be her friend just so they could hear the sad story, but she would not give it to them. She had watched people change the way they looked at her when they found out she was not just Leda, but *Leda the motherless girl,* and she resented the idea that a life should be defined by a single moment. So day after day, Leda sat on the rocks of Crows Nest straining to think of something else that would allow her entrance into Paulette's club of troubled souls, and finally one day she did.

I need to talk to you sometime.

This was the password.

The chapel benches were twelve-foot-long pine logs sliced in half, their bowl-shaped bottoms wedged into the terraced hill. There were two rows, eight logs deep, with an aisle up the center. At the bottom was a stone pulpit, and behind it, the lake. Paulette sat sideways on one of the benches hugging her knees, her pink toenails on tiny sandaled feet pointing toward Leda. Her hair was wet and newly combed and lay flat against her back. Leda straddled the bench, her feet flat on the ground. She spent a few awkward minutes examining the chigger bites on her ankle before getting up the nerve to say what was her mind. "I don't think I can believe in God anymore."

Leda was prepared for Paulette to be shocked. Nobody she knew didn't believe in God except her father, who had good reason. The way Leda saw it, if you say *See you later* to your wife then, later, end up identifying her car-mangled body on an emergency room stretcher, you earn the right to believe anything you want. But her father never talked to her about God or her mother or much of anything, so she was left to decide for herself if the prevailing wisdom about God trumped her father's particular and personal loss of faith. She did not think so. The prevailing wisdom where Leda grew up in Chattanooga, Tennessee, where the only question regarding church was not *do* you go, but *where,* did not even allow room for faith. God was real the same way dirt was real, and no one struggled over whether to believe or disbelieve in dirt. She suspected there were people elsewhere in the world who felt the same way she did, and though she did not suppose Paulette was one of them, she had decided it was worth the risk, because what she was hoping for were dark, brooding deliberations over what might be Paulette's toughest challenge yet. Because Leda's problem was not only personal, but theological, an archetypal cry in the wilderness. It might take days. Leda was not at all prepared for what she got.

"Dave doesn't either!" exclaimed Paulette, in a voice that made Leda think of a contestant on a television quiz show. "Do you want me to ask him to talk to you?"

Leda wore hiking boots in case Dave needed a reminder that they had something in common, but he showed up in tennis shorts, his hair pulled back in a terry-cloth headband. He would have no way of knowing, but Leda also played tennis. She wondered if she should mention this. He was sitting on the ground at the front of the chapel with his back propped against the pulpit, throwing tiny pinecones toward the lake. She sat down on a bench and pretended to be watching the pinecones hit the water, but, really, she was having a hard time breathing. When finally she spoke, explaining her problem, it was with half a voice. He did not even look up. "It's no big deal."

"It's not?"

"Nah."

That seemed to be it. She thought for a minute he might even stand up and walk away, but instead he picked up another pinecone.

She had assumed certain philosophical questions did not require elaboration. It was like the Beatles; if you had to explain why the Beatles were great to somebody, they weren't going to get it anyway, and here was Dave, with no sense of the depth of her predicament, so she decided to bring it down to a practical level. "You don't understand. I'm going to be president of my church youth group next year. How can a person be president of a church youth group and not believe in God?"

"Don't be president?"

Leda turned her attention to the lake. It was a dark gray-green and impossibly cold, fed by a mountain spring; it knocked the breath out of you when you dove in. Leda remembered the summer before, earning her Senior Lifesaving certificate in this lake, not because she wanted to be a lifeguard but because she wanted to swim a mile. It was required, the swimming of the mile, and as Leda watched other girls drop out because it was too hard, or because the water was too cold, she became even more determined to finish. Never in her life had she been discouraged by physical discomfort. She was aware of being admired for this quality. She was aware also that she was considered sort of an oddball, and it was these conflicting notions, that she was an admired oddball, that explained why she had been elected president of her church youth group. It was not popularity, but competence, that swung the vote her way, or, as the past president told her when he talked her into it, "Nobody else can do it."

What he could not know was that nobody else would face the same dilemma. Would she be considered a successful president if she merely did a good job running the fall carnival, or was more required? Was it enough to stick to the predictable *how-even-one-person-can-make-a-difference* theme for the Youth Sunday sermon, or did she have the guts to talk instead about the hypocrisy of a Christian congregation with no black faces, no poor faces, only well-dressed Episcopalians? Because it was no joke; these Episcopalians were getting to her. A tour through the pews could turn up pastel linen shifts and white leather sandals that smelled as sweet, Sunday after Sunday, as when they first came out of the shoe box. Midnight blue velvet dresses with white lace collars, wool skirts, cashmere sweaters, silk shells. Leda had decided there might as well be a sign on the door to the sanctuary: POLYESTER NOT WELCOME HERE. (Also, while they were at it, no dark skin or anyone with an income of less than six figures.)

She did not imagine she had the guts. But she argued back and forth with herself over the relative morality. Was it better to be kind? Or principled?

The one option she had never considered was quitting, but as she watched Dave throwing pinecones, she decided she could not explain why, so she steered the conversation back to the original question. "I used to, you know, believe in God, but one day, it was like it didn't make sense anymore, and once you get started, the whole thing kind of unravels. Is that like what happened to you?"

"I never thought about it."

"The problem is, I feel so guilty."

"Then don't."

Leda took a few minutes to consider this advice, partly because it was Dave, with the muscular forearms and the wide shoulders and the silky hair, who had given it, but mostly because it pointed to an area of logic she had never explored. Guilt gone with the wave of a hand, could thus fall obligation? Worry? The implications were mind-boggling. Dave had stopped throwing things at the lake and started pulling pine needles apart like wishbones. Black smudges of sap stuck to his fingers. He looked, maybe sincere, but it also could have been slightly bored, and though she was beginning to feel sorry she had brought the whole thing up, she persisted anyway. "Don't? That's it? Just don't?"

He looked surprised to have his words played back to him. "I guess." His hands scrambled for another pinecone, which he sailed nearly to the other side of the lake. "Why do you feel guilty?"

"I don't know. I just think that I should. Believe in God, I mean. It's something people *ought* to do."

He sighed as if relieved to be back on ground he recognized. "Don't let other people tell you what to think. That's what I do." But already he was standing up, dusting pine needles off the back of his tennis shorts, teaching her another lesson entirely from the one he spoke with his words, and that was: *Boys like me don't look at girls like you.*

On the last night of the camp session, Leda was sitting by herself with her back against a tree, watching the bonfire, which had shrunk from a huge inferno to a smoldering collage of yellow, scarlet, blue, purple, and green under a web of disintegrating logs. Back at the cabin, her friends were exchanging addresses and phone numbers, promising to write, promising to call, promising to get together in the fall, at Christmas, sometime, promising to come back next year, promising to remember. *To never forget.* And they would mean it. Leda knew; she had seen it every year, because they would think it was not possible to get this close to people, then never see them again. But Leda knew it *was* possible, that it was not only possible but probable, that the initial flurry of letter writing would fall off, then it would die, and that would be it. She closed her eyes. When she opened them, she realized she was not alone. On the other side of the fire stood Daniel Greene.

Leda knew Daniel. She knew all the cooks, Fritz and Peg and Maggie and Big Sam, because of the kidding around in the mess hall between the cooks and the CITs when they set the tables. Daniel was not the biggest teaser (that would be Peg or Big Sam), but he was friendly and called her Tennessee, because they were the only two Tennesseans at the camp that summer. He said it with a voice of solidarity as if they were some brand of underdog, which he believed, because, as he explained once, there were two notions about Southerners, and only one included sitting on big porches, drinking Mississippi toddies, saying *y'all,* and writing like Faulkner. The other involved going around barefoot and toothless, sleeping with family members, saying *yu'ins,* and lucky even to read. "Most people," he told her, "even fellow Southerners, *especially* fellow Southerners, assume people who come from Tennessee are the second kind."

Leda never knew if he was joking or not. But the girls in her cabin had labeled him as strange, and he did look different with his long dark hair that was so curly, it twisted in tendrils. (Later, when she knew him better, Leda called him Medusa to tease him, but instead of laughing, he looked horrified. She was sorry and assumed he was upset because she had compared him to a monster, but that was not it. It was because she had picked the wrong Greek. "Bacchus," he declared, as if she should have known.) But on the last night of the camp session, when he came around to her side of the fire and sat down beside her, Leda noticed for the first time all summer that his eyes were the color of chocolate.

They talked about camp for a while, about some of the things they had done and what they would miss and, in particular, some of the people they liked and did not like. Then, right in the middle of something he was saying, Daniel stopped and admitted that, having called her "Tennessee" all these weeks, he did not remember her real name. "Of course," he said when she told him, slapping his head in surprise to have forgotten. "Do you happen to know the poem . . ."

"Yes."

"I didn't know if maybe . . ."

"I've read it," she said and blushed. Leda was a difficult name to carry around. Chances were, those who had not read the William Butler Yeats poem *Leda and the Swan* had never heard the name and tended to spell it wrong, such as Leida, Leada, Lida, Lita, or Leta (although some simply bagged it and called her Lisa), but the burden was greater around those who had. She imagined them conjuring up images of strong white-feathered fingers pushing against the soft flesh of her thighs.

"Did you know," Daniel was saying, "Leda was the mother of Helen of Troy."

Ah, yes, Leda thought, as she had so often. *The mother of the beauty; never the beauty herself,* but before she could reply, Daniel added, "I'm an English major, you know."

"At the University of South Carolina?"

"Why would you think that?"

Leda shrugged. "I don't know. A lot of people around here seem to go there. My counselor goes there. Also Dave; you know him, the hiking counselor?"

"That asshole?"

"Yeah. Him."

When the fire died down, Daniel led Leda to a garden behind the barn which, in all the summers she had been at this camp, she never knew was there, and they picked corn and shucked it and ate it raw off the cob. And they took a handful of beans and two tomatoes back to the top of the hill near the mess hall and ate them, the tomatoes like apples, juice rolling down their chins, which they wiped with their shirts. Daniel explained that he had gotten his job through his friend Brian, whose father knew the owner of the camp. Brian was supposed to have come, too, he said, "But something came up." He lay back on the grass and put his arms under his head. Leda was trying to decide whether it would be appropriate to ask what it was that came up, when Daniel continued, "He got himself arrested for drunk driving the week we were supposed to leave. I don't know; it shook him up, I guess."

"I guess."

"Brian's dad is a jerk, by the way. Just to let you know."

Leda nodded as if she did.

"Brian would have liked it here. Let me tell you something, Tennessee; things can get crazy out there."

"You mean . . . out in the world?"

"Suburbia."

"Ah."

"You can get lost." And he snapped his fingers to show how quick. "You can forget who you are and end up selling out for the sake of, I don't know; you name it. Stupid things like making money, being top dog, shit like that. You are my witness, Tennessee; that is the one thing I will never do." Leda was struck by the explosive quality of Daniel's voice, as if he had been silent for a long time and was bursting now with a profusion of pent-up words. It was exciting just to hear him; she would not deny that. He told her about a time when he and Brian had tried to catch fish using a string with a hook on one end and a worm on the hook. They dangled it into the creek, but the fish ignored it, some of them shoving the worm as if it were in their way as they headed downstream. So he and Brian ended up trying to hit the fish with rocks, although they were equally unsuccessful. "I don't know what I'm saying, really, except that I think stuff like that is good for you. It's humbling to be bested by fish." He paused. "Not in the same way as a night in jail."

"I guess not."

"Brian should have gotten himself up here anyway. He wouldn't have had to give up drinking or anything like that." He sat up. "I've been thinking a lot, sitting up there alone in the loft of that cabin all summer, and here's the thing. I want my life to mean something, you know? I'm not interested in accidents. I don't want to wander around wondering what the hell I'm doing. The way I look at it, if we only get one life, why shouldn't we live it exactly the way we want?"

"We should."

"That's what I mean! Screw expectations. Next time I bump into somebody else's idea of how I should live my life, I'm running the other way. I might even run off and build my own log cabin in the woods someday."

Leda suspected that he was talking more to himself than to her, but it did not bother her, because she was busy thinking about how lately she, too, had been questioning her own life. She had been feeling caught in a cheated generation, too late for Vietnam (which, okay, so she knew that was a good thing), only her concept of what it meant to be a young person in America included protesting against the war. She had looked forward to the day when she could stand on a university lawn with a sign, and now what? She could burn her bra, but nobody would notice. Civil rights marches were already in history books, and being a hippie had become a fashion statement. The way she saw it, people older than she had stories to tell; people younger were forming different notions about what it meant to be young in America, leaving Leda in a sliver of a generation that did not belong anywhere. What she had not known was, if anyone else felt this way.

"Brian would have us sailing around the world, but I keep telling him, we don't know how to sail, so now we're talking about hiking the AT, if and when he ever gets his shit together. I'll tell you right now what Brian ought to do. Start a band. Everybody knows what Brian ought to do but what about me?" He threw his hands in the air. *"How should I begin to spit out all the butt-ends of my days and ways?"*

"Oh!"

"T. S. Eliot."

"Would you really build a log cabin in the woods?"

For a brief moment, Daniel looked alarmed. Then he shrugged and lay back down. "My parents," he said, "have some land."

When her father arrived to pick her up the next day, Leda told him about Daniel, and when she mentioned the college in North Carolina where he went to school, her father nodded. "That's a good school. You ought to consider a school like that." Peering out the car window as Leda pointed to the figure behind the mess hall, he added, "He must be a pretty smart boy."

So it happened that when Leda was a freshman, Daniel was a senior and lived already in a log cabin of sorts, although he did not build it. It was better described as a shack made of wood that had at one time been painted a pale shade of green but now looked gray and sunken on one side, so that you could see under the half that was still propped up on cinder blocks, while the other side looked rooted in mud. A cinder-block step in front of the door was also crooked. So was the door. There was no running water, but it had electricity, because, as Daniel pointed out, "No one can be expected to live without a stereo." There was also a phone jack, but Daniel did not have a phone, because, he explained, "This way my parents can't reach me."

The shack was about a mile from campus on property owned by an art professor who sometimes took students there to paint nature scenes. Daniel lived there by himself with his books and his guitar and his Leo Kotke records, and Leda thought his was about the most romantic life she had ever seen. The first time she went out there, she stood in her dorm room in front of a mirror for an hour trying to decide which jeans to wear, although, it turned out, it did not matter anyway. He already had a girlfriend.

Her name was Pat. She was three years older than Daniel and already out of school, working as an artist in Chapel Hill and living in a rented garage, which also served as her studio. Leda never met Pat, but in her picture, which Daniel kept on a table beside his bed, she was a tiny woman with dark hair cut as short as a man's. In the picture she wore a long black skirt and black vest with no shirt so that her thin arms angled outward from her body like branches on a sapling. The expression on her face indicated she did not much care whether her picture was being taken or not. Pat painted huge, dark, multitextured pictures that depicted women with distorted bodies and tortured faces floating in abstract images that evoked hurricanes and tornados. There were also random drippings of red paint that you could take for blood or tears. Either way, the effect was disquieting. Daniel admitted that he did not like them, either, but he kept one hanging above his bed.

Daniel spent a great deal of time complaining about Pat. *I swear something's up with the guy who owns the deli down the street. We go in, she orders extra guacamole, there's something more than guacamole going on.* Leda just listened. Every day after classes she walked the mile to his cabin, where they would study together, Leda at the small wooden desk, Daniel propped up on the bed, reading Chinese poetry or picking out Graham Parsons tunes on his guitar. She got used to going out to the cabin, and Daniel let her use it even when he was gone. He was gone every weekend to Chapel Hill.

But one weekend in the spring he surprised her, and they drove the two hours to Camp Woodsong, where they had met. The camp was closed for the winter, the driveway covered with rank, wet leaves, although scattered through the forest were the bright green nibs of new leaves. They parked the car on the shoulder of the road, climbed over the gate, and headed for a trail that started behind the junior cabins and followed a creek for about a mile before climbing to the top of a ridge opposite Crows Nest. The trail had been one of Leda's favorites, but never had she seen it lined with spring wildflowers, and Daniel knew the names: jack-in-the-pulpit, golden seal, chickweed, trillium. At the top, they came to a grassy bald where they ate a lunch of French bread, cheese, grapes, M&Ms, and a pint bottle of Jack Daniel's, which they poured into plastic cups and mixed with warm Coke. To the west, the Pisgah National Forest stretched all the way to the horizon, and Daniel pointed out that there were no traces of civilization anywhere. "What I like to do," he said, "is pretend it's a thousand years ago, and there are no humans around, and I'm standing up here, the first to lay eyes on this whole expanse of untouched land."

Leda looked at the expanse and saw a radio tower to the right, and though she decided not to contradict him on this point, she could not help reminding him that there certainly were humans around a thousand years ago.

"I know that."

"I see what you mean, though."

Then he, too, spotted the radio tower. "Shit," he said, and stood up. His father, he said, did not believe in untouched land. "The way he looks at it, idle land is as bad as idle people." Daniel was pacing back and forth on the rock now, shaking his hands from the wrist down, like a swimmer warming up for a plunge into water, a nervous habit he slipped into whenever he paced and talked at the same time. "It's like a moral thing with him. He had me and my brother out there working on the farm as soon as we could walk, but it was always Bob he was planning to give the land to, you know? He probably thought I'd run it into the ground. Starve the cows or sell them and give all the money to the Sierra Club. Watch it turn fallow, grow wild, and choke on cedar trees; I don't know. The real problem was, I was second son, see. He never even tried to hide it. We'd go out with him, and he would turn to Bob and say, *Bob, this is how you change a scraper blade.* Then he would turn to me and say, *Daniel, get me a screwdriver.* What was he thinking? And don't assume he didn't expect me to be a farmer, but on what land? And how was I supposed to learn, from listening to him teach Bob? He never got it either. He never understood. Still doesn't."

Until that precise moment, Leda had known Daniel as someone who talked passionately and frequently about freeing himself from the trap of suburbia, and now he was telling her he had grown up on a farm, and she did not know what to think. Her first impulse was to be hurt, because she had thought she knew him better, but the longer he talked, the more she began to wonder what kind of feat it had been for him to come from being the son of a farmer to someone who, among other things, possessed a sharp eye for cultural hypocrisy and a staggering knowledge of English and American literature. She conceded that she could be wrong. There was no rule that said he could not have come from an *educated* farm family, and she winced at her own prejudice. But wherever the truth lay, she concluded that Daniel would resist easy definition. She studied his face and missed the conflict that was there. Instead, she saw only a complexity that changed her hurt feelings into something like awe. "I never knew you wanted to be a farmer."

"I don't," he said. Then he blushed and looked down at his feet. "Pat doesn't know any of this," he said.

"I won't tell."

He began stuffing food back into the backpack. They hardly spoke as they walked back down the trail. When they reached the creek, Daniel stopped, picked up a rock, and skipped it across the water. Leda watched him, and in a minute tried it herself, but her rock sank when it first hit the water. She tried another and another, but they all sank. Daniel said, "I don't think you're flipping your wrist."

"I don't think my wrist flips."

"Don't be ridiculous."

"I can't throw a Frisbee either."

"Watch," he said. He threw another rock, *one, two, three, four, five.* Five skips! His whole body curved into the throwing, easy, and he spun around to face her, grinning. Creek water dripped off his arm. Sunlight shone through his hair and onto his skin. He walked to where she stood, reached down, then slowly, watching her face as if waiting for her to stop him, pulled off her shirt. And in the rush of spring air, her tiny naked breasts were beautiful, and in his kneading hands, her big bottom was beautiful, and by the time they lay down on her shirt, which he had carefully spread on the ground next to the creek, they did not take the time to get their pants past their ankles. "No promises," he whispered, and feeling beautiful, she whispered back, "I know."

The next weekend, Daniel drove up to Chapel Hill to see Pat, and Leda never went back to the cabin again.

SEVEN

LEDA

Pat left Daniel for a drummer in a rock band. After that he got in his car and drove across the country to California, where he lived with a friend from college in an upstairs apartment on Main Street in Tustin and picked strawberries on a farm until it was sold off to developers. Next he got a job teaching seventh grade English at a private Christian school, but when he was fired for spending more time talking to the students about politics than comma placement, he moved back to Knoxville, where he worked for Brian at his restaurant, the Flying Dog. He had just been accepted into a graduate program at the University of Tennessee when he remembered Leda, looked her up, and called her.

It would not be true to say she had waited all that time for him. Five years had passed, and by then she had finished college and part of a graduate degree in education, which she abandoned after deciding she did not want to be a teacher after all. She switched her sights to journalism and got a job working as a reporter on a small newspaper south of Raleigh. She had other boyfriends, a whole series of them, some more serious than others, so it would not even be true to say she thought about Daniel all of that time, although she might have conceded that he served as a kind of measuring stick.

Leda would remember she was living in the blue house when he called. The walls were Carolina blue; the carpet, a turquoise shag;

the curtains, royal; and the couch, navy. The blue house, which looked as if it had once been somebody's elegant home, was now divided into four apartments, two upstairs, two down, of which Leda's was downstairs at the front. It was a dangerous place to live, a fact she discovered early each morning when she entered the police department and opened a file drawer and flipped through the reports to see what had happened the night before. Officer Mike was usually standing right there, but he would not tell her, even if she asked. This was the game. A murder report could be waiting on one of the note cards in that file drawer, and he would not let on. Most days there was nothing but speeding tickets, which was why she had to stay alert. You could get lazy, flipping through all the speeding tickets and miss an armed robbery, and the one time she did, Officer Mike went out of his way to stop by the newsroom and grin at her, but he never said a word. The one piece of information she did not miss was the fact that almost all the crimes happened in her neighborhood. She mentioned this one day to Officer Mike, who nodded, and said, "Yes, ma'am, you sure picked one hell of a place to live."

But the police beat was not as bad as writing obituaries, which was the other assignment that had been given to Leda, police and obits being the two beats assigned to all new reporters, with the understanding that they would move up. It took Leda about a day and a half to realize there were only two other reporters at the newspaper, and they had been there forever, and they weren't going anywhere. So there was no way to move up. Up was taken. The only thing she could do when she got tired of police and obits was leave.

Writing obits was not merely boring; Leda could stand boring. It was also heartless, because, a few months earlier, the editor (who suffered from thwarted ambition and believed that, just because it *was* a small-town newspaper did not mean it had to *act* like a small-town newspaper) had instigated a new policy that required every obituary to follow the same rigid form. The form allowed only for the name of the deceased, age, date of death, a listing of survivors, and funeral arrangements. People would bring in announcements with angels taking their mother away, and Leda had to say, nope.

There could be no more Calling Home to Jesus or Going to Glory or Resting in the Arms of the Savior, and nobody was going to get to be Sorely Missed or Forever Etched in Memory either. Leda found herself in the position of enforcing a rule she thought unnecessary, even cruel. "If these people want angels, they should get angels," she told Daniel the night he called. "Anything they want is all right with me."

"No angels?" Daniel said.

"It breaks their hearts."

There was silence on the other end of the phone. And after all these years, with no hope left, Leda could not stand even one second. "Daniel? Are you still there?"

"How about you come to Knoxville."

For the wedding, Leda's grandmother suggested lilies. "They're elegant but not flashy," her grandmother explained. "And, please, not too many. A few on the patio, a centerpiece for the table, and a bouquet for the bride, but that's enough."

"I don't *have* to have *any* flowers," Leda said, but her grandmother gave her the weary, on-the-precipice-of-patience look that she used on salesclerks, waiters, and children. "Yes," she said, "you do."

The wedding was to be a small, simple ceremony under a rented tent on the lawn with a reception to follow inside. Leda had attended just two weddings before, one given for the daughter of one of her father's partners and featuring more than two hundred guests, six bridesmaids in pink satin, six groomsmen in black tails, a flower girl, and a ring bearer. The bridal gown, because that's what it was, a gown, not a dress, reportedly cost $4,000 and made the bride look like a no-kidding princess, even though she was one of the girls Leda knew in high school who snuck behind the bleachers to smoke cigarettes. At the reception, a band played "Jeremiah Was a Bullfrog," the cake was four feet high, and Leda considered the whole thing ghastly. The other wedding was for a cousin she hardly knew, held in front of only twelve people in her aunt's living room. Leda was only eleven and did not find out until several years later that the groom had left a wife and two children to marry this cousin, but she sensed something was wrong, because all the grown-ups looked as if they had stomachaches. Leda had a feeling her own wedding would be something like that one. A disaster.

Plan Number One, to hold the wedding at St. John's Episcopal Church, fell through when the priest refused to allow singing. The song in question was from an oratorio by Handel, and the singer, a soprano, was one of her grandmother's many friends from the local opera company, where Leda's grandmother was a benefactress, her name permanently at the top of donor lists. She and Leda met with the priest one afternoon to go over the arrangements for the wedding, which included pieces for trumpet and cello as well as the Handel. The priest, a man close to her grandmother's age named Eric Hahn, listened without interrupting, taking notes and nodding, but when they finished, he smiled, and said, "No singing."

Her grandmother smiled back. They were sitting in Mr. Hahn's office, which was small and shabby but, Leda guessed, only for effect. Pictures on the wall hung slightly crooked, as did the curtains, but they did not have to be that way. Somebody, anybody, could have reached over there to straighten them if they had wanted. Stacks of books and loose papers were everywhere, piled on the chairs opposite the priest's desk, so when Leda and her grandmother had walked in, he had made a big deal about moving them so they could sit down. But, Leda thought, people came to talk to him all the time. Why go through this, if not to make people think you are something you aren't? Say, a disheveled genius too important to clean up after himself, for instance.

Leda had little use for priests anyway. In the first place, she suspected they did not buy all the words they said, which made them hypocrites in her eyes. But her low opinion plummeted when a friend confided she had been seduced by one at church camp. Her friend had insisted on not calling it rape, saying, "I let him," although when she said it, she was sobbing so hard she could barely speak. Leda never attended church camp, but she knew of the priest. He was thirty-eight years old, exceptionally handsome, exceedingly popular, quite married, and all the girls were crazy over him. Her friend swore no one would believe her and told only Leda, who called it rape anyway.

Mr. Hahn was not exceptionally handsome; he was not even attractive. He had stiff gray hairs sprouting outward from the side of his head and a belly that pressed against his belt like a large egg and seemed obscene in the way it drew attention away from everything else in the room. It was hard to take your eyes off that belly. Leda's grandmother, on the other hand, seemed to have no such trouble.

"I understand your position, Eric," she said. "I am not proposing to bring a guitar-strummer in here to sing . . ." She snapped her fingers in the air. . . . "What's that song, Leda?"

"'Turn, Turn, Turn'?"

"Not that one; the other one."

"I think it's just called 'The Wedding Song.'"

"How unfortunate." She turned her attention back to the priest. "I assure you, what I am proposing is in good taste."

"I have no doubt, Adele. You must understand, however, that if I allow one, I have to allow them all. It's simpler, you see, to draw the line. No singing."

"It's Handel, Eric." Her grandmother's voice was icy now.

"It's still my policy."

Leda looked back and forth at the two of them, so perfectly matched, and knew neither would give in. She felt certain that, if her grandmother walked out of the church without getting what she wanted, she would not go back. She would give up thirty years of membership in this church, not for a principle, because on another day she might hold to a different principle, but because she did not tolerate no.

"Then we shall hold the wedding elsewhere," her grandmother said. They walked out, and true to Leda's prediction, the next Sunday, her grandmother was across town in the pews of St. Timothy's.

Plan Two, to hold the wedding in the backyard, began with the arrival of the tent the day before. The lawn was long, narrow, and bordered by flower gardens in front of a tall brick wall. At the back were huge old rhododendron bushes, which were still in bloom, and smaller but just as old azaleas, which were not. The house and its yard were as much Leda's as they were her grandmother's. She and her father had moved there during the confusing weeks after her mother's death, while her father was still wandering around the house in pajama bottoms, sleeping on couches, and not answering the telephone. Meals had appeared, but nobody ate them. Cakes collected on the dining room table. Leda was allowed to eat all the icing off the cakes, then show up for supper too full to eat her peas, but one night she overheard her grandmother say, "Enough," and they moved. In her grandmother's house, her father came to the kitchen every morning wearing a suit and tie, where he ate two eggs over easy, bacon, and toast, then went to work, and after that, Leda hardly ever saw him. He was a surgeon, and people said he was the best. They came up to her after all the school functions he did not attend and told her so.

Your father is a genius.

He is a saint.

Your father saved my life.

Great.

The house was large but not showy, an understated brick with white trim and working shutters. Her grandmother occupied the large bedroom at one end; her father, a smaller one down the hall, which left the entire upstairs to Leda. With this arrangement, it was easy to climb out a window onto the roof without anyone knowing, and often she did, to sunbathe or read or spy on the neighbors, if ever there were neighbors out to spy on, which there hardly ever were. When she was in high school, she was perfectly aware that she could sneak out of the house any night she wanted by getting on the roof, then climbing down the nearby maple tree, but it aggravated her when friends pointed this out. Were they blind? Did they know nothing about her? Leda was not the kind of person who *snuck out*. But at the same time, it irritated her that her father and grandmother took for granted her good behavior.

The morning of the wedding, Daniel and Brian arrived early to arrange the chairs under the tent. Her father stood on the patio with a cup of coffee and watched them. Moving the cup from the saucer to his lips and slowly back again, he resembled a man overseeing workers on a summer morning, a man who could turn and walk back into his house if he wanted, but he put the coffee down and joined them in the yard, where he was transformed into a man with the stiff, self-conscious movements of an older person intimidated by teenagers. Daniel and Brian, who had been leaping over chairs and chasing each other like puppies, stopped. Chairs were brought upright and straightened. Awkward sentences were produced.

"I understand you own your own restaurant," Leda's father said to Brian.

"Yes, sir."

"So. How's business?"

"Great."

Leda's father unfolded and arranged a single row of chairs before slipping back into the house.

Leda was watching all this from the window seat in her bedroom, where she had spent hours of her childhood reading, thinking, or simply staring at nothing in particular. She had opened the window and sat perched on the sill, with one foot on the roof outside, the other on the window seat inside, and soon she heard the music of the *Eroica*. Leda's father always closed the door to the study behind him whenever he went in there to listen to his music, but he turned the volume so high, it hardly mattered. Anyone could hear it, anywhere. When Beethoven was playing, Beethoven was playing in every room, and it affected everything. The television, for instance; if she or her grandmother turned it up loud enough to hear over the music, he would storm out of the study. *What is that noise?*

Leda watched the florist drive up and her grandmother walk out to meet him. She heard her grandmother calling her name when the caterers came, and she went downstairs to show them the kitchen. It was only when she returned to her room that she heard Daniel laughing. The window was still open, and *Eroica* had stopped, but, of course, she never would have heard Daniel if the music had not stopped. It was the distinctive high-pitched laugh that came out of him only when he was high, which was not often, because Daniel did not make a habit of smoking dope, and that's exactly what she was thinking as she hurried to the window. *Why on earth did he have to pick today?* The chairs were lined up in neat white rows like gravestones under the tent. Daniel and Brian were sprawled across them, Daniel in the first row, Brian in the second. They looked, not so much stoned, but all-puppied-out. She watched as Brian pulled a small silver flask out of his back pocket and handed it to Daniel, who raised it above his head. "Here's to Pat."

Then Brian raised it, too. "To Pat."

An hour later, Leda was still sitting there in the corner of the window seat, holding a pillow against her chest with one hand. In the other hand, she held a photograph of her mother standing beside a car in a driveway, her hair fixed in a pageboy, secured by a yellow headband. She was wearing a matching yellow cotton dress, cinched at the waist by a wide belt that showed how tiny she was, fine-boned and graceful. The key attributes related to Leda about her mother were that she was petite, well dressed, and tidy. She kept a clean house. She was good at arranging flowers. She was, in fact, nothing like Leda, but Leda refused to see this when she looked at the bright eyes of the woman in the photograph, at her rakish smile. She saw a woman stuck in time. And what she believed was, her mother would have changed. *She* would have changed her.

She was still sitting there when she heard the voices of the first guests gathering under the tent. When Daniel's parents arrived, she saw them seat themselves on the front row, even though they had been told at the dress rehearsal to wait for the processional. Leda had been there and heard it; they had been told twice. She scanned the yard for her grandmother, but there was no sign of her, and Leda found herself hoping that, if she did come out, she would leave them alone. Leda felt sorry for them. It was sympathy wholly unexpected, but Arliss looked so small in his ill-fitting cream-colored suit, and

Merle's slip was showing beneath her lime green dress, and nobody was talking to them. Merle wore black shoes with thick rubber soles, which could indicate either ignorance or defiance (as in, *I'll be damned if I'll stick my feet into any flimsy girl shoes*). Leda wished she knew which.

Daniel's brother, Bob, was better dressed and appeared comfortable in his suit and tie, but he worked as a financial consultant down in Atlanta, so was used to dressing this way. He was handsome, blond and fair like Arliss, and no one would pick him out of a crowd to be the brother of dark and wild-haired Daniel, although they shared certain facial expressions, and both gave the impression of being agile and athletic. Leda knew Daniel was not fond of his brother, but she had no reason to think badly of him, unless you count the fact that, already, he had tried to interest her father in an investment opportunity, a move that could be considered tacky, although Leda was willing to blame it on simple enthusiasm. Bob was standing near the entrance to the yard, having taken on the role of greeting guests alongside his wife, Tina, who, with her Tinkerbell voice, was the one who got on Leda's nerves. She was wondering why her father wasn't the one out there greeting guests, when he stuck his head through the door.

"Ready?"

But he knew the answer when he stepped into the room and saw her sitting in the window seat, her dress still lying on the bed. She saw him take in the fact that something was wrong, but she could count on him not to pester her about it. With some regret, she realized how little credit she gave him for thinking well of her, and quickly she hid her mother's photograph under the pillow. Leda's father hardly ever came to her room. He stuck his hands in his pockets and walked awkwardly over to where she sat. Together they watched out the window as her grandmother scurried from the patio to the tent to speak to Arliss and tug at Merle's sleeve, ushering them out of their seats and back inside the house. They watched Brian, his red hair uncombed, his shirttail hanging out over his tuxedo pants, talking to the cello player. They watched Bob and Tina shaking hands with her grandmother's friends as if they had known them all their lives.

"If this doesn't work out, you can come on home."

"I know, Daddy."

When he left, Leda walked over to the bed and picked up her dress. It was a white cotton sundress with an empire waist, puffed sleeves, and a pale blue satin ribbon woven into the neckline. She had chosen it, following her grandmother's advice to *keep it simple,* but simple to her grandmother meant white linen suit, so when Leda brought it home, her grandmother had gasped.

"It will go with my sandals," Leda had argued.

"You can't wear *sandals.*"

"What's wrong with sandals?"

If your mother were here. The words never had to be said anymore, they were so obvious; bigger than flesh, this hole where her mother ought to be. Maybe her mother would have sided with her grandmother on the question of the sundress and sandals, but here was the point Leda would never concede. Nobody *knew.* She was standing in the middle of her room, holding the dress, when her grandmother walked in. "What are you waiting for?"

"I should have eloped."

"Maybe so."

Here's to Pat.

Okay, so Daniel could have meant one of two things.

Here's to Pat, the love of my life, the one who got away.

This was the one Leda assumed first, before she had time to think about it, but driving to the beach the next day, she came up with a second and more acceptable possibility.

Here's to Pat for leaving, thereby making way for Leda, the true love of my life.

Both made sense. There was no reason to rush judgment. She could ask him, of course, but Leda understood the implications of the before-and-after-moment, as in, before the phone-call-in-the-middle-of-the-night, and after, the difference between innocence and that other thing, Eden and beyond. She remembered the moment, just before she learned of her mother's accident, when she had been thrilled that the principal of her school had called her into the office and handed her a full bottle of ice-cold Fanta Orange. So there was risk in knowing the truth, even if Daniel said the right words, because, what if he hesitated? They were barely out of Tennessee when she decided to assume the second meaning, even if it meant living in a perpetual *before,* because, no matter how interesting life can become after, before is always better.

They were driving to the Outer Banks of North Carolina for their honeymoon, because Daniel had been there once with Brian and swore it was *the greatest place,* which meant only that Daniel's vocabulary did not allow for *good* or *pretty good* or even an unadorned *great.* The plan was to camp near a town called Salvo, and when they passed the sign by the side of the road, Daniel pointed to it, and said, "Does this mean we'll be gunned down by cannons?"

"Maybe it means salvation."

"Mowed down by artillery fire, and our lives just beginning."

"Maybe it doesn't mean anything, Daniel."

The campground was just off the highway in a flat, dusty clearing, surrounded by squatty pine trees that promised privacy but killed the wind. Leda and Daniel selected a campsite in the corner, where they spent their first sleepless night battling mosquitoes. The next morning they went to the beach, walking across the street to the nearest public access, a boardwalk behind a general store. When it got too hot to sunbathe, they swam in the ocean, but the surf was rough and the undertow strong, and after a little while, Leda got out and spread a towel on the sand and, because she was exhausted, fell asleep.

She woke up to the sound of Daniel's voice. "Pick it up," was what she thought she heard him say. Looking around, she saw a man standing on the boardwalk. He was facing away from Daniel as if he were deliberately not listening. "Now." Leda spied the candy bar wrapper on the sand below the boardwalk. It was caught in a tangle of dried seaweed, but the wind was tugging at it, and it was likely to break free any minute. "Pick it up now, or I'm calling the cops." Daniel was pointing to the NO LITTERING sign at the end of the boardwalk. Leda would have thought that would have been enough, but Daniel was still talking. "You think everybody ought to be able to throw trash on the ground? You want to guess what this beach would look like? You like living in a dump?"

The man appeared pinned to where he stood on the boardwalk, as if he did not know whether to proceed toward the beach or turn around and walk away.

"I'm not asking you what you think of littering, asshole; I'm asking you what kind of world *you* want to live in. That's what I'm asking."

The man turned and started to walk away.

Daniel yelled, "I swear to God, if you don't pick it up, I'm calling the cops," then he started toward the boardwalk. Instantly the man turned back around and came toward Daniel, and Leda could see how it would be if neither one backed off. The man was younger and a good deal bigger than Daniel.

"I think you should drop it, Daniel," Leda said, and, to her surprise, Daniel stopped. Maybe it was like pulling a dog away from a treed raccoon, but for whatever reason, when Daniel stopped, the man hurried down the steps, stepped across the sand, and picked up the candy wrapper.

"Next time . . ." Daniel started to say, but Leda interrupted.

"Hush."

They watched the man walk away from them down the beach, the trash still clenched in his hand. "Watch him," Daniel said. "He'll probably throw it in the ocean now." He was shaking. Leda reached out to steady his arm. She did not know whether to feel angry or proud, because, no question, what he had just done was crazy. He could have gotten hurt, could have gotten killed, could have gotten *her* killed, but who else did she know who would have dared speak up like that? It was gutsy; there was no taking that away from him, and he was right. That was the part that was hard to get around; he was right. Still, it scared her, thinking about how far he might have gone, just because he was right. "How about if we get out of here," she said.

They drove up the beach and ate lunch near the pier at a cafe that also sold wind chimes made from shells. The wind chimes clanged ceaselessly. Next door was a store selling sea kayaks, and when Daniel went to look them over, Leda walked out on the pier, where the same wind that rattled the wind chimes blew her dress against her thighs. It made her feel naked, but when she tugged at the skirt, it only slapped back against her thighs. Her skin was tight from a fresh sunburn, and she could feel the heat from the pier through her flip-flops. Halfway out, Leda passed a man sitting behind a small wooden table where a handwritten sign advertised: PALMS READ, $5. His feet were propped up on a bucket where a second sign read: WORMS FOR SALE. The man wore no shirt, and his skin was deeply tanned. The way he grinned at her, she knew any attempt at freeing her thighs from the clinging dress was absurd. He stretched out a hand. She shook her head no.

"For you, only three dollars," he said, and he patted an empty stool.

Leda hesitated, glancing up and down the pier as if she might see someone she knew, then fished in her purse for three dollars and sat down. The man stuffed the bills in the pockets of his shorts, then reached his hand toward her again. She did not understand what he wanted.

"Your hand," he said.

"Oh." She held out her right hand. He turned it palm up and stared, and when he did, his smile disappeared.

"What do you see?"

He shook his head.

"Don't I have an unusually long lifeline? I mean, compared to other people. I know it sounds silly, but it's hard not to notice. I don't know if it means anything, though. What do you think; does it look long to you?"

He shrugged. "No doubt you will live a very long life."

"Or continue to live with a particularly long wrinkle on the palm of my hand."

His smile came back "No, darlin'. You will live a long time."

Not that this man knew what he was talking about, but she did have a sense that her life would be long. It was not superstition, exactly; she assumed everyone had the same sense, including her own mother, who had been wrong, so she put no faith in it. Until she met Daniel, she had simply considered it human nature to hope for the best, but Daniel, whose lifeline happened to be short, believed he would die young. "Why would you say such a thing?" she had asked him, alarmed when he told her. "It's just a sense I have," he had said.

"What else do you see?" she asked the man.

"I see that, in your very long life, you will have two great lovers."

As it happened, this was the moment Daniel stepped onto the pier. Leda saw him, jerked her hand away, and stood up. The man was saying, "Count yourself lucky. Most people don't even get one." Daniel had not seen her yet. He was heading toward a crowd that had gathered on the opposite side of the pier. "But for you," the man continued, "two," and he held up two fingers as if to emphasize the bounty.

"Can we not *talk* about this now," she snapped at him. "I am on my *honeymoon,* for God's sake."

She turned and ran across the pier to meet Daniel, who, if he noticed she was breathless, did not mention it, and together they moved through the crowd until they could see what everyone was looking at. It was a shark, swimming in the breakers underneath the pier, feeding on fish heads thrown from a cutting board. Another crowd of people watched from the shore.

"Whoa," Daniel said.

Leda was thinking the same thing, remembering how they had been swimming not so far from this very spot that very morning. She shuddered. Daniel said, "How fast do you think that guy could cover a couple of miles?"

"Too damn fast," said a man standing next to them.

"Its fin is underneath the water," Leda said.

They all looked.

"I thought that was the thing about a shark; you would see it coming, you know, because of the fin," she said.

"What difference would that make?" Daniel said.

Leda shrugged. "I just always thought you'd see it coming."

"So what? You could swim away?"

"They won't hurt you none." It was the man next to them again. "This one here's just in for the fish heads."

Daniel whistled. "He's fucking huge."

"You got that right," said the man.

The usual way to get from the campground at Salvo to the ocean was to cross the road and take the boardwalk behind the general store, but Leda and Daniel had discovered, if they walked down the road a bit, then cut through the dunes, they could have the beach to themselves. They did not do it every day. There were many more rows of dunes than appeared from either the road or the beach, and they were tangled with wind-dwarfed trees and vegetation, which made walking tough, plus they harbored mosquitoes and greenhead flies. The trick with greenheads, or so claimed the man at the general store, was to kill them after the first bite, because it's on the second pass that they inject the poison that makes the bite at least as painful as a bee sting. Leda considered this a fine tip but hard to follow, because the flies were as big as pennies and harder to kill than you would think. But on the last night of their honeymoon, she and Daniel hacked their way over the dunes to the deserted beach. Daniel carried a bottle of wine. They walked down to the ocean but stopped shin deep in the water. They had not been swimming since the day they had seen the shark.

In the sky over the western side of the island, the sun was setting behind a large purple cloud, and shooting fanlike from it were multicolored rays of sunlight, pink and red and gold and an unearthly shade of silvery blue. Leda was facing toward the ocean and did not see it, but Daniel was turned the other way. He unscrewed the top off the wine, took a drink, then pointed to the sky. "That, right there, is where they got the idea for heaven," he said.

Leda turned around. "You're just thinking about those pictures of Jesus with the halo that looks like light beams shooting out of his head."

"Maybe." He handed her the bottle. "But I wasn't thinking about Jesus. I had in mind people who lived thousands of years ago, looking up and seeing a sky like that. I'm guessing they would have already come up with the idea of life after death, because, I mean, think about it. Who wants to imagine the alternative? But they need a place, an idea of a place, a picture they can put in their minds, so they look up, and, *voilà*."

"These are French-speaking primitives?"

"Okay, so they grunt an appreciative exclamation, but that sky does appear supernatural. Admit it; doesn't it look like God lives there?"

The cloud was moving. Soon it obliterated the sunbeams and revealed the sun as a sphere turning an orangish red and sinking. "I think you're wrong," Leda said. "I think heaven was invented by the good guys."

Daniel, who until that moment had been absorbed in his own logic, seemed brought up short by her words. He grinned. "The good guys?"

"I mean people like me, you know? People who play by the rules, fasten their seat belts, stop at stop signs, don't speed, do their homework."

"And don't litter."

"Right. Also people who don't risk their lives fighting over candy bar wrappers."

"We weren't really going to fight."

"You fooled me."

"How about people who don't eat meat?"

"Okay, I'll give you that, although I know plenty of people who would argue with you."

"And don't use Cliffs Notes."

"What's wrong with Cliffs Notes?"

Daniel shrugged. "They've always seemed like cheating to me."

"Let's just say the good guys are people who clean up after themselves and wait their turn. That pretty much covers it, I think. And the reason they had to invent heaven was because the bad guys were winning."

"Ah, yes. Enter the bad guys. Rogues, scoundrels, scallywags." He bowed deeply from the waist.

She smiled. "I mean the line-breakers."

He reached over and undid the top button of her shirt, but Leda kept talking. "You've been there, patiently standing in line, when suddenly some jerk butts in ahead of you, and what? You can't believe his nerve, right? But while you're standing there with your mouth gaping, not believing his nerve, the line-breaker gets there first. I mean, what else? Does lightning strike him down? No. He cheats, he wins, that's it, and all you've got is the hope that, in the end, he'll wind up in hell, while you'll go to heaven. Justice, that's where heaven came from." She paused for a minute before adding, quietly, "Or maybe heaven is letting the line-breakers have it."

Daniel took a long drink of the wine and said nothing. Leda smiled. "That's why you married me," she said. "Because I'm the only person in the world you'll let have the last word."

Daniel dropped the wine bottle and shook his head. "Oh, no. That's not it at all."

As they kissed, he unbuttoned the rest of her shirt and spread it flat on the sand. Leda put her hand on his shoulder. "How about we use your shirt this time," she whispered.

"What difference does it make?"

"No difference. It's just that I always end up with the wet spot, you know? I thought we might use your shirt for a change."

He stepped backwards and stared at her.

"But it's no big deal."

"I can't believe you care."

"Really, it doesn't matter, Daniel. We'll use my shirt."

But he was already walking away. Leda put her shirt back on but did not follow him. She sat down on the sand and watched the ocean in the dimming light, before she stood and walked back through the dunes to find him.

EIGHT

LEDA

Leda cringed as the right rear tire slipped into a rut, and the bottom of the car scraped against the gravel. She put her hand on her stomach. Daniel slowed and eased the wheels back on track. The driveway was steep and eroded, which did not matter to Arliss and Merle, who owned trucks, but it was hard on cars. Daniel pulled the car behind the house and parked. Leda got out and peered underneath the car to make sure nothing had knocked loose, but Daniel crossed the yard, opened a gate, and entered a field of tall grass up to his knees. Grasshoppers scattered in front of him as he walked. A few yards in, he stopped and turned back to Leda. "Aren't you coming?"

She stood up and nodded to the house. "Shouldn't we tell them we're here?"

"They know we're here."

"Shouldn't we say hello?"

"You can if you want," he said, and walked on. Leda watched him move through the grass, which appeared to open, then shut behind him. She went as far as to the edge of the field but stopped there. She did not know yet that it was a hayfield and not simply grass allowed to grow unruly. It spread out in front of her like marsh grass rippling in the wind, swallows circling low like seagulls cruising for food. Somewhere in the woods on the other side was where Daniel wanted to build a log cabin.

"Are there snakes?" she called.

"Probably."

She looked down at the stalks of grass at her feet, thick and strong like rope. A cloud of gnats surrounded her face. She glanced back at the house. It was the kind of house she could drive by every day and not notice, she thought, box-shaped and dingy, with metal-rimmed windows that gave it a hollow-eyed, unfinished look. She wondered if Merle were in there watching, but the windows were dark, and she could not see in. Daniel was so far across the field by now she had to shout to make him hear. "I'm not going in there, Daniel."

He stopped, turned around, and put his hands on his hips, but he did not argue. He cupped one hand around his mouth and pointed with the other. "Walk up to the barn, hang a right, then follow the dirt road as far as you can. I'll meet you there."

Leda had never been up there before. In fact, they hardly ever came to the farm on Bearpen Lane. She was working as a secretary at a public television station, a job Daniel considered beneath her intellect and abilities, although she felt lucky to have it, having moved to Knoxville the same year the city's two newspapers were merging into one. As one of the editors had explained, not only were reporters not being hired, they were being laid off. He was a kind man, though, and sympathetic, and suggested she call a friend of his over at the public television station, where the only position open was the secretarial job. She had taken it with the promise that there was room for promotion, but now she was pregnant, and everything had changed. Her supervisor had agreed she could bring the baby to work, and whenever Daniel argued she should find a better job, she reminded him there were some things more pressing than a better job.

Daniel had his own problems. He had passed his oral examinations, but just barely, and it had taken him two tries, and he was still sensitive about it. Often he looked for clues that would reveal who in the department might have been working against him. But now he was busy working on a dissertation on the obscure subject of Sut Lovingood, the fictitious narrator of a book written by an almost-forgotten nineteenth-century Tennessee writer named George Washington Harris, who, some believed, influenced both Mark Twain and William Faulkner. It excited him, not just the particulars of Sut Lovingood as a character, but the idea that he was working on something no one else had thought of. The few literary critics who had bothered were all over the place on the subject, some saying Sut was nothing more than a mean, disgusting, stupid redneck who had nothing of value to say, while others compared him to Socrates. Daniel loved that. He did not mind saying that he dreamed of one day being in the center of pre-Twain studies.

Because of these things, the jobs, the dissertation, and especially the baby, Daniel and Leda were not serious about building the log cabin, although they did still talk about it as something they might do, someday, but they had not driven out to Bearpen Lane that afternoon for the purpose of looking over the farm. They had come to pick up a box of old record albums for Brian, whom they were planning to meet later at a Smokies baseball game, and Daniel had said, as long as they were there, they might as well take a look at the land. And when Leda reached the top of the hill, she saw what could not be seen from the road, the pasture behind the barn and the ridge beyond that. The cows were at the far end, some of them grazing up the side of the ridge. One cow was in a pen by itself next to the barn. It looked back at her, and as she approached, Leda shuddered at its size, much bigger than she had thought a cow might be. Then she realized it was not a cow but a bull, and she backed away. She looked at the bull, and the bull looked at her, and the fence around him looked old and rickety, but almost as unsettling was the fact that, although she knew there were bulls in the world, it had never occurred to her to think about where they lived. An entire mythology of bulls was missing from her consciousness. *Elephants live in Africa, penguins live in Antarctica, kangaroos live in Australia, bulls live in . . . ?* Surely nowhere near where she might be.

The narrow dirt road led to the woodlot between Arliss's farm and the one next to it. Halfway there was the abandoned house where Daniel had said his grandmother used to live. He called it Belle's House, although his grandmother's name had been Marion, so it was confusing. When she had asked him who Belle was, he had answered only, "Damned if I know." Behind the house was an ancient-looking graveyard, surrounded by a low rock wall. When she passed between it and Belle's house, she was tempted to stop and read the names on the wooden crosses, but Daniel was waiting at the end of the road where the woods began. He was pointing down the hill. "See those big poplar trees?" he asked.

Leda looked. From where she stood, she could see the farm across the street where Arliss leased land for part of his herd and a small to-bacco crop. Beyond it, a river and a valley and the mountains in the distance. She said, "Would we have a view?"

"Better than they do," he said, pointing to his parents' house, which was ridiculous in his mind for not having any view at all. Leda nodded. She knew Daniel blamed his parents for an endless list of errors in judgment, some not even theirs, as was the case with their house, which was not built on the top of the hill but halfway up and facing the barn. The fact that they were not the ones who built it there did not matter. What mattered was the pattern, the crimes against reason that dogged their lives and added up to one conclusion: They could not do anything right. She looked behind her at the farm. Listening to Daniel talk, she had pictured it as a farm you might see in Kansas, with acres and acres of neat cropland, a farm like you might see in a movie or on the cover of a magazine. Even when Daniel got through to her that it was a *cattle* farm, the image she held on to was something out of Texas, not a scruffy little farm perched on the side of a rocky hill. Now that she saw the land and stood on it, she had a new thought. "Maybe we ought to pay him for it."

"It's his land," Daniel said. "If he wants to give me some of it, I'm going to take it."

It was then that they saw that Arliss was walking toward the woods from the pasture. He came slowly, as if he were happening along, not intentionally heading their way, although he could have been. He was carrying a metal canister with a small hose attached and wore a long-sleeved shirt. Daniel stood with his hands in his pockets, and when his father got close, he said, "We're thinking of building in the woods, over there in the middle of those poplars, so we wouldn't disturb the hay. That sound okay with you?"

"This is hay?" Leda interrupted.

"What did you think it was?"

"Grass?"

"It's hay."

Arliss said, "If I'd known, I wouldn't have put the saw here."

"Don't worry about it, Dad."

"I could have put it up on the ridge."

"It's not a big deal, really."

Arliss pointed across the field. "You could have Belle's House. It don't lack much in fixing up. Save you a lot of trouble."

"I know that, but we'd rather be over here in the woods."

"Your mother always thought Bob would move into Belle's House."

"Well, he's not going to."

Arliss nodded. "When do you plan to start?"

Daniel sighed. "Not anytime soon, but you don't worry about it, okay?" Arliss started to say something, but Daniel cut him off. "I mean it, Dad. I'm not asking you to help."

Arliss nodded. When he started to walk away, it was without a *good-bye* or *see you later;* he simply moved off, but then he stopped. "You're going to have to take down those poplars if you build there."

"No, Dad," Daniel said. "We're going to build it *next* to the trees. We like the trees; that's the point. I want to sit at my breakfast table every morning and look out my window at those trees."

Arliss walked away.

When he was out of earshot, Leda put her hand on Daniel's shoulder. "Just don't cut them down, that's all."

"Don't worry, I won't."

"You don't have to make a big deal about it."

"I know that."

Merle could be counted on to serve one of four meals: meat loaf and mashed potatoes, fried chicken and rice, ham and potato salad, or

hamburgers and slaw. Daniel called it a rotation like a pitching rotation, and each time they ate with his parents, he would whisper to
Leda, "Who's pitching?" and she would know he was not talking
about baseball. Daniel had told his mother they would not be staying
for dinner, but the smell of fried chicken met them even before they
reached the back door. "Dammit," he said.

"You told her we were going to the ball game?"

"Twice." He spit and stepped through the door. The air in the
house was thick with the smell of cooking plus another sour smell that
was always there, as if part of the flooring had gotten wet a long time
ago and was still not completely dry. The ceilings were low, and the
rooms, dark. The windows were covered with heavy green curtains,
the same curtains Arliss's mother had hung before Merle came along.
Every spring, Merle took them down and washed them and hung
them back up, but no spring did she take them down and think to replace them with something different.

"Y'all wash your hands," Merle said.

"We're not staying for dinner, Mother. We're going to the ball
game, remember."

The grandfather clock in the living room chimed six o'clock. It
was like a bolt of sound that came out of nowhere, and each time it
went off, Leda jumped, which seemed to amuse Merle. Merle loved
that clock, and no one knew why. It was huge, the first thing you saw
when you walked in the room, made from a flimsy cut of wood,
overcarved with gaudy, tendrilous designs and studded with glued-
on florets. It had no identifiable sentimental value. Merle had simply
gone to a furniture store one day and had it delivered, unannounced.
Daniel had been seven at the time and said he remembered the day.

Merle placed two drumsticks on plates and handed one each to
Daniel and Leda. "You ought to fix up Belle's House. Your dad's already done most of the work."

Leda looked at the greasy drumstick. It had been presented to her
like a snack, a snack of chicken, which seemed more like a sneaky way
to serve dinner and would have made her feel queasy even if she had
not been pregnant. She set the plate on the kitchen table as discreetly

as possible, but Daniel picked up his chicken and bit into it. "We just walked over there and looked at the woods, Mother," he said. "That doesn't mean we're going to build anything."

"Your dad always thought Bob would move into Belle's House."

"I know. But he's not going to."

"You never know."

"I know."

"Go ahead and sit down."

"We really have to go." He finished the drumstick and set the plate on the table next to Leda's. For a minute it looked as if he might pick up her piece and eat it, too.

"You can stay long enough to eat supper," Merle said.

"I told you; we're going to the ball game. We're meeting Brian."

Merle turned to Leda. "Don't you want some of this chicken?"

"I'll just eat at the game, but thank you anyway."

But Merle followed them, and when they reached the car, she handed Leda two more pieces of chicken wrapped in a paper towel.

"I'm not eating this, Daniel," Leda said, when they got on the road.

"You don't have to."

"You shouldn't either."

Daniel turned on the radio. "I'll give them to Brian."

Leda turned off the radio. "Brian won't want chicken. Brian's going to want a hot dog. He's going to buy himself popcorn and peanuts. Nobody shows up at a baseball game wanting fried chicken, Daniel."

"Brian'll eat anything."

Leda tossed the chicken into a barrel trash can in the parking lot when they got to the ballpark.

Brian had brought his son, Seth, with him to the ball game, and the two of them were already seated behind first base when Leda and Daniel got there. Seth was five years old now and lived with his mother, Susan, but Leda often saw him at the Flying Dog, riding on Brian's shoulders, the waitresses teasing about the new helper being taller than everybody, and once she had seen him at one of Brian's parties, hiding with Brian's dog, Chicken, in a back bedroom. Leda had gone back there to get away from the smoke and the loud music and the beer-bloated voices competing with each other to see who could outshout the others. Seth was a quiet boy; Leda would have said tense. She had watched as he dropped a plastic dinosaur off the edge of the bed over and over again and had not told him, even once, to stop. He had his daddy's red hair, but he also looked like his mother, whom Leda had met but did not really know.

By the time she and Daniel got to the ballpark, Brian was on his third beer. Bottom of the first inning, the Knoxville Smokies were already behind by two, but with the bases loaded, two out, and the count 3 and 0, the cleanup man swung and missed. Strike one.

"DON'T SWING AT THAT," Brian yelled. He turned to Daniel. "What's he swinging at that for? IT WAS UP AT YOUR GODDAMN NOSE."

"It was over his goddamn head," Daniel agreed.

"Watch, he'll throw a slider now. STRIKE! YOU CALL THAT A STRIKE? IT WAS OUTSIDE!"

"By a fucking mile," Daniel said. "Now watch him go back to the fastball."

"Like the sun's not coming up tomorrow. JESUS CHRIST! He didn't even swing. YOU DIDN'T EVEN SWING, YOU MORON!"

After the batter struck out, Brian patted Seth on the knee. "Want a hot dog? Let's go get us a hot dog."

Brian and Seth left together, but only Brian came back, holding two hot dogs in one hand and a plastic cup of beer in the other. He was looking out at the field and screaming, "YOU CALL THAT A BALL?" Seth was not behind him.

"Where's Seth," Leda asked.

"He's coming."

Leda turned around and was relieved to see the little boy at the top of the aisle. He was clutching an extralarge cup of Coca-Cola in both hands and making his way down one step at a time. Leda watched him, but when, finally, he reached his seat, Brian only pointed to the field. "Hey, buddy, we got ducks on the pond; it's a brand-new day."

Leda turned to Daniel. "Ducks?"

"Men on first and third." But just then the pitcher picked off the runner on first, and Daniel said, "Cancel the ducks," and Brian said, "Shit."

The next time Brian got up, Leda offered to watch Seth, but the little boy broke away and ran to catch up with his dad, who was already halfway up the steps.

"Brian," Leda yelled.

Brian turned around.

"Wait for Seth."

He did, and Leda turned to Daniel. "He's not keeping an eye on that boy."

"They'll be okay," Daniel said.

But when Brian returned, it was the same as before, Brian with a beer and a bag of popcorn, Seth far behind with another Coke. The stadium was grime-coated, littered with sticky trash, filled with hard, smoke-worn people with thin, snarly lips, puffy eyes, and dirty hair. Leda was sure any one of them could snatch a five-year-old, while his father, oblivious, would not even know. Hours later, would he look around? *Has anyone seen Seth?* The next time Brian and Seth got up, she followed them.

Seth fell behind just as she feared he would, but what surprised her was, instead of panic, there was a look of determination on his face, as if he knew all he had to do was put one foot in front of the other and eventually he would get where he needed to be. Leda did not know whether to call it ignorance or courage. She parked herself behind a T-shirt kiosk and watched him until he reached his father, who was waiting in the concession stand line. Brian put his hand on Seth's head as if there were never a question he would make it, the assumption of a man who does not fear the worst because, how can you be afraid of something you don't believe in? Brian bought a beer, a package of M&Ms, and, was that another Coke for Seth? How much caffeine can a forty-pound body take, was what Leda wanted to know. She ducked into the bathroom when Brian and Seth started back to their seats.

The Smokies lost, and Daniel and Brian believed it was because of a call the home plate umpire made in the eighth inning: bases loaded, two outs, and once again their best hitter called out on strikes that were *clearly balls*. That's what Brian kept saying, and each time Daniel would answer, *In the damn dirt*. This outrage consumed them as they walked to the parking lot together. Leda followed, holding Seth's hand. Car doors slammed, people cussed, radio music poured out of open windows, dust rose from the parking lot, as one by one, cars sped away. Twice Brian stumbled, almost stepping in front of a moving car. When they got to Brian's car, Leda spoke up. "Let me drive Seth home."

Brian and Daniel looked at each other.

Leda turned to Daniel. "He shouldn't drive, and you know it," but Brian interrupted.

"I believe I can handle it."

"Well, I don't," Leda said.

"Shit," Daniel muttered, and covered his face with his hands.

"Get in the car, Seth," Brian said.

"If you want to kill yourself, fine, but you're not taking this boy," Leda said.

"You sound like his mother," Brian said.

"Wouldn't it be nice if you sounded like his father."

"That's enough," Daniel said. Brian and Leda both stared at him, daring him to take a side, and he knew it, too. Leda could see his brain working out the relative advantages and disadvantages of favoring his wife or his friend. Finally, Daniel turned to Brian and put an arm over his shoulder and walked him to the other side of the car. "Let me drive you home, man," he whispered.

"I'm fine," Brian said.

"He's not fine," Leda called.

"Hush," Daniel snapped at her, then turned back to Brian. "Come on, man."

The parking lot was empty. Lights from the stadium burned into the sky, then, suddenly, they turned off, leaving them in darkness, the sky restored to black. Brian slumped against the car door, defiance gone, arms hanging limp, keys dangling from a finger. He looked away as the keys fell into Daniel's hand. Seth ran around the car and pressed himself against his father's legs, but Brian rubbed his hair, and said, "Go on with Miss Leda, buddy. I'll catch you tomorrow."

They worked it out that Daniel would drive Brian home while Leda took Seth to his mother's, then she would swing back by Brian's to pick up Daniel. Daniel gave her directions to Susan's house, then added, "How about you don't tell her the reason."

"Okay, sure."

Daniel held her arm and made her look him in the eyes. "I mean it, Leda. You have to promise."

"I promise."

Seth would not talk on the ride home, and Leda did not make him. She did not feel like talking anyway. She felt bad about what she had done, because, the truth was, she liked Brian. Sometimes, when he joined them for dinner at the Flying Dog, for instance, he could be subdued, even shy, and there were times when he had been particularly kind to her. Daniel had a habit of interrupting her, and not just her, but everyone, because he did not have an ear for when people were finished speaking, mistaking pauses for his turn to break into the conversation. Brian always came back to her, as if he had put his finger on the moment she left off to save her place—*Now what were you saying, Leda?* It was a little gesture, but Leda had noticed it. Of course, none of this made any difference when Brian was drinking.

The house where Susan lived turned out to be only a few blocks from Brian's apartment downtown in a neighborhood of small, brick bungalows and old sidewalks split by the roots of large maple trees. The covered porches were deep and supported by thick, concrete pillars, some swallowed by ivy. Susan's porch was overrun with hanging planters of impatiens and handmade ceramic wind chimes, which made it possible to sit on the porch and not be seen from the street. Susan was not expecting them. When she opened the front door, Seth walked past her without a word and disappeared into the back of the house. In a minute, the sound from a television broke the silence. Susan looked embarrassed. "I'll make him turn it off," she said.

Susan was a short, athletic-looking woman with sand-colored hair cropped short like a boy's. All Leda had ever heard Daniel say about her was that she was cold, and looking at her, she could see why there might be something to that. It was in the set of her square-shaped jaw when she closed her lips and narrowed her dark eyes, sending an unambiguous message, that she might be small, but don't mess with her. What she knew about Susan was this: She owned her own land-scaping business and was an artist of some local renown. At the moment she was dressed in an old T-shirt, running shorts, and ankle socks, and Leda remembered Daniel saying that she had recently had some success at running marathons as well. It was not with admira-tion that he had said it. He and Brian talked as if running marathons were deviant.

"I'm sorry to bother you," Leda said. "Brian asked me to bring him home."

"He was drunk, wasn't he?"

Leda looked down and said nothing.

"That's okay. You don't have to tell me."

Leda nodded. She was turning to walk away when she noticed the tears in Susan's eyes. She hesitated, and Susan covered her face with her hands. "That asshole," she whispered.

"Are you okay?"

"I'm fine."

"I can stay if you want."

"No. Really, I'm fine."

"Okay then. Well. I guess I'll be seeing you."

Susan nodded, then closed the door. Leda was halfway to her car when she heard it open again. "Thank you," Susan called, and waved.

Driving back through the darkened streets that night, Leda could not quit thinking about the way Susan had looked standing in the threshold of her simple house, defeated in the same way Brian had looked defeated when he had stood limp beside his car, dangling his keys from a finger. She felt sorry for both of them. Leda's life to that point had not included many friends, certainly no close ones, the reason having something to do with the fact that she kept people away. She admitted it. It felt like something she could not help, an instinct for knowing how much closeness she could stand, and as a result, she neither spent time blaming others nor feeling sorry for herself, but that did not mean she did not need a friend. She turned the car around. When she got back to Susan's house, she knocked on the door. "You want to talk about it?"

NINE

ARLISS

Arliss walked out with a chain saw and cut down the big maple tree in the middle of the back pasture. He did not tell anybody; he just did it. When it hit, the ground shook. Branches broke and flew into the air as if they had exploded. He looked back toward the house, half-expecting to see Merle running over the hill to see what had happened, even though he knew Merle was working down at Carr's Big Orange and would not be back for hours.

He started first with the branches, gathering up loose ones and cutting the larger ones into logs, which he loaded in a wagon, then drove with the tractor to the small sawmill he had set in the woods at the base of the ridge. The mill was intended to provide supplementary income, and over the winter months, too, which was something he could not say about tobacco, although the money was not as good. It took too much out of him to grow tobacco anymore, and he was thinking about dropping the lease. Or he could keep the lease and plant hay for the horse people, but he reminded himself that, unlike cattle, horses require square bales, which are harder to work. Arliss had never forgotten that his best hand, Freight Train, had gotten himself shot the same year he had bought his first round baler, which allowed him to single-handedly cut and bale his own hay, drastically reducing his dependence on other people. He did not believe in trusting luck, but neither would he deny he had been lucky.

Some of the income from the sawmill came from other farmers who brought their own wood, but most of the money came from selling rough boards from his own trees to a wholesaler in Grainger County. He had located the saw where he did so he could drive a truck to it on the old dirt path that went between Belle's House and the graveyard. It was just uphill from the place where Daniel wanted to build a log cabin, and Arliss had been turning over the possibility of moving it. He didn't know where. But when he thought clearly, he would remember that building a log cabin required not only thinking up the idea but going through with it. He would see then that Daniel was never going to build any log cabin. That was just Daniel talking.

He had not until that morning considered taking down the maple tree. His father had left the tree standing for shade, but there were other ways to get shade. What Arliss saw when he looked at the tree that morning was not just board feet, which was considerable; he saw a solution to the problem of where to put a pond. The drain tiles he had buried next to the creek had helped dry up the mucky areas along the bank, but if the cattle had a pond, he could fence off the creek, keeping them out of it entirely. The problem had always been finding a way to dig a pond without sacrificing pastureland. Now he could see, if he cut down the tree and put the pond in its place, the loss would be minimal. That was it, then. He cut it down, glad to have thought of it in the winter before the leaves came out.

But by the time he heard Merle's truck, he was not even half-done. A car followed the truck up the driveway. It was Bob's car. Arliss had forgotten his son was in town, but he did not go in right away. He saw no reason to alter his plans just because one of his sons happened to show up, and he was determined to get most of the tree cut up and stacked before lunch. He finished piling in another load and started the tractor and headed toward the woods on the dirt path, where he found his thoughts wandering back to New Hope and another dirt path, the one that had run through the woods to his uncle Luke's house. Whenever he looked back at his childhood these days, he did not think about how cold they were in the winter or that they did not always have enough food. He would remember Rose-mary. He would remember listening to her sing and to his uncle Roy telling stories and other things like sitting in a patch of sunlight on the porch on a chilly autumn day and catching crayfish in Stickpin Branch. He would remember being six years old and walking by himself through the woods on a dirt road that in his mind had come to stand for possibility, the idea that anything could happen right around the next curve, before the time came when he knew how hor-rifying the possibilities could be. Before he knew better than to hope for surprises. For most of his life, he had assumed they were better off on the farm on Bearpen Lane because they did not have to strug-gle so hard just to live, but recently he had begun to feel as if some-thing had been lost on the way from New Hope.

He was remembering these things when, near the end of the road, one of the tractor tires threw a rock. It hit him hard on the arm, so hard he took his hands off the wheel and slammed his foot down on the gas pedal and ran through his own fence and into a ditch at the edge of the woods. The rock tore his jacket. He tried to move his arm and saw that it still moved, and he closed his eyes and held his breath against the pain. He knew he was lucky. He knew, if the rock had hit his head, he might be dead, or, if he'd jerked the wheel right instead of left, he and the tractor might have careened down the hill instead of into this ditch, and it was not likely he would have sur-vived that. He tried to restart the tractor, but the wheels just spit mud, so he shut it off, and, with hardly another thought, lifted three logs from the wagon and carried them on his shoulder the rest of the way. He went back for another load and another until the wagon was empty, then he rigged a temporary fix for the fence he had flattened. The cows were across the pasture, far enough away to trust they would not discover the break, but Arliss knew, just as soon as you're sure what a cow will do, she'll do something else.

The pain in his arm was no longer piercing, but it had spread through his entire body, making him ache as if he might be coming down with something. His stomach felt queasy. The cut was on his upper arm near the shoulder, and though he had not yet looked at it, he could see out of the corner of his eye that there was blood on his jacket. He had been determined to keep his arm moving, not let it lock up, but lock up was exactly what it was doing, and by now, every little movement brought tears to his eyes.

He found the rock. It was on the floor of the tractor, and he picked it up and threw it into the woods, knowing he need not have bothered. There were hundreds just like it. He could spend a month, two months, three, trying to pick them all up, but there were always more rocks. Every time it rained, a new crop surfaced. He would not forget the hours and days and years he had spent picking up rocks beside his mother, who had tried to convince him that the rocks were God's will, and, whether punishment or test, it was not his place to know which. He remembered a time when, listening to his mother talk about the world that had been wrenched from them, he had believed there had been no rocks in New Hope. He no longer thought that was true, but he did not believe there could have been *as many.*

He checked to see if Bob's car were still there. It was. Bob never stayed long, though, and he never stayed overnight. If he were in town for more than a day, he stayed in a hotel, which ticked Merle off, but living all the way down in Atlanta, he still managed to come by the house more often than Daniel, who lived just across town. His excuse was he was too busy, but all he did was go to school. Twenty-nine years old and still in school! Arliss never knew what to say to his sons or their wives, anyway, so he did not care how often they came home, or did not come home, but Merle did, and he had better things to do than listen to her gripe.

He washed his hands in the spigot outside the barn, then remembered that he was covered with sawdust and mud. It was in his hair. It was crusted in the folds of his neck. He stuck his head under the spigot and did the best he could.

"What are you doing with your hair wet?" Merle said, when he stepped inside.

Bob walked over and shook his hand.

"What happened to your jacket?" Merle said.

"Yeah, Dad. Are you okay?"

"I'm fine."

Arliss was surprised to see that Bob's wife, Tina, was there, too, and he looked around for their children. They had two, his only grandchildren so far, and every once in a while, Arliss gave himself a moment when he imagined having grandchildren who might show some interest in the farm, although the likelihood was slim, since Bob and Tina had only daughters, and Tina had been heard to say the farm was a dangerous place for children. Daniel and his wife were expecting, but in whose fantasy would Daniel encourage a child of his to love the farm? So he did not hope, but he did not let the idea die either, because, whatever he had done or not done to set his own sons against the farm, it seemed reasonable to want a second chance. Tina explained that the children had stayed back in Atlanta with her parents, but when Arliss glanced at Merle to see if she were disappointed, he saw that she was not listening. She was sitting at the kitchen table, looking at brochures of Florida. She handed Arliss one that advertised a retirement community, and said, "Bob is building this one."

Tina placed her hand on Merle's arm and explained, in a voice dripping with patience, that no, Bob was not *building* it, exactly. He and his partners (and by partners, Arliss had no idea what she was talking about) had just gone in on the financing. "I don't know what all's involved—you know *men* when they get together—but I can tell you it's a prime investment opportunity." Tina was a tiny woman with wrists the size of chicken wings. She spoke with a high-pitched, singsong voice, and every time Arliss heard it, he was just glad the cows hadn't. Merle had asked him just the other day if he liked his daughters-in-law, and he had stared at her, not knowing what to say. She had not waited for his answer; she never did; Merle only asked questions for the opportunity to hear herself answer them, and so it was this time, as she explained why she liked Tina more because, even though she was a Methodist, she at least *went* to church, while Merle did not know about the other one. Leda would not commit one way or another, but Merle knew something was not right in the church department. She had a nose for it. Arliss had listened. He would not have argued with Merle's logic, but if he had to choose which one he'd rather be around, he would pick Leda, because she was calm, whereas Tina was as bad as Daniel for fidgeting. But did he *like* them? How was he supposed to answer such a question? Half the time he swore he did not know what Merle was talking about.

Bob walked to the window and stood with his hands in his pockets. Arliss watched him. No matter how many times he saw it, he could not shake the idea that his son dressed like a banker. It was as if somebody else had raised him on the sly. "I ain't got any money to invest," Arliss said. "I hope you didn't come here thinking I did."

"No, Dad."

"I ain't never had that kind of money."

"Arliss, hush," Merle said. "He don't want your money. I was the one who asked to see his brochures because, who knows? I just might up and get the urge to move there someday."

"To Florida?"

"I don't see why not." Merle stood up, at which point Bob and Arliss both grabbed the table to hold it still. It was a habit; everybody in the family had developed it, because Merle's getting up from the table involved a series of lurching movements that often resulted in sliding silverware and spilled drinks. Sometimes it was her sturdy arms pushing against the table; other times it was her thighs bumping against it as they turned her around, but, regardless, she was oblivious to her role in whosever glass of milk might tip over, whosever fork might fall to the floor. "I hope y'all are hungry," she said. "I'm making fried chicken."

Tina spoke up, saying they would not be staying for dinner, but Merle waddled into the kitchen anyway. "Fried chicken's his favorite," she said, pointing to Bob.

Tina looked alarmed, but Bob held up a hand as if to calm her down and followed his mother into the kitchen. "We've made dinner plans in town tonight, Mother, but you could wrestle us up a snack."

"I got a made-up mind."

"I'll bet you can unmake it."

Merle opened a package of vanilla wafers.

Arliss excused himself and went to his room. Carefully now, moving as little as possible, he took off his jacket, then his shirt, and examined his arm in the mirror. The cut was not deep, but it was messy, and already there was a bruise forming on the skin around it. He raised the arm over his head and back down, then again, sucking air through his teeth. Sweat popped out over his face, and he wiped it off with a washrag. He stood over the bathroom sink and cleaned the cut by squeezing water over it out of the same washrag, then patted it dry and wrapped it in gauze. He turned his attention to the jacket. He opened the narrow drawer at the top of his dresser and rummaged through fingernail clippers, an eyeglass repair kit, crumpled store receipts, several balls of string and one of twine, handkerchiefs, a flashlight, batteries, and an extension cord until he found what he was looking for, a roll of electrical tape. He spread the sleeve of his jacket flat on the bed and patched the tear with pieces of the tape, which he tore with his teeth.

He emerged from his room to find that Merle had placed four bowls on the table. In each bowl were a handful of vanilla wafers topped with a scoop of vanilla ice cream. Merle and Tina were at the table with their bowls in front of them, but Merle was the only one eating. Bob was back at the window, looking out. "I see you got rid of the tree," he said.

Arliss nodded. "I'm going to put a pond there in its place."

"What do you need a pond for? Did the creek run dry?"

"No, but they're telling me they'll shut me down if I can't keep the cows out of it."

"Who told you that?"

"I don't know. Some fellow come out here and told me."

Bob nodded. "It's probably running into the river. Not that it hasn't always run into the river, but nobody's cared until now."

"I don't know, but I ain't got time to argue with him."

"I don't know why you had to take down the tree, though."

"Better than losing pasture."

"What about shade?"

Arliss peered at him. He did not know why Bob all of a sudden should get interested in a subject he never cared for before. In fact, Arliss had considered the problem of shade and, without Bob's or anybody else's help, had already made plans to build a tin-roof shed. He looked at the ice cream melting on top of the vanilla wafers. He had gotten in his mind the idea of a ham sandwich, but knew it was not worth hurting Merle's feelings to change the menu, so he sat down. He decided, then, to tell Bob about his plans for the shed, but before he could finish, Merle interrupted, suggesting that, as long as he was in a mood to build something, he should put a new roof on Belle's House. "You get Belle's House in shape, maybe Daniel will get that log cabin business out of his head."

"What log cabin?" Bob asked.

"My point exactly. Shitfire and a cat's ass, you can't raise no baby in a cabin in the woods. Not these days anyway."

"He better not ruin it," Bob said.

"You can't ruin the woods, Bob."

But Bob was not listening. He sat down and leaned over the table toward Arliss. "Do you have any idea how much this land will be worth when it's time to sell it, Dad? Please don't let Daniel mess it up."

"How much money?" Merle asked.

"A boatload. Please, Dad?"

"Who's saying I'll sell?"

"You can't farm it forever."

Arliss did not answer. He ate a bite of the ice cream but had a hard time swallowing it. He pushed his chair out and stood up. "I got a tractor in a ditch."

Merle turned to Tina. "If Daniel ever did build him a house, you and Bob could move into Belle's House. I don't know why in the world y'all have to live in Atlanta anyway. My friend Dorothy Mills has a sister who moved to Atlanta and was mugged at the mall in full daylight. They knocked her to the ground and stole her purse and broke her arm. Pure meanness is all it was. There weren't no reason to go and break her arm."

Arliss turned to Bob. "I suppose you couldn't help."

Bob hesitated. He looked at the expression on his wife's face, which was hovering now on the line between alarm and panic. He looked down at his clean shirt and slacks. He sighed. "Sure," he said, and started rolling up his sleeves. "I want you to think about what I said, though. It's not too soon for you and Mom to be thinking about your future. That's what I *do,* Dad, help people plan for their future, so don't forget, okay? I can help you."

"I've always wanted to live in Florida," Merle said.

TEN

LEDA

When their daughter, Hannah, was born, Leda and Daniel were living in a small rental house on Dogwood Street in a neighborhood like Susan's but on the other side of town. Leda considered the house dark and stuffy, but she loved the yard, which was shaded by two large oak trees that pelted the ground with acorns every fall, and a mimosa, which, with its low branches, looked like a perfect climbing tree for children. Daniel liked the fact that the house was close enough to the university to ride his bike to work. Leda was aware that other people were impressed by this. They came up to her at the Flying Dog, for instance, to make sure she knew how much they admired him. People she did not even know, telling her things about Daniel!

Leda took Hannah to work with her at the public television station. Her job involved some filing and typing, but mostly all she did all day was keep the daily production schedule straight—who was working which camera, where and when; that sort of thing. Hannah became a bright spot in the days of disgruntled production workers, who used Leda's office as their lounge. The real lounge was next to the executive director's office, but they were not allowed to use it because, regardless of the complicated and multifaceted organizational flowcharts, the television station operated on just two levels. The bottom level consisted of the people who did what they considered the real work of the station; they ran camera, sound, or lights, wrote scripts, directed television programs, designed logos, drew animation, applied makeup, and typed letters. The bottom level people swore the top level people did no work beyond dressing for lunch, but for doing all this nothing, they made twice the money (and got to use the lounge). Their crimes were cited over and over and over again in Leda's office as if the outrage were a scab that kept coming off. Here were some:

—The executive director was a man named Sam Phelps, who was famous for requiring massive doses of ass-kissing, which was not difficult for a person who worked in, say, Development (where a certain amount of ass-kissing was part of the job description), but excruciating for someone who stood behind a camera all day. He also had a bad habit of promising his high-paying donors that "his people" (and by that, he meant the people who worked in production) would produce programs that they absolutely loathed. Documentaries on a certain person's oil company, for instance.

—The head of Production was having an affair with the head of Development. Actually, nobody cared; they were both famously unattractive people, and the consensus was: more power to them. But problems arose if they could not be found *anywhere* when one of them was needed, for instance, to sign a purchase order for an essential piece of equipment.

—The director of Programming was a lurker who docked his employees' pay for making personal phone calls on company time. In addition, he kept the window blinds in his offices closed, so his secretaries would not become distracted by what they might see outside. *Like what, trees?*

—And Peggy Boatwright, the director of Marketing and Promotion, was a cocaine head.

Peggy's office was located next door to the Production Department, where Leda worked, but before she ever appeared in the doorway, Leda would hear the warning signal, the click, click, clicking of high heels on industrial-strength linoleum, a sound that had the ability to freeze her intestinal system for years. *Would you mind,* Peggy would say, handing her something to type, explaining that her own secretary was too busy. Leda's own boss, the director of Production, was never around to save her (holed up, as he was, in some closet with the director of Development). But lounging on the brown velvet couch on the other side of the room, the cameramen, artists, writers, sound engineers, or whoever else might be taking a break, would be sending her eye-messages, *Say no, Say no, Say no,* like her own personal cheering section.

But Leda found it impossible to say no to Peggy Boatwright, dark-eyed, thin, and intimidating in her Anne Klein suits and Ferragamo shoes. The day Peggy handed her a thirty-five-page report to type, there was only one other person in the room, a graphic artist named Micky, who, when Peggy left, shook his head. "You are such a sucker," he said.

On her way home that evening, Leda drove out to Carr's Big Orange to pick up a box of diapers. She made a point of going once a week as an offensive move to keep Merle from complaining that they never came to see her, but she had learned to buy only certain things there, and meat was not one of them. Carr's was in an old building with a concrete floor and cinder-block walls and a ceiling streaked with brown, amoeba-shaped water spots. On rainy days, you would find buckets under the leaks, but neither Merle nor the Carrs seemed to have any inkling that people might question the safety of the meat if they had to walk around buckets to get to it. Strangers might be drawn to the shelves of homemade jellies and jams and honey and beans and pickled okra and relish and beets, but Leda looked at those dusty mason jars and saw botulism, so she stayed away from there, too. Chances were, the crackers and cookies were stale, but the vegetables, when they were in season, were better than any you could find at a supermarket, because they were locally grown, so Leda felt safe with them and certain household items such as tinfoil, paper towels, dish soap, and, of course, diapers, which Merle always handed Leda for free along with advice, such as the tip she offered this afternoon. "There are no bad children," she said, "only spoiled ones, and those you can cure with a good spanking and a Little Debbie." Leda took the box of diapers and a bag of freshly picked corn but ignored the advice. Before she left, she watched Merle tease a couple of men who came in wanting Slim Jims and cigarettes and shotgun shells, and they teased her back. Daniel never saw this side of his mother, because he never went to Carrs, but Leda could see it. Guys like these thought Merle was *fun*.

Hannah was crying by the time Leda got home, hungry, no doubt, so Leda scanned the window of her neighbor's house next door when she pulled into the driveway, and, damn! There it was. The lace curtains opened and closed. Leda knew it would take almost no time now for the old woman to get outside, and sure enough, by the time she got Hannah out of the car, her neighbor Mrs. Grable was standing in the driveway in front of her.

"The bone was sticking out of his leg," she said.

Mrs. Grable never said *Good evening, Leda* or *Hey* or *How's the baby* or anything that might suggest the beginning of a conversation. She simply started in the middle of a story that was, if not gruesome, then at least hard to ignore. She did not do this to Daniel. Leda did not think she did this to any of their other neighbors. Mrs. Grable was the kind of old woman who was getting skinnier with age, as if the flesh between her bones and her skin were being sucked away, but the lines around her mouth told the real tale, that this was a woman who, in her whole life, hardly ever smiled. The way Daniel liked to describe her, Mrs. Grable could play Death onstage with no makeup. This evening, Mrs. Grable did not proceed with her broken bone story, but then, she never did. Her routine was to deliver the initial pronouncement of bad news, then stare at Leda, presumably waiting for a reaction, and Leda almost always obliged.

"How awful," she said.

That was the cue for Mrs. Grable to continue the story, which involved her sister's daughter's son who had broken his leg. It was impossible for Leda to extract herself from this conversation with anything like civility. Nodding and saying, "Uh-huh," she carried Hannah, who was screaming now, to the front door, while Mrs. Grable followed like a puppy, describing as graphically as possible the nothing-less-than-horrible surgery this child was in for. Leda put the key in the door and, at the exact moment Mrs. Grable took her first intake of breath, interrupted. "I've got to go now," she said, then closed the door in the woman's face.

There was no other way to do it; Leda had tried. Most days she felt at least a trace of guilt for closing the door in a lonely old woman's face, but not today. Today she was too tired. She changed Hannah, then fed her and waited for Daniel to come home.

Most nights she watched through the window as he rode over the hill on his bicycle. He would pedal fast, then throw his head back and stick his legs out sideways, the hem of his corduroys tied with shoelaces. Then he would careen down the hill in a sort of bicycle free fall until he reached the bottom, where he would catapult over the curb, wobble through the yard, then leap off the bike before it stopped, letting it fall in the yard somewhere. He never looked where. Daniel believed in the world as it ought to be, which meant if you left your bike lying unlocked in the middle of your yard all night, it should be there the next morning. That he'd had two bikes stolen already did not change his mind. You *ought* to be able to leave your bike where you wanted.

But tonight he was late, and when the sun went down, she fixed herself a sandwich, and when he still wasn't home, she gave Hannah a bath and put her to bed. There she stayed, because if left alone at night, Hannah would cry and bang her head against the side of the crib. Lots of people, including her friend Susan, had advised Leda and Daniel to let her cry and bang away, because eventually she would stop, and they had tried it. For an entire week they tried it, seven whole nights, but Hannah never gave up. "What if she dies?" Daniel had whispered one night as they huddled in the hallway outside her door.

"She won't," Leda said.

"It's a cruel trick, though, isn't it? To give us a baby to love that could turn around and die on us. It's sick, is what it is. If there is a God, he's sick as hell."

"Stop it, Daniel."

"I still think, as a plan, it sucks."

Listening to Hannah go on for an hour, two hours, banging her head, even Leda sometimes thought it sounded as if she were killing herself. A baby killing herself; it seemed too serious a business for a baby, but there were times when she swore she caught in Hannah's eyes a sadness that should not have been there in someone so young. Or was she reading things into Hannah's face that were not there, guessing at something serious when it easily could be a stomachache? It did not matter. On this, Daniel and she agreed, they would ignore the advice and stay with Hannah for as long as it took until she fell asleep.

Sitting in the darkness, Leda remembered the report she had to type for Peggy Boatwright, and she began to speculate on the nature of suckerdom, wondering if she might qualify. Where was the line, she asked herself, between being nice and being used? No idle question, it had become a joke between Daniel and her that, in a crowd of people, she was always the one approached for directions or donations or bus fare. She had never even told him about the time in New York City, when she had been picked out of a crowd by a desperate young woman who had begged her for groceries. It was a big crowd. As impressive as anything else she saw in New York was the number of people on the sidewalks at all hours, and the idea that she had been the one selected from all these other people was troubling. The woman had a frenetic manner of speaking, which Leda guessed was drug-induced, but not until much, much later. It had taken her several minutes to understand that the woman was telling her she was pregnant and hungry, but when Leda tried to give her money, she had said no. The cops would throw her out of the store if she went in there by herself. She had wanted Leda to go with her and buy the food, and—this is what still amazed Leda—she did it. She walked down the street with the woman, went into the store, and pushed the cart while the woman put in bread and crackers and cheese and Vienna sausage and a box of Tampax. (*Wait! Tampax? Didn't you say you were pregnant?*) Leda did not say a word. She paid for the groceries under the scrutiny of a policeman who clearly knew her companion from past adventures in shoplifting, but when it was over, her main thought was not that she had been duped. It was that she could have been killed. How easily the woman could have walked her, not into a grocery store, but into an alley, where someone waited with a knife. Thus be to suckers! Leda wished she knew what it was about her that attracted these people. Maybe a bland face is a kind face, she thought. Maybe big-hipped women look motherly, or else, too slow to run away.

An hour later, she was sitting at the kitchen table typing the report when Daniel came through the back door. "You won't believe what I did today," he said. "Told them Faulkner was redundant. Nothing a good editor couldn't fix—my exact words."

Leda watched him. He looked flushed, as if he had biked a long distance and not just the mile and a half from school. "I thought you liked Faulkner," she said.

"And that new girl, Beth from somewhere, not from around here, Kansas or Nebraska, maybe. Could be Iowa. Where in God's name is Iowa?"

"You know where Iowa is."

"She practically had a heart attack and marched down the hall to the office of our beloved Faulkner expert, Ambrose Carmichael III. You remember the guy. Wears bow ties. Hates me. The next thing I know, he's telling me that if I ever, and by ever I mean you haven't lived until you've heard this guy say ever. *Evah.* If I *evah* say anything against the late, great William Faulkner again, he is going to personally see to it that I never, and by that I mean *nevah,* work in this school again."

"He's harmless, right?"

"A cupcake. What I want to know is, how they got three different women to name their sons Ambrose." He went over to the refrigerator, opened the door, and peered inside. "Ambrose pissed me off so bad, I sat down and read *Absalom, Absalom!* all over again."

"That's why you're late? You've been reading *Absalom, Absalom!*?"

He looked at her. "Not the whole thing."

He pulled a can of beer from the refrigerator and came over to the table and turned a chair around backwards and straddled it. It creaked under his weight. The chairs, hand-me-downs given to them by Arliss and Merle, were made with frames of thin metal tubing, the seats, an orange plastic attached with hollow screws. The same metal tubing held up the table, the top a mottled Formica, sand-colored with orange flecks. The most startling thing about the kitchen set to Leda was the fact that, when Merle bought it, she had thrown out the wooden table and all but one of the chairs that Arliss's father had made when he moved his family to the farm. The remaining chair was sitting in front of the desk where Merle kept her sewing machine, and when Leda commented on how much she liked it, Merle had told her about the rest, including a few pieces of furniture Arliss's family had brought with them from New Hope. All of it, she said, had been thrown out or burned. "You wouldn't have wanted it," Merle had told her. "It weren't nothing but junk," to which Leda had been tempted to say, "Junk you couldn't afford to buy now," but she refrained. If Merle preferred Formica to hand-crafted wood, there was no point in arguing with her. Leda was starting to suspect that the way Merle and Arliss looked at the furniture they had thrown away was not far from the way they viewed the past in general. All her questions about the early days of the farm, for instance, went unanswered. *What do you want to know that for,* was as far as she got with Merle. Arliss ignored her. Even when she asked him about New Hope, he acted as if he had never lived there. To buy the kind of table Merle and Arliss had thrown away, Leda and Daniel would have to save their money, and even then, it would be a brand-new table with none of the dents and scratches that only a history can bring. For now, Leda had to be content with orange furniture that was practically falling apart. (Actually, the table did not worry her, but she was holding her breath over those chairs.) Daniel hung his arms over the back of his chair and drank the beer without looking at her. "I didn't really mean it, you know," he whispered after a few minutes. "Faulkner doesn't need any editing."

"I wouldn't think so."

"I don't know, Leda; sometimes I think there's something wrong with me. I mean, I was sitting at my desk reading *Absalom, Absalom!*

and did not know the sun had gone down until I realized I was squinting, and even then I did not quit. It was not until I couldn't see the words at all that I even thought to turn on a light. All that time, I could not quit thinking about the improbability of somebody writing such a book, or any book. I don't get it, see, how this odd species of ours developed the kind of consciousness that can write books, or why. That's the question. Why? So I was sitting and reading and wondering; it's like I could not help but wonder if there might be a God after all. Or something. Does this ever happen to you? Because I don't know how else to explain something like the genius of Faulkner, see, or, forget him. Take Shakespeare. All I'm saying is, I'm on the same page when they're talking about why ants build anthills; you know what I mean? Birds fly south, wolves hunt in packs, but then there's Shakespeare, for Christ's sake. It's hard to believe it's just neurons firing."

"Nothing is, but believing makes it so."

"That's *Hamlet*."

"I know."

"Except it's *thinking*. Not *believing*."

"Okay. My mistake."

"And it's nothing *either good or bad* but *thinking* makes it so."

"I said, okay."

"If you're going to quote Shakespeare, you should get it right."

"Listen, Daniel. You can believe anything you want."

"But you don't."

"I could."

"But you don't."

"That's true. I don't."

"I don't know how you can be so sure."

"I'm not. But that's sort of the point."

"You don't have to be sarcastic."

"Sorry."

"You always do this, you know. Right in the middle of when I'm trying to say something important, here you come with some sarcastic remark."

"I said, I'm sorry."

Abruptly he stood up. "I'm thinking about giving Sut Lovingood a rest, by the way."

She watched him pace, shaking his hands at the wrists. She could not say she was sorry, having always questioned the wisdom in staking a reputation on a man named Sut. She had grown tired of the questions that pushed the bounds of minutiae. Is Sut merely a witless example of human depravity, or can he shed light on the human condition? Questions like that. Did Faulkner name his character Sutpen in *Absalom, Absalom!* after Sut? And what to make about that last name, the combination of Loving and Good? Leda did not care and was glad now that Daniel would not, either. Still, she was worried. For all the ridicule Daniel threw at Dr. Ambrose Carmichael III, she had always suspected he wanted to be in the same club.

"You mean quit?"

He shrugged. "What are you working on there?"

She looked down at the typewriter. "Nothing," she said.

As he walked back toward the refrigerator to search for something to eat, he reached behind his head and pulled out the rubber band that held his hair back. He tossed his head, and she watched as the hair fell to his shoulders. He was wearing glasses now, a large, dark-framed pair that was out of style, but on Daniel, they looked like a style that should be, as if he might be the precursor to the next new thing. "This Beth," she asked. "Is she pretty?"

He turned around and smiled. "You, Leda. You're my rock."

ELEVEN

DANIEL

Daniel always knew Sut Lovingood was problematic. It was not the dialect, either; that came easy after a while, once you got the rhythm. Brian was the best at it. Sometimes when Tom Fields came down to the Flying Dog with Daniel, Brian would join them and start talking like Sut and have everyone at the table laughing. *"I'se a goner I 'speck, an' I jis don't keer a durn,"* was one of Brian's favorite things to say when he was drinking. But that was part of the problem. Daniel had researched the material long enough to know that Sut Lovingood could be complex and symbolic. He also knew that the author George Washington Harris had impacted American literature. Maybe not deeply. No one was going to claim there would have been no Mark Twain without George Harris, but the influence was not disputable. The problem was, nobody else seemed to care.

He could admit it now; he had fallen for the chance to do something different; I mean, how many dissertations do you want to see on Walt Whitman? He had loved it when people asked him what he was working on, so he could watch their faces when he answered, "Sut Lovingood," stopping there, no explanation, just a look in his eye: *You mean you don't know who that is?* He always waited to see if they would ask, but hardly anyone did. "These assholes never want to show their ignorance," he had told Leda. For a long time he worried that Tom Fields might tire of him and offer the idea to another student, or two or three; then he would be forced into a race to see who could write the better book or who could get it out quicker. He worried that someone younger and faster would come up with an idea more profound than his, because his was looking less and less profound every day.

His premise was that Sut was a fool, but a wise one, the trickster in the Shakespearean tradition, and though it was not a wholly original idea, the possibility that Sut might be mythically grounded had sucked him in, because it reminded him of when he had charged out of college with a newly found conviction that all literature, all art, all of life, for that matter, can be broken down into a handful of mythological archetypes, similar to the way matter is broken into atoms. It was like an epiphany for him and then an epidemic, because everywhere he looked, he saw these archetypes, but he could hardly help himself. His idea had become more than a convenient hook for literary criticism or even a nifty psychological theory. It was his religion. One Christmas he even forgot himself and tried explaining it to his parents in a scene he would remember always, sitting at the kitchen table, a plate of stale cookies between them, Olivia Newton-John singing Christmas songs from the television on the other side of the room. The cookies were store-bought, with red and green sprinkles on top, and when he bit into one, it tasted like sawdust. He ate half of it, then started with the story of Prometheus as a way to get their minds around the subject, but each time he mentioned Zeus, his mother interrupted. "He weren't no real god."

"For that time and in that culture, Mother, yes. He was considered a god."

"But he weren't real."

Finally, he looked at her. "I can do this same thing to the Bible, Mother."

"I'd be happy if you'd just read it."

"If it will make more sense to you, I can break the story of Jesus down to its mythical roots."

"Jesus will break you right back."

"You're missing the point."

"Arliss, make him stop."

"Stop hurting your mother's feelings, Daniel."

"What feelings? She doesn't have any feelings. If you want to talk about feelings, what about mine?"

Arliss stood up, his hands, shaking. "I ain't listening to you talk to your mother that way."

"At least I talk to her. You don't even talk to her."

"Sit down, Arliss," Merle said. "You know you can't tell him anything. He's been too big for his britches ever since he was born."

"Excuse me," Daniel said. "Is the TV on? Can we please turn off the TV? I can't hear a goddamn thing."

"He's cursing. Did you hear that, Arliss?"

"Or down. Can we at least turn it down?"

"Don't curse," Arliss said.

"*She* curses all the time. What's shitfire? Poetry?"

"There's a difference," Merle said, "between strong language and taking the Lord's name in vain. Tell him, Arliss. I told you something like this would happen if he went to North Carolina."

Arliss looked back and forth between his wife and his son. Then he went to the door, put on his hat and coat, and walked out of the house.

"Forget it," Daniel said. He started to leave the table, but Merle stopped him.

"You didn't eat your cookies."

"I ate one."

"Half."

He sat back down then and ate the other half of the cookie while, on the television, Burt Reynolds and Angie Dickinson sang "Frosty the Snowman."

Over at the university, Tom Fields was all for giving Sut Lovingood mythical importance and helped Daniel design a thesis with the goal that it become a published book, although Daniel's expectation of the popularity of such a book differed drastically from Tom's. By the time he understood Tom's fondness for modest texts written for a small but discerning audience of American literature scholars, the myth idea had started to unravel anyway. It was not that it did not make sense, only that it did not seem important anymore. Nothing seemed to *hinge* on archetypes, and sometimes he had to make himself run through his own theory just to remember how it went. "Think if you had to relearn chords every time you picked up the guitar," he explained to Brian.

"It's a bummer, man."

"It's not working out for me."

But Daniel did make it work out, for a long time, because he did not want to disappoint Tom.

Then one day Celia Montalvo stopped him in the hall and fixed him with her dark Italian eyes and told him he was the last person in the world who should be defending such a person as Sut Lovingood. He is cruel and he is racist, she said with particular emphasis on the latter, achieved by pursing her lips in a particularly provocative pout. Daniel, who had led campus protests over higher wages for the janitorial staff, had never before felt the need to clarify his political or social righteousness and, to anyone who cared to ask, he would argue that Sut's racism was universal, including not just black people, for instance, or Jews, but Yankees, lawyers, sheriffs, preachers, men who used big words, and, in particular, his own father. There was a difference, he claimed, between simple racism and an all-encompassing, unyielding (he sometimes came on out and added mythical) hatred of the world. But here was Celia Montalvo, six feet tall with black hair that hung halfway to her ass, which she considerately displayed in skirts and pants that were, at least, one size too small. Celia Montalvo, who was writing her dissertation on Henry James in both English and Italian. Celia Montalvo, who had never condescended to speak to him before. It got his attention.

"I'm going to have to be honest with you," he told Tom the day he gave up on his dissertation. "The longer I work on Sut, the meaner I feel myself."

"That's good, Daniel. Maybe that's an angle you could explore."

"I can't."

He was standing in front of Tom's desk and all of a sudden felt

how strange that was. How many times had he come into Tom's office and slumped into a chair and spent the next hour, or two, talking
about baseball, politics, cars, the writings of William Kennedy and
Jim Harrison, or Celia Montalvo's red cashmere sweater, and now
he was standing and did not know if he ought to sit down or not.
Daniel could not look at Tom. Instead, he looked out the window at
the two students who were just outside, throwing a football on the
lawn below.

"You want to quit?" Tom said after a long silence.

Daniel did not know what to say.

"Don't quit. Just take some time off. Take a year."

"They're not going to let me do that."

"Why don't you let me take care of that."

The boys throwing the football on the lawn outside had the kind
of beefy bodies that made Daniel think they had played football before, in high school maybe, but they weren't good enough to play
anymore. They would be the kind to wake up after graduation and
wonder where the party went and get jobs selling something, maybe
insurance or cars or home appliances, so they could afford football
tickets and tailgate for the rest of their lives. They would never get it,
the fact that they were going to die.

"Don't give up," Tom was saying.

Daniel looked at Tom. "I won't."

Tom did two things for Daniel for which he should have been grateful, although Daniel's memory for such things was short. First he
made him an instructor, then, to cushion the contract nature of that
job, he made him director of the new Writing Center, which was a
salaried position, including benefits, and not subject to yearly review.
He did not carry the same status nor engender the same respect as a
tenured professor, but he soon reached the point where his classes
were filled every semester, with long waiting lists of disappointed
students forced to wait another term for the chance to take English
from Mr. Dan. (Those who called him Dr. Dan by mistake, he did

not correct.) He earned the reputation of being an easy grader, but that wasn't all. If you went over to the Flying Dog, you were likely to find him there, surrounded by students, who had pushed tables together to sit around with him, talking about Shakespeare.

So sometimes he was late coming home. So what? You can teach more about literature over pizza at the Flying Dog than from a hundred textbooks, but Leda did not want to hear it. She persisted in asking if he would ever start back on his dissertation, but Leda was the kind of person who thought it perfectly okay to work at a job she hated, as if that did nothing to your soul. Daniel did not mean *soul* in any religious sense, but *soul,* as in the core of his being. He did not want to die wondering whether he'd done the best for his. As he liked to tell his students (stealing from Joseph Campbell), "You've got only one life. Follow your bliss or it's not worth living." Tell that to an eighteen-year-old and see how much he loves you.

If you were Daniel, though, and you said it enough, you might start wondering if you were following the right bliss.

Daniel's office at the university was in the Writing Center, and when he was not in the classroom, he could be found there. His job was to help students with their writing assignments, anything from one-page essays to full term papers, but he had a staff of work-study students and a few salaried employees, so there were times he had nothing to do but sit and stare, for instance, at the carpet, which was gray, but if he looked closely, he could make out shades of blue, even pink, woven through it. The walls were covered in the same carpet, which was one reason the Writing Center was almost irritatingly quiet. The carpet swallowed people's voices. Sometimes he got sucked into staring at the electronic message board on the opposite wall. WELCOME TO THE WRITING CENTER. 103 AND 104 STUDENTS BE SURE TO TALK WITH A WRITING TUTOR AT LEAST ONCE BEFORE SEMESTER'S END. WRITING CENTER HOURS, M–W 9–7:30, THURS 9–6, FRIDAY 9–3. DRIVE SAFELY, CITIZENS. The messages were uninteresting (except for the *citizens* part, which Daniel thought lent a refreshingly socialistic slant to this Go Vols stronghold), and endlessly repeating, but the patterns were mesmerizing. Sometimes the words scrolled from right to left across the board. Sometimes they came in from the right, then disintegrated, either from the top or from the bottom, as if they were consuming themselves. Other times, they came in from the right or the left, stopped in the center, and dropped down, giving the real impression of some solid thing falling to the floor, so that you might find it and pick it up. The colors of the words were traffic light colors, but these, too, were tricky. Daniel liked to stop students and ask them to identify them, without looking. Invariably they said either red or green or yellow, never picking up on the fact that they were all three at random intervals. He was aware that this was a waste of time.

Over the next four years, Daniel and Leda had their second child, a son they called Andy, and in that time, Daniel won teaching awards and increased the use of the Writing Center by 40 percent, which earned him a raise but not the same respect he believed those with a *Dr.* in front of their names received. It began to affect the way he looked at his colleagues, the English professors and want-to-be professors, or as he saw them now, the strutters and fretters. Brian's work, making pizzas and drawing beer, seemed to him more authentic than these yellow-stockinged Malvolios, yet they were the people who continued to look down on him, year after year. He was certain they called him "quitter" behind his back. Called him "loser." They thought they were the insiders, the ones with the answers, but Daniel could see from his seat in exile that their little club was a joke, and he gave up thinking he would find meaning for his life there.

More and more he had had difficulty sleeping at night. He would listen as Leda gradually drifted off to sleep but feel himself, in direct proportion to her slumber, waking. He would lie still, willing himself to quit thinking, but it rarely worked. His mind was a tumultuous think factory that could not be distracted from its determination to ponder such questions as justice, evil, desire, and death, forcing him out of bed to read or watch television. Some nights he practiced his guitar, but he compared himself to Brian and felt like a pretender, because, even though Daniel could play anything Brian taught him, Brian could play anything he *heard.*

One night he saw a movie that affected him deeply. It was about an artist who uses his conflicted, often violent, relationships with people, specifically his girlfriends, to inspire his art. Daniel watched the movie with Leda, then, when she went to bed, rewound the tape and watched it again with the volume turned low so she would not wake up. He stayed up most of the night, rewinding the tape and watching it again, five times in all, and when he was through, he had to ask himself what he would do for art. He guessed the answer and was ashamed. The next day the world looked different to him, and what he saw was this: It is the job of a secondhand man to talk and talk and talk and talk about the work somebody else has done.

He put down the guitar and, for the first time since college, began to write again. He started with little things, poems. He began a novel, abandoned it, then started another. He wrote in spiral notebooks, which he took with him to work, where he would look over what he had written the night before. It was devastating, really. He did not know why he did it to himself. He felt as if he must be two people inhabiting one body: at night, an infinitely hopeful and gullible person, impressed by the words that flowed from his pen, but by the light of day, a cynic, duped and seething, capable of seeing the very same words for what they were. Garbage. Every day he vowed to quit; then night would come again.

He remembered something he once heard about a painter—he thought it was Edward Hopper—who, despite much acclaim, considered himself a failure, saying at the end of his life that all he had wanted to do was paint sunlight on the side of a house. Most people, Daniel believed, would not understand how a person as successful as Hopper could feel like a failure, but he understood. Every time he tried to describe yearning (which was all Daniel believed he ever wanted to do) with the clumsy tool of language, he understood. He considered his the hardest of all the arts, in fact. Anger, loneliness, unspeakable joy; he could imagine any of these easily evoked in paintings, music, or dance, but words, unless they were exactly right, could make even the most profound human experience sound silly.

Often during this time he found himself drawn to a photograph hanging on the wall over his desk in the Writing Center. It was a photograph of an old log cabin in the woods, taken early one morning before the fog had lifted. It was an inadvertent and ironic result of his work on Sut Lovingood that Daniel had become an expert on Appalachian culture and knew, exactly, how it was built. Leda had bought it for him from a photographer friend of Susan's who specialized in images of the Great Smoky Mountains. "This is us," she had said when she gave it to him, which had surprised him, and he had looked closely at her to see if she meant it. She was smiling. Even though Leda was not the most beautiful woman he had ever known, he still found himself surprised by her warm and complicated eyes, especially when she smiled.

"Do you remember . . ." he had started to say.

"Yes," she had said. "I do."

Then one afternoon, instead of going home, he drove out to the farm. He guessed his mother was still at Carr's, and his father was either in the barn or out in the pasture somewhere, but Daniel did not want to take a chance of running into them and parked the car on the side of the road and walked directly into the woods. It was a hot summer day, and Daniel was sweating before he was even halfway up the hill. He had forgotten how quiet it was out there, and how thick were the smells of ripe leaves and sun-heated tree bark and the soggy earth under his feet. Also in the air were the smells of cattle and the tang of newly cut wood, and these forgotten smells brought back the memory of his father's nasty mixture of diesel fuel, which he had made Daniel spray on the cattle to rid them of face flies. It had made him gag; that's how bad it was. His brother, Bob, always got out of it by volunteering, like a regular Boy Scout, Daniel thought, for harder jobs, such as digging up cedar trees or stacking square bales in the barn loft to store for sick cows, but Daniel never would forget the secret smirk Bob would give him, as if to say, he knew he was getting the better deal. Daniel was convinced half the stuff on the farm would make him sick, and one day he remembered telling his father straight to his face, "If I get cancer someday, I'm blaming you."

More than the diesel spray, though, Daniel had feared the job of culling the cows, when his father would make him stand by the barnlot gate and let only one animal in at a time. These were creatures that weighed close to a thousand pounds, and he was supposed to hold them back with a rickety wooden gate, but that was not nearly as crazy as Arliss, who would be walking around in the barnlot with them. And this with the knowledge that *his* father had been trampled to death by cows! As Daniel once told Leda, "My dad's got shit for brains."

It had been a long time since he had thought about any of this.

By the time Daniel got to the grove of poplar trees, he felt a breeze blowing through the trees, and he stopped and thought again how quiet and peaceful it was. He had to ask himself why he had never noticed it before.

After a while he heard a tractor start up, and he walked to the top of the hill and stepped out of the woods onto the narrow dirt road that led to the barn. Now he felt the full force of the wind coming off the ridge, and he turned his face toward it. The cows were on the top of the ridge, and his father was running the tractor back and forth across the lower pasture. It looked strange out there without the maple tree. Soon the tractor turned and headed his way. Daniel watched as Arliss drove over to where he stood, cut the engine, and got off. "Cutting hay?" he asked.

Arliss looked back at the pasture as if Daniel might have seen something he hadn't. Then he shook his head. "Just topping it," he said. "It bothers their eyes for that grass to go to seed, so I keep it trimmed. Cuts down on the pink eye."

Daniel stared at his father. Putting cows and pink eye in the same sentence sounded like a joke waiting for a punch line, but Daniel never could tell when, if ever, his father was kidding. "I don't know why you had to take down the tree," Daniel said, changing the subject.

Arliss took his gloves off and stuffed them in his back pocket. He lifted his hat and wiped the band of sweat off his forehead, then put the hat back on. He pointed to the clearing in the woods. "You're going to let me know when you're fixing to build, aren't you? I'll have to move the saw."

Daniel shook his head. "I'm just looking around."

"You need to take down those poplars first. You ought to do it before I move the mill so we can cut them up."

"I'm not cutting down the trees, Dad."

"You could use the lumber."

Daniel did not answer.

"You still thinking about building?"

"Not really."

Which was true. He and Leda never even talked about it anymore. Chances are, they never would have tried to build a log cabin had Daniel not stumbled on help.

TWELVE

LEDA

Their names were Fred and Walter. Daniel met them at the outdoor equipment store where they worked, and they agreed to build, not quite a log cabin, but something very close, even though their main line of work was not construction but selling sleeping bags and hiking boots and freeze-dried food. To Daniel, this was even better. "It's perfect," he told Leda. "These guys are true craftsmen; you know what I mean? It's not the money, either, because they don't build anything they don't want to build. It's the work, pure and simple, and how often do you find that anymore?"

This was the fourth time Leda had heard Daniel say the same thing, and she did not feel like answering again. They were in Arliss's truck driving back from the building supply store with a load of concrete blocks on a warm October Saturday morning, Daniel in short sleeves, steering with one wrist the way Leda imagined him as a teenager, driving around in his daddy's truck with Brian, a six-pack between them, Joe Cocker on the eight-track. She loosened her seat belt and scooted over next to him.

"What are you doing?"

"Nothing." She laid her head on his shoulder.

"Don't do that."

"Why?"

"That's what rednecks do."

"So?"

"We aren't rednecks."

"I know that."

"Just because we're in a truck . . ."

"I *know*, Daniel." She moved back to her side.

The blocks were for the foundation. Already, Fred and Walter had cleared the site and cut a crude driveway up from the road. Daniel drove up to where Fred and Walter were waiting beside Fred's truck, which was also full of blocks. Fred leapt into the truck bed and handed down the blocks two at a time to Daniel and Walter, who carried them to a stack at the end of the driveway. Fred was a tall man, six feet, seven inches, and strong, despite being extremely thin. He lifted the blocks as if they were nothing. He had small eyes, crooked teeth, and a cigarette dangling from his mouth almost continually, because he was one of those people who can smoke without hands. His skin was tanned. His hair was long, stringy, and multicolored: bleached blond on top but brown underneath, although most days he wrapped his head in a blue bandanna, so all you saw were the ends. He tended to wear layers of clothes, such as a pair of shorts over army fatigues and more than one shirt, and for this Leda called him Raggedy Man, although not to his face. Standing in the truck, backlit by the sun, it looked as if the rays of sunlight were extending from his blue bandanna. Leda had to shield her eyes to see him clearly. She could not take the blocks directly from him. They were too heavy to catch, the way he swung them into the hands of Walter and Daniel, so she lifted them directly off the truck and carried them one at a time to the growing stack. She did not have to be doing this. She had left Hannah and Andy with Merle and could join them back at the house anytime she wanted, but Fred had told her they did not need her help. There was something about the way he said it. The blocks cut into her wrists, but she gritted her teeth and did not complain.

"So this man pulls up to the store in a Jaguar," Fred was saying, standing in the truck bed swinging blocks. "We know, because that's what me and Walter do, don't we Walt? We check out what they're driving before they walk in the door."

"Did you do that with me?" Daniel asked.

"Sure. Toyota. We called you Toto, right, Walter?"

Walter was a short muscular man whose clothes never seemed to fit him. His shoulders were too round, his thighs, too thick. He had pale skin and a large round head, balding from the forehead back, which caused Leda to call him Mr. Onion Head although, again, not out loud. He nodded to Fred, but kept his pace between the truck and the steadily growing wall of blocks, back and forth, two blocks at a time, easy.

Fred continued. "So Jag Man walks in, suit and tie, lawyer type, and asks to see the sleeping bags. I know what you're thinking, Jag and all, but I don't show him the top of the line, no way. I pull out some of the lower lines, maybe second-best, get him all lathered up before I give him a glimpse, you know, like a tittie tease, of the model you'd need only if you were headed for fucking Everest. That's when I say, *Now of course, if you're looking for the best* . . . See, that's the thing gets those Jag guys every time, thinking they barely missed out getting the very best. So he says, *I'll take it,* and I move on to ground covers. There was no limit to this joker, was there, Walter?"

"Nope."

"Ended up sticking him for almost nine hundred dollars." Fred flicked his cigarette to the ground.

Daniel was grinning, but Leda had decided Fred could burp and Daniel would think it was funny. Recently he had even begun to quote him, such as the other night, when he had handed Brian a Schlitz beer, saying, "A poor man's piss is better than a rich man's poison. That's a great one; isn't that great? I didn't make it up. Fred did."

Andy, who was three years old by now, was delighted with his new word, *piss,* but Brian set down the beer, and said, "You're wearing me out with this Fred business."

"You're just jealous."

"Maybe," Brian had said, "but whatever you're doing, I'll be glad when you're done."

Fred's cigarette butt was smoldering on the ground between the two trucks, dangerously close to a cluster of dry leaves. Leda looked to see if anyone else noticed, but nobody did. She walked over and stubbed it out with her shoe.

When both trucks were unloaded, Fred and Daniel sat down on the wall of stacked blocks. It occurred to Leda that this was a wall built to be unbuilt, and thinking of it in this way reminded her of an installation she and Daniel had seen in a New York art museum. It was a room entirely empty except for one tiny chair, the size of dollhouse furniture, sitting in the middle of the floor. A caption on the wall said, simply, CHAIR. The instant Leda read it, she laughed out loud and called to Daniel, who could have ruined the moment by theorizing on *chairness* or *smallness*, but he didn't. He laughed, too, and later even extended the joke, pointing to a window, saying, *Window*, to a car, saying, *Car*, to a door, saying, *Door*. It became an inside joke between them that had lasted for years and covered everything: *Mailbox. Fork. Stop sign.* So Leda knew if she pointed to the blocks and said, *Wall*, Daniel would probably laugh. But then, he might not. In front of Fred and Walter, she did not know what he would do.

At the moment, he and Fred were making bets on the World Series, which would be played that year between the Toronto Blue Jays and the Philadelphia Phillies. Daniel was pulling for Toronto, mainly because Fred refused to back any team that wasn't American. He and Fred traded drinks of water from a large plastic jug, leaning backwards, holding the lip of the jug above their mouths so the water splattered on their faces and down their chests. Fred filled his mouth with water and threatened to squirt Daniel, but at the last minute turned and spit it out on the ground. Then he lit a cigarette.

Daniel shook his head. "I don't know how you can smoke those things, man."

Fred just looked at him.

Walter was standing in the clearing trying to get Fred to decide how high they should build the foundation, but before Fred could answer, Daniel spoke up. "Just clear eighteen inches."

Fred seemed to consider that advice, then nudged Daniel's arm. "Why?"

"To keep out termites."

"What? Do they get dizzy?"

"It's a superstition. Go up there in the mountains sometime; you won't believe the shit you'll hear."

Walter turned so he was looking out over the valley at the rows of mountains behind other mountains, three or four layers deep, visible on this haze-free autumn morning. Fred was staring at Daniel. "Are they afraid of heights?" he asked. "Hey, Walt, you ever seen a termite afraid of heights?"

Walter shook his head but did not turn around.

"I told you it was just a superstition," Daniel said.

"You won't have no termites," Fred said. "Because you're going to call the exterminator, right, Toto? You wouldn't pull something stupid like not calling the pest man, would you?" Again he shoved Daniel's arm, but this time the shove was harder, and Daniel fell backwards off the wall. Leda rushed over to help him up, but he waved her away. He stood up and brushed off his pants. Fred stubbed his cigarette out on a block. "Hey, sorry, man."

"No big deal," Daniel said.

Walter never turned around.

"Your mother invited us down for lemonade when we're done," Leda said.

"We're not done," Daniel said.

The men worked the rest of the afternoon and into the evening on the foundation, but Leda quit early. She walked along the dirt path at the top of the ridge, past the graveyard, past the barn, then down the driveway to Arliss and Merle's house, where she found Andy covered with chocolate icing from a boxful of doughnuts.

"Them chocolate's his favorite," Merle said, wiping Andy's face and hands with a wet rag.

Had Leda arrived ten minutes later, she would not have known about the doughnuts, so she had the option of staying quiet if she wanted. Or, she could tell Merle one more time that Daniel did not want his children to eat junk food, which, of course, he told her all the time. *Don't give them cookies,* he would say, while his mother muttered, *What's one little cookie going to hurt?* Sometimes he ran down a list: *No cookies, no candy, no Cokes, no potato chips, no ice cream, no fast food, and I mean it, Mother.* Doughnuts were so off the chart he never thought to mention them. But Daniel never went to Carr's Big Orange, because if he did, he would see how much of not-a-big-deal a doughnut was compared to Merle and Lydia Carr coming at you with a Little Debbie snack cake, and if you did not take it, you'd find yourself face-to-face with a hunk of butterscotch fudge the size of your hand. Hannah, who was seven now, managed to ignore it. She would find an upside-down orange crate to sit on and read, and when Merle or Lydia Carr offered her a piece of candy, she might take it and say thank you, but just as often Hannah would say no thank you and keep on reading. She was polite; there was no way to argue otherwise, but she did not behave like a normal child in Merle's book, and Merle always ended up saying so, loud enough so everybody in the store could hear. Andy, on the other hand, would eat whatever was offered—candy, cookies, soft drinks, a Slim Jim—until Leda stepped in. Usually she succeeded in stopping him at a couple of cookies.

Leda decided to forget the doughnuts, but she would not have had time to say anything anyway, because just then the grandfather clock chimed, and Andy screamed. He ran around the room screaming, through six deafening rings, before throwing himself in Leda's arms.

"Has he been like this all day?" she asked Merle.

"Only when the clock rang."

"Can't you turn it off?" But Leda knew the answer, because she knew about the switch inside the clock's door that muted the chime to an innocuous clicking noise. Usually she remembered to turn it off herself.

Merle only shrugged. "He'll get used to it."

Arliss came through the door, as he did every day at six, and hung his hat on the hook next to the door. He stood there, watching Andy screaming. Only when it was quiet again did he come on into the room. "Is Daniel coming to supper?" he asked.

Leda nodded toward the window. "Looks to me like they're going to keep working."

Arliss looked. You could just see the men through the trees on the other side of the hayfield, working in the dusk by the headlights of Fred's truck. The sound of rock 'n roll from somebody's car radio rose into the night air. Merle put supper on the table, meat loaf, mashed potatoes, and frozen peas, but Arliss kept staring out the window.

"He should have taken them trees out first."

"Why do you say that?"

"He's going to lose them anyway. He can't build on top of their roots and expect them to survive."

"Does he know that?" Leda asked.

Arliss shrugged. "I told him."

THIRTEEN

LEDA

Winter came, and they worked on the house on weekends when they could, the days dismal and drizzly, marked by the scraping of rain jackets and the squealing of truck tires stuck in mud. When the air was clear, it was cold, and their hammers echoed like gunshots, but between each shattering hammer fall was a wonderful stillness, a gray silence. *A terrible beauty,* Daniel would shout, quoting Yeats, his voice ringing in the brittle air. Leda thought some painter ought to come out there and see these men against the pale light, should come and paint this gray before it was gone.

By the end of March, they had finished the foundation, the sills and sleepers, and most of the framing. Soon they would be ready to attach the exterior logs. Fred and Walter had talked Daniel into buying precut logs, even though Daniel had showed them how to hew your own. Hew was the word he used, an old-fashioned-sounding word, and sometimes Leda said it softly to Andy, who liked to put his hands up to his mother's lips to feel the gust of breath it produced. Daniel believed there was a difference between precut, prefitted, store-bought logs and logs you hewed, but he could not defend the idea with anything like fact, and Leda did not know. She wondered if Arliss knew, but she would not ask him. Daniel would hate it if she asked, if she allowed his father to think they welcomed his opinion. It wouldn't even matter, the opinion. Even if Arliss gave his blessing on store-bought logs (because that's what it would sound like, a blessing), he would be set free to comment on other things. Drywall, for instance. Plumbing fixtures. How to raise their children. Anything. As it was now, Arliss kept his distance, pausing outside the barn to watch from time to time, but that was as close as he got. Maybe he was thinking they were making a mistake not using hand-hewn logs. Maybe he wasn't thinking anything at all.

Daniel's brother, Bob, on the other hand, called them several times a week to ask about the house, and one Saturday morning in early spring, he showed up to see it for himself. He parked his car behind Arliss and Merle's house and walked along the dirt path at the top of the ridge toward the construction site. Daniel was on the roof with Fred and Walter and saw him first; then Leda, who had been given the job of marking two-by-fours for electrical outlets, saw him, too. Watching how he picked his way along the path, careful to keep his shoes and the hems of his pressed khakis out of the mud, it was hard to believe he had ever considered being a farmer, but either it was true, or else he had fooled a great many people. At least when he entered UT as an agriculture student, it was assumed he had done so with the idea of taking over the farm from Arliss, so when he graduated with a degree in business instead, no one knew what happened. It appeared as if he had changed his mind at the last minute, but, as Daniel pointed out, no one knew how long he had been thinking about it. He could have been walking around the farm with his father for years, nodding, looking exactly like a person taking serious mental notes, all the while knowing he had no intention of spending his life on a farm, none at all. Or, he could have had a sudden change of heart, a waking-in-the-middle-of-the-night realization that something was utterly wrong. Or, it could have been a gradual drifting away from farming, so slow, he did not see it coming until it was over, but no one knew, because no one ever knew what Bob was thinking, so unlike Daniel, who hardly had a thought he did not think worth telling somebody else.

Bob stopped when he got as far as Belle's House. He put his hands on his hips. Belle's House was situated about twenty yards down the hill from the road. The narrow path that led to it went down a short, steep slope before leveling out into a small yard, where once there had been a vegetable garden. Some of the fencing that had surrounded the garden was still there. Bob left the road and walked down the path to Belle's House and put his foot on the back porch, as if to test whether it still held up. It did. Arliss had kept the house in shape, even though no one had lived there since his mother died. Every few weeks he swept it clean of dust and nesting animals and washed the windows, and just recently he had replaced the roof. Bob walked across the porch and looked in a window, before climbing back up the hill and proceeding along the road. Daniel had come down from the roof by then, and when Bob reached the clearing, they shook hands. Daniel pointed back toward Belle's House. "You could move there anytime, you know. He's been saving it for you."

Bob smiled. "Yeah, well, you could, too. Listen, you remember that guy, Freight Train?"

"No."

"Sure you do. Freight Train. That crazy guy who worked for Dad and got himself shot, I think, right down there on Bearpen Lane. He was always making these stupid train noises with his mouth, and he used to slip us licorice sticks. I haven't thought about him in years."

"Maybe he just slipped *you* licorice sticks."

"I can't believe I forgot about that guy." He was smiling and shaking his head and running his fingers through his hair. People often commented about the fact that Bob and Daniel did not look like brothers, but Leda could see, if you disregarded the color of their hair and eyes, there was a definite resemblance in their smiles. He said, "I see where Dad moved the sawmill."

"I'm not sure he really wanted to, but yeah. It's on the other side of the barn now."

"That's a better place for it anyway." Bob pointed to the poplars standing beside the house. "Aren't you worried about losing those trees?"

"No," Daniel said.

Bob walked around the house. He stopped to look in through the opening where the front door would go but did not go inside. Fred and Walter were still on the roof, but either Bob did not notice them or pretended not to. When he had walked once around, he stopped in front of Daniel. "Let me just ask you this. Why did you bring your driveway up way over here?"

"Where would you have put it?"

Bob pointed toward the field between Arliss and Merle's house and the woods. "Closer to the middle there."

"Through his hay ground?"

Bob shrugged. If the driveway were centered, he explained, they could convert it to a road if they ever wanted to develop the property. "We could sell lots on both sides, see. Where it is now, you're cutting into some prime lots just for a driveway."

"We're not going to develop the property, Bob."

"Not that it won't still work; it'll just cost more."

"What do you mean by 'lots'?" Leda said.

"I'm just planning ahead for when Dad sells the farm."

"Why would he sell the farm?"

He looked at her. Then he looked up at the sky, a habit of his, Leda had noticed, as if he expected to be struck by divinely inspired patience. "He can't keep this up forever," he said, finally.

Leda persisted, "But he wouldn't have to *sell* it."

"I'm just—what is the word I'm looking for? Thinking ahead?"

"You are so full of shit," Daniel said, but Bob was smiling as if he did not hear. He pulled a package of gum out of his pocket and offered a piece to Leda.

"I don't guess Daniel's told you about that time he and his pal Brian stopped by my place on their way to Fulton County Stadium. Drove all the way to Atlanta to see the Braves play, prepared like a couple of Boy Scouts they were, with their gloves, their cooler full of beer, their Braves caps, except, what was it they forgot? Money?"

"You want your money back? Is that what you want?"

"Don't be an ass."

Daniel dug through his pockets but came up with only two dollars. "You got any money on you?" he asked Leda.

"In my purse. It's still in the car."

"I told you I don't want your money," Bob said. "That was a long time ago."

"You're damn straight it was a long time ago. Centuries, but you're still bringing it up."

It was then that Fred jumped down from the roof. Bob pretended to look as if he were not startled.

"How're y'all doin'?" Fred said, grinning at Bob, and Daniel smiled.

One of Arliss's dogs was lying on the ground, chewing on a stick. Arliss had a number of dogs. (Daniel pretended there were so many he could not count them all, but Leda knew there were only four.) This was the tan one with the little-dog body on the big-dog legs. Fred picked up the stick and threw it. When the dog chased it and brought it back, Fred threw it again. They did this a couple of more times, Fred throwing the stick, the dog chasing it and bringing it back, Fred grinning, a cigarette hanging from his lips. He took it out of his mouth and, squinting through the smoke, looked at Bob. "You ever watched a dog with a bone?" But he did not wait for Bob to answer. "He won't give it back to you like this here. No, sir. He'll sneak off with it, give you that suspicious look, like he thinks you're going to take his bone away, and don't you try neither, unless you're just wanting to lose a hand. What I want to know is, what's the difference? And how does he know?"

Bob was well known for being a hardnosed shark when it came to dealing with a variety of tough characters—lawyers, developers, bankers, doctors, real estate executives, board chairmen, company owners, politicians—men (because they were, for the most part, all men) who could snakebite a snake, but it was clear by the baffled look on his face that it had been a long time since he had come up against someone like Fred.

"You reckon there's some kind of bone gene?" Fred asked.

For help, Leda thought, Bob should have looked to her, because she was accustomed to being dumfounded by Fred, but he turned to Daniel instead. Daniel only smiled. "We're not selling any lots, Bob," he said.

"You don't know what you'll want in twenty years," he mumbled. Then he started walking away.

"I know we're not going to all this trouble just to end up in a sub-division," Leda called after him.

"You could think of it as an investment," Bob said, still walking away.

"Except it's not," Daniel said. "It's our land."

At that, Bob stopped and turned around. "It's not just *yours.*"

Leda waited for Daniel to say something back, but he did not. She watched Bob get farther and farther down the road while Daniel just stood there. Finally, she could not stand it any longer. "We're not going to all this trouble just to end up . . ."

But Daniel cut her off. "I know that Leda."

"I'm just saying . . ."

"I know."

Daniel followed Fred back to the roof. They were nailing sheets of plywood to the framing, and it made Leda suddenly tired to watch how quickly they worked, even Daniel, who seemed to know what to do without asking, even though he had never done anything like construction before. Leda always had to ask what to do, but—here was something she had noticed—Fred never answered. He ignored her. Sometimes Walter would let her hold a board straight for him, but mostly it was Daniel who would give her some small job, something that, if it never got done, no one would care. She stood on the ground and listened to them laughing over dog bones and bone genes. Then Daniel, for what seemed to Leda like the thirty-thousandth time, called Fred a moron, and Fred called Daniel an idiot, causing Daniel to remind Fred of the money he won off him when the Blue Jays stole the World Series off an unlikely, bottom-of-the-ninth, three-run homer by Joe Carter. It was, Fred conceded, a spectacular moment in baseball, topped only by one in 1986 when Boston first baseman Bill Buckner let the ball slip through his legs, enabling the New York Mets to win that World Series. Daniel hated the Mets. Fred knew that. He shrugged. "We all have our cross to bear," Fred said. Expanding on the subject of improbability, Fred changed the subject to tell his story about the bear he had met up with while camping in the mountains near Cosby. Leda had heard this one. More than once. Then Daniel piped up with the story about the shark they had seen off the pier in the Outer Banks. "I swear to God it was ten feet long," he said, which was when Leda decided to speak up.

"Six," she said.

All three men looked surprised to see her still standing down there. "I was there, Daniel, and the shark was no more than six feet long." Daniel blushed. "Eight," he said. "At least."

"I'm quitting," she said.

"Fine."

As usual, she had left Hannah and Andy with Merle, but she did not go there right away. She walked along the dirt road until just beyond the graveyard, where there was a gate into the pasture. She checked to see where the cattle were and saw that most were either spread across the slope of the back ridge or congregated at the base, so they were reasonably far away. Still, the idea of being on the same side of the fence with them felt risky. She opened the gate slowly and went through, keeping her eyes on them while she headed toward the pond Arliss had built. It had become family lore that Arliss had run into trouble filling it up. Water, any water—rainwater, water from a hose—soaked right through the ground and disappeared when he had tried. After two or three hard rains and still no water in the pond, Arliss had been forced to spend several days sealing the bottom with soda ash. It held water after that, but Arliss had stayed mad about it for a long time, which had tickled Daniel. He told Leda it served his father right for cutting down that tree.

"Why do you care?" she had asked him once.

"Because," he had said, "Dad looks at a tree and sees board feet. He sees shade. Firewood. That's what it means to be a scorched-earth farmer, see, incapable of appreciating something like a tree for its own worth. Never does he say, *lookee there; that's a beautiful tree.* You don't know him like I know him."

"I'll buy that, but I still don't know why you care."

Daniel had looked surprised. "Because he's wrong."

So there was a philosophical difference between father and son. Leda understood that, but she did not understand why Daniel was not more concerned about what it might be like to live next door to him. She had asked, of course, the day he met Fred and Walter and several times after that. *It'll be fine,* he always said whenever she brought it up, but she did not bring it up so much anymore, and the reason had less to do with Daniel's contradictions than the fact that she was beginning to like it out here. It was peaceful, like nothing else in her life.

Over at the public television station, she had been promoted from production secretary to a writer in the Marketing and Promotion Department, but while the salary was better, and the work more stimulating, the new position had the drawback of making her answer directly to Peggy Boatwright. So it was more stressful. It also meant she had leapt from a lower level job to one in an upper-level department, which gave her the odd feeling of having crossed over to the other side. Now she was embarrassed around the cameramen, sensitive to the fact that they might think of her as a traitor. If anyone had asked how she was these days, she might have said, out of kilter.

But driving out from the city, she could tell the instant her body started to calm down. It was right after Glen Pike turned from four lanes to two, there at the big horse farm with the white fencing and the house you could not see from the road. Most days, she would not even be aware of how tense she was until she began to feel her shoulders relax. Then there was the left turn onto the narrow, tree-covered Raccoon Road, the S-curve that made you slow down before the bridge that went over the creek, and the big cattle farms with their round bales sitting in the sun. By this time, she would have turned off the radio and opened the windows so she could hear the sound of the rushing water in the creek. If there were honeysuckle, she would smell it, and if a skunk had been around, she would smell that, too. Chances were good that by the time she turned right onto tiny Bearpen Lane, she would have seen a deer or two.

Arliss's troublesome pond was full of water now; the shore on the other side where the cattle tended to drink was marshy, and there was a thick boggy smell around the place. Dragonflies hovered over it, and mosquitoes. Leda found a dry spot where she could sit and keep an eye on the cows. It was incredibly quiet here, and she realized that nowhere in her range of vision could she see a man-made structure other than the barn. No houses, no roads, no electric or gas lines. She could be miles and miles from civilization, and it would feel the same. The sun warm on her face and arms, and the smell of new grass and mud and manure brought her back to the summer she was thirteen and she had owned a horse.

Cricket was her name, a three-year-old filly borrowed from a family friend, broken only during the four weeks in June while she was at camp, which was not nearly long enough for a beginning rider, but she did not know that. This, she had believed, was going to be her summer of horseback riding, which had followed her summer of sailing, which had followed her summer of dancing, both at which she had failed, but she had promised herself this time it would be different. Because the dancing and the sailing had been her grand-mother's idea, while a horse, well—she had wanted a horse all her life. They boarded Cricket at a stable only five miles from Leda's house, and the plan was for her to bike there each morning, ride all day, then bike home in time for dinner, which might have worked out fine, except it turned out that Leda was terrified of this horse.

And it was not just the horse. She was afraid of the sneering sta-bleboys who had to hold Cricket still, because she spooked and crab-stepped when Leda tried to saddle her. She was afraid of the stable owner, a rough old man named Cowboy, who was supposed to be her riding instructor, but who grew visibly weary of teaching her to trot, because she absolutely refused to go any faster. And she was afraid of the other girls at the stable, who easily cantered their horses across the fields and into the woods, while she walked Cricket around and around the ring, pleading that she not attempt a break for the barn every time she passed the broken gate.

Yes, she had always wanted a horse.

No, she had not known what she was talking about.

But she could not tell her father. Looking back on what it was like to grow up in her family, the image she got was of three independent souls operating out of the same house, an arrangement that depended on her being happily occupied during the summer months when she was not in school. It was a question of pride, a matter of *what one did,* to be happy with your situation, and if you weren't, to keep it to yourself. So she told no one. Every day she biked to the stable, begged the stableboys to saddle Cricket for her, then rode around the shadeless ring, sweating, batting flies, breathing air so thick you could swim in it, but even on the worst days, when the stableboys refused to help, and Cricket broke through the broken gate and ran like hell for the barn, Leda made herself believe that it would get better. *Ride around that ring enough times,* she told herself, *and you're bound to wind up having some fun.*

But the truth was, she never did. When the summer ended, she gave the horse back to her father's friend and never rode again, but forever after she felt ashamed. After all, how many people are afraid of their own horse? Now she was surprised to realize she did not feel that way anymore. What had changed, she did not know, whether the memory had lost its sting, or her shame had been a mistake all along, but remembering her summer with Cricket now, it was with some fondness for her young self who had stuck it out.

So it was with an unaccustomed feeling of accomplishment that she left the pond and walked toward the barn, where she found Arliss. He was in the barnlot emptying a bucket of corn into a trough for the bull and a couple of first-calf heifers, one who had delivered, and another who was due. Leda stopped to watch the calf. Arliss followed Leda's gaze. "His mama didn't want to feed him," he said. "But we straightened her out."

"How'd you do that?"

Arliss looked surprised that she would ask. Then he explained how he had tube-fed him with his mother's colostrum first, to give him the immunity he needed to survive more than a few weeks. Then he bottle-fed him with her milk, which he got by putting her in a headgate twice a day and milking her himself until she came around. It took maybe three weeks, he said. Two and a half. "Now lookee here; she won't let you near him," and to demonstrate, he started to walk toward the calf, but the cow turned her body so she was between him and Arliss, and Arliss stopped. He stepped back and picked up the empty bucket to put it back on a hook, then asked Leda if she wanted to come through the barn. He opened the gate, but she hesitated.

"They won't hurt you," he said.

"What about the bull?"

He shook his head.

It was a big bull. Leda was nervous, but she followed him through the barnlot anyway until they reached the safety of the barn. Inside, the barn was dark and musty and ripe with the smells of manure and grease and hay.

"Have you always had cattle?" she asked.

"Yes." Then he took off his hat and scratched his head. "You mean here?"

"I guess. Where else?"

"Corn was all my people ever raised back there in the mountains, you know. Daddy got talked into switching, but he didn't much care for the cows."

"Daniel told me that's how he died. Killed by a cow, is that right?"

"It was an accident." Arliss put his hat back on.

A tractor was parked in front of the barn door. Arliss walked her around it and out of the barn, and they stood at the top of the driveway looking down at the house. Leda saw that Bob's car was gone already. She said, "Bob was talking to Daniel about selling the farm someday. Did he say anything to you about that?"

"Not today."

"Because I think he was trying to talk to Daniel about developing it. But I guess it's crazy to think you would let anybody come in here and tear up this place."

"I hardly ever know what Bob's talking about."

Leda nodded. She was halfway down the hill when Merle came

out of the house with Andy and Hannah. Andy, who loved coming out to the farm, was reciting the rhyme he always said when he was there. *"Little Boy Blue, come blow horn. Feeps in mimi. Cows in corn. Where's boy? Gone night night."*

Merle looked surprised to see her. "We were just going to get us a little something to eat at that new McDonald's."

Leda took in the scene. Andy had run to the truck already and was bouncing up and down in the front seat, but when Hannah saw her mother at the top of the hill, she slid into a chair on the porch and crossed her arms. Merle was clutching her new orange-and-white plastic Go Vols pocketbook shaped like a football. "You want to come with us?" she asked.

Leda pointed to the truck. "There's no car seat in the truck."

"We're just going down the road."

"You can have a wreck in the driveway, Merle. Don't you know that?"

"How come you ain't working on the house?"

"I changed my mind."

Andy was still bouncing up and down. Now he was singing, "Ee I Ee I O," his standard response to the prospect of going to McDonald's. Leda had a hard time getting him out of the truck until she told him they were going to Susan's house. Then he bounded out and raced to his car seat in the back of her car. If anything, Hannah looked relieved. Merle waddled up to where Arliss was watching from the top of the hill. Just before she closed the car door, Leda heard her say, "Those children would be a whole lot better off if she worried less about car seats and more about their souls."

FOURTEEN

LEDA

They could hear Seth's guitar from the street. Hannah put her hands over her ears when she got out of the car, and by the time they reached the porch, Andy had his covered, too. "Do I look like the last sane person standing?" Leda said, when Susan opened the door.

Susan looked down at Hannah and Andy with their eyes closed and their hands over their ears. "It's too loud, isn't it? I'll have him turn it down."

"Don't bother him," Leda said, but Susan was already walking down the hall toward Seth's bedroom. The music ballooned when she opened his door, but then it stopped. Leda could not hear what Susan said, but she heard Seth.

"But *Mom,* it won't *sound* the same. I might as well not even *play.*"

Hannah and Andy liked going to Susan's house, because on the coffee table was a huge ceramic bowl, and inside the bowl was an iron ball the size of a marble, which they could start rolling near the rim and watch it spin in ever-smaller circles all the way to the bottom. Susan's house was full of bowls like this and other assorted pottery, crowded together on shelves that had been built just to hold them all. She had painted the walls of her living room a deep red, then covered them with artwork, some of her own, but much of it given to her by friends. From floor to ceiling, paintings and photographs filled the surface of the walls like a giant collage, with thin strips of red showing between. It was the boldest decorating move Leda had ever seen, even though she knew she was the last person on the planet to have an opinion on decorating. She did wish sometimes for Susan's kind of nerve.

Several of the small, penciled sketches on the wall were Brian's, many of them drawn when he was still in high school while he and Susan were dating, although no one who knew them then would have used the word *date* to cover what happened to them. They fell in love is what happened. They did it against odds and the opinion of their classmates, who told them they were crazy, who considered them perfect foils. He was boisterous and crude, while she was quiet and serious. He was disheveled and disorganized, while she was neat and orderly. He abused his body with alcohol and cigarettes and parties that lasted until dawn, while she was an athlete, a cross-country runner, who did not drink or smoke or even bother to show up at his parties. But they were both artistic, and they were both stubborn, and, because of that, there were people who swore they were made for each other and were not surprised when they got married. These same people were also not surprised when, two years after Seth was born, they split up. Every one of Brian's sketches was of Susan, although some were not as obvious as others. From a distance, they looked like intricate abstract drawings, but if you studied them, you saw what they were: pictures of Susan's hair or Susan's knees or Susan's hands or Susan's thighs. It was hard not to consider them awfully sophisticated for a high school boy to manage. Once, when she caught Leda looking closely at them, Susan had said, "You think I ought to take them down, don't you?"

Shaking her head, Leda had answered, "I don't think anything."

Hannah started the ball rolling in the ceramic bowl for Andy; Seth turned down the volume on the amplifier, and Susan returned to the living room, but within a couple of minutes, the music was cranked back up again. Susan turned to march back down the hall, but this time Leda stopped her. "Let's just go outside."

Susan's backyard was divided into several small gardens connected by wide grassy paths. There were flower gardens and vegetable gardens and various rows of short and tall bushes and intimate groves of trees, and in the middle of one grove, Susan had built a pond. It was not nearly as big as Arliss's pond, which was a good thirty or forty feet across; Susan's pond was small, only about six feet long and lined with plastic. She used her own yard as a demonstration for her landscaping business, and the pond was an example of something else she could do. Goldfish, frogs, and turtles lived in it, although they were hard to see under the lily pads. While they walked through the yard, Susan told Leda about a recent client who had ordered sixteen azalea bushes but, after they were already in the ground, paid for only ten, despite an invoice that clearly stated sixteen along with a detailed drawing of where each bush would be planted, signed by the man himself. "He called me Honey," she said.

"Jump back," Leda said.

"And he must have thought he was going to get away with it, because you should have seen the look on his face when I came for my six bushes."

The story made Leda smile. What often surprised people who mistook Susan's small size for an easy pushover was how tough she was, except, Leda thought, listening to the discordant chaos seeping out of the house from a jacked-up amplifier, when it came to Seth.

"Brian tells us he's really getting good on that guitar," she said.

Susan nodded. "He is. He also wants to go live with Brian."

"What does Brian say?"

"He says he's not responsible enough to take care of a kid."

"At least he admits it."

They sat down on a bench next to the pond. Leda had come over to see what Susan might say about Bob's visit to the farm. But Susan, who had known both Daniel and Bob longer than Leda, shrugged it away and said not to worry. "Bob likes to make Daniel mad, but that's the end of it," she said. "Making Daniel mad is the sport, and it's not hard. It's never been hard."

Leda nodded.

"I guess you knew that. Listen, what's that Fred joker up to these days? Brian says he's trouble."

"Brian said that?"

Susan nodded. So Leda told her how she was starting to think that Fred did not even want her near the cabin now, and how Daniel still seemed incapable of seeing anything wrong with Fred. "Maybe," Susan said, "Daniel's just enjoying all the attention. He's not used to being so admired."

"I find that hard to believe."

"That's because it's probably not true anymore, but when he was a kid. That's what I mean. It was different then. You have to imagine how tough it was for him to be accepted when he was the only farm boy who did not run with the other farm boys. By the time I met him, he was already good at faking it, but I can guarantee you, he was the only one of Brian's friends who ever shoveled manure out of a barn."

Leda tried to imagine. She spent a great deal of time, in fact, imagining, piecing together the discrepancies between Daniel and his family, figuring out what, if anything, they cost him. "You would think he'd talk about it more than he does," she said.

Susan shrugged. "Like I said, maybe it's not such a big deal anymore."

Hannah and Andy were kneeling beside the pond, looking for fish. Andy had his own pet goldfish at home, which Daniel had bought for him when he said he wanted a dog. He first named it Leonardo after his favorite Teenaged Mutant Ninja Turtle, the one with the sword, which had horrified Daniel, who objected to television influences. "How about Arthur?" he had suggested, referring to the king, whose sword was nothing to scoff at, but, Andy argued, King Arthur did not eat pizza. Leonardo turned somersaults, and not only that, he liked to dive-bomb straight down to the bottom of the bowl, then, as if playing chicken, pull up at the last minute and swim away slowly like some crazy James Dean of a fish who could care less. He also swam upside down. Andy changed his name to Crazy Fish.

Crazy Fish lived in a two-gallon glass bowl with blue rocks, a toy pirate ship, and a plastic conch shell, which might have given Andy the idea he could put other things in there, too, like plastic Teenaged Mutant Ninja Turtle action figures, Hot Wheels cars, Lego blocks, and broken pieces of dried spaghetti. Leda had discovered the spaghetti the day before, but not until after it had turned limp and swollen, as if a colony of fat white worms had invaded the water. "What are you trying to do, Andy, kill your fish?" she had said, not intending to hurt his feelings, but he collapsed into tears. Andy cried easily and at seemingly everything. He was only three, so it was hardly time to worry, but Leda wondered if she should anyway. She had been worrying about Andy since he was born, blue and unwilling, or unable, to breathe. Eight nurses dressed in green had burst through the birthing room doors with an explosive sound like a gunshot. How long did Leda get to see him before they whisked him away? Five seconds? Ten? Long enough to know that Daniel was not exaggerating when he told the story later, swearing that Andy had been born blue. It was a shade in the Wedgwood family. Sometimes she distrusted her memory and doubted he could have been as blue as all that.

Daniel, on the other hand, had been white. Leda had stared at his white face, and demanded, "Why doesn't he cry?" Other questions had been on her mind, such as, *What's wrong with the baby?* and *Why are there so many nurses in this room?* but she could get only the one out, and she had asked it over and over. She remembered thinking that the answer to this question was the key to the chaos around her, that if somebody would just get to the bottom of it, the baby would be okay, but nobody was talking. The nurses were huddled on the other side of the room with her baby between them; the doctor was watching the nurses, and Leda, listening to James Taylor singing "Sweet Baby James" for the twenty-seventh time, developed a sudden hatred for the birthing room, with its cheerful balloon wallpaper and pictures of clown children on the wall, the rocking chair with the red-and-yellow cushions, and the bright yellow chenille rug on the floor. It was ludicrous, all of it, as if you could banish death with decorating. She kept her eyes on Daniel's white face and screamed at him one more time. "Why isn't he crying?"

"He can't."

The words were whispered, and, had Andy not cried at that instant, Leda would have remembered them as the most devastating words of her life. It was not a full-blown scream, the voice of an angry baby yanked into the world of light and air; it was closer to a whimper, but the room changed. The huddle of green nurses broke apart; the doctor turned and gave her a weak smile, and after a few minutes, someone laid Andy across her chest. The doctor explained how a knot in the umbilical cord had tightened when Andy started down the birth canal, and how, seeing the heart rate plunge on the monitor, he had gone in with forceps. Leda had not remembered anything about forceps. She had some notion that this talking man and the army of green nurses had saved her son's life, but it was dim. She found it possible to hold only one thought in her mind at a time. "Is he going to be okay?"

"I think so."

And he was, a perfectly normal little boy so far as Leda could tell, but she was always watching, not ready to trust that what she saw as okay today would hold. Now she watched as he spied a tiny frog on the rocks beside Susan's pond. He shrieked but quickly settled down, focusing his whole body until he managed to catch it. He held it in his hand for two seconds, three seconds, maybe four, before it jumped away; then he could not find it again. Suddenly Hannah stood up, saying she was bored, although with Hannah it was hard to tell if she was truly bored or just pretending. Leda watched her go off by herself to sit under a tree.

Hannah was turning out to be a beautiful little girl, with blue eyes and a pale shade of blond hair that made Leda think of moonlight. She took after Arliss, that's all; there was no mystery to it, but the one time she had said so out loud, Merle shook her head. "Rosemary," she had said. Leda did not know about Rosemary, so Merle had to explain. "Arliss's sister," she said. "Not Virginia, the other one. The one who burned up in the fire."

"What fire?"

"My land, you ask a lot of questions."

Leda had seen a photograph of Arliss's family, taken when he was about nine or ten. It showed Arliss and his mother and father, his sister Virginia, and his aunt Belle, but that's all. Merle said Rosemary was already dead by then, and there were no pictures of her that anybody knew of.

"So how do you know what she looked like?" Leda had asked.

"Virginia told me. You won't get nothing out of Arliss."

But Leda had asked Arliss about the resemblance anyway. He said he did not remember.

Leda was having a hard time believing she had a daughter who was beautiful. She herself had never been beautiful. She was prepared to advise a daughter how to buck up when no one thinks you're pretty, how to be thankful you're a late bloomer, how to consider the prom a gigantic waste of time, so what would she have to offer Hannah?

These days Hannah spent much of her time sequestering herself in various corners to read the books Daniel brought home to her, the way-over-grade-level books he insisted she could read, while Leda argued, "Sure, she can *read* them, but can she *understand* them?" It was an old argument between them, one Leda had already lost, because Hannah had taken on her father's pride in what she could do, so smart so young. She enjoyed the reaction she provoked in people when, at seven, she was seen with Isak Dinesen in her hands. Hannah worked at not being obvious, but Leda did not miss that flash in Hannah's eyes when somebody made a remark, *Look at what that little girl is reading!* Leda did not know if Hannah minded, or even if she knew about, some of the other comments made about her, such as the ones from her teacher, who reported that she had trouble making friends, or asked if Hannah might be depressed, or suggested she might have a problem picking up on social cues. Daniel had been rude. "Next time she picks up a social cue, I'm telling her to put it right back down," he had said to the teacher, but to Leda he offered this perspective: "Hannah's just different, and why shouldn't she be? Look at her parents."

Sometimes Leda wanted to hide in a hole for the way Daniel embarrassed her, but secretly she considered him a good parent, better than her, because he believed in things she did not. He believed, for instance, his children were capable of great things, and a child, she knew, could do worse than know something like that. She was the one who saw the pitfalls, the hurdles, the thousand different reasons to hedge against disappointment.

The guitar music coming out of Seth's room stopped, and in a few minutes Seth himself came out of the house and got on his bike.

"Where are you going?" Susan called.

"Nowhere."

"Wear a helmet."

But he was already gone. Susan stood with her hands on her hips watching him ride down the sidewalk, then for a long time after he was out of sight. Leda wanted to tell her it was going to be okay, but she did not know that it would, and Susan hated sympathy, anyway. Susan watched after Seth for several minutes before she turned and walked over to sit back down on the bench next to Leda. "Three years ago I bought him a raincoat. Now I'm going to ask you, why do you suppose I did that?"

"To keep him from getting wet?"

"Why does anybody buy a raincoat?"

"It's a reasonable thing to do, Susan," she said.

"He told me at the time he did not want the raincoat, but he was ten years old, for heaven's sake. I bought it, because that's what parents do, right? They do things to protect their children, even if the children don't think they need it, and besides, what's the alternative? Not buying the raincoat? That's the Brian philosophy of parenthood."

"In his defense, most people don't know they need a raincoat until it rains."

"I know. Like snow boots."

"And by then it's too late."

"So I hung the raincoat in the closet, thinking if he got tired enough of getting wet, he would put it on and be glad to have it, and that is where it's stayed, untouched, for three years. I should have left it alone, but I swear, Leda, it's like I can't stop myself sometimes.

This morning I opened the closet, and there was the raincoat, and I had to look at Seth, and say, *Are you ever going to wear this raincoat?* in that tone of voice, I swear, would make God feel guilty, but not Seth. Seth won't bite. He just looked at me as if I were an idiot, and said, *I told you I didn't want it.* It's like he hates me."

"He doesn't hate you."

FIFTEEN

LEDA

Leda had been watching Peggy Boatwright for signs of erratic behavior, because this year's speaker for the annual fund-raising dinner was Louis Rukeyser, host of *Wall Street Week,* which made him a celebrity in the world of public television, and everyone knew Peggy could not be trusted around celebrities. Both Leda and her office mate, Kevin, were on alert. When they heard Peggy's high heels on the floor outside their door, they stopped whatever they were doing, held their breaths, and looked at each other until she passed by their door. Unless, of course, she stopped. Leda conceded it would not be unreasonable for Peggy to conclude that she and Kevin spent a good deal of time these days breathlessly looking at each other.

Peggy never actually came all the way into the room. Typically, as was the case on this day, she stuck her head through the doorway, and said, "See me when you're done." Leda hated that. Peggy did not mean, *when you're done,* either. She meant *now.* Leda followed Peggy across the hall.

"Close the door," Peggy said.

Peggy's office was decorated with abundantly pleated draperies in a green-and-pink floral fabric and three chairs upholstered in a matching green-and-pink stripe. Two of the chairs were roomy and overstuffed, but one was smaller and had no arms, which Leda assumed was fashionable, but sitting in it made her feel unbalanced, and she made a point to avoid it. Dark green carpet gave the room a cool, se-questered atmosphere that reminded Leda of the ladies' lounge at her father's country club, where closing the white-slatted doors could make you believe that money can insulate you from the world. She sat down and waited, while Peggy picked up the phone and called her friend Ariel Masterson. This was not unexpected. There were two things you had to know if you worked for Peggy Boatwright; one, she liked to make people wait, and the other was, she used cocaine.

That was the rumor, the evidence being that she never ate, she almost always had black circles under her eyes, she was an emotional nutcase, and she hung around Ariel Masterson, but it was the Ariel Masterson charge that made Leda wonder if it might be true. Ariel had a great deal of inherited money, which she gave generously to civic or-ganizations around town (the art museum in particular, where there was a Masterson Sculpture Garden), but it was her parties that had made her famous. There were always people who knew people who had been there, and word was, there were lines of cocaine right next to the spinach in puffed pastry and crab-stuffed mushrooms.

Peggy finished her phone conversation with Ariel and looked at Leda. "I want you to take over the Rukeyser event," she said.

Leda tried not to show her surprise. "I thought that was Kevin's job."

Peggy shook her head. She had hair other women envied, per-fectly straight and shiny and black, blunt cut just above her shoul-ders, and in so many other ways, she was, unquestionably, a striking woman, alarmingly thin and dressed every single day in designer suits. She picked up a gold pen and slid it between fingers so bony they looked like claws. "Kevin's work has been slipping; haven't you noticed?"

"I'm sorry, no."

"He's lazy. Resting on past success, and that won't cut it, but it's what happens when you're not hungry anymore. I'm onto him, though. I'm quite confident I don't even need to say this, Leda, but this conversation is just between me and you."

Leda nodded.

"Good then." Peggy explained that she needed both a press release on the fund-raising dinner and a brochure, which would advertise the station's Friday night public affairs lineup, starting with *Tennessee Times,* a news program hosted by a local celebrity named Nate McPherson. *Tennessee Times* was followed by *Washington Week in Review,* then *Wall Street Week.* Leda's challenge was to highlight Rukeyser without slighting McPherson, whose ego was legendary and whose friendship with the station's executive director habitually complicated a great many things. "It's your classic dueling dick situation," Peggy explained. "But you can handle it."

When Peggy finished listing all that she wanted out of the brochure, Leda said, "It will be a tight fit."

"I can't see what we can leave out, though."

"I'm just saying it might be crowded. Not a lot of white space."

Peggy smiled. "People don't need white space, Leda. They need information. We're not in business to dumb down content for the sake of appearance. As for those too simple to understand the information, I would argue, it's our job to cure them. People rise to the level you expect of them. I say we don't expect enough."

Leda returned to her office. "She's doing it again," she told Kevin. "This time it's you she's calling lazy."

"Let me guess. She took the Rukeyser brochure away from me and gave it to you."

"Lord help me."

"You'll need something."

Leda spent the rest of the day working on the brochure, getting it to look as close as possible to the way Peggy had prescribed, but the next day, Peggy called her into her office and, when she finished her phone conversation with Ariel, placed her hands on top of her desk. "I suppose," she said, "you could go on writing press releases all your life, if that's what you want."

Leda had learned a trick from Kevin: When you don't know what Peggy is talking about, don't say anything.

"Is that what you want? Because you have the potential to go far in this organization, but not if you insist on producing trash," and at the word, *trash,* Peggy picked up the Rukeyser brochure and let it go, so that it floated down to the green-carpeted floor. "This was all you could come up with? And forgive me; what is that color? Yellow? Beige? There's no spark here, no crackle."

"No white space."

"Exactly."

Leda took a deep breath. "So what information, exactly, would you want me to take out?"

"I should not have to tell you everything."

That afternoon, Kevin found Leda at her desk with her head in her hands. He shut the door and sat down. "You can't win."

"I know."

"How're you going to reason with a brain on cocaine? Want help?"

"Like what do you propose we do?"

"I don't know. Let's go down to the art department and see if they can't give us a graphic."

"And she'll find something wrong with it."

"Actually, yes. She will."

But Kevin did manage to produce a design that was artistic but still included most of the information Peggy had asked for, and, not for the first time, Leda wondered if she lacked imagination when it came to this job. Kevin, not Leda, was the one who had come up with the Big Bird Pizza Parties, and the *Mystery!* ties and scarves, and the *Ken Burns Civil War* tours through area battle sites, and any number of clever ideas that slipped from his mouth like butter. Clearly he was the pro here, but Peggy never seemed to notice.

At the end of the day, Leda put Kevin's brochure and her press release on Peggy's desk. Peggy often left work early, so Leda was surprised to find her still there, sitting with the lights turned off, flipping through a report in a thick blue folder. Peggy took off her glasses and rubbed her eyes. "We should both go home," she said. The late-afternoon sun shone through the window and fell across part of the desk, but Peggy was behind it in shadow, and though it could have been an illusion caused by the darkening room, she looked tired, the shadows under her eyes more pronounced, her bony shoulders slightly sagging. Leda hesitated without knowing why.

"Sit down," Peggy said.

What happened next was so strange Leda later had a hard time believing it ever happened. Peggy began to talk about an incident she remembered from her childhood, a relatively unremarkable incident, Leda thought, involving Peggy and a few friends, who intentionally hid from a girl they had invited over to play. "That was cruel, wasn't it?" Peggy said. "You don't have to answer; I know it was, and I was old enough to know it then, but I could not stop myself. I wonder what that is, when people can know something is wrong and do it anyway?"

"What did she do? The girl, I mean."

"She cried like a baby, of course."

"Oh."

"Her name was Melanie."

"Do you know where she is now? I only ask because, you know, maybe, if you saw her again, you could apologize."

Peggy looked at Leda. "I don't feel *that* bad. I would tell you that, soon after, these same friends of mine pulled that number on me, you know the one, changing lunch tables when I sat down. And there was poor pitiful Melanie, right there in the thick of them this time. She was in; I was out. But you see, Leda, the difference between Melanie and me is, she went back to being friends after we were so mean to her. Not me. I never went back. I never spoke to those girls again. So it feels like we're even, Melanie and I, as if there might be some universal justice system at work. Do you believe such a thing is possible, Leda?"

"I'm a skeptic by nature, but anything's possible, I suppose."

Peggy smiled. "I've kept you long enough. Go. Shoo," and she waved her hands playfully, motioning Leda out the door.

The gesture was friendly, and Leda could not help it. She saw Peggy through kinder eyes. It was not so much that she related to Peggy's story, not exactly. She could not look back and say anyone had ever been deliberately mean to her, but more than once she had felt ignored. Invisible. Not forced out, but not asked in, either. Just as often, though, she had kept herself apart for reasons she did not completely understand. It freed her from people who might bug her about her mother's death, for one thing. It gave her room to think, for another. And thinking about the way the sunlight had shone from the window onto the desk, and behind it, Peggy in shadow, looking small and utterly alone, she wondered if there might be something to the idea of universal justice, or just dumb luck, that she had been given this opportunity to reconsider Peggy Boatwright. Maybe, she thought, Peggy would not act as crazy if someone were nice to her.

Leda had picked up her purse and was turning to leave when Peggy stuck her head through the door. "This is unacceptable," she said, holding up the press release. She tossed it on Leda's desk. "Please do it over."

Leda looked down at the red marks littering the page. "I'll get on it first thing tomorrow," she said.

"I'll need it before you leave today."

"But my children are at day care, and I'm already late."

"They'll have to wait."

Leda had not been expecting to see Brian's car in the driveway when she got home that evening, so she was distracted and did not notice Mrs. Grable until she came up from behind to report that her brother's wife's sister was in the hospital with pneumonia.

"You know what? I can't talk right now, Mrs. Grable."

"Her husband borrowed my brother's chain saw and never gave it back. That was her second husband. She's been married three times."

Leda sighed and wondered if she didn't smell whiskey on the old woman's breath. She stopped and turned around. "Is she very sick?"

"They say she might die."

"Then you better get that chain saw back quick."

Mrs. Grable did not smile, but that was okay. She never did. Leda walked toward the house, slowly, so that Mrs. Grable could keep up, until they reached the door. "I think I've got company," she said, pointing toward Brian's car. Then she opened the door and walked inside.

From the driveway she had heard the sound of someone playing the guitar, but it did not sound like Brian, who had a habit of stopping halfway through one song to start another, which tended to annoy Leda, but once inside she saw that it was Seth instead. He was sitting on the couch, leaning over the guitar, his long red hair falling in his face. It was Daniel's guitar. The familiar case with the blue felt lining was open on the floor, and there was Andy, sitting beside him. Daniel had picked him up and Hannah, too, whom Leda found reading in her room. From the kitchen came the voices of Daniel and Brian talking, and was that the smell of chili cooking? She closed her eyes and let herself smile. For all her worry, everything had turned out okay. She opened her eyes in time to see Andy dropping peanuts in the fishbowl.

"Andy, stop!"

He looked startled, jerked his hand away, then burst into tears. Seth quit playing the guitar and looked at her.

"He's going to kill his fish if he doesn't watch out," she said, then wondered why she was defending herself to a teenager.

Everybody said Seth looked like Brian just because his hair was red, although Seth's was a brighter shade, a true orange, and it was wispy fine like a child's, which gave him the appearance of being younger than he was. But Leda thought he looked more like Susan. It was not so much in his features, but the expressions that appeared then disappeared on his face. Or was it in his eyes that looked, not wounded like his father's, but angry, like his mother's. Today he was wearing half of a baseball uniform, the pants, but, instead of a jersey, he wore a black Metallica T-shirt, and instead of socks and cleats, he wore flip-flops. The pants hit him midcalf, which made his bare, skinny legs look frail. He put down the guitar and walked over to the fish bowl. "This your fish?" he asked Andy.

Andy stopped crying and nodded. "He's crazy."

"I can relate."

Andy stood next to Seth, the two of them peering over the bowl, waiting for Crazy Fish to turn a flip.

Leda went to the kitchen, where Daniel and Brian were talking, and Daniel was, indeed, cooking chili. Brian was sitting at the table, leaning backwards against the wall with only two legs of the chair touching the floor. She hated it when he did the chair like that. She dropped her purse on the table. "I swear I'm going to quit," she said.

"Better not," Brian said.

"I might."

"You can't afford it and still build this silly log cabin."

"Did Daniel tell you that?"

Brian looked at Daniel. "Of course, you could always ditch the log cabin."

"Since when do you believe everything Daniel says?" Leda said, then turned to Daniel. "Is it true?"

"Not exactly."

"Have a beer," Brian said.

She shook her head and sat down at the table to listen to the rest of the conversation Brian and Daniel had been having before she walked in. They had been talking about Brian's efforts to buy the vacant building next door to the Flying Dog so he could start his own radio station, WFLD, Flying Dog radio. He had bought the store on the other side several years earlier, doubling the size of the restaurant so it now included a bar, complete with a performance stage, where local bands played every night, and it was for these bands, plus the need for somebody to play music not heard on commercial radio, that he wanted to start the station. His plans included cutting out a soundproof window in the adjoining wall, so people in the bar could see through to the DJs working on the other side, and he planned to renovate the top floor of the building, turning it into an apartment, similar to the one he had made for himself above the restaurant. That, specifically, was the subject he and Daniel had been discussing when Leda walked into the kitchen. Brian wanted Daniel and Leda to buy it and move there instead of to the log cabin. His motives were partly selfish, he admitted, because he needed a buyer to help him afford the deal, but the point was, he could find a buyer, any old buyer. He wanted Daniel to have the first option. "I mean, think about it, man. We'd be next-door neighbors."

But Daniel, stirring the chili, kept shaking his head, and saying, "We're already in too deep."

"So what you're saying is, you'd rather live next door to your parents?"

"I never said that, but one thing's for sure; I'd rather live in the country than the city."

"You can visit the country."

"But if you live there, you can do what you want."

"What the hell is that supposed to mean?"

Daniel shrugged. "I don't know. Like you can let your dogs run wild. There's no such thing as leash laws in the country or anything else to tell you what to do."

"You don't have a dog, Daniel."

"You can shoot off fireworks if you want. You can shoot a gun."

"You don't have a gun either. Have you gone insane?"

"I'm speaking theoretically."

"Since when did you turn into Mr. Wild West?"

"It's not like that."

"Oh, really?" Brian dropped the chair down to all four legs. "Allow me to remind you of the Daniel I used to know, the one who believed it's not such a great idea to let people do whatever the hell they want. How many times have I heard you say, we either live in community, or it's dog-eat-dog? Haven't I heard you say that? Back me up here, Leda; he's been listening to that Fred character too long. Somebody else has jumped inside his brain."

Daniel was silent. But something Brian said must have reached him, because now he looked as if he had just been slapped. Then, suddenly, he grinned a big, wide, guilty grin. "You're right, man."

"Of course I'm right, you moron."

Leda was relieved that he backed down, but she was thinking more about her own reaction to Brian's offer. She hated it, although just a few months earlier, the idea of abandoning the cabin, and ditching Fred and Walter, might have sounded good. But Fred and Walter would be gone soon enough, and she realized now that the farm meant more to her than she could explain. Already she had imagined herself in the kitchen, looking out the windows at the mountains in the distance, walking slowly down the long driveway through the woods to get the mail, sitting on the front porch listening to the wind through the hay. She looked forward to nights when she and the kids could spread a blanket in the yard and look up at the stars. She had told herself stories that there would be more time when they lived in the country, that life would be slower, and that their children would escape some of the fast-paced, soul-sucking lifestyles of their peers. She believed they would find peace. She even hoped that it would be good for them, especially for Hannah and Andy, to see firsthand the way Arliss and Merle lived. It would give them a connection to the past and a way of looking at their lives that was deeper in some unspecified way, and she assumed that's what Daniel meant, too.

She made a salad, and, when the chili was ready, Daniel asked if Brian didn't want to stay for dinner, but Brain said he and Seth were heading out. "I promised I'd take him to look at amplifiers. I mean, throw me the hell in the briar patch, you know?"

Daniel said, "I thought Seth had a baseball game tonight."

Brian looked embarrassed. "He's not playing," he said.

"He's sick?" Daniel said.

Brian shook his head. "I mean he's not ever playing."

"He quit?"

"I can't make him play, Daniel, Jesus." Brian lowered his voice. "He can't even throw the ball from third to first."

"You want me to work with him?" Daniel said.

"He says he's done with baseball, and shit, Daniel, I don't blame him. I know how it feels."

"Don't give me that, man. You loved baseball."

"But I was no good."

"You were, too, good."

Brian turned to Leda, and said, "My dad had this idea I could catch, because that's what he did in high school, see; he was a catcher, but I was too little to be a catcher."

"Not too little," Daniel said. "Too chicken."

"This guy" —and he pointed to Daniel—"nearly broke my hand with his fastball."

"He used to stuff a washrag in his glove," Daniel said.

"The only reason I stayed on the team was so me and Daniel could play ball together."

"No, so you could score weed in the parking lot."

"Besides that. Then there was the small problem that my dad would have killed me if I had tried to quit."

"That's true," Daniel said. "He would have killed you."

"So there I was, lousy and miserable, and my dad wouldn't let me quit, while Daniel here was a goddamn superstar, and his dad couldn't have cared less. I think he would have paid money for you to quit."

Daniel shook his head. "He was too cheap."

Brian turned back to Leda. "Did you know that Arliss never watched him play a single game?"

"Never?" Leda asked.

"Never," Daniel said.

"But he loves baseball. He watches it every night on TV."

"Now he does, but not then."

They stopped talking again and listened to Seth. He was improvising his own version of "All Along the Watchtower" and, after a few minutes, Brian sighed. "He's better than me."

"He's not better than you," Daniel said.

"Not yet, but he's going to be."

"Nobody's better than you."

"Seth is."

Brian stood up and got another beer. On the counter next to the refrigerator was a stack of books. Brian picked up the one on top. "Now here's a memory," he said, flipping through the pages. It was a Jim Harrison book, *Legends of the Fall.*

"I'm taking it to Fred," Daniel said. "You would not believe what that man has not read. I'm catching him up a little."

"You can't give Harrison to a man like Fred."

"He's all right," Daniel said.

"Yeah? And you're crazy."

SIXTEEN

ARLISS

Arliss saw Angel walk over to the fence and stand there waiting for him even before his truck reached the bottom of the driveway. She was across the street in Lloyd Pitt's field, because that's where she had wandered off to give birth a week earlier, having escaped through a gate that had been left closed but not locked. He guessed she had walked down the driveway to the road (where there was no telling how long she stayed) before she found her way to Lloyd Pitt's backyard and delivered the calf. Now both mother and baby were going to have to stay over there until the calf got bigger, and Angel did not look happy. When she was not waiting for Arliss to bring her a bucket of corn, she was watching the herd on the hill across the road. She seemed to know her brief bid for freedom could cost her place in the herd, and it would be a dear price; Arliss knew, because Angel was relatively high up in the herd hierarchy, and there was a chance her position would be taken when she returned. Arliss did not think she would be gone long enough for this to happen, but Angel did not know that. Cows could be hard to predict, though, and if her status were knocked down to the bottom, she would be last to get water and shade, and she would have to walk farther and work harder for her food. She might be shoved and bullied by the other cows, some of whom she had shoved and bullied herself only a week before. Her calf bucked and pranced beside her, unaware of what might be in store for her and her mother.

Arliss knew there were people who would tell him he was crazy for attaching feelings to a cow, but he never cared what people thought. He figured if somebody wants to be ignorant, it was not his problem.

The Pitts' main driveway was long and straight and lined with cherry trees, which made an impressive entrance in the spring, but there was a short driveway on the far end of the pasture where Angel was waiting. Arliss drove there and parked the truck and took the corn and dumped it into the tub he had attached to the fence for this purpose. He rubbed Angel's head while she ate and told her to quit worrying.

The unlocked gate through which she had escaped was the one between the old graveyard and the barn. Arliss could not prove who left it open, but he could guess. Next to Luke's grave he had found a waxed paper cup and a wadded-up sack from Burger King. Cigarette butts were scattered everywhere. Arliss had been tending the graveyard ever since his mother died and left him the job. While she had placed fieldstones at the head of each grave, he had gone further, sticking a wooden cross next to each stone. He had made the crosses himself and painted them white, and Merle had written the names in gold. At the head of Rosemary's grave, he had planted purple crocuses, and he maintained a border of day lilies around the inside of the wall. Each spring, a fresh crop of Queen Anne's lace and buttercups would come up as well, but he always mowed them down, because he did not tolerate weeds in the graveyard. At least once a week he trimmed the grass, swept the fieldstones, and wiped the dust off the crosses with a rag. To his way of thinking, you take your lead from what you see; if something's clean, you don't dirty it. People shouldn't need signs or rule books; just the sense to look with the eyes God gave them. He had zero tolerance for those who could see what's right and did wrong anyway.

He had picked up the trash and carried it over to where they were building the house. Daniel was not there, but he wasn't looking for Daniel. He held out the trash to the tall one and did not say a word. After a minute, the shorter one came over and grunted something that had a long way to go before it would sound anything like an apology. He took the trash from Arliss's hands and shoved it through the window of his truck. The tall one never moved and never spoke but had on his face an expression that was familiar to Arliss but one he had not seen in a long time. Not since he was a boy, and it came to him; his cousin Eli, Luke's boy, had looked like that. Times when, say, a gun would go off, and here would come Eli up from the woods, and somebody would ask, *Did you shoot that gun? Nope,* he would say, and look just like that. Arliss felt his heart speed up. He had not thought about his cousin Eli in a long time, and the memory surprised him. He did not know what had ever happened to Eli, or even if he were still alive. His uncle Roy had died of lung cancer; he did know that. Roy had been forced off his farm in Anderson County when the government moved in there and built the Oak Ridge National Laboratory, and that's the last he ever fooled with farming. He moved to town and got work as a janitor for a school until he got sick. Arliss's sister Virginia still came for a visit exactly once a year, but never more, because she and Merle did not get along. It seemed peculiar to him that he had not thought about Eli for such a long time, and now what he remembered were not specific incidents so much as images and impressions. What was it that could make a person appear contemptuous and amused at the same time? Arliss knew this much; it was the look of a man who doesn't care what happens to him, and you have to watch a man like that.

Daniel had driven up then, and Arliss told him to make sure his friends cleaned up their trash from now on. He said it in a voice meant to be heard, because he wasn't talking to Daniel. But Daniel had blushed and stammered an apology, then mumbled some nonsense about Fred and Walter not knowing better, and for the second time in a day, Arliss was brought back to the past. Specifically it was a time he had watched his uncle Luke swear for the umpteenth time that Eli never meant to set that cat's tail on fire. Arliss was not in the habit of analyzing the characteristics of other people the way Merle and her friend Lydia Carr prattled about how much like Aunt Ina that person was, or how this other person was the spitting image of Cousin Herb, and so on and so on. If you listened to those two, there were no new people in the world, only recycled ones. Arliss had always believed Daniel took after his own father, because they were both careless and not sorry about it, but maybe, he thought for the first time, Daniel was closer in spirit to his uncle Luke. He remembered the time Bob had told Daniel, if he spun the wheel of a bicycle fast enough, it would make a Popsicle. Daniel could not have been more than five and did not even have a bike, but he turned Bob's upside down and commenced to spinning it, until Merle came up and asked him what he was doing. She laughed so hard when he told her that Bob abandoned his pretence and broke down laughing, too, but Arliss did not see one thing funny about it. He told Daniel to quit wasting time. But Daniel set his jaw and would not quit. He stayed out there through dinner, and when it got dark, he was still at it. The next morning, Daniel swore he had made more Popsicles than he could eat, but they could not find the bike anywhere. Daniel said he did not know where it went. When Bob found it later in the woods and dared Daniel to make another Popsicle, Daniel just crossed his arms. "I can't," he said. "It's broken." Daniel always thought he knew so much, but he did not fool Arliss. It was in his eyes. Just exactly like Luke, Daniel was willing to believe almost anything.

Arliss let himself in the pasture with Angel and checked her over and checked over the calf, too. Newborn calves are flighty and cannot be trusted to follow their mothers, but in past years, he might have judged it safe enough to cross the road with a calf. Arliss could see those days were gone, with Bearpen Lane so busy now that they had widened Glen Pike to four lanes all the way to the horse farm. There wasn't anything out Bearpen Lane, but people were using it as a cut-through road to avoid the congestion on Glen Pike. It bothered him to see this kind of inefficiency. The way it looked to him, they had widened Glen Pike to accommodate the businesses that were already there, but now they were building more. So what would they do for them, add more lanes? He stood next to Angel and counted the cars that passed in the next five minutes. Eight.

While he was standing there, a truck driven by the tall one sped down Daniel's driveway, spitting out dust and gravel as it came too fast down the hill. It barely slowed at the bottom before launching onto Bearpen Lane and screeching away. Anyone coming would have had to brake fast, because the tall one had no intention of stopping.

Arliss drove back across the street, but instead of turning in his own driveway, he headed up Daniel's and found Daniel at the top, sitting on the floor of his new house. Arliss got out of his truck and took off his hat. He stopped himself from saying the first thing that came to his mind. *You got nothing better to do than sit?* Instead he took Daniel's offer to have a look around. They walked through the rooms. It weren't no log cabin, was what Arliss thought as soon as he got a chance to poke around. It might be a house with logs stuck on it, but that was a far cry from what he remembered. There were too many rooms, and the walls were going to be covered in drywall, and whoever heard of building a log cabin without a fireplace? Arliss could not see a sign of one anywhere. He did not fault Daniel. He never understood why on earth the boy had wanted to build a log cabin when he could just as easily build a house, but now he understood. Daniel was not building a real log cabin. He was just pretending, and in this case, that was better. If he was going to fault Daniel for anything, it would be that the house was simply not well built. Arliss saw evidence of shabby work and shortcuts everywhere he looked, but he knew, if he said something, Daniel would just argue with him.

Before he got back in the truck to leave, he looked at Daniel, and said, "That tall fellow you got working for you? You ought to watch him."

But Daniel shook his head. "He's harmless, Dad."

"I don't much like him."

"You don't like anybody."

The unexpected memories of New Hope that had beset Arliss that day stayed with him. He drove up to Ted Minton's Feed and Seed later in the afternoon, and when he passed the sign to Norris Dam on the way home, he slowed down. He had never been there. When he was younger, he had listened to his mother telling him that bad things were part of God's plan, but if anybody mentioned the dam, there was no question that *it,* without any help from God, was the cause of all her sorrow. Arliss was aware of the contradiction, but he had long ago, without thinking too hard about it, decided his mother was the expert on God, and if there were contradictions, they were due to failures of his own intellect. Visiting the dam while his mother was alive had never been possible. It would have been a betrayal. But the memories of the people he had known in New Hope had stirred up feelings he was not used to, and this time when he saw the sign it occurred to him that his mother had not been alive for a very long time. He turned the truck around.

Once off the highway, he found himself driving through a forest. A road to the right led to the town of Norris, where his uncle Roy had worked for a while, but Arliss kept straight, and soon he could see the river through the trees on the left. The water was dark, and over it hovered a ragged fog. Soon the woods gave way to a meadow, and there! A blue-and-white sign by the side of the road. Big letters: TVA. He was staring at the sign so, possibly, missed the first instant he could have seen the dam itself, but then he looked, and there it was.

He was prepared to be stunned but was not. It was smaller than he had imagined, and dirty, streaked with something black like tar. It fit neatly, even naturally, between the two rocky hills on either side of the river. A web of power lines stood on a platform to the right, and at the base of the dam was a building studded with so many windows it looked like the way a child might draw a picture of a house, with windows stuck in every available space. Arliss saw that the building would be considered large anywhere else, on a street corner or beside a highway, but next to the dam it seemed small. He decided maybe the dam was bigger than it looked.

He parked the truck and got out. The river looked dangerous, a metallic gray, a deathly color, not of water but of something mixed with water, like poison. Otherwise, it was peaceful there beside the dam, and surprisingly quiet. A low electrical noise hummed in the background, but the chirping of a cricket in the grass was louder and more insistent. As Arliss walked toward the building, he felt like a trespasser, sure that somebody would ask him to leave, and here were two men just coming out of the building. But they merely waved and walked past him. Closer to the dam, he could see that the black streaks were not tar but some combination of grime and algae.

He went inside. A sign on a glass door at the end of the lobby read AUTHORIZED PERSONNEL ONLY, but there were public restrooms in one corner, a bronze bust of Senator Norris on a pedestal, and annotated photographs of the dam under construction lining the walls, all clearly intended for visitors like Arliss. He studied the pictures. They revealed the chaos of any construction site, no magic here, no evil intent, just bulldozers and dump trucks and wheelbarrows and lumber and rocks and mud and dozens of people, tiny against the magnitude of the mess they were in. On one wall was a bronze plaque embossed with a column of figures.

> HEIGHT: 265 FEET
> LENGTH: 1,860 FEET
> CONCRETE: 1,002,253 CUBIC YARDS
> STORAGE: 830 BILLION GALLONS
> RESERVOIR AREA: 40,160 ACRES
> POWER: 250,000KE GENERATING UNITS
> LENGTH OF LAKE: CLINCH RIVER, 72 MILES
>   POWELL RIVER, 56 MILES

It was a memorial. Arliss recognized it at once. All of a sudden he felt dizzy and had to sit down on a bench in the center of the room.

He understood, of course, that the people who designed the plaque and fastened it to the wall did not mean to memorialize the dead or the lost; no, this was a recounting meant to impress. It did not matter. He wondered how many others had found their way here, to this dark little room, this hidden-away museum in the guts of a dam, to stare at these numbers, the way you might go down to Chickamauga to read the numbers of the dead and wounded on plaques at the base of statues. Forty thousand acres submerged. Casualties: Luke Greene, Rosemary Greene, Joseph Greene.

Arliss felt the urge to grab somebody up and shout the names but, at the same time, remembered how long ago he had tried to tell Merle about the sunrise over Spinner Ridge, the road through the woods to Luke's house, the pools in Stickpin Branch where he had gone swimming, but Merle had interrupted him. "Shitfire and a cat's ass, Arliss, I'd trade you a million swimming holes for one thermostat." So he had never mentioned it again.

He realized he had not seen what he had come to see. He hurried out the door and across the parking lot, where he saw the road to the top of the dam and the lake. What surprised him when he drove up there was that the road crossed over the dam. The dam was also a bridge! It was hard not to admire the efficiency. He pulled over to the side of the road, got out of the truck, and walked to the edge, where again he found himself startled. What had he been thinking all these years? That having seen the ocean, this lake, this body of water that happened to cover everything he remembered of his childhood, might be as big? It was not even close. His own sons could swim across it. If he threw a rock, he had a good chance of hitting the other side. Arliss walked back and forth across the dam, from the lake side to the river side, trying to comprehend the thing, but he could not. He got back in his truck and drove across the dam to the top of a hill on the other side, where there was a viewing platform.

Now he could see it, the scope, the implications, the mechanics of what was going on: a preposterously huge volume of water was being held back by one, simple wall. No doubt, there was violence here, if only in potential.

But when he blocked the dam out of his sight, the lake by itself looked benign. It meandered in two directions, split down the middle by a finger of land. On all sides, the lake was surrounded, right down to the water's edge, by dense forests that looked familiar to Arliss. He had walked through forests like that. He knew those trees. No matter how much he wished it so, the lake did not look shoved down where it did not belong. No, it looked as if it could have been here forever, catching sunlight, lapping against the shore, beaconing waterfowl on their way southward and then back home again. He whispered the names to remember that they ever existed: Andersonville, Loyston, Oak Grove, Wolf Hollow, Indian Creek, Forks of the River, and, yes, New Hope.

SEVENTEEN

DANIEL

Daniel was surprised by how happy it made him that Walter was not coming with them. He slid into the front seat of Fred's truck and closed the door. "Let's get on out of here," he said, saying *git* instead of *get,* and giving two syllables to the word *on,* hoping to make Fred grin, and he did. He was holding a list of the things they needed at Home Depot, including gutter pipe and nails, and he tossed it on the dashboard in front of him and reached back to grab his seat belt, then remembered it was gone. Fred had cut it out, because, he said, he did not believe in seat belts. Heading down the driveway, Fred's head was surrounded by gravel dust pouring through his open window and by smoke from the cigarette hanging from his lips, but it did not seemed to affect his breathing. Daniel had decided Fred had lungs of steel. They passed Arliss, his head in a cloud of dirt, on the bush hog, clearing any trace of brush that dared spring up along the fence line next to the woods, keeping up his reputation for having the cleanest farm on Bearpen Lane. Daniel glanced through the rearview mirror in time to see that Walter had stopped working and was standing in the door of the cabin, watching them drive away.

Daniel liked Walter okay, but sometimes he reminded him of a little Buddha, with his chubby face and impenetrable eyes, or one of Yeats's ancient-eyed Chinamen made of lapis lazuli. Walter watched everything but said nothing. Sometimes he looked wary, as if he might be afraid of Fred, or if not exactly Fred, of what Fred might do next, giving Daniel the feeling that he knew something Daniel did not. Other times, his face took the shape of a silent judge, which made Daniel equally nervous. But there were just as many times when Daniel looked at Walter's blank face and decided it was just blank. That Walter was what he was, a simple man who was not thinking much of anything. In any case, Daniel found it more difficult to talk to Fred when Walter was around, especially when the conversation turned to subjects of any depth, such as literature, because there would be Walter on the outskirts, looking left out.

Fred reached down and picked a tape off the floor, gave it a quick glance to make sure it was Lynyrd Skynyrd; yes it was, but before he could slip it in, Daniel put his hand over the tape player. "What the fuck?"

"I've got something I want you to hear," Daniel said, and he pulled a tape Brian had made for him out of his pocket and stuck it into the tape player instead.

"What's wrong with this?" Fred asked, holding up his Lynyrd Skynyrd.

"Nothing. You just listen to it all the time."

"That's because I like it."

"I thought you might want to hear something new for a change."

"I like Lynyrd Skynyrd."

"I know that, but I think you'll like this, too."

Honestly, Daniel thought, he could be so much like a kid. He had lent him a whole stack of books, which he had selected carefully—really, he had put a great deal of thought into this—Steinbeck, Hemingway, Vonnegut, Salinger, Harrison, but the only one he would read was Harrison. At least he read it. Leda would not concede that Fred was intelligent, but Daniel believed she misread him in every way. What did she think, that he was some kind of Sut Lovingood character? That was where stereotyping could go awry; you could look at a man like Fred and make all kinds of assumptions, when the truth was, given half a chance, he could turn out to be the smartest guy in the room. That was the problem, though, wasn't it? Nobody ever gave him a chance.

"Brian gave this one to me," Daniel said, pushing PLAY.

"What is it?"

"Just listen!" But Brian had written the singer's name in huge black letters across the front of the tape, Robert Earl Keen.

"Sounds like a tomcat screaming," Fred said. He tossed his cigarette butt out the window and lit another.

"Well, I think it's good to keep up with what's happening, even if you don't like it. It's exactly what I was talking about the other day, remember? When I told you that being educated does not mean just books? It means staying curious about the world around you."

Fred did not answer.

There was then in the car several minutes of silence (Daniel would have called it excruciating) while they listened to the first song. Daniel wished he had played the second one first because it was livelier, or better yet, the fifth one, which was about chewing tobacco and might have made Fred sit up and listen. Daniel could have kicked himself for not thinking of that.

The Home Depot was on the other side of town, about a half hour drive by interstate. The way they were headed, north on Bearpen Lane away from Raccoon Road, was the long way to the interstate in actual miles, but the shortest route; taking Raccoon Road to Glen Pike took longer because of all the traffic on Glen Pike. They passed the Tyler farm, the Wilson farm, the Kelly farm, and the Powell farm before reaching Bucket Road, which would take them over the creek, past Carr's Big Orange, and, eventually, to the interstate. According to Daniel's mother, who kept an ear out for rumor, there was talk of getting a Home Depot on Glen Pike someday soon, which would eliminate the need to travel all the way across town. Either that, she said, or a Lowe's. After two Robert Earl Keen songs and Fred still frowning, Daniel spoke again. "I guess it takes some getting used to."

Fred did not answer. He ejected the tape, handed it to Daniel, then put his Lynyrd Skynyrd in. "This," he said, "is what I like."

"Good for you," Daniel said.

"Damn straight."

"I have to hand it to you, man; you know your own mind. You probably don't even know how rare that is, do you?"

"Nope."

"My students are proof of that. I swear, every year it gets worse. They don't want to have to think, much less do any work. They'd be happy if I'd hand them a sheet of paper that tells them what they're supposed to think so they can memorize it, as if English were like fucking math, with right and wrong answers. It kills them when I insist they come up with answers of their own; you know what I mean? Kills them. You should hear the whining; talk about cats screaming. Shit." He glanced sideways to see if Fred were paying attention. He could not tell. "Or I'll tell you what's worse is the silence. You ought to come see it for yourself; it's classic. Picture this, I'm standing in front of the class after having asked a perfectly reasonable question, and I'm waiting for an answer, waiting, waiting, waiting, for somebody, anybody, to speak up. Because I'll do that to them, see; I don't mind just standing up there, letting them squirm, but I swear, most of them aren't even embarrassed to show their ignorance. They don't know their own minds; that's the real problem. It's occurred to me, and stop me if I'm wrong, but I'm just wondering, if the simpler you make your life, the clearer you can think. That's one of the reasons Leda and I decided to build out here in the country, see. Simplify things. I mean, take a person like yourself, willing to live a simple, no-bullshit kind of life, and what have you got? I say you've got your priorities straight; am I right?"

"Whatever you say, professor."

"Let me just ask you this. Do you believe in God?"

"No shit."

"That's what I thought."

Suddenly Fred jerked the wheel and turned into the parking lot of Carr's Big Orange. "I'm out of cigarettes," he said.

"You don't want to stop here."

"Yes, I do."

"My mother works here, man."

"I know."

Daniel stayed in the car. He watched Fred cross the parking lot, then, because he was so tall, stoop to get through the door of the old building. Daniel did not know how old it was. Older than sin. Too old even to think about wanting to buy *food* in there. He looked down at the tape still in his hands. It was amazing how different it had sounded when he listened to it with Brian, but the thing with Brian was, he was crazy about all kinds of music, and it was hard not to be crazy right along with him. Listening to music with Brian was like doing a close reading of a difficult poem; *Did you hear that,* he would say, jabbing you in the shoulder, rewinding the tape, making you pay attention until you heard things in the music you might not have picked up on by yourself. It was going to pay off for him; Daniel knew it, because there were tons of people who had the technical know-how and business sense to start a radio station, but only Brian could make it a *great* radio station. He particularly liked finding musicians no one else had heard of and spreading the word, such as Robert Earl Keen, who was nowhere to be found on the radio dial. Stealing unapologetically from *Star Trek,* Brian's slogan was **WFLD! Playing boldly what no one else will play**, which he had already put on bumper stickers and key chains. Daniel could not remember if he had told Fred about WFLD, but if not, he certainly would. Today. He made a mental note to say something as soon as Fred got back in the truck.

He had been wanting to take Fred down to the Flying Dog anyway, but Fred always had some reason he could not go. He imagined introducing him to Tom Fields, for instance. He imagined sitting at the bar with Fred and Brian and Tom Fields, the four of them talking about Jim Harrison. The bar Fred and Walter talked about going to all the time was called *Eats,* although they joked about the fact that the "s" had been torn off the sign, so it now read only EAT. Daniel was curious to see what it was like, but he did not know how to get there. Somewhere in Sevier County was all Fred had told him.

Fred was taking a long time to get cigarettes.

But Daniel told himself to relax. He did not have anywhere else he needed to be. Hannah and Andy were spending the day with Susan, while Leda worked in a public television booth at a festival downtown. She was in charge of the booth, which had meant coordinating volunteers to walk around in the Big Bird and Elmo suits, designing and ordering enough buttons and bumper stickers and program guides to hand out, producing a promotional video to display on a monitor set up especially for the booth, and what all else, Daniel could not imagine. It amazed him sometimes how much stress Leda was willing to put up with for a job she did not like, and recently it had gotten worse, with rumors spreading every day about impending layoffs. Leda was worried about her office mate, Kevin, although rumors had also named Peggy Boatwright as a possible victim, which had given Leda hope that things would get better. Daniel did not know what she meant by better. Peggy or no Peggy, he had always wished she would get a different job, something more interesting, more worthy of her abilities. You did not need more than half a brain to write a press release about *Sesame Street*.

But listen! He knew how easy it was to tell yourself a story to keep from having to change, and, for an example, he needed only to go back a couple of days, when he and his students (talking about *Who's Afraid of Virginia Woolf?*) had concluded that, sometimes, it's easier to delude yourself. I mean, what the fuck, he thought; some days it beats reality, and Daniel suddenly felt bad about what he had told Fred about his students, because it was not true. The truth was, every year he had more than a few who were easy to teach, fantastic, passionate about their literature, and willing to suck up everything he had to tell them. He let himself imagine how cool it was going to be to invite them out there for dinner when the cabin was finished. He would serve something they weren't used to getting on campus, like a seafood pasta with fresh vegetables and grated cheese and good bread and an unlimited supply of expensive wine. And they would take their wine out to the front porch, where they could listen to the sounds of the country and breathe in the fresh air and watch the stars, and they would sink into their chairs and thank him for rescuing them from the chaos of campus life. The drudgery of the dorm. Every year then, new students would look forward to the day they got their invitation. The Dr. Dan break; he would be known for it. He couldn't wait.

Daniel looked at his watch. He did not remember what time Fred had walked into Carr's Big Orange, but it seemed like a long time ago. He let five more minutes pass before he got out of the truck, slammed the door, and went in himself.

He had heard his mother's laughter before he got inside, and there she was. And there Fred was, standing at the checkout counter, talking to her. He was drinking a Coke and eating from a bag of Cheetos that lay opened between them. "Come get you something to eat," she said when she saw him.

"No thanks."

But she had already turned her attention back to Fred. "You don't want blue," she said. "Lydia, where's them orange bandannas at?"

Lydia emerged a few minutes later from a back room carrying a box, which she placed on the counter and opened. Merle took out an orange bandanna and handed it to Fred. He tied it around his head.

"You never told me how cute your friend was," Lydia said to Daniel.

"Shitfire and a cat's ass; I'm like to take him to the cornfield and kiss him between the ears," Merle said.

"Not if I get there first," said Lydia.

Fred grinned.

If Daniel had been thinking straight (which he did, several days later, when it did not count), he would have come up with something clever to say. He would have had the whole room cracking up. But he was not thinking straight. "We have to get going now," he said to Fred. "Walter's waiting for us."

EIGHTEEN

LEDA

Fred pulled the cigarette from his mouth and let it drop to the ground two stories below. He was sitting sideways in the open window of the half-constructed log cabin, his back resting against the edge, a boot wedged up against the opposite side. His other leg dangled out the window, and Leda could not help but see how little it would take to push him out. She did not know he was going to be there, or she would not have gone upstairs.

She had hoped to find Daniel, and his car was there, parked in the gravel in front of the house, but there was no sign of him. There were no trucks in the driveway, which she had assumed meant that Fred and Walter had not shown up again. Fred and Walter had been not showing up a lot lately, or sometimes Walter came but not Fred, and several weeks would pass without any progress on the house. If it made Daniel mad, he came up with excuses for them anyway. After all, he would say, defending them to Leda, they had real jobs at the outdoor equipment store, and once he had even told her, "We can't forget, they're doing us a favor." The one time he questioned Fred about it, suggesting that he might at least call when he was not planning to work, Fred had told him to lighten up.

Fred had not used the words *lighten up.* "He instructed me to get the burr out of my butt," Daniel told Leda. "I'm just wondering. Do you think it's possible I take things too seriously?"

There was no way Leda could respond to this question on short notice.

"I mean, really."

Leda thought carefully. "I don't think," she had said, "it's a good idea to listen to Fred."

Although she was surprised to see Fred in the window, he was not surprised to see her. She knew that much instantly. He would have seen her drive up and get out of the car and call Daniel's name. He would have heard her footsteps on the wooden floor below. He would have known when she started up the stairs. "Where's Daniel?"

"They went to Burger King."

"No. My husband does not eat Burger King."

Fred shrugged. "That's where they went."

He was wearing a pair of red shorts over green camouflage army fatigues and no shirt. His stomach was flat and hard. The blue bandanna he usually wore on his head was orange and was tied around his wrist, and his hair hung loose and tangled to his shoulders. He was looking right at her. She blushed and hated him for it. She whispered, "I want you to leave my husband alone."

He smiled, then leaned his head back against the window frame and laughed.

"I don't see what's funny."

"The professor can take care of himself."

Leda did not think so. She started back down the stairs, then stopped. "Tell me something. What is it you like so much about Jim Harrison?"

He rolled his head sideways as if to get a different view of her. "I like the way, when a man needs to kill another man, he just does it." He slipped a cigarette between his lips. Leda heard a truck coming up the gravel drive, then she heard the sound of the radio coming from the open window of the truck, but Fred lit the cigarette, blew smoke out of his nose, and continued. "There's this one guy. Walks into a barn, rams the head of the man he's after right through a pitchfork. You ever read that one?"

Leda shook her head.

"Well." He swung his legs around so that both feet rested on the floor in front of him. "That's what I like."

There would be times in Leda's life when she would look back and wish she had stayed there and stared him down, but, instead, she ran down the stairs and across the wooden floor to the driveway, where Daniel and Walter were getting out of the truck. Daniel was carrying a large sample book of roof shingles, which he laid on the truck bed, then Walter came behind him with another one. Leda noticed there were no paper sacks or drink cups from Burger King in the cab of the truck, and she asked Daniel about it.

"I don't go to Burger King," he said.

"I know that, but that's where Fred told me you went."

"Well, he was wrong." Daniel shaded his eyes and looked up at Fred, who was still sitting in the window. "There's a boycott on against Burger King. You should know that."

"I don't think he cares," Leda said.

"Did you hear that, Fred? She doesn't think you care."

Fred had turned and was dangling both legs out the window. He kicked his boots against the side of the house, one after the other, but the sound died on the thick logs.

"Maybe we should take a look at those roofing samples," Leda said.

Walter opened one of the books. The shingles were organized in shades of gray, from a near-white fog color all the way to black, and shades of brown, from tan to muddy red to dark chocolate. Daniel did not look. All spring he had been insisting on hand-cut wooden shingles, even though Fred had been telling him he did not know how to make them and would not have time even if he knew, which was why he was pushing for the asphalt. So while Leda turned the pages, Daniel turned to Walter and tried to explain why he ought to boycott Burger King, although Leda noticed that Daniel skipped over the fact that the official boycott had ended years earlier, when Burger King canceled its contracts with rainforest beef producers. Leda decided not to correct him. She knew that, for Daniel, the fight was never over. Even now, with a Democrat in the White House, he was not happy (a position he held by himself among their friends, for whom it was enough to be content) because he believed the powerful were all the same. He clung to the clichéd distrust of anyone over thirty, even if that included himself. (*"I mean it; don't even trust me,"* Leda had heard him tell Hannah.) Walter just wanted to talk about the price of stone.

"I got a cousin who can get his hands on stone cheaper than what we saw this morning," Walter said.

"Fine, but next time you bite down on a Whopper, I want you to picture a million acres of rainforest destroyed in Nicaragua."

He was about to add that he meant all fast-food hamburgers, when Fred, who had come down from the window and was standing in the driveway, interrupted, "All them people in South America can kiss my ass." Nobody even knew he was there.

Daniel stopped talking to Walter and turned to look at Fred. "What did you say?"

Fred spoke louder. "I *said,* all them people . . ."

"Nicaragua is in *Central* America not South America."

Fred shrugged.

"It's a big difference, Central America, South America. I can't believe you don't know that, man."

"But I don't care," Fred said.

"You should," Daniel said.

"I like this gray," Leda said, pointing to a sample in the roofing book.

Daniel glanced at the sample, then shook his head. "It would destroy the whole thing."

"Destroy?" Fred walked across the driveway. "Jesus Christ, did you hear that, Walter? What do you think he means by that?"

Walter drew half circles in the gravel with the toe of a boot, then smoothed them over.

"It's going to look tacky," Daniel said. "I told you that already."

"Asphalt shingles don't have to be tacky, Daniel," Leda whispered, but Fred cut her off.

"What if tacky was all you could afford?"

"Custom shingles will sure cost you a bundle, because we'll have to hire them out," Walter said.

"But maybe the professor can afford it," Fred said.

"Don't call me that."

"What?"

"You know what."

"How about tin?" Leda asked.

Nobody said anything for a minute. Then Walter nodded. "Tin's good. Noisy in a rain, though."

"Goddamn blow you out of your house," Fred said.

"But my grandmother lives in a house with a tin roof," Walter said. "She seems to do all right."

Daniel nodded. "Tin might work if we could get it in green."

"Or red," Leda said.

"Green."

"I'll call some people," Walter said.

Fred started to say something, but Walter cut him off. "It's their house," he said.

Three nights later, Leda woke up in the middle of the night and found Daniel sitting at the kitchen table grading papers. A small lamp shone a single beam onto the table, but the rest of the room was left in darkness. Most nights, Leda slept through the hours Daniel was up at night like this, but she always found evidence in the morning, books piled on the table that had not been there the night before, wads of yellow legal pad paper in the trash, cereal bowls in the sink with small puddles of souring milk and forgotten flakes encrusted on the side. It was like a secret life. "You ought to get some sleep," she said.

"Is the light bothering you?"

"No."

A package of cigarettes lay on the table, and Leda picked it up. "What's this?"

Daniel put his pen down. "Don't worry. I'm not hooked."

"What do you mean 'hooked'? When did you start?"

"I didn't *start*, Leda. You make it sound so sinister. I've smoked a couple of cigarettes; that's not the same as *starting*. Jesus." He took the package from her and set it back down on the table and picked up the pen and went back to grading papers.

Leda pulled out a chair and sat down. "Fine," she said. She watched him while he worked. There were times when she wondered if Daniel possessed more energy than the average person, and every so often she looked through his desk, his briefcase, his dresser, or she might check the medicine cabinet or under the sweaters in his closet, for signs that he might be taking something, but she never found anything.

Daniel looked up from his work. "What's the definition of *spherule*?" he asked.

"Spell it."

He did.

"I don't know."

"Me neither."

"Could have something to do with a sphere."

"Then why didn't she just say sphere?" He left the room and came back with a dictionary. When he found the word, he shook his head. "I don't think she knows either."

"Plagiarism?"

He nodded. "It won't be hard to catch, because she's only got three sources in her bibliography."

"Who's to say she put all her sources in her bibliography?"

"She's not that bright."

"Who is she?"

"You don't know her."

Leda watched as Daniel wrote an unnecessarily large *F* across the top of the paper. "Don't you want to talk to her first? Give her a chance?"

"Oh, I'm going to talk to her all right."

"I mean . . ." She did not finish the sentence. "You ought not to use red ink. It's too brutal."

He slid the paper under the stack. "What would you say if I went camping this weekend?" he asked.

She looked at him.

"Fred wants me to go with him."

Leda picked up the package of cigarettes, rattling the cellophane between her fingers. She brought it up next to her face and breathed in the sweet sharp smell of tobacco, remembering when Daniel had told her how the smell of tobacco on his father's farm was so sweet it used to suffocate him. "Is this because of Fred, too?"

Daniel took the cigarettes out of Leda's hand and tucked them into his shirt pocket. "Walter can't go, so Fred asked me."

"I really don't like him, Daniel."

Daniel sighed. "He's okay."

"He's sneaky."

"He's not smart enough to be sneaky."

"That's not what you've been telling me."

He took another paper from the stack and began reading it. "I was wrong," he said. In the dark, under the beam of a single light, Daniel reminded her of the way he used to look so many years ago, when they had studied together in his dark and dilapidated cabin, he under one lamp, she under another, and everywhere else was darkness. This could even be one of those same lamps, thin, green, bendable metal. Yes, she believed it was the same one. She remembered peeking at Daniel from behind her books, amazed that he was over there on his bed reading, and she was sitting at his desk, and that he was not going to stop and say, *Jig's up, dream's over, time to get real.* There was a time when all it took to make her happy was to sit in a dark room with him.

"I don't want you smoking in the house," she said.

"Oh, really? I thought I might go stand over Andy's bed and blow smoke in his face."

"I mean it, Daniel."

"I swear, Leda, I don't know what's happened to your sense of humor."

NINETEEN

LEDA

Fi-yerd. Fyrd. Fired! Leda said it so many times it ceased sounding like a real word. Faard. Fired. It was a word unmoored. Without meaning. Preposterous. Driving home, she kept thinking she had missed something, some crucial bit of information that would make the whole thing make sense. She kept thinking that it might be possible to go back and make things turn out differently. She could not even remember all of what had just happened to her; why, for instance, had she sat down in the armless chair? She never sat in the armless chair! And Peggy behind her desk, sitting up straight, with the emotional warmth of a fence post, dispatching the bad news as if it were simply one more thing to do today. She could not remember the words Peggy had used to call her into her office. Not to be fired; she knew that much. She never would have walked in that room if she had thought she was going to be fired. What exactly had Peggy said?

This is not working out.

That was it, exactly, but what did it mean?

Then there was the awful moment when Peggy stopped talking, and Leda knew it was her turn to say something. What could she say?

Oh, but now she had them, perfect, pithy comments that could have laid Peggy out (and right there in the car, Leda began storing them up like gold), but at the time, from the armless chair, she could not have sounded weaker if she had tried. "Wait. Are you saying I'm fired?"

She did not understand. Really. Not at all. There was zippo understanding on her part, and still she had to pick up the kids and pretend everything was okay and go home and dodge Mrs. Grable and think of something to cook for dinner. Of all the times for Daniel to run off with Fred!

She would not cook. There, she thought, that was easy enough. They would order a pizza, or even better, they would go to Burger King.

The phone rang a couple of hours after midnight. Because she was half-asleep, Leda's first thought was that Daniel would get it. It rang twice more before she remembered he was camping. With Fred somewhere; she did not even know where. She fumbled for the receiver.

Daniel. It was Daniel, calling from the hospital with a broken arm. Leda sat up in bed. "How?"

"I'll tell you when you get here."

"I can't leave the kids."

"Can't you bring them?" His voice sounded scared.

"Do you know what time it is?" But he had already hung up.

She carried Andy in his pajamas to the car and buckled him in, then turned to go back for Hannah, but Hannah had already changed out of her nightgown into a pair of shorts and a shirt and was standing in the doorway. "What's wrong with Daddy?" she asked, as if it were Leda's fault.

"Let's go get him and find out."

But Hannah was not that easily put off.

"Please, Hannah, can't we just go."

Hannah did not budge. She crossed her arms and studied her mother, waiting just long enough for it to look as if it were her idea to get in the car.

Leda drove down streets emptied of traffic, familiar streets turned unfamiliar in the night. She listened to the exaggerated swish of the tires on the silent road and, for the second time that day, had the feeling that she was missing something. She felt out of sync with the darkened houses she passed, as if she were no longer in the same world as the people who slept inside, but in an entirely different world. Strange things could happen here. If the road had suddenly tilted upward, leading straight into the endless black sky, she would not have been surprised.

Leda expected to find Daniel with a cast on his arm waiting for her in the lobby, but he was not there. A woman behind the desk did not know where he was but pointed Leda to a hallway. He was not there either, but at the end of it was a small waiting room, where she found him sitting in a chair, leaning his head against the wall as if he had been trying to sleep. His arm was in a cast, but what he had not mentioned over the phone was that one side of his face was swollen and turning colors, purple and red with a shadow of greenish yellow, and that his lip was cut, and that there was a Band-Aid on his forehead and dried blood in his hair. Hannah gasped. Andy started crying. Daniel stood up. "Let's get out of here."

"What . . ." Leda started to ask.

"I'll tell you later."

That's all he would say.

Andy stared at his daddy all the way home, but Hannah would not look at him and stared out the window instead. Daniel went straight to bed, but Andy insisted on breakfast, and Hannah demanded an explanation, so Leda fed them both bowls of cereal and told them their daddy fell off a cliff, but he would be okay. By the time she got them back to bed, it was almost dawn. She slid in beside Daniel, thinking he would be asleep, but she could tell by his breathing, he was not. "Did you fall?" she whispered.

"People usually fall when they're pushed."

"What do you mean, pushed?"

"I'm trying to get some sleep here, Leda."

"You got in a fight?"

He did not answer but threw the covers off and went to the kitchen. Leda followed. She watched him pour whiskey over ice, then sit down at the table. A streetlight lit a corner of the otherwise dark room, and it occurred to her that people in passing cars would think theirs was a house of people sleeping, but they would be wrong. She sat down. "Was it Fred?"

"It was stupid."

"Was it the cabin? Did you fight over the cabin?"

He shook his head.

She waited for him to say more, but he drank the whiskey and breathed as if it hurt him to breathe. "How did you get to the hospital?"

"I hiked out, hitched a ride to a pay phone, and called an ambulance."

"You *hitched* a ride?"

"That's what I said. Jesus, Leda, you aren't deaf."

"I suppose Fred's still there?"

"I don't care where the hell he is."

Then the phone rang again.

Daniel laid his head on the table and covered it with his arms, so Leda had to answer it. "It's your dad. It sounds like we better get over there."

She smelled it before she saw it, the acrid smell of sodden smoke. A lime-green-colored county fire truck passed her when she turned onto Bearpen Lane. The driver waved. She had sent Daniel, with his glass of whiskey and his multicolored face, on ahead to keep from having to wake the children and drag them, sleep-starved, to one more catastrophic scene. They were still sleeping when Susan came over and told Leda to go on.

The cabin was still smoldering. Arliss was standing beside it in ash-covered boots. Daniel was sitting on the ground. There was hardly anything left besides fragments of charred wood standing in the morning mist like soldiers after a battle, dazed and uncomprehending that they are the ones alive. Everything was soaking wet.

"There weren't no way to save it," Arliss said.

It was the sound of a truck spitting gravel as it wobbled up the hill that woke him, he said. By the time he got outside, the man was pouring gasoline. "I could smell it clear across the field." By the time the first match was struck, Arliss was shouting and running toward the flames. "I reckon I chased him away."

"What man? Was it Fred?" Leda asked.

Arliss looked at Daniel. "Whoever done this is your business, not mine."

"Damn straight," Daniel said.

"And God's," Arliss whispered, adding, "Don't never misjudge the power of fire."

"Spare me the sermon, Dad. I'm going to get plenty of that from Mother."

Daniel waited until Arliss left. Then he picked up a piece of scrap wood and hurled it as hard as he could down the hill. He kicked a half-burned two-by-four until it crumpled, then another and another, grunting as if he were the one taking the blows. She walked up to the top of the ridge and sat down in the grass and watched him, but she was not thinking about what he was doing or whether he ought to be doing it. Really, she did not care. She was thinking about the fact that, all the while she had been busy living her life, *other things were going on.* It felt as if someone had pulled back a curtain to show her that what was true in the world was not necessarily the same as how she experienced her life. Unsettling was what it was. Terrifying. It was like being made to walk on ground that was moving, and it occurred to her that the older she got, the less she knew, which was backwards from the way she always thought it would be. When Daniel quit throwing pieces of two-by-fours into the woods, he walked up the ridge to sit down next to her.

"Whoever idea this was to build a log cabin, it was stupid," he said.

"It was both of us."

"Then we're both stupid."

"No, we're not."

"Goddamn fucking bastard."

"I lost my job yesterday," she said. She could not say fired. It was, possibly, going to be the one word in the English language that, absolutely, she could not bring to her lips.

"What do you mean lost?"

She shook her head.

"You were *fired?*"

She tried to hold on to the tears, but they came anyway. Daniel put his arm around her shoulders. In the silence they understood, one thing, then another, that in a single day they had lost half their income, and every penny of their savings had just burned up.

TWENTY

LEDA

Crazy Fish did not survive the move to Belle's House. Leda noticed he was not moving and asked Andy when was the last time he had seen him turn a flip, but he could not remember. She scrubbed his bowl, washed the blue rocks, cleaned the pirate ship and the conch shell, and refilled the bowl with clean water, but when she put Crazy Fish back in, he sank to the bottom without even trying to swim.

People began to notice, for instance, the man who came to hook up the dishwasher. He was a young man who chewed gum with his mouth open and frequently flicked it from one side of his mouth to the other with his tongue. It was not a trick anybody would choose to see. She felt as if she were in his way and alternated between hovering in the kitchen and making up something to do in another part of the house. She was in the kitchen when he finished and, putting his tools away, pointed to the fishbowl, and said, "I think your fish is dead."

"He's not dead."

The young man shrugged and flicked his gum and began stuffing his tools back into a satchel. Leda studied Crazy Fish, who was clearly breathing, even if he was not moving. "But he might be sick," she said. "You think it could be the water?"

"I wouldn't know about that."

"Because he was fine before we moved out here."

"I don't know a thing about fish."

"We're on a well out here. Could be he doesn't like well water, or else he's just getting old. How long do goldfish live?"

"Look, lady, I'm telling you, I don't know anything about fish. All I said was he looks dead."

"Well. He's not dead."

They had moved into Belle's House after the fire. It was free; they were broke and, on top of everything, they had no insurance on the cabin. Leda's father did not understand that. He also did not understand why no one was saying the word *arson*. He would call, and Leda would try to explain, then he would hang up until the next time he called with a new reason they ought to prosecute, as if that was what they were lacking, a good reason. Daniel refused to press charges, but he had his own reason. *I never want to see that man again.*

Leda never found out what happened in the mountains, why Daniel and Fred had fought or how. She was left to imagine the scene, although she could not imagine it, because Daniel was not someone who fought with his body. With words, yes; with words there was hardly anyone his equal, but he was not one to push or hit or kick or punch or shove or grab other people, and no matter how Leda tweaked the image in her mind to make it fit, it did not fit. It remained forever a gap between them, but she had come to the conclusion that gaps were not the worst thing and left him alone.

They never talked about the fire. It was embarrassing the same way having your yard rolled with toilet paper is embarrassing, as if somehow you are the dupe, the sucker, the one singled out to play the fool. There was something so unseemly about the act, the pouring of the gasoline like subrogated pissing, degrading, menacing, if only by its smell. There would have been time for Fred to stop there, a moment to consider whether it would be enough to leave the cabin gasoline-soaked and reeking, the point made (whatever the point might have been), yet no real harm done. But it had not been enough. There followed the striking of the match, and real harm was done.

———

Crazy Fish could not feed himself. Before he got sick, he would lunge at the fish food flakes as soon as they broke the water's surface and eat them before they got to the bottom of the bowl, but no more. The best he could do was wiggle in a furious attempt to move forward, but he went nowhere. It was horrible, like watching someone try to swim away with his feet held fast.

"Something is seriously wrong with your fish," Seth said one day, when he and Brian were over, helping Daniel knock out the wall between the living room and the kitchen.

"Maybe you should take him to the vet," Brian said.

"You can't take a fish to the vet," Daniel said.

The two men were sitting on the floor of the kitchen admiring the hole they had knocked in the wall. They were planning to replace the wall with a built-in cabinet and countertop that would divide the two rooms but still make it possible to see through from one to the other. It was one of the many projects (which included painting all the walls, throwing away the curtains, changing all the bathroom fixtures, and screening in the back porch) that Daniel had come up with to change Belle's House until it was unrecognizable to anyone who had known it before. He said it was the only way he could stand living there.

Seth was standing beside the kitchen sink, watching the fish. His hair was short now but starting to grow back from the day Brian had cut it in a desperate and misguided attempt at discipline, after he and Susan discovered that he had been skipping school. Susan had been begging Brian to help her with Seth for a long time, because she was having trouble getting him to do anything she asked. She wanted him to do his homework, for instance, but he did not want to do his homework. She wanted him to go to bed at night, but he said he did not need to. She wanted him to clean his room and help with the laundry, but he did not want to do that either. The only thing he cared about was his music, and if she tried to punish him by taking that away, by locking up his guitar or his amp or his CD player, for instance, he just ran away to Brian's, who might let him stay for a day but always brought him back. Then the school called, and Susan went down there and talked to two of his teachers and the guidance counselor and the principal, and when she got home, she called Brian. We have to *do something*, she told him.

So he marched Seth down to the barbershop.

Susan did not refer to what Brian did as desperate or misguided. "That is the stupidest thing I've ever heard of in my whole life," were the actual words she used before adding, "I don't care about his *hair*. I want you to make him stop smoking pot!"

Then something happened to Brian. He said, "Okay."

Then *he* stopped smoking pot. He threw out all his drugs, except for alcohol, which he said did not count.

At first Susan did not know whether to believe him, but Daniel swore it was true, and Leda told Susan she felt pretty sure Daniel was right about this. Then she sat with Susan in her kitchen while Susan made the second-hardest decision of her life (the hardest being leaving Brian in the first place). Seth moved in with Brian, which seemed to be having some effect. He had, at least, quit skipping school. But Leda watched him whenever he came over with Brian, not because Susan had asked her to, but because she wanted to be able to tell Susan whatever she could, although she did not know exactly what she was looking for. Shaky hands? Bloodshot eyes? A funny smell to his clothes? She did not see any of that. If anything, Seth looked calmer when he was with Brian, but she felt disloyal to her friend for even thinking it.

Andy scooted a chair to the sink and climbed up next to Seth to have a look at Crazy Fish. He stuck his finger in the water and wiggled it to see if that might scare the fish into swimming. He turned to Leda. "He's not going to die, is he, Mom?"

"Of course he's going to die," called Hannah from the living room, where she was reading a book in a chair by the window.

Andy and Seth stood there side by side watching Crazy Fish for a long time. Finally, Seth whispered, "She doesn't know everything."

The only way Leda could get Crazy Fish to eat was to feed him by hand, so that's what she did. All that summer she fed him and discovered that, no matter how dead he looked, when she held a fish flake directly in front of his mouth, he gobbled it like a starving creature. She was aware of the fact that she was probably prolonging his suffering, that it might be kinder to let him die, but she could not shake the feeling that he trusted her. She knew it was stupid; goldfish don't feel trust, but she did not care what might or might not be true. Once Crazy Fish accepted food from her hand, it was the same as a promise: *I will not let you starve to death.*

She tried to get Andy interested in helping her. Not Hannah, who had made it clear she did not understand the concept of keeping a small yellow fish in a bowl. It was enough for Leda to see how well Hannah took to living in Belle's House. Sometimes she caught her walking from room to room, talking to herself, as if she were a character in one of the novels she read. Belle's House was bigger than the rental house Hannah had lived in since she was born (and a great deal bigger than the log cabin, a fact Leda was careful not to mention to Daniel). It had a secret closet under the staircase and an attic you could get to through a tiny door in Andy's room. The front porch had a view of the mountains; the back porch had a view of a graveyard, which, if you were Hannah, must have seemed more exotic than anything she could have dreamed up by herself.

Andy was just as excited to live where there were four dogs living right next door and an entire herd of cattle practically in his backyard. He was so excited that Leda and Daniel had to sit him down and tell him about the time his great-grandfather got trampled by the cows, and the other time when one of Arliss's dogs got caught and chewed up in the corn grinder. They made rules about where he could go by himself and when he had to be with a grown-up, and Andy was young enough, and enough prone to fear, that he did not argue. Arliss brought over a half dozen hay bales to stack in the backyard, so Andy could build forts and climb up on them and jump off. (Daniel never got over the fact that his father let go of so much hay.) Feeding a sick fish could not compete with all that. Whenever he tried, Andy got impatient and did not want to hold his hand still long enough for the fish to eat anyway, so, more often, Leda just asked if he wanted to watch her do it. Sometimes he would stop what he was doing and climb on a stool and peer into the bowl, but not always. She suspected Andy was getting tired of watching Crazy Fish die.

Even Susan was unsympathetic. "You know," she said to Leda one day, "it's just a fish."

"I know."

"It's not even a dog."

"I know, Susan."

But on a scale of who was patient, and who was not, Daniel was not. Every time he saw Leda feeding the fish, he told her he was going to flush it down the toilet. He spent the summer cutting out want ads from the newspaper and bringing home HELP WANTED signs from the bulletin boards at school and placing them on the kitchen table, so she would see them when she ate her cereal in the mornings. Daniel insisted he was not unsympathetic to her misfortune. He did not dispute the fact that she had gotten a crummy deal, that she had been misused, kicked around, screwed over, treated like shit, treated like a dog, hosed, and hung out to dry, but the way he looked at it, welcome to the world. She could not just *stay home*.

One morning in midsummer, Leda found a silverfish in the kitchen sink. Silverfish are hard to kill; she knew from experience. If she tried running water over them to push them down the drain, they would climb back out of the drain again and again, as if they could hold their breath under water. She wondered if they were aquatic animals, thus impossible to drown. Leda decided she was going to have to look this up, or else ask Susan, who knew more than the average person about insects. Then she saw that the one in the sink was already dead, its legs splayed out like fringe, the back legs spotted in an intricate design. Leda did not share Susan's fondness for insects, and her first impulse when she saw the silverfish was to jerk her hand away, but since it wasn't going to bite or crawl on her, she allowed herself to see that it was beautiful. The thought came to her to wonder about the mind of

God, who cares enough about the back legs of a silverfish to make them lovely. She recognized this as the sort of thing Susan would say and believed, of all the ways there were to think about God, she could almost live with this one. Susan had no trouble believing in God. For her, the world worked in a certain logical way, and God was simply a part of that way. Leda did not agree with her, but she understood the reasoning and decided not to wash the silverfish down the drain, but to leave it on the sink for a while, just to look at it.

There were a great many silverfish in Belle's House and even more camelback crickets, which looked to Leda like hulking brown spiders if she came around a corner and spotted one, suddenly, on the floor at the end of the hall, for instance, or on the other side of a room. Leda was getting used to them. She was even starting to like having them around. It made sense to live with some disorder, now that so much in her life was out of her control, and when she said so out loud one day, Susan pointed to a flower bed choking with weeds and introduced her to the idea of entropy. If you leave something alone, she said, if you don't touch it, if you apply zero energy to it, it will move in the direction of maximum disorder. "Scientists know it as the second law of thermodynamics and use it to measure disorder," she explained, "and some have called it time's arrow, because, theoretically, the potential for greater disorder is always in the future, but I like to think of it as the tendency for things to fall apart." Glass breaks but cannot unbreak. Tea left on the counter will grow colder but never hotter. Time moves forward not backward. People get older, never younger, and (unless they do something about it) they are, and always will be, alone. Wood rots, houses burn, money disappears, confidence is shaken, then shattered, to the point where the fact that you were elected Most Likely to Succeed by your high school classmates means nothing in the face of so much failure.

Leda managed to show up for three job interviews that summer. One rejected her on the spot. The other two did not call back, and she had to call them and find out from some secretary that, yes, they were sorry but they had hired somebody else. She woke up every morning wanting to go back to sleep. She wanted to sleep like Rip

Van Winkle, like a baby, like a dead person. She followed Andy and Hannah through their days and dreamed of naps.

Susan said that some people use entropy to describe one theory about the motion of the universe. They maintain that, like the cup of tea, the universe will grow steadily colder as it expands outward, until there is no more heat. Susan called it heat death. Daniel, she knew, would think of T. S. Eliot and call it a whimper. There was another theory. This one describes a universe more like a giant rubber band that will slow down in its expansion until it stops, reverses itself, then speeds inward again toward a single point where, who knows? It might explode again.

One night Crazy Fish did not eat. Leda held the food flake closer to its mouth. Nothing. "He's not eating," she said to Daniel, who was lying on the sofa, reading a magazine. He sighed and put his finger on the page to hold his place and looked at the fish.

"That's because he's dead."

"How do you know?"

"He's not breathing."

She nudged him gently, but Crazy Fish only floated away from her finger, as inert as a twig in the current of a stream. "Supposed to be a funeral," she whispered, and Daniel looked at her. There was no mistaking it; she could see he was jolted by the memory of the old Graham Parsons song where these lyrics had come from. It was a song they had both loved a long time ago. She returned his look. Really, she was as surprised as he was that a memory had so much power, that five words could throw them both back to a time when they were young, before, she thought sadly, they had exchanged one unkind word.

"It's been a sad, sad day," he whispered back.

She held her breath.

"You want to know something stupid?" he continued. "I used to tease Bob. We'd be out there doing some chore for Dad, and I would tell him that Mother was going to get to him someday. She was going to wear him down until he ended up crawling home to Belle's House, and you know what he would say to me? He would say, if he ever did, shoot him."

"Maybe it will work out, Daniel. You don't know."

"Maybe."

Leda sighed. "I was voted Most Likely to Succeed by my high school class, and now look."

He picked his book back up. "I wouldn't have thought of you as a person who went in for that high school crap."

For a coffin, Leda opened a box of Animal Crackers, and while Hannah and Andy sat at the kitchen table stuffing the cookies in their mouths, they talked about what to do. Following her father's lead, Hannah suggested they flush him down the toilet, but Andy yelled, "No," and threw a cookie at her. It was drizzling when they went outside. Andy held the box while Leda dug the hole in a corner of the graveyard, and when she was finished, she suggested they all say what they remembered about Crazy Fish. Daniel spoke up first. "He was crazy," he said.

"Besides that."

"He turned flips," said Andy.

"He swam upside down," said Hannah. "And he's the first animal to die in Belle's House."

Daniel opened his mouth to say something, but Leda knew what it was (that this was a house that had seen death before), and interrupted him. "He was pretty," she said.

"He liked toys," said Andy.

"He did not," said Hannah. "Fish are not capable of liking or disliking anything."

"He did, too."

Leda sighed. "Andy can say whatever he wants, Hannah."

"I just think it's important to tell the truth."

"It doesn't matter." Leda was surprised to feel tears building behind her eyes, but she held them back. "He was a survivor," she said.

Andy placed the box in the hole, and no one said anything while Leda covered it with dirt. There was only the sound of the shovel and of the rain, and when it was over, Hannah and Daniel ran back inside. Leda and Andy walked slower.

"I can get you another fish."

"I don't want another fish."

A shaft of sunlight shaped like a windowpane shone on the kitchen counter in Belle's House. Leda had not noticed it before. There was a particular slant and color to it, which Leda wanted to call blue-tinted, although it was not blue. But just as skim milk is bluer than whole milk, its quality seemed thinner than the rich yellow light of summer, and there were other signs that autumn was near. The leaves on the trees, for instance, might still be green, but they were growing brittle and dull, and the orb spiders had appeared, spinning and respinning their webs each night, and Hannah and Andy were back in school. She could take all the naps she wanted, and nobody would know. The windowpane pattern of light on the kitchen counter had the sharp edges of a solid object that would not shift or even disappear in a few hours, which, of course, it would. Leda decided to take a picture of it.

She was wearing her gray suit and white blouse, because she was supposed to be going to still another interview, this one for a job in the development office of the art museum. She was running late but knew that if she waited, the pattern of light on the counter would be gone. She had been taking photographs of objects around the house for several weeks. Walking by Andy's room, for instance, she would catch a glimpse of his little plastic chair sitting by itself in a pool of light and feel the need to get it on film. Shadows on the stairwell. Empty flowerpots on the porch. A shirt hanging on the bedpost against an unadorned wall. She had seventeen rolls of undeveloped film sitting in a row on her dresser. She went upstairs to get the camera.

When she returned, she looked out the window over the sink and saw Arliss walking toward her on the dirt road from the barn. She took the picture of the light on the counter, shifted her position, and took another. Arliss left the road and was coming her way. Leda put down the camera and met him on the porch.

He took off his hat and held it in his hands. "Can you help me for a minute?"

FALLOW GROUND

TWENTY-ONE

LEDA

Leda sat on the front porch watching the hay. Sometimes it billowed and swayed like a sea in a storm, but tonight it lay still under a full moon, rustling fitfully from an occasional breeze. By June the hay would be gone, cut down the way it was every June, only to grow back, to assert itself again as something that appears permanent.

In the dark, the new subdivision going up across the street looked no more dreadful than a scattering of oddly shaped shadows, but Leda knew that daylight would expose the red, muddy scars of earth never meant to be laid open, and the thin boards of cheap houses piling up like litter. She remembered when she could look across the valley and see nothing but farmland and huge tracts of forest all the way to the Smoky Mountains. Now she could see Walmart. And every week it seemed as if there were new roads, new subdivisions, and new shopping centers in bright, jarring colors. Lloyd Pitt's farm across the street was only the second one sold on Bearpen Lane, but the farm next door was for sale, and Leda knew there would be others. Someday, Arliss's farm was going to be an island in an asphalt sea.

A light was on at Arliss and Merle's house down the hill, which meant Arliss was up watching the Braves. Leda reasoned it was a West Coast game for him to be up so late. It did not matter how many innings a game might run, he would stay up until the end, then tell her who won in the morning. The joke was that Merle, not

Arliss, had wanted cable, that Arliss had even argued against it, until he found out that a man named Ted Turner had fixed it so he could watch every game Atlanta played. America's team. Merle had only wanted to watch the Christian Cable Network.

Leda would not be surprised if Arliss knew she was out there on the porch. It was some trick of his to know everything that was happening on the farm. She remembered eight years earlier when she first started working with him, he would nod toward the dog food bowls beside the barn and say, *That old coon's been back,* and Leda would study those bowls, sitting exactly where they had been the day before, dented in the exact same way they were every day, and she would say, *How do you know?* Or they would stand by the fence looking over thirty head of cattle, and Arliss would point to the one who was sick. *How do you know?* It was like that so much back then that Arliss had taken to pausing after every new thing he said to look at her, the slightest sparkle in his eyes, the beginnings of a grin, and she would not disappoint him. *And just how do you know that,* she would ask. Then they would chuckle. He never actually answered the question though. The answer was something Leda had to learn over time. Arliss knew what he knew, because the farm was like a living person to him, someone you love. The smallest change in the look on a face, the cadence in a voice, and you know something's wrong. It was one of the many things Daniel refused to appreciate about his father. So what if you could run a farm? To Daniel, that was like being proud of pulling your pants on right, because what good was it? It wasn't Shakespeare. The scope of a farmer's world extended no farther than the seventy-odd acres of land that defined his life. Daniel could not see how it was one bit ironic that he had closed himself off in the ten-foot-by-twelve-foot world of the back screen porch to write a book, but Leda did. As far as she could see, it was like father, like son when it came to stubbornness.

Three days earlier, Daniel had come home from work in the middle of the day, which was especially odd for spring, because spring was when he taught poetry, and after class, he and a small group of students always walked down to the Flying Dog to sit around talking about William Butler Yeats over pizza. Leda was in the barnlot, or she might not have seen his car pull in the driveway. She figured he must be sick. She pushed her hair away from her face with the back of her wrist, stuffed her gloves in her back pocket, and washed off in the spigot. Arliss had nailed a board to the side of the barn for shoes. She pulled off her muddy boots, slipped on an old pair of loafers, then walked to the house to see what was wrong.

She found him on the back porch moving furniture. Already he had cleared out a space by shoving the glider, two lawn chairs, and a wrought-iron end table to one corner so they were stacked like rejects in the back room of a furniture store. She caught up with him as he was moving a small desk from the living room through the kitchen. "What are you doing?"

"Moving this desk."

"I can see that."

"You want to help?"

"No, I want to know what you're doing. Are you sick?"

The desk was not big, but it was heavy, and as he walked backwards with it, scooting it toward him by inches, Daniel explained that, no, he was not sick. He had come home because he had decided to write a book. She assumed that meant he was reviving his Sut Lovingood dissertation, but he said no. He wasn't going to write anybody else's story but his own; in fact, he already had a title. *Caramel Dreams,* he said.

"Stop," Leda said. "You're scratching the floor."

"I am not," he said.

She knelt and ran her hand across the floor until she found the scratch. The old pine floor was covered with hundreds of dents and scratches, but they were worn down, while this one was still jagged. Leda tried to rub it smooth with her finger. "Why not chocolate?" she said.

"Chocolate what?"

"Chocolate dreams. The name of your book. I've never heard of anybody dreaming about caramel."

"That's why. Anyway, caramel better symbolizes my theme."

"Which is?"

"That dreams can be sticky."

He heaved the desk over the doorjamb, banged it down the step between the kitchen and the porch, then pushed it to the cleared area and positioned it so that when he sat down, he would be looking toward the barn. She could hear Arliss's tractor in the barn, but the sound did not seem to mean anything to Daniel, who treated farm-related sounds like background noise, like the whirring of an air conditioner, like wind, like anything easy to ignore.

"Were you . . . (She almost said *fired* but, even now, after all these years, she could not bring herself to use that word) . . . let go?"

"I cannot believe you asked me that."

"Well?"

"No way."

"You quit, then?"

"No, Leda, I did not quit." He hopped up on the desk and sat kicking his legs back and forth. "I'm taking some time off, that's all."

"In the middle of a semester?"

"I talked to Tom this morning, and he said, no problem. *Go for it,* were his exact words, and I'm quoting him, so don't try to tell me I didn't hear him right. I heard him just fine. He said he wishes he were me. Too few people ever actually do what they want with their lives, he said."

"I didn't know you wanted to write a book."

"Is that my fault?"

"You never told me."

"Well, now you know." He jumped off the desk. "Excuse me," he said, walking past Leda back into the house.

She stared at the desk. It had been her grandmother's, not a valuable piece of furniture, but Leda remembered it because of the glass dish of cinnamon candy her grandmother had kept on it. As a little girl, Leda had loved sneaking into the living room to snatch a piece of candy, because, while it was not explicitly forbidden (How could it be, when her grandmother kept filling it back up?), it felt that way, because her grandmother never actually offered the candy. Her grandmother had died five years earlier, never understanding why Leda had chosen to work on a cattle farm, although she was careful never to say so. If Leda tried to explain, she would grace her with a patient smile, then suggest, gently, that they go shopping, treating her as if she had been indoctrinated by a cult and required skillful reintroduction into civilization. Toward the end of her life, she began to tell Leda the same stories over and over, such as the one about the opening performance of Verdi's *Otello,* after which the audience had followed the composer back to his house and kept him up all night with their cheering, the suggestion being that civilization has been declining ever since. Leda missed her grandmother, but it was not with sentimentality that she regarded the desk on the porch. She looked at it the way you would look at a cow in the living room. It did not belong. It belonged in the living room next to the front door, because that's where Leda put the mail, specifically in Crazy Fish's old bowl, which she kept on top of that desk for that purpose. She went inside and found the fishbowl sitting on the floor in a rectangle of dust.

Daniel came downstairs carrying a heavy, black typewriter, the one she remembered him using in college. When she suggested he work inside on the computer, he said, "There's no soul in a computer."

Which was her cue that she might be in for more trouble than she had thought. She followed him back to the porch and sat down on the stoop. "So," she said. "This is like a sabbatical?"

He blew the dust off the typewriter keys. "Sure."

"What I mean is, you're getting paid to write this book, right?"

"I know what you mean."

"Well?"

"Not exactly."

"Then what? Exactly."

He looked at her. She crossed her arms and waited.

"Hold on a sec," he said, and bounded past her into the house, returning with a chair, which he placed in front of the desk. He slid into it and sat with his hands hovering above the typewriter.

Leda waited, but when, still, he said nothing, she stood up. "I suppose I can find another place to put the mail," she said, letting the screen door bang shut behind her when she left.

She walked across the backyard, past the swing set nobody played on anymore, past the crepe myrtles planted in a row, past her small vegetable garden, up the railroad tie steps that climbed the slope to the graveyard and the dirt road that led back to the barn. Arliss was still on the tractor, mucking out the barn with the scraper blade. Leda hoped he had not seen Daniel's car, but as soon as she got to the barn, he cut the engine. He waited until it sputtered out before he asked. "Is he sick?"

"In the head," she said.

She slipped out of the loafers and pulled her boots back on. Arliss said nothing more, but she knew he wouldn't. She shrugged then, and said, "It's probably nothing. Some sort of cold."

The next morning, Leda woke up to a broken ice maker. Andy discovered it when he tried to put ice in his orange juice. "There's no ice," he said.

Leda was making his lunch. He was eleven now, old enough to make it himself, but she did not necessarily want him to. Next year, was what she told herself. There would be plenty of time next year for making lunches and whatever else boys needed to do to grow up. Andy did not like mayonnaise or mustard, and he did not like regular bread, so she spread a bagel with cream cheese and one thin slice of ham. Then she took his water bottle over to the refrigerator and pushed the ice lever. "The ice maker's broken," she said.

"He just told you that," Hannah said.

She was fifteen and overrun with sarcasm, which tended to elicit responses from Leda along the lines of, "What did you say?"

"He just got through telling you . . ."

"Don't get smart with me."

"All I said was . . ."

Leda stopped listening. There was no end to this argument; Susan kept telling her that, and Leda closed her eyes, wishing she had kept her mouth shut. She pressed the lever again and heard a motor whine from somewhere inside the freezer door. "What's wrong with it?" Leda asked.

"How should I know?" Andy said. "Can I have money for a Coke?"

"No."

"Why not."

"Just take plain water. You don't need ice."

"All my friends drink Cokes, Mom."

"You are not all your friends."

She saw the look he and Hannah exchanged with each other and wished, for a second time that morning, for a muzzle on her mouth. "Don't tell your dad," she said, shoving change into his hand.

"Where is Dad?" Hannah asked. Hannah was sitting at the table, drinking a cup of hot tea and ignoring the cinnamon toast in front of her. She had recently started skipping lunch as well; at least she refused to pack one or even take lunch money, claiming she could not give up precious study time for lunch, and, besides, she hated people watching her eat. Leda suspected she was sneaking candy bars out of the machines and secretly hoped it was true. As for dinners, they had all made the concession to Hannah to become vegetarians, at least for part of the time. She did not know how to answer Hannah's question, even though she knew her hesitation would signal to her quick and perceptive daughter that something was, indeed, awry. Most mornings Daniel was the first one up, and the kids would find him dressed, sitting at the table, drinking coffee, and reading the newspaper, but instead of some normal greeting such as, *Good morning,* Daniel would throw them a question along the lines of: *Why are so many people in Africa dying of AIDS?*

I don't know, Dad.

Hannah and Andy never knew. Regardless of what the question was, they were too sleepy to know anything that early in the morning, but no matter how many times Leda encouraged Daniel to wait at least until they had eaten, he always forgot. But this morning, he came into the kitchen in his underwear, barefooted and sleep-rumpled, scratching his head and looking around the room as if surprised to find so many people there.

"The ice maker's broken," Andy said.

Daniel blinked. "What do we need an ice maker for?"

"For ice," Hannah said.

Daniel sat down. "There are children all over the world who are lucky if they get clean water. They're grateful for even one meal a day, and you are worried about ice?"

"That's enough, Daniel," Leda said.

"Aren't you going to work?" Andy asked.

Leda answered for him. "Dad's working at home today. Now hurry, or you'll be late for school."

Andy's school was at the end of Bearpen Lane on Raccoon Road. It was the same school Daniel had gone to (and Arliss before him), although it had undergone extensive renovation and had doubled in size to accommodate the children coming out of all the new subdivisions. This side of town was growing so rapidly, it was hard for anything to keep up, but it seemed to Leda that there was a haphazard quality to the development, as if nobody were in charge, or whoever was, was crazy. The new subdivisions were all self-contained communities built independently on individual farm property, which made them dead ends. To get from one to another, people had to drive out to roads like Raccoon Road first, an exercise similar to pouring buckets of balls into small tubes. It ended up putting too much traffic on a lot of narrow curvy roads originally built for tractors. Because there were no sidewalks, or even decent shoulders, it was dangerous to walk, so Leda drove Andy to school every morning on her way to taking Hannah to the high school. Hannah rode slumped down in the backseat, sulking, because taking Andy meant she was late to school. (She wasn't. Leda always got her there at least fifteen minutes early, but Hannah never let facts get in the way of an opportunity to criticize her mother.)

Later that morning, Leda found Arliss in the far corner of the northeast pasture fixing a fence. She could see the section he had already strung, and it looked too loose. It was not terrible; the cows would not break through or anything like that, but Leda knew it was not a job he would be proud of.

"Sorry I'm late," she said. "I had to call somebody to check the ice maker."

"What's wrong with it?"

Leda winced, wishing for a third time for more control over what came out of her mouth, but it was too late now. "It's broken."

"I'll look at it."

"I've already called somebody, Arliss."

He pulled at the wire, then threaded it through an insulator on the post in front of him. Leda picked up the reel and walked backwards, winding out enough wire to take him to the next post. They worked fast, both of them looking over their shoulders at the herd in the pasture below, because cows can tell when the electricity is turned off. Arliss said they could smell it. And sure enough, just as Arliss was turning it back on, a calf went through.

Leda saw it and quickly followed him into the woods. For a few minutes, the calf ran up and down the fence line, trying to find a way back, but Leda knew he would not attempt to take the shock again, and when she came near, he bolted. She and Arliss chased him in and out of the trees for nearly an hour, coming close a dozen times but not close enough to catch him. Finally, he lay down, exhausted, near the fence within sight of his mother, who had only intensified the bedlam with her nonstop bellowing. Leda circled behind him, signaling Arliss to stay out of the way. She got down on her belly and began to crawl. Slowly, slowly, slowly, she crawled, stopping whenever she saw his ears twitch. Crawl, stop. Crawl, stop. Crawl, stop, until, there! She reached out her hand and grabbed his leg. He jerked and tried to wrench himself away from her grasp, but she held on until Arliss got there and took over. Arliss had the strength to pick him up and carry him back to the pasture.

Back on top of the ridge, Arliss handed her a thermos of water, then nodded toward Daniel's car, sitting in the driveway. "Must be a bad cold," he said.

The car parked there in the middle of a workday looked like something you don't want to be looking at, like a stain on a shirt or somebody's unzipped fly. She turned her attention back to the cows. "Who's that, walking over there by herself?"

"That's the one who keeps kicking at the dogs. I'm keeping an eye on her."

"I thought so. Her tail's up."

He nodded. "She's come fresh just this morning."

"Isn't that early?"

"She did the same thing last time."

Leda handed the thermos back to Arliss, then sighed. "He wants to be a writer."

"What does that mean?"

"I'm not quite sure."

They both looked back toward the house, but there was nothing to see except Daniel's red car. Then up the driveway came a white truck.

"Must be the refrigerator repairman," she said. As she walked away, she thought she heard Arliss start to say something, but she did not look back. "I don't even want to hear it, Arliss," she called, running down the hill.

When she got to the house, she found out that Daniel was not being a writer. He had gone back to bed. The refrigerator repairman put a new motor in the ice maker for $138.41. Leda hid the bill.

Over the next few days, Daniel transformed the back screen porch into his office. He replaced the kitchen chair with a new chair that swiveled and glided up and down on a glossy, black pole, and under it he put a three-by-five rug with an oriental pattern he bought at Walmart. He nailed a bulletin board to the wall, where he pinned a picture of a star nebulae he had torn from a magazine and one of the photographs she had taken of sunlight against the side of their house. Tacked up beside it was a note card where he had copied a quotation from *Hamlet:*

> *Sir, in my heart*
> *there was a kind of fighting,*
> *that would not let me sleep.*

On another piece of paper was a schedule:

> 5 a.m.—wake up
> 5:15 a.m.—exercise (run - 4 miles? stretch?)
> 6–8 a.m.—write
> 8 a.m.—coffee (Get the poppy-seed from Brian)
> 8:15–11:30 a.m.—write
> 11:30 a.m.—lunch
> 12–2 p.m.—write
> 2 p.m.—take walk
> 3 p.m.–6 pm.—write
> 6 p.m.—dinner/talk to kids
> 7–midnight—write/read

Ha! Leda wanted to laugh. So far in his career as a writer, Daniel had arranged furniture, shopped, and slept. She went inside and called Tom Fields.

"All he told me was that he was going to be gone for a few days," Tom said. "I figured he was sick. I put a substitute in there to cover his classes, but that can't last forever. What did you say he was doing?"

"Writing a book," Leda said.

"He didn't say anything to me about a book."

"He told me you said, *Go for it.*"

"I said no such thing."

"I see."

"You don't think he means to really quit, do you, Leda?"

"No," she said. "I mean, absolutely not."

TWENTY-TWO

LEDA

By the time Daniel had installed himself on the screen porch to begin his life of fiction, Leda had been working on the farm for eight years, but she had learned most of what she needed to know about Arliss in the first year. She had been working with him for only six months when Susan gave her the first bluebird box. It never occurred to her to ask him first. She was nailing it to a fence post when he drove up in the tractor and stopped her. "What are you doing?"

She had assumed, because he worked outside with animals, that he liked birds. Arliss got off the tractor and took the box in both hands and ripped it off the fence. Leda couldn't speak. She watched him throw it in the back of the trailer with the rest of the brush he was hauling away. "What's wrong with bluebirds?" she asked.

"I can't mow with that thing in the way."

She looked at the fence where the box had been. She looked at the box in the trailer. She looked at the ground, still covered with winter stubble. "What are you talking about?"

Arliss climbed back on the tractor. "I'd run right into it," he said.

She still did not understand. If he absolutely had to mow that close to the fence, she figured he would lose, what? A couple of feet of hay in the seconds it would take to drive around the box, but when she told him that, he said, "A couple of feet is a couple of feet." Then he started the engine and drove away.

From this incident, Leda learned that the principle of a thing was more important to Arliss than how it played out. He believed, for instance, that a farm should be operated with no waste, yet, in real life, he lost anywhere from 20 to 40 percent of the hay in each and every round bale he left in the fields for the cattle to eat over the winter. There were ways to minimize the loss, but no way to eliminate it. Cows pull on the hay, some of it drops to the ground, cows trample on it, ruin it; that's just how it works. So the idea that a couple of feet of hay left unmowed would make a difference was ridiculous.

Unless it's not the hay. Unless it's the principle that matters.

Leda believed it was the hay. She believed the spirit of the law trumped the law. And she believed the sight of a bluebird flying across a field was worth a couple of feet of hay, so she did not give up on putting bluebird boxes around Arliss's farm, but she waited to bring it up again until she was indispensable.

When she first began helping Arliss on the farm, she did not work every day, only when he asked her, but in a couple of year's time, she had learned enough about the farm to know what needed to be done without his having to say a word. Some days she wondered what on earth he had done without her. But to answer those people who thought she had lost her mind (and there were plenty), she came up with a list of reasons she enjoyed working on a farm:

1. You don't have to wear hose
2. Flexible hours
3. No boss to tell you what to do
4. No meetings/no memos
5. An infinite number of photographic subjects
6. You get exercise on the job (no need for a gym)
7. Fresh air
8. The cows are entertaining
9. The dogs are amusing
10. There's something new every day

There were some things she could not explain and would not have bothered anyway, such as the afternoon she spent digging up cedar trees, saplings really, the largest not more than a couple of feet high. They were like warts, Arliss had said; you can file them down to nothing, but if you don't get at the roots, they'll grow right back. It was a windless day in July, and, in minutes, streams of sweat started running through her hair and down her face and neck and back and chest. The ground was hard and rocky, and her muscles ached; blisters formed on her hands; sweat bees stung her arms; gnats dogged her eyes; and she came to a point when she did not think she could stand it. But then she stood it. *She passed through it,* there was no other way to describe it, and she found herself no longer fighting the heat, but part of the heat, which made her feel strangely powerful, as if she were in possession of a strong and supremely capable body. She remembered the fortune-teller on the pier in the Outer Banks, who had told her she would have two great lovers in her life. She had not believed him then and did not believe him now, but it occurred to her, if ever she were to love another, it might not be a person, but a place.

She would not forget the first day Arliss had stood on the back porch asking for help. She had said yes, impulsively, without thinking about whether it was a good thing or a bad thing to cancel the job interview she was supposed to go to, without wondering what Daniel, or anyone else, might say, without considering the risks. She had found it unexpectedly refreshing not to weigh the pros and cons. She had said, simply, yes, then changed her clothes and followed him to the barnlot, where he had corralled half of the cattle. Stationing her beside a gate, he had told her to open it when he said to, long enough only for one cow to pass through into a chute, which led to the barn. Then she was to close it quickly. The job had sounded simple enough, until she got right there close to the animals and saw how big they were and realized it was just her and a flimsy gate keeping thousand-pound heifers from going where they wanted to go. Arliss appeared unaware or, more likely, unconcerned about their size, and got in the barnlot with them, reminding her of the way Arliss's father had been killed, which until that moment had been only a story to chill the spine, but now seemed uncomfortably real. She asked him about it and was surprised when he took the time to tell her exactly how it had happened. The message was clear; not simply that it was an accident, which was all he had ever said about it before, but one that could have been prevented. It was then that he began teaching her how to look for what a cow might be seeing: a reflection off the pond, for instance, a discarded Coke can, a sweatshirt hanging on a fence, or a cup of coffee sitting on a post, knowing that cows fear things they don't understand, and that goes for strange smells and noises, because a cow's senses of smell and hearing are more sensitive than a human's. He told her how to look for signs of aggression in body movements and in their eyes but warned her never to look directly into an animal's eyes. It was the first of Leda's many lessons on how to think like a cow. Then, with her operating the gate, Arliss lured the cows one by one with a bucket of corn into the chute, where they had nowhere to go but to the end. There, he trapped them in a headgate and poured liquid wormer over their backs. He and Leda finished the first half of the herd that day with the understanding that they would finish the next, and when Daniel got home, she told him she was not going to touch up her résumé, not going to put on the gray suit, not going to look for another job. She had found the one she wanted.

He had stared at her while she talked. Then what he said next surprised her. "Don't you know by now that my father cannot be trusted? He will let you work and work all you want, but in the end, he will spit you out." At the time, that was all he would say about it, and she was left to believe him or not.

Her father was more enthusiastic, walking around the farm with her, poking his head in the barn. The first time he came for a visit, they sat on the ridge, eating apples and watching the cows in the pasture below. He confessed that he had once thought about getting a farm of his own. When she looked surprised, he said, "I was thinking, actually, of Montana."

"You would have given up medicine for farming?"

He thought for a minute. "Probably not." Then he smiled. "Your mother never would have let me do that."

The mention of her mother startled her. She watched her father stand up and stretch and walk toward the woods behind them, where he threw his apple core deep into the trees. She listened to it smash through the leaves on the branches but never heard it hit the ground. He walked back and stood with his hands on his hips, looking as if he might be surveying the herd below, but as always with her father, it was hard to tell what he was thinking. She remembered the years she had spent, convinced he was on the verge of telling her something important, until finally she realized he never was. What she did not know was whether he was just that way, or if grief had changed him.

"Why?"

Her father had not answered right away. Then he said, "She never liked to get dirty."

Leda nodded. "I'm not anything like her, am I?"

"She wouldn't have wanted you to be."

She got up and stood beside him. "Arliss says there's a fox who lives up here somewhere. He's seen him. I never have, but I've heard him. It's pretty creepy. It sounds like a little girl screaming."

He nodded. "I'd give anything to see something like that."

"You know, Dad, you can come here anytime you want. I'd even put you to work." He never did, but it meant something to Leda to have her father's approval.

Daniel still left occasional HELP WANTED notices on the kitchen table, but his initial disapproval of her working on the farm did not appear to last long, and there was even a period of time when he collected obscure facts about cows, which he used to delight the children. He found out for instance, that different moos mean different things, that, in fact, animal scientists had discovered at least six different cow vocalizations. Some nights they would sit outside and listen to the cows and make up a cow language of their own. He liked to toss out random facts such as in 1860 there were 31 million people in this country and 25 million cows, and he told them that in certain Indian traditions, a person who kills a cow will become a ghost and be forced to experience twenty-one kinds of hell. Hannah, in particular, loved the idea of those numbers and would challenge him.

Twenty-one?
Yes.
Not twenty-two?
Twenty-one.

But his favorite story was the one about the Dun Cow of England who went mad when she learned she had been tricked by the villagers into giving them an unlimited supply of milk. She was killed by the earl of Warwick, who was cursed then for his efforts, forever after seeing her ghost just before the deaths of family members. Her hooves were silent and left no trace of hoofprints on the grass, Daniel would whisper, while Andy and Hannah shivered with the thrill of it.

Daniel's stories, plus the fact that he was busier than ever after Tom Fields increased his teaching load, giving him a poetry class he had always wanted, fooled Leda into thinking Daniel supported her working on the farm. But one night at a party at Tom and Elaine Fields's house, he said something that made her think it bothered him more than she had known. She and Daniel had never met most of the guests that evening, but that was not unusual, since Tom and Elaine were known for bringing together interesting people who had never met before. Most were congregated in the kitchen, but Leda had spent the first part of the evening sitting on a sofa in the living room with Elaine, looking at a book on bird photography. Elaine was an artist who specialized in naturalist painting and was interested in hearing about Leda's bluebirds, among others, including a bird Leda had spotted that week but could not identify. Leda could hear Daniel's laughter over all the other guests in the kitchen, and when she and Elaine finished looking at the book, she headed that way. She was only a few feet from the door when she heard someone (she did not recognize the voice) ask Daniel what his wife did for a living, and that's when she heard him say, "She's between jobs."

She stopped. *Between jobs?* At the time she had been working on the farm for two and a half years. She turned around and returned to the living room to wait for dinner.

And thank goodness for Brian, she remembered thinking, who also happened to be there that night. She made a point of sitting next to him at dinner, and the two of them, using code words and surreptitious facial expressions, made fun of some of the more pompous guests. But Daniel was impressed, as Daniel so often was, and on the drive home, he chattered about the people he had met. Leda was not speaking to him, but there was no silence big enough that Daniel could not fill. He was particularly taken with a woman who managed to make her living as a freelance writer and photographer and had published articles in a number of different magazines, magazines Leda had never heard of but Daniel obviously had. Recently, however—and Daniel was totally sympathetic here—she was having a hard time selling her work.

"Maybe she's between jobs," Leda said, before getting out of the car and slamming the door.

Daniel did not say anything more about it, and neither did she, and they went to bed, but in the middle of the night she woke up and found Daniel gone. Leda generally did not wake up in the middle of the night, but when she did, she was used to finding the other side of the bed empty. Usually she simply turned over and fell back to sleep, but on this night she turned over, then she turned over again. She got out of bed, pulled a sweatshirt over her nightgown, and went downstairs.

He was sitting on the kitchen floor in front of the back door, watching a raccoon on the other side of the glass. Leda tiptoed closer, slowly, even though the raccoon did not appear even mildly skittish, and sat down beside him. The raccoon was eating dog food out of the bowl Andy had left on the porch in hopes of encouraging one of Arliss's dogs to start hanging around their house. (Andy had asked if he could take one to sleep in his room at night, but Arliss said no. He said he would not stand for any dog of his turned into an inside dog.) The raccoon picked up the dog food, one nugget at a time, and placed it into its mouth with fingers as nimble as a monkey's, all the while staring directly at Daniel, with an expression on its face that, if it could talk, would say, *What are you going to do about it?*

"He's brazen, isn't he?" Leda whispered.

"He's beautiful."

"Yes. He is."

They watched him for a few more minutes. Leda said, "Some people consider them pests, you know. Your dad; he'd have them all shot. You don't suppose they carry rabies, do you?"

"That's only in Virginia."

"What makes you say that?"

"Or somewhere. Could be South Carolina."

Leda reached out and tapped the glass with her fingernail, but the raccoon did not flinch. It did not blink. "I still think we ought to screen in this porch."

They watched the raccoon eat the dog food until the bowl was empty, but even then it did not scurry away. It slunk around the bowl like a cat for several minutes before it turned and, moving with the hollow-boned swiftness of a phantom, vanished into the darkness.

"I'm sorry," Daniel said.

"It's all right."

"You like living here, don't you?"

"I do."

"We couldn't exactly go nose to nose with wild animals anywhere else, could we?"

"No."

"Maybe Africa."

"Maybe."

"And there's no law that says one of us shouldn't be happy."

She had to think for a minute to come up with something to say that would not make her sound impatient, but finally she gave up. "I don't understand why you aren't."

They watched as a June bug hit the glass and landed on its back. It flopped around the porch, buzzing like an angry hornet in its struggle to flip itself upright. "Most days," Daniel said, "I wake up worrying that this will be the day they knock on my door and tell me the game's over. No more fooling around; they know."

Leda waited. Then she asked, "Know what?"

"Who I really am. A fake. A fraud, and not particularly good at it, either."

Leda nodded. "Don't you think everybody feels that way at one time or another?"

"Not everybody."

Leda did not argue with him.

"We'll stay here, then," he said. "In Belle's House. If that's what you want."

"I would like that."

After that night, Leda never heard Daniel say another critical word about her work on the farm. She had been working there for almost a decade now, and in that time, she had put up nine bluebird boxes, the last three with Arliss's help, and once she even saw him showing them off to his neighbor Lloyd Pitt, before Lloyd sold his farm and moved to town.

TWENTY-THREE

LEDA

Two days after the ice-maker repairman left the first time, Leda woke up and found a puddle of water on the floor in front of the refrigerator. It was easy to trace it to the ice dispenser in the door, because there was a steady trickle running from the lever to the catch basin, which was full and spilling water over its side and down to the floor.

"Daniel!"

He had spent the night before in a sleeping bag on the floor of the screen porch and was still asleep, but he could, by golly, *wake up*. She mopped up the puddle and placed a large bowl under the refrigerator door to catch the water. Daniel stumbled from the porch into the kitchen. Together they pulled the refrigerator away from the wall, then Leda reached behind to turn off the water.

"Didn't we just have this thing fixed?" he asked.

"I'm calling them back right now."

"I don't know how much more fixing we can stand."

She dialed the number while Daniel stood in the middle of the floor looking as if he were trying to decide whether to stay up or go back to bed, but she felt as dog-tired as he looked and had no sympathy for him. She did not know how she was supposed to get used to the fact that he was sleeping out there, alone, on the screen porch.

"Hello?" A woman came on the line briefly, then clicked off again.

Leda shifted the phone to the other ear, and told Daniel, "She put me on hold."

"Figures." He poured himself a cup of coffee.

Andy came downstairs and saw the refrigerator in the middle of the kitchen. "Cool," he said.

The woman came back on the line. Leda explained the problem, then, after a pause, said, "No, you aren't sending somebody out next Monday. You're sending somebody today. . . . Tomorrow at the latest, then. Are you listening to me? You were supposed to fix it the first time. . . . Fine, but I can't wait until Monday. Don't you people understand? My floor could have been ruined! . . . Okay, but this time I want it fixed, period." She hung up.

"Go, Mom," Andy said.

"They'll be here Monday," she said, adding, "Arliss is going to freak out when he sees that truck."

Hannah had not come downstairs yet. Leda went up to see what was going on and found her still sleeping, despite the clock radio blaring in her face. Leda shook her.

"Ohmygod, ohmygod, ohmygod," Hannah said, pushing past her mother on her way to the bathroom. "Why didn't you wake me *up*?" Leda looked over at the desk, which was covered with books and papers and several empty cans of Diet Coke. She counted them. Five. She did not need a degree in higher math to calculate the amount of caffeine. She wondered how long it would take Hannah to discover speed.

Leda's day did not improve when she walked out later and found Arliss getting ready to spray the pastures with herbicide and in a bad mood himself. Leda knew something had made him mad the day before when he had gone to the feed store up in Clinton and found it sold and under new construction. It was going to be turned into a Pilot gas station complete with its own McDonald's restaurant inside, but she did not understand what the problem was. There were feed stores a whole lot closer than Clinton. He could go to one of them anytime and not have it take up a whole afternoon, but she had pointed that out to him before, and it did not matter. He always insisted on going up there anyway. He had never taken her with him. Now he was hitching a rented sprayer to the tractor, and when she walked in the barn, he did not give her a chance to say hello. "I'm not listening," was what he said.

"And I'm not saying anything," she said back.

But just her presence seemed to remind him of the arguments they had fought over the use of herbicides, and as he went about his business, he seemed determined not to look in her direction. *Fine*, she thought. Over the years she had tried to interest him in other methods of weed control, but even she believed she had made a mistake the last time when she had suggested he switch for Hannah's and Andy's sakes, hinting they might show more interest in taking ownership of the farm someday if it were chemical free. He had stopped her cold with an upraised hand. "If you think them kids are ever going to work on this farm, you got another think coming," he had said, and she knew he was right. It had been a disappointment to Leda, something she viewed as a waste, a misfiring of intention that sometimes even seemed comical, that neither Hannah nor Andy showed any interest in the lives of their grandparents or the farm. Hannah had slipped seamlessly into the frenetic lifestyle Leda had hoped to protect her from by moving to the farm, and Andy, well . . . Andy had discovered baseball, something Arliss seemed to take as a personal insult, as if Andy were anything like Daniel. Leda would concede that farm life might never have appealed to Hannah, but she partly blamed Arliss for turning Andy away. She could point to the day. Andy had been seven or eight, no older for certain, and he was playing in the creek, which was one of his favorite things to do in those days. He liked to look for crawfish and water spiders, and he had taught himself to skip rocks at the wide place near the road. On this particular day, he was back toward the ridge where the creek was narrow and had built a dam of rocks. He had worked all morning, fighting a current that kept finding a way over or through his wobbly wall, but finally he made it work, and the creek began forming a pool behind it. He was busy building up sides for the pool with mud and more rocks and did not see his grandfather marching toward him. Leda saw it, but did not understand what was happening until it was too late. Wordlessly and without warning, Arliss kicked down Andy's dam while his grandson yelled, "Wait! No! Stop, Granddad, stop!" But Arliss walked away, still without a word. Even when Leda demanded an explanation, he said nothing. She made it up to Andy that afternoon by letting him play in the barn loft, something Arliss frowned on, because he said it messed up his hard-earned supply of square bales, but they were Leda's square bales, too, and she dared him to say one word against it. He didn't. But Andy lost interest in the farm quickly after that, and whenever he played outside, he tended to stay in his own small backyard.

Leda had given up fighting Arliss over the herbicide issue, and when he did not ask for help with the spraying, she was not disappointed. She walked up the ridge to the northeast pasture to hunt for cedars, taking her camera with her. She kept her eyes open for tiny saplings as she walked along the edge of the woods and considered her conflicted feelings about Daniel's writing. She did not fool herself into thinking he had the talent or perseverance to make a success of it (although no one can say for sure what another person is capable of), but neither was she sorry to see him try. What she wanted for Daniel was simple, or as Merle would say, if it were a snake, it would have bit him. She wanted him to explore his past and that of his father, and she had told him so, because she had sensed for a long time that something was missing there. So twisted were his perceptions of his Appalachian heritage that he refused to see how it might have something to do with the reasons they had moved to the country. Arliss was almost worse. He had cut off his past like you'd cut off an arm and pretended it didn't hurt. She had told Daniel about his father going up to the feed store and finding it gone. "It meant something to him," she had said. "I don't know what, but you could start there."

Rolling his eyes, Daniel had said that was a subject that had been ridden harder than a cow pony.

"Since when do you know anything about cow ponies?"

But she believed, if she left him alone, he might change his mind. She found a crop of small cedar saplings pushing through pine needles, but before pulling them up, she got down on her belly and snapped a picture.

There was another reason she hesitated saying anything against Daniel's writing. Guilt. Having spent the last eight years doing exactly what she wanted, she was hardly the person to tell Daniel he couldn't do the same. What made it scary, of course, was the prospect of Daniel losing his job, pointing them toward an uncertain future. The only real question then was could they do it? She wanted to be able to say yes.

The refrigerator was still in the middle of the floor later, when Leda came in for lunch and found Tom Fields in the kitchen sitting across the table from Daniel. Daniel was staring at his hands. Tom was leaning back in one of the kitchen chairs so that only two of the legs were on the floor. Andy had a habit of treating chairs the same way, leading Leda to warn that he was going to fall backwards and break his neck if he wasn't careful. Andy ignored her when she told him things like that, so next she would inform him that he would have to pay her back if the chair broke. That did not work either, because he did not believe, either that the chair would pitch backwards, or that its legs would break. Susan (who was full of advice these days, now that it looked as if Seth was going to come out okay) once told her that threatening children with impending danger would not work if the children did not perceive the danger themselves. "Eventually," she said, "they will come to the conclusion that you are just crazy and won't believe anything you say." Leda liked Tom. She was glad he had come and decided she would not say anything to him about the chair. She offered him coffee instead.

Tom nodded and explained that, if Daniel would agree to continue overseeing the Writing Center and finish up the semester in the poetry seminar, he would cover him for the other classes. "That way he can keep his job," Tom said. "But that's all. He'll need to come back full-time in the fall."

Leda almost winced at the generosity; Tom had been so good to them for so long. If nothing else, he was the one who consistently refuted Daniel's claim that he was disrespected for never having earned his doctorate. According to Tom, that was a notion that existed only in Daniel's imagination. But Tom had never wavered in his support for Daniel, and that included giving him opportunities he would have given no one else. "That sounds good," she said. "Doesn't that sound good, Daniel? That way you'll have the rest of the spring and all summer to finish your book."

"I can't write a book in a summer."

Leda turned to Tom. "Cream?"

"No thanks."

"Sugar?"

"No. I want you at least to think about it, Daniel."

"The answer's still no."

"How about I give you until the end of next week to make up your mind." He stood up.

"Don't you want your coffee?"

"That's okay, Leda."

"You should come over more often, Tom."

"I will."

"Come to dinner sometime. You and Elaine."

"Well. Okay then."

When he was gone, Leda set the coffee cup down, put her hands on her hips, and faced Daniel.

"Quit staring at me," he said.

TWENTY-FOUR

DANIEL

Daniel was coming to the conclusion that you can hardly write a book anymore unless it's about Africa. Or India. Sri Lanka was also good these days, and Bosnia, and you could always count on Russia, China, or the Middle East. Anywhere there were floods or earthquakes or hunger or disease or horrific living conditions or revolution or war or armed militia or torture. Torture was especially popular, particularly if you, yourself, had survived it and could talk intimately about the cruel gleam in your torturer's eye. One good gleam of a torturer's eye, and it did not matter how well the book was written; it was like mainlining it to publication.

"People like to be startled these days. They seem to *want* to be grossed out, have you noticed?" he had asked Brian.

Brian said, "You forgot Burma."

But it was better if the book could be written well, and by well, Daniel meant in a raucous style. A little torture and maybe a natural disaster like a flood, sex of course (sordid was best), all with a healthy sense of humor; that was the trick. Edgy, frenetic, ironic, hard, explosive, unsparing, rollicking and . . . funny! That's what was called for these days. Daniel was no dummy; he could see it everywhere he looked, and he felt conspired against that he was not well traveled, that the scope of his world was so pitifully small, that he did not have the necessary credentials to make a go at the writing game.

"Have you noticed this?" He had asked Leda, who, if she had tried to be more unhelpful, could not have done a better job. Leda insisted his subject was right in front of his face, but she was referring to the whole Appalachia thing, Sut Lovingood all over again, that flogged-over, run-through, worn-thin yawn factory. *Talk to your father,* she kept saying, *talk to him before it's too late.* She had in mind a cozy father/son chat, Daniel with the legal pad taking notes, Arliss spilling his guts about his childhood in the mountains. Right. Like that would ever happen. Leda's problem was she had stuck her head in a cow's butt and never pulled it out. Daniel's concept of Appalachia was nothing like the noble photographs of Walker Evans, or the raw desolation of Faulkner's Snopes family, or even Sut Lovingood, who at least could claim the complexity of symbolism. What he saw instead was a hillbilly in a red-checkered shirt and overalls, barefooted, holding a cane pole or a shotgun or a corncob pipe or a jug of moonshine, grinning under a wide-brimmed straw hat, with a look on his face that, if it only defined stupidity would be tolerable, but it did not. It was silly. The joke of the South. The one icon that embarrassed even Southerners.

It was nowhere near as interesting as his book, *Caramel Dreams,* which told the story of a university professor who falls in love with a beautiful, brilliant, but extremely troubled young student, although so far there was sex but no violence, and the novel was set in Knoxville, a long way from Africa, and Daniel's style tended toward rambling, which was not the same as raucous.

He had decided to model the character of the brilliant young student after Hannah. Not Hannah exactly, but the way Hannah might look in ten years, ultrathin, long blond hair in her face all the time, sullen expression on her face, which, on a fifteen-year-old looks like a phase, but, on a twenty-five-year-old, can reveal a psychological disorder. Daniel felt guilty about this and hoped no one would accuse him of exploiting his own daughter's looks, so he made distinctions. Hannah's eyes were blue; his character's were brown. Hannah was of average height; his character was unusually tall. But there was the matter of the self-destructive personality, which, he could hardly deny, came straight from his daughter. It was something Leda liked to spend time worrying about, but Daniel understood it. He would watch Hannah not eating and remember what it was like the first time he stayed up all night and was okay, but of course Brian was the pro. He knew the feeling better than anybody, to abuse your body and get away with it, to push the limits and prevail, although, Daniel would admit, there was something to be said for degree. Hannah was not as accomplished as Brian when it came to the art of self-destruction, but here was the point: Cheat death, there's hardly a better high.

The problem was, Daniel was having a hard time giving this particular personality quirk to his character without making her sound crazy. And he had lost control of his structure, or, rather, he had no structure, stuck, as he was, in the professor's childhood, with no clear way to get back out. Then there was the whole language thing. He felt as if he were competing with all the other writers in the world to see who could come up with new ways to describe the same old things. At the moment, for instance, he was struggling with pale. He could try substitute words, like ashen, pallid, or wan, but he had to be careful. A pale face is not always ashen, and pallid and wan can sound pretentious.

He knew one thing; if Tom Fields had not made him so mad, he'd be getting a lot more work done. Daniel could not get over the gall of the man to drop by without calling, as if he had come to see for himself if Daniel had flipped his lid. And the way he had talked, to Leda, especially, with such courteous restraint, as if what he asked were reasonable. So a couple of classes needed to be taught, *okay, already;* Daniel did not begrudge Tom that. What pissed him off was the insinuation that he could write a book in three or four months, when Tom knew better. Good Old Tom sure tipped his hand there. It was clear to Daniel that Tom considered his book a joke. He was humoring him, and Daniel knew exactly what he thought about people he, himself, had humored. He thought they were fools. He ripped up the pages he had written since Tom had left that morning and drove down to the Flying Dog.

"Updike has a new story in the *Atlantic Monthly,*" he said to Brian.

"Shall I puke now or later?"

It was in the afternoon, between lunch and dinner, and both were slumped over the bar, drinking orange juice in their vodka for the vitamins.

"The man could get a grocery list published," Daniel said. "It's not fair."

"What is?"

He tried to get Brian to drive up to the mountains with him, but Brian said he had to work, so Daniel left by himself. Instead of toward the mountains, however, he headed for a lake where he and Brian had gone as teenagers to drink beer and see how fast they could drive around the curvy roads. He was driving and listening to WFLD when Steve Earle came on the radio and, son! He felt his whole body settle back into the seat, and without warning, he found himself thinking about a girl he knew when he was younger. It wasn't so much the girl, but the time when he knew the girl, when his life was uncomplicated, or at least it seemed that way, when the only important decisions involved what kind of music to play on the stereo, or whether to drink beer or vodka, eat pizza or a sub, sleep in or get up for an eight o'clock class. He *knew* things then, in a way he did not know them now, and there was an urgency to his thinking. If he had to choose a single image to represent that time, it would be of himself and this girl (or any number of girls), leaning over tables, sitting in hallways, walking down sidewalks in the middle of the night, talking, talking, talking about things that *mattered,* about whether it was better to be happy or strong, for instance, or what was the greater virtue, love or courage, or if there were principles worth losing your life over—things that still mattered, but no one talked about them anymore. He rolled down the window and felt the spring air hit his face. It occurred to him that there was a difference between Steve Earle, who could sound like he was trying too hard, and the easy, unself-conscious way people like Graham Parsons had just sung their songs, or was it not the music at all, but himself that had changed? Certainly, if not changed, then he was a great deal more tired than when he was the person with his arms around this girl. He remembered her name. (Not Pat. He made a point of never thinking about Pat, because if ever there were a road not taken, that was it.) Caroline. Such a beautiful name, he thought, like music. He was thinking about what it would be like to run into Caroline unexpectedly and see the smile that would form on her face—the one that says, *I remember you*—and be transported to the time when he *was* the person she used to know, when suddenly it came to him that he could round the next curve and die.

It was nothing new or unusual for him to think about death, although the whole subject had become even more real to him since the crash of the Concorde. If, he reasoned, you can be sitting in a hotel room in France, minding your own business, playing it safe, taking no risks, and the Concorde (not just any airplane, but the *Concorde!*) can crash through the wall and kill you, all bets are off. So lately he had been doing certain things to ward off death. He would leave his worn blue jeans, still molded to the shape of his own legs, lying across the bathtub, and, looking at them, it was unthinkable that the soul who had shaped those jeans could cease to exist. It was like leaving a piece of himself, his jeans hanging over the side of the tub; as long as they held their shape, he would not die.

On another level, he was aware he was making up his own superstitions, which, in itself, could portend death.

What would happen, he wondered, if he died right now in this car, listening to the radio, thinking about a girl? This is what would happen: Steve Earle would keep singing, but this person called Daniel, this complicated (or was he fooling himself) bundle of thought processes that can hear a song and bring back instantly an entire world that does not exist anymore, would be gone.

The next morning he walked into the kitchen and sat down at the table and looked at Leda. "Do you think I'm going to die today?"

Leda did not hesitate. "No."

TWENTY-FIVE

LEDA

Leda parked the car and sat there for a minute listening to WFLD. It still amazed her that Brian had managed to make his radio station work without any funding source other than private donors. No advertisers, no government, pure underground, although (despite Daniel's efforts to the contrary) Brian also had kept it free from political statement of any kind. Its purpose was music only, and it played a variety of styles, most of which could not be found on commercial radio stations—bluegrass, alternative country, folk, jazz, blues, and some alternative rock, often from other countries. The DJs were volunteers and sounded like people who had dropped by the station with a handful of their favorite CDs. They coughed on the air, giggled, dropped things, and forgot what they were going to say, incidents that to Brian and Daniel were as entertaining as the music. Leda liked listening to all but one, a woman named Georgia, although she could not say why. There was something about her voice, abrasive as a smoker's, yet cute at the same time, so what was that? Phony, was what Leda called it.

Several nights a week, the station broadcast live whatever band might be playing onstage at the Flying Dog next door, and, on Thursday nights, Brian always played the lead-in set. Leda liked to tune in to hear him play, although she had never been there in person to see the show. Several local bands had recorded albums from the shows. *The Culture Shocks, Live at the Flying Dog. The Grass Kickers, The Flying Dog Sessions. Buddy Pope and the Band: Dog Time.*

Leda was sitting in her car in the parking lot of the baseball field, where she had dropped Andy off. She watched him attempt to run down the sidewalk in his cleats, his bat bag slung over his shoulder, bouncing against his thigh. His bag was not as big as some she had seen, the megabags, almost as big as the boys who carried them; still, Andy had to stop twice to readjust his on his shoulder before he could continue. He did not want to be late for practice. He got nervous when he was late, and when Andy was nervous, he did not twitch or flutter or jiggle or pace the way his father did, but, instead, became utterly still, so still that, if he did not absolutely have to breathe, he wouldn't. It was unnatural how still he could get, and Leda had watched it today all the way to the ballpark, Andy sitting tense and motionless, his hand on the door handle, his eyes on the road, as if he could make the car go faster by the force of his own will. The instant she brought the car to a rolling stop, he was out and hobbling down the sidewalk as fast as his cleats would let him go.

The song on the radio ended, and Georgia's raspy voice came on. *"Georgia here, now you be there!"* she gushed. Leda cut off the car and walked down to the field, which was hardly what you could call where Andy played baseball anymore. It was located in the same spot where Daniel and Brian had played baseball, but instead of the two rutty diamonds in the middle of a cornfield next to the Baptist church, it was now a baseball complex holding twelve fields with combed dirt and clean white bags and green-painted fences and spacious dugouts and grass infields, protected as fiercely as golf greens. There were sidewalks and landscaped flower beds and, in the center, a concession stand and a covered picnic area. Daniel hated it. "It's not a ballpark," he said. "It's a country club."

And what had been the modest Raccoon Road Baptist Church next door was now attached to a two-thousand-square-foot sanctuary with a forty-foot steeple and brand new Family Life Center that featured two full kitchens, a preschool, a recreational room with Ping Pong tables and wide-screen TV, and a basketball court. From anywhere on the farm you could see that steeple, and at night you could hardly see any stars anymore for all the lights.

Leda found Andy's field and was surprised to see Brian sitting on the top row of the bleachers. She climbed up and sat next to him. Andy's coach was yelling.

"Pull that trigger, boy. Murder it. Christ almighty!" The coach was sitting on a ball bucket he had emptied and turned upside down, and he clearly resented having to stand up and walk over to the boy behind the plate. "You're swinging too late; that's your problem, son. And what are you doing with the bat? Jesus Christ, you're going to break your nose with it. Get it behind you, see? *Behind* you. Now, try it again." He stepped away and pointed to the boy on the mound. "Fire one in here."

"Who knew baseball was so violent?" Leda said. Brian smiled.

Andy was in right field, knees bent, glove up, ready to catch a ball even though there was almost no chance a ball would head his way off the bat of that particular batter. Boys elsewhere on the field seemed to know it. The shortstop and second baseman were talking to each other. The boy at third had left the bag to throw grass at the left fielder. The boy on first was sitting on his base, and in center, the boy had his back turned and was watching another team practice on the next field over. Unexpectedly, the batter hit a ground ball to third, only no one was at third. The left fielder chased it, picked it up, and threw it back to the pitcher, but the coach was not watching any of this. The coach was telling the batter, "That's contact at least. That's getting the old bat on the old ball, but let's see you do it again, only this time turn your hips. Your *hips,* see? Forget it, just watch the ball." He pointed to the pitcher again, "Okay, Con, rock and fire."

"Con?" Brian asked.

Leda sighed. "I think his real name is Conrad, but don't hold me to it."

She and Brian were the only ones on the bleachers. There were four or five dads there, but they were standing behind home plate, hanging their fingers through the holes in the fence and talking to each other in loud voices about their sons on the field. They had come from work, the sleeves of their dress shirts rolled up to their elbows, their ties loosened and shifted sideways. When they walked, their slacks stayed precisely pleated, but their shirts were wrinkled in such a way to make them look casually wealthy, the same way wrinkles strategically placed around the eyes can look sexy on some people. These men were always at the ballpark. Daniel called them the Dad Club.

"Andy wants to pitch this year," Leda told Brian. "But I don't know. These other guys all seem to have an inside track with the coach. I can't prove it, of course, but their sons seem to get more attention than Andy and a few of the others, like that poor little boy at bat."

"I could work with him, if you want."

"Daniel's always saying he'll do it."

"Where is Daniel anyway?"

"He said he was going to the Flying Dog to see you."

"Well, I'm not there, am I?" Leda detected a note of testiness in his voice, but he quickly softened it. "I assumed he would be here."

Leda sighed. "Do you know what's wrong with him?"

"You mean, more than usual?"

"I mean, I want to support him, but first I'd like to believe he knows what he's doing."

Brian shrugged. "I really wouldn't know, Leda. He hardly talks to me anymore."

Leda and Brian watched the next batter step up to the plate. "Look at that boy," Leda said. "He's huge."

"Somebody ought to check his birthday, but nobody will," Brian said. They watched the batter hit the first pitch over Andy's head to the fence. By the time Andy got back there, he had hit three more. "He wants to hold poetry readings at the Dog," Brian said.

"Daniel?"

He nodded.

"Are you going to let him?"

"The Flying Dog is a musical bar. It's not a poetry bar."

Leda switched her attention to Andy, who was fielding balls from the right field fence now and throwing them all the way to the first

baseman. Leda was impressed and looked to see if the coach might
be watching. He wasn't.

Brian said, "The guy on the mound?"

"Con."

"Yeah, him. He's the coach's son."

"How do you know?"

"I can tell. It's going to be some trick to get Andy a chance to
pitch with that kind of competition, but I'll do what I can."

They watched the next two batters take their turns. Neither was as
big as their slugging predecessor, but both could hit the ball just as
far. Preposterously far, but Andy was catching many of them and
throwing the balls all the way back to first base. The coach still was
not looking.

"Seth is gone."

Brian whispered it, so it took a minute for Leda to realize he had
spoken again, then to understand what he had said. "What do you
mean, gone?"

"He's been working for me for a while; I guess you knew that."

Leda nodded.

"It's not like he's ever been punctual, but this morning he did not
show up at all. Susan went over to his apartment, and it was empty.
I mean, the furniture was there, but his clothes weren't, and his guitars were gone. All of them."

"No note?"

Brian shook his head. "I called around. One of his friends said
he'd been talking about heading west. I'm guessing Austin."

"So he's probably fine. You don't know that he's not."

Brian didn't answer.

"I need to call Susan," Leda said.

"She's probably trying to call you."

The coach was off his bucket again yelling. "Holt, get your ass
out of left field and cover first. Con, take shortstop. Harding, move
to third."

"Can I pitch?" Suddenly Andy was there in front of the coach, almost tripping him on his way back to the bucket. The way Leda saw

it, the coach did not look angry or even surprised. He looked like he
did not remember Andy's name.

"Porter's going to pitch," he grumbled.

"Can I pitch next then?" Andy asked.

"We'll see."

Andy bounded back toward right field, and Leda's heart broke to
see it, not simply because the coach had told him no, because clearly
that's what he meant. Leda understood. The dads along the fence
with their ties askew and their sleeves rolled up understood. The
boys slouching in the field understood. Only one boy did not. Leda's
heart broke because when everyone else heard *No,* Andy heard *Yes.*

Leda did not see Daniel at first when she and Andy walked into the
Flying Dog. It was not until Brian brought them their pizza that she
looked over and saw him across the room near the stage in the bar,
talking to some people who looked as if they were setting up for a
show. He waved. Through the glass window in the wall, Leda could
see into the studio of the radio station next door, where a disc jockey
was talking into his microphone. Hannah had not come with them,
having gone from school to track practice, then to a study group, ad-
hering to a schedule that, to Leda, seemed designed by an insane person, but you could not pry Hannah away from it, nor any of her
friends, who seemed to be competing with each other over how
much they could do in a day and how little food or sleep they could
get away with in the process. It had been almost a relief not to sit
across a table from her, watching her nibble the crusts off the pizza,
then exclaim how full she was. Brian sat down next to Andy and,
when she asked, identified the people Daniel was talking to: a guitar
player, a technician who worked for the radio station, and the disc
jockey named Georgia.

"That's Georgia?"

He nodded.

"She doesn't look anything like she sounds," she said, but he was
not listening. He was leaning over the table with his face in his

hands. Leda wanted to kick herself for not picking up on the fact that he had left the ballpark hoping to find a message from Seth waiting for him at the Flying Dog. "He didn't call, did he?" she said.

He shook his head. "And I'm the fool who's always told him how good he is. All these years. Shit, Leda, what have I done? Somebody out there better be giving him a chance; that's all I've got to say."

"I suppose no news is good news," she said, because she could not think of anything else.

"Because I swear to God, it's like he's Duane Allman reborn. I'm not kidding."

"Yeah?" Daniel had walked up then. He put his hand on the back of Brian's chair. "You're the one who plays like Allman, man."

"Did I tell you he had started writing his own music? He's like fucking Townes Van Zandt, I swear to God."

"All these dead guys. Jesus, Brian."

"Writes like Townes, plays like Stevie Ray."

"*You're* the one who plays like Stevie Ray."

"He's better than me."

"You keep saying that."

"I keep knowing it."

Daniel pulled out a chair and sat down next to Brian. "How about Tuesdays?" he said.

Brian grimaced and poured himself a beer from the pitcher he had brought over from the bar. Daniel declined Brian's offer to pour him one and leaned over the table. "We'd do an hour of poetry, then the band could take over."

Brian looked over at Leda for help, but, at that moment, she was thinking that wanting to organize poetry readings at the Flying Dog was not the most alarming thing Daniel had done lately.

"A half hour. Think about it; this is poetry for the masses. Democracy in art. Our chance to elevate the intellect of the average man. Shit, Brian, what else is going on around here on Tuesday nights?"

"I think it's a great idea." That was Georgia, who had come over from the bar and was standing now beside Daniel. Leda could not get over how much she did not look like her voice. In person she was a tiny thing and much younger than she sounded. She had blond hair that fell over her shoulders. One side was tucked behind her ear, but the other side was not, and a strand of it fell partway over her face. A thin gold chain with a small gold cross hung from her neck. "We could broadcast it live over WFLD like we do the bands," Georgia was saying.

"People turn on the radio expecting to hear music," Brian had said.

"Okay, one Tuesday a month," Daniel had said.

"I don't see how it would fit."

"People come in here all the time to play their own music. Why not poetry and other stuff?"

"Other stuff isn't music."

"Play music in the background then."

"That could be my job, picking out the music," Georgia had said.

Brian had looked back and forth between Daniel and Georgia. "You already have a job," he said.

TWENTY-SIX

LEDA

Leda went to bed that night thinking she owned two pairs of reading glasses, but when she woke up the next morning, she could not find either one. The reason she had bought two in the first place was because she was always losing them and hated wasting time looking for things she already owned. Two pairs, she had figured, would give her one to use while waiting for the missing one to turn up. Or not. Some glasses stayed lost forever, which was why she bought cheap drugstore brands rather than prescription glasses, which the eye doctor had said she did not need anyway. All she needed, he had told her, kindly, was a little magnification to help out her aging eye muscles.

What to do about the aging muscles in her belly, she had no idea. And she would have appreciated some warning that her skin was going to stretch like an old elastic waistband. She was not asking to be pretty all of a sudden. Everybody got older; she knew that; she just did not know why she had to do it so fast, while Daniel down there on the screen porch writing poetry seemed hardly to be aging at all. Only his hair, which used to be nearly black, had taken on some gray highlights, but that only made it more interesting.

She stood in front of the mirror in her room and looked at herself. She kept her hair a medium length, not long, but long enough to pull away from her face in a ponytail. She took the rubber band out and shook her head so the hair fell evenly below her ears. Then with her fingers, she combed a little of it so it fell in front of her face. This was a trick; she had not understood it until now. To invite someone to reach out and lift your hair out of your face was not all that different from offering a blouse to be opened, a skirt to be lifted. Leda had never cared for tricks. Flirting, push-up bras, high-heeled shoes, even makeup; she saw no use for any of it, sticking instead to the philosophy: What you see is what you get, which was noble and honest and true. But what if her motivation were not? That was the question that bugged her now, because the defense of the underachiever asserts that, if you try and fail, you really fail, but if you don't try? Ah, then at least you leave yourself with an excuse.

But she had made a point of asking herself, hadn't she? Yes, she had. She had asked herself, and asked again, if being pretty would have made her happy, and the answer was always and emphatically, no. She saw no reason to change her mind now. She pulled her hair back in its ponytail and went downstairs to look for her glasses.

Daniel was writing poetry because his novel was not working out, and at that moment he was fussing over a poem about his typewriter. "I'm playing around with the metaphor of the typewriter being like a giant eye into my mind," he said.

Leda sat down on the stoop. "Tell me something, Daniel. Do you think I'm beautiful?"

He looked at her. "I cannot believe you asked me that." He returned his fingers to the keyboard as if he were getting ready again to type, but he did not type. Instead, he said, "Beauty is a construct of our modern marketing society. That's the problem with this country, you know. All flash and no substance."

"I don't care."

"You used to."

"It's a simple question, Daniel."

"And I'm telling you; beauty's not everything."

"I didn't say it was."

He picked up a magazine that had been lying on the desk and started flipping through it. "You look fine to me," he said.

She went back to the kitchen to wait for Susan who, in training for her next marathon, was running the twelve miles from her house to the farm on Bearpen Lane this morning. The radio on the windowsill was tuned to WFLD. Susan walked in the door at the same time a song ended, and Georgia came on the air. Leda flipped it off. "Something about that woman's voice makes my skin crawl," she said, handing Susan a glass of water.

Susan drank down the water and nodded. "It's like she's trying too hard, isn't it? She's too eager. Suggestive, maybe. Whatever, it's kind of embarrassing."

"What do you guess she looks like?" Leda asked.

"How should I know?"

"Take a guess."

"Have you seen her?"

"Last night at the Flying Dog. Andy and I went in for a pizza, and she was there."

Susan shrugged. "I don't know. I hate to typecast."

"Do it anyway."

So Susan thought for a minute and came up with a description of a middle-aged woman trying to look younger: dyed blond hair, heavy makeup, tight jeans. "And if I had to guess," she added, "she's from the Midwest or somewhere, not from around here." Leda was shaking her head. "Am I wrong? Don't tell me she's attractive."

"No."

"That's what I thought."

"She's drop-dead gorgeous. You were right only about the blond hair, but I don't think it's dyed. And, not only did she grow up right here in Knoxville, Brian says she's rich, or at least her daddy is. He owns a whiskey distributorship."

"I've always heard there's money in that."

Leda led the way out to the front porch, where they would not disturb Daniel. The construction across the street was particularly loud today. The dump trucks hauling dirt were making shrill beeping noises when they backed up, so along with the rumbling of engines and the screeching of brakes, there was this incessant *beep, beep, beep, beep, beep, beep*. Leda and Susan talked over the noise, and soon their conversation turned to Seth. It had been two days since anyone had heard from him, but while Brian had spent most of that time trying to track him down, Susan said she was not worried. "He's twenty-two years old," she said. "He didn't run away. He just forgot to tell his parents where he was going. There's a difference."

Brian suspected Seth had gone to Austin, Texas, because the musicians down at the Flying Dog were always talking about breaking into the music scene there, but Susan did not know why Brian was so quick to rule out Seattle. Or Boston or Los Angeles, even Nashville. Her guess was that Seth would not call home until he had good news. "He doesn't want to feel like a failure, you know, taking this big leap, then falling on his face. Especially to his father. Brian won't believe me, but he hasn't stood where I've stood, watching that boy knock himself out for his dad."

"Hannah's like that."

Susan nodded.

"But you know, Susan, it's nearly impossible to live anymore without feeling like a failure, if you're paying attention, I mean. If you're even half awake, you know you ought to be eating five to six servings of vegetables a day, am I right? Drinking eight glasses of water. Stretching. Washing your kitchen counters with antibacterial soap, getting eight hours of sleep, and what else?"

"Flossing."

"Oh my God, how could I forget dental floss?"

"You're also supposed to organize your house so it stays clean. Rubbermaid bins, I'm told, are the trick."

"And you better not forget your PIN number. And where you put your insurance policies and your appliance manuals and your warranty agreements."

"Don't forget to make time to meditate. Live in the moment, you know."

Leda nodded. She knew Susan was still making fun, but she was reminded of Daniel's recent and solemn proclamation that he was incapable of living in the moment, because then all he would think about is death. Each moment, he said, if he had to think about it, could be his last, and it would drive him crazy. She never knew how to respond when Daniel said things like that, because it was not as if he were wrong, exactly. It was not a matter of right and wrong, as much as it was a way of thinking that never occurred to her.

But she did not feel like telling Susan. She did not suppose Susan would understand, anyway, because, despite her protestations against the tyranny of perfection, Susan ate right, got plenty of sleep, remembered her PIN numbers, and kept her house clean. And a great deal of life's details worked out for her. Teflon, for instance. Susan literally wiped out her dirty pots and pans with a washrag so they stayed as clean and shiny and black as when they were new, while, for reasons Leda could not figure out, hers never came clean without a hard scrubbing, which rubbed the Teflon off, so what good was it?

"Yes," Leda said, "if you're paying attention, you have the opportunity to feel like a failure, not just every day, but several *times* a day."

"I surrender," Susan said.

"Me, too."

Leda looked up and saw Arliss waving from the barn. "Just a minute," Leda yelled. "I need to help him with a bloated cow," she explained to Susan, then motioned toward the commotion across the street. "We can't hear ourselves talk out here anyway."

"I can run home, if you need to go," Susan said.

Leda shook her head. "He can wait."

Leda drove her home, and when she pulled up in front of her house, Susan said, "I'll call you if I hear anything from Seth."

"In the meantime, Brian thinks he going to find him."

Susan did not get out of the car right away. She looked down at her hands. "I know," she said.

They sat for a minute longer without talking. Then Leda said, "You still love him, don't you."

Susan sighed. "I know it doesn't make any sense."

"It doesn't have to."

When she got back home, Leda hurried to the barn. Arliss had not been having a good spring with his cows. Besides the one that had become bloated, he'd had his first stillborn calf in four years; one of his heifers had died of acorn poisoning, and, not one, not two, but three cows had fallen down with the grass staggers. The vet had revived them easily with an IV of magnesium, but when he drove away for the third time, Arliss had looked disgusted.

Arliss had named the bloated cow Trouble, and, when Leda got there, he had already run her through the chute and put her head in the headgate so she could not move. He picked up a cut-off piece of hose, handed Leda a block of wood, and said, "Ready?"

Leda put on her gloves. "Go."

Teasing Trouble with a handful of corn, Arliss got her to open her mouth, and Leda wedged in the wooden block so she could not close it. Arliss then threaded the hose down the cow's throat and into her belly, where he poured a bottle of mineral oil. Leda knew if the oil did not break up the gas that had filled her to bursting, he would have to cut a hole in her belly to let it out. She hoped it would not come to that. When the bottle was empty, Arliss pulled up the hose, knocked out the block of wood, and rubbed the heifer's neck. Leda backed out of the way to give them room. If there was anything she knew from the years of working with Arliss on the farm, it was that no one, vets included, was better with his animals.

His gift, because that's the way Leda saw it, was partly due to his deep understanding of his cows, and he had taught her as much as he could. His lessons ran like a list of dos and don'ts in her mind. Talk to them, he would say, but don't look directly in their eyes and don't hurry them. Understand that there are differences between individual cows, just as there are differences between people; some are more nervous than others, for instance, so pay attention to that. Pay attention, anyway. When a cow drops a shoulder, she is about to turn to that side, and if the skin on the shoulder rolls or twitches, she is preparing to turn quickly. Rapidly moving eyes can mean the cow is scared or nervous, but slowly moving eyes can mean you are being evaluated as a threat. A steady stare can mean aggression, and any animal that slings its head or holds its head low is very aggressive and may be poised to charge. Plan an escape route, but in an emergency, don't run. Stand your ground and stare the cow down, and if she charges anyway, yell. (Leda had never been charged, but it was some comfort to know what to do.) She had learned to watch for signs that a cow might be sick, if she is slow, for instance, or keeps to herself, or spends more time than usual lying down, or breathes fast when it's not hot, or has trouble swallowing. An overly active animal can signal one in pain. Cows like their pastures clean, so she and Arliss kept them that way. They prefer new growth to mature plants, so Arliss rotated his pastures and kept a watch out for hemlock, burdock, and cocklebur. He had seen a cow develop an abscessed lump jaw as big as a tennis ball from a simple seedpod that happened to be sharp enough to puncture her mouth.

If you asked him, Arliss would say he was only following good business practices to treat his cows so well, because it was a fact: Stressed cows do not resist disease as effectively as healthy ones, and they certainly don't grow as big. So it made sense, economically, to know all you could about the animals, but Leda believed there was more to it. She had memorized the list of dos and don'ts and followed it step by step; still she was not as good as Arliss around the cows. There was something else that happened when he walked among them, and the more Leda saw it, the less she understood.

While Arliss was taking Trouble out of the headgate, Leda went to the spigot outside and washed her hands, and that's when she spied a small booklet on the shoe shelf. She picked it up. The front cover had been torn off, but she could read the title page. *A Mountain Boy's Life on the Farm,* it was called, written by somebody named Ted Minton. It was spine-broken, thumb-smudged, page-frayed, and red-dirt-stained, which surprised Leda, because the only books she had ever seen Arliss read were technical ones on farming and cattle. She turned to the first page and read the dedication.

So people won't forget
what it was like growing up
in the town of Loyston
that is no more

Clearly Arliss had read this little book and more than once, and one could assume he had memories of his own, so it seemed like a shame, and even a puzzle, to Leda that he hardly ever spoke of them. No stories about his family, his home on the mountain, even what he did for fun or what he missed. There was a whole way of life back in New Hope that simply wasn't anymore, and she was reminded again of the loss that would occur when Arliss died. It made her sad, especially when she thought about Hannah and Andy and how little they knew about who they were. And Daniel had spent so much time studying Sut Lovingood, he had missed the bigger story, the one about a real Appalachian life that lived right next door. She wondered, now that Arliss was older, if it would mean more to him to remember, and to remember out loud, so that somebody else might hear and remember what she heard. She found him and, without saying anything, handed him the booklet.

He rolled it up and stuck it in his back pocket. "It weren't exactly like he says."

"If you ever feel like driving up there, I'd love to go with you."

"There ain't nothing there."

"There's a lake."

"It's just a lake."

She became aware then of the silence in the barn. She went out the back to the barnlot, where she could make out the sounds of the trucks and bulldozers across the street, but they were muffled. In fact, as she listened, she realized it was quiet enough back there to hear the wind. She could see the steeple on the Raccoon Road Baptist Church across the pasture; otherwise, the farm looked the same as it always had. She imagined it looked very much the same as when Arliss first moved here, except for the pond, of course, and the bluebird boxes.

A week earlier, she had overheard him boasting about the bluebirds to a man who had come to look around the farm. He was a young man, dressed in khaki pants and a yellow golf shirt. He drove a white Jeep Cherokee. A friend of Bob's was all Arliss seemed to know about him, but Leda was not so sure, and when Bob showed up the next day, Leda had walked right up and asked him what he was up to. Bob seemed happy to talk to her, and they had driven out to Weigel's and brought back coffee in large styrofoam cups, which they drank, standing in Arliss's driveway. "You know, Leda," he had said, "there's nothing intrinsically wrong with development. As a concept, I mean. What's wrong is ill-planned development," and he used for an example the project across the street on the Pitts' farm. "I know that guy, and I can tell you he's greedy. Cramming too many houses on too little land, which is not catastrophic like, for instance, a trailer park would be, but it's not good. He doesn't care, and he's going to get away with it, but that doesn't make it right." Bob cited other examples, including twenty-seven acres on Bucket Road that had been in the same family for 150 years. The man who bought it promised the old woman who lived there that his intentions were to build a single house for himself and his family, but he turned around and sold it, for three times as much as he paid for it, to a developer, who proceeded to cut down every tree. Then he got the property rezoned for condominiums. "It's a crime," Bob said, "but not illegal. It seems to me, there's a way to look at this issue that's not black-and-white, because—don't get me wrong—I have no patience for people who are against progress, either. I'm the kind of guy who says, okay, here's the problem; how can everybody win?" And in the driveway, drinking her Weigel's coffee, Leda had thought Bob sounded reasonable enough; it was only later, she realized, that every time she asked Bob if he were trying to talk Arliss into selling the farm, he never gave her a straight answer.

You mean, Mr. Stubborn? He'd say something like that, or else he would laugh and say, *Nobody talks Arliss Greene into anything.*

Leda went back inside the barn and found Arliss straightening the shelf where he kept the mineral oil. "I'll make you a deal, Arliss," she said. "If the time ever comes that you feel too old to work anymore, I won't let anything happen to this land. If I can't keep the farm going, I'll let it grow back to the way it was, but I won't let anybody come in here and tear it up. I promise."

Arliss just stared at her.

She went home for lunch and found Daniel in the kitchen. He had pulled the refrigerator out from the wall again and had taken the ice maker out. When she asked him why, he told her it was making a noise. When she told him it's supposed to make noise, he said, "Not that kind of noise. I think it's broken again."

"Again? I'm calling them back right now."

"We don't need an ice maker. We can use trays."

She looked at him. He was sitting at the table, eating a sandwich and flipping through a magazine on astronomy. He was taking notes.

She went to the refrigerator, opened the door, and stood there deciding what to eat. She stood there for a long time. Even after Daniel stopped what he was doing to inform her that letting all that cold air escape was a waste of energy, she did not budge. Finally, she picked up an orange.

The problem, though, with oranges is they have to be peeled, and that was what she was thinking about, holding the orange in her hand, calculating whether it was worth the mess, when she heard Daniel say, "We aren't going to make it, are we?"

She took a deep breath and turned around. He had stood up and was pacing now, one hand dug into the back pocket of his corduroys, the other fingering his tangled hair.

"You aren't talking about us, are you?" she said.

He stopped. "Hell, no. What do you think?" He spread his hands out wide in front of him. "The *Earth,* Leda. Our *planet.*"

"That's what I thought." She took the orange and a paper towel to the table and sat down.

Daniel resumed his pacing and began talking about the sun's scheduled expansion due in several billion years. It was not going to *maybe expand,* in the same way a person is not going to *maybe die,* he said. It was part of the life cycle of this particular kind of star to grow larger with age, and, given the exacting parameters needed to sustain life on Earth, he added, "We're fried." Leda was tempted to make him repeat the part about several billion years but understood that Daniel was not really talking to her. She could be anyone sitting in the kitchen chair in front of him, or no one. She could imagine him talking to an empty room. But then he looked in her direction, and said, "You have to wonder what kind of god would put us on a collision course with the sun, which, of course, only proves you right, doesn't it? There's no such thing. *Ain't no use in calling out my name, babe;* am I right? Although, it might interest you to know, Leda, that there are subatomic particles that don't behave anything like they're supposed to, which tells me there might be a whole lot that we don't know about how the world works, leaving room for possibilities for God you haven't even thought of. It doesn't matter. We're not going to make it that far. I used to think we had a chance, but not anymore."

Leda lifted the orange. *There is a trick to the first cut,* she thought. If she dug her fingers in too deeply, she would squirt juice in her face, but too shallow, and she would come out with a thumbnail full of rind. That was why she always thought twice before eating oranges, because they can be difficult and messy, unlike apples, which you simply wash and eat. But Leda did not like the taste of apples nearly as much as she liked oranges, so it was worth it, mostly. She eased her thumb into the peel slowly and felt a spray of juice shower her hand.

Daniel was still pacing. "Reason number one," he said. "We are going to blow ourselves up. Between nationalism and religion, we don't have a chance, and let me tell you, in the minds of fools, destruction will be preferable to figuring out how to get along."

Even if she could peel the orange without disturbing the pulp, the mist that emanates from the rind makes your hands sticky anyway. She licked the inside of one of her wrists. The taste was slightly sweet but mostly bitter.

"Reason number two. We won't be able to sustain our own population. I'm talking about enough food or clean water or even clean air to keep all of us alive, and what a shock, you know what I mean? Like we couldn't have predicted this? Which takes me back to reason number one, of course. How much do you want to bet we blow ourselves up before we starve into oblivion?"

Leda was considering another danger to peeling an orange, the fact that, no matter how careful she was, her fingernails got jammed with white, spongy rind, and it hurt. Leda tried to scrape it out with her teeth, but her fingers still ached, partly because she could not get to all of it, but partly because the pressure had bruised the tender flesh under the nails. So she had to work with sore fingers, and she was only half-done.

"Which leaves only one question."

"What's that?"

"You know. What's the point?"

"Right." Leda reached up to push a strand of hair out of her face, and now both her face and hair were sticky. She wondered if she would have to take a shower just because she had decided to peel an orange. She tore away the last piece of peel and set the jagged fruit on the paper towel, which was wet with juice and disintegrating. She stared at it. Then she cupped the naked orange in the palm of one hand.

Daniel looked at the orange. He sat down. "I mean it, Leda."

And she knew he did. She even knew he was right, that every word he said was true, and that every true word wounded him in some profound way, and she did not know what to do about it. She raised her hand above her head and squeezed the orange. Pulp oozed between her fingers as the juice streamed down her arm. Daniel opened his mouth to say something, then did not say it. He grabbed her raised wrist and began licking the juice off her arm. She let go of the orange. She listened as it hit the floor, ran her sticky hands through his hair, and slid to the floor beside him.

Their lovemaking was awkward and uncomfortable but not unwelcome, and when they finished, they lay naked on the floor in a square of sunlight coming from the window over the sink. Leda noticed her shirt lying crumpled next to the table leg, artistic in presentation, and the word that came to her was *shirtness*. She smiled. She considered pointing to it. *Shirt,* she would say and nothing more, then decided she did not want to break the silence. Daniel's eyes were closed. He was flat on his back, his feet splayed outward, his chest rising and falling as if he were sleeping. Leda's hip loomed over him like a mountain. She did not think they looked beautiful lying there; they looked middle-aged, which, Leda decided, had a beauty of its own. Two sagging and mottled bodies on a wooden floor in the sunlight.

After a long while she whispered, "Isn't this enough?"

She waited to see if he would answer. She let several minutes go by before she picked up her clothes and left him lying naked on the floor.

"What do you mean trays?" said Hannah.

"How are we going to get ice?" asked Andy.

TWENTY-SEVEN

ARLISS

Arliss had been watching Leda walk out of the barn and along the road toward her house, which was why he had not been paying attention to Trouble when she turned around and kicked him. He was lucky. She kicked him in the thigh and broke nothing, no arm, no rib, no skull, but it knocked him down, and, as he hit the ground sideways, his hands came across a stack of two-by-fours, and he grabbed one up and stood and swung and hit her square in the head and killed her. She dropped like a stone. *Fwump,* right there in the barnlot, as if somebody had let the air out of her. The impact of the board on Trouble's skull almost wrenched Arliss's shoulder out and sent him falling again, backwards this time, on his rump. He blinked. The bull was in the barnlot and so was a first-calf heifer. He stood up, slowly, not calling attention to himself, and walked backwards to the gate and let himself out. He leaned on the gate then and breathed and listened to himself breathing, as if he were the one dying, the one sucking air, as if each breath would have to last longer than the one before, because there might not be another. His heart was beating so hard that his chest hurt, and he thought he might be having a heart attack. He leaned on the gate and breathed and waited for his heart to slow down.

The bull and the heifer were looking at him. Trouble was still on the ground, of course, but they were not looking at her. He became aware of the noise of trucks and walked over to the edge of the hill and watched the construction going on across the street. He wondered how much he would have to pay a man to drive a bulldozer up here and help him load Trouble in the back of his truck. He looked back and forth between his truck in the driveway and the pasture behind him and decided he could tie her legs to a chain and drag her without anybody's help. He went inside the barn and found some chains and attached the front-end loader bucket to the tractor so he could dig a hole.

Back outside, he stopped the tractor next to the barnlot. The bull and the heifer had wandered over to the far corner and were poking their noses under the fence to get at the grass on the other side. He got down off the tractor and walked to the fence. He meant to keep going, through the gate and into the barnlot, but he stopped instead and knelt. His hands were shaking. He stuck them through the slats in the fence and rested them on Trouble's still-warm flank.

He did not know why Leda was taking so long to eat lunch, but he was thankful for it. For once he wished she would just stay away.

That afternoon, when she discovered the dead cow on the ground and Arliss digging the pit, she exclaimed, "I don't believe it!"

He said, simply, "I never asked you to."

That night he did not mention the cow to Merle, and when she turned on the television, he went outside and sat down on the porch. He could not shake the feeling of the animal falling to the ground under his hands, which was not like him. Usually he could put things out of his mind. He remembered how his mother, especially toward the end of her life, believed that they had brought misfortune on themselves by leaving New Hope, even to the extent that they had gone against God. She never called it a curse, but that's what it was. When he was able to push aside the image of the fallen cow, what emerged in its place was worse: his uncle Luke hanging in the barn, or Rosemary on fire and running down the hill, or his father, screaming under a torrent of hooves. He looked at the sky over the barn turning a purple shade of red and wondered if there had been some sign he had ignored. Merle's religion was of no help when it came to questions like this, but his mother's seemed as far from him as the grave.

He went to bed early but had a hard time falling asleep. When sleep finally came, it brought him, not peace, but a familiar dream that began with a dam. In the dream, he watched as the dam was built, not with concrete, but with gigantic blocks, lifted by cranes that fit them together until they locked tight. He did not see the cranes, only their booms as they swung in and out of view. It was like looking through the small, circular lens of a telescope: the steel arms of the cranes appearing and disappearing, the dam rising, one block on top of another, until the moment when the last one slid into place. The lake began filling immediately, and in the way dreams have of transporting a person from one place to another without explanation, Arliss found himself standing on the top of the dam, watching the water rise.

The chickens went first, a burst of squawking then gone, and the dogs, a staccato of barking, and they were gone too, then hogs, squirrels, cats, raccoons, possums, chipmunks, mice, and snakes. Deer on spindly legs were flipped facedown by swirling water, but even the sturdy-legged cows were swept off their feet by the accelerating current before the water reached their heads. Some of the deer managed to right themselves and, with the frenzied, bug-eyed mules, tried to swim, but the shore kept moving as the lake grew wider, a foot every second, until they tired of chasing a receding target and were sucked under by the current. Birds flew upward, all of them at once as if startled by a shotgun blast, and formed themselves into a great screeching cloud that moved across the sky until it was gone. People climbed on porches, then roofs, pulling each other with outstretched arms, handing babies up through windows, shoving old women from behind. These were not a people of boats. They had nowhere to go.

Under Arliss's feet, the dam shuddered as the river crashed against it. The noise was explosive, as if boulders were tumbling into each other, but over the roar he could hear people screaming and crying, some praying, some unable to utter a sound, their gaping, voiceless faces more horrible than screaming. He watched as houses came off their foundations. Spinning, top-heavy, they tipped over and sank. Some people leapt to floating timbers, but the water was too violent to hold on, or here would come a wagon or a barn door to knock them off. On stronger houses, people stood watching the water rise, past the first story, past the second, to their feet, to their knees, holding children over their heads to give them the last gasp of air.

Last of all came the trees, shortened in the end to bushes, then to shoots of what could be mistaken as scattered weeds atop a glassy plain, and when the last leaf of the last tree was covered, there was silence, suddenly, as if somebody had turned off a switch and left the world with no sound. The lake in turn became instantly still, a mirror reflecting clouds and the massive, immovable dam where Arliss stood.

He was transported again, this time to a small rowboat in the middle of the lake with the dam in front of him like a wall at the end of the earth. Arliss had never been in a boat, yet here he was, and after the tumult of the rising water, he found it peaceful. Slightly eerie, unworldly, due to the sudden silence and the silvery smooth water and the looming dam, but peaceful still. Then something scraped against the bottom of the boat, and he looked down.

What he expected to find was a floating log, and he was poised to shove it out of the way with the tip of his oar, but, instead, it was somebody's boot, and beneath the surface of the still and silent lake he saw everything that had been destroyed. Trees, houses, a crop of corn waving like seaweed, cats, dogs, tables, chairs, and bodies. He picked up the oars and rowed away from that spot, but wherever he went, under every part of the lake, teamed mules, shovels, plows, saddles, hogs, outhouses, hay bales like giant sponges, fences, and the bloated bodies of people he knew, his father, his uncle Luke, his sister Rosemary, all floating in the water, twisting and bumping into each other. Arliss could not stick his oar in the water without striking something, but in all the carnage there was no blood, no color at all but a dull blue-gray, the shade of a fading bruise.

Then out of the silence he heard a noise. He looked up and saw that it came from a wave, born of some wild, satanic current that had slammed into the dam to be propelled backwards, sucking water like a vacuum, building higher and higher. By the time Arliss looked up, it was taller than the dam and racing straight toward him, screaming speed, but it never reached him. The turbulence that ran before it knocked him out of the boat, and he found himself in the water, battered by sodden mules and fence posts and wagon wheels and bodies. Then he woke up.

This was the point in the dream when he always woke up. He had dreamed the same dream countless times, and each time, he would be the same age in the dream that he was in real life. When he was six, he was six in the dream; at twenty, he was twenty; at forty-two, he was forty-two; and so on until now; he was seventy-four, an old man, and so it was in the dream, as if it would not allow him to outgrow it. Each time, it was newly horrible. He would watch the dam rise and the valley fill as if it were all brand new. In the rowboat on the silent lake, he never remembered what came next. The scrape against the bottom of the boat was always a surprise. He felt laid open by this dream, like Prometheus bound to the rock. He knew the story of Prometheus from Daniel, who would have been stunned to learn that his father remembered, but Arliss did remember. He knew what it was like to be bound, to be unable to stop the inevitable. He sat up in bed and held his head in his hands and cursed himself for letting it happen again.

Merle was still asleep. He got out of bed quietly, although he did not have to; Merle slept through anything. What he was accustomed to doing, whenever he woke up like this in the middle of the night, was to walk outside and stand in the yard and listen. To nothing in particular, the wind if there were any, and, depending on the season, spring peepers or cicadas or a deep-winter silence, and, recently, the sound of a late-night car over on Glen Pike, but it gave him solace to hear that everything was all right. Tonight he got as far as the door, then stopped. There was no moonlight through the window, but his eyes adjusted to the dark room as he stood there with his hand on the doorknob. He was sweating. After a while, he became aware that his shoulder was hurting, and he remembered Trouble and the two-by-four. He did not remember how long he had been standing there before he found his way to the refrigerator and poured himself a glass of milk and took it to his chair, the one he sat in to watch baseball, the one that had conformed to the shape of his body, because no one else ever sat there. It was where Merle found him the next morning, asleep, his mouth open, a glass full of milk on the floor beside him.

TWENTY-EIGHT

DANIEL

Daniel did not know how long he had been staring at his shoes. Maybe just a minute, but it could have been all morning. It was hard to tell. The shoes were an old pair of loafers, softened like a seasoned baseball glove, so they were comfortable, but they revealed how misshapen his feet were, the toes crooked, the toenails yellowed, the balls like tree burls. He wanted to know when his feet had grown old. He was trying to write but having a hard time concentrating, with all the noise coming from the bulldozers across the street. It reminded him of the time he and Leda had gone to New York and stayed with an old college friend from the city. The first morning, they had been awakened by a jackhammer on the sidewalk below, then, every morning after that, there was the jackhammer plus an increasing number of trucks and electric pumps and men shouting to each other, until the last morning, when they woke up to see a giant crane, ten stories high and beeping like a shrill dog barking, and they felt as if they had been sentenced to machine hell.

He did not know where Leda was. Her car was gone. He remembered her standing in the door to the screen porch, telling him she was going somewhere, but he forgot where.

He looked across the hayfield and noticed the barren limbs of three tulip poplars sticking up above the rest of the trees in the woods. He did not have to walk over there to know they were the poplars next to the site of their burned-down log cabin, but he could not remember if they had been dead the year before, which gave him another reason to panic. What if he were not an observant person? This was no minor question, no passing concern. He was not sure he could *be* a writer if he were not an observant person.

He went inside and got a cup of coffee and spied a magazine lying on the table, opened to an advertisement for life insurance. It showed a close-up of a woman, not a particularly pretty woman, but one with an interesting face. There was something about the wrinkles around her eyes that suggested she had a history that might not have been easy, but she had *pulled through,* and now she had her priorities straight. She had her ducks in a row. And what she was saying was clear. *I know the secret.*

It was the plainness of the woman's face that alarmed him, a subversive move from people who must have figured out that glamour won't work in an age of irony. *I know the secret, and you don't,* she said with her perfectly normal face, a face that could be anybody. Really, anybody at all.

He hated her. He hated the photographer who took her picture, and the insurance company who pretended to be something it was not, and the advertising company that believed him so easily duped, and the magazine editor for caring less. He closed the magazine and closed his eyes. He did not know how to live in a world where insurance was good for a spiritual path, and what passed for happiness were shopping malls, Hot Pockets, and wilderness you could drive to in an SUV. He did not know how much fight he had left in him. Suddenly, it seemed important to him to get away. Where he should go and how long he should stay, he did not know, but it was something to do, and he trusted the rest would come to him.

The attic was located behind a small door in Andy's room. A window at the end offered the only light, and he waited a minute for his eyes to adjust. He did not know exactly where to find the camping equipment, but he had not had an occasion to use it for a long time, specifically, since the night he had gone camping with Fred. He knew he was lucky still to have any of it, because he had left all his camping gear with Fred in the mountains and, hiking out that night, he had believed he would not see it again. That was before Walter called and agreed to meet him, secretly, in the parking lot behind Shoney's. "You left it," was the only thing Walter had said, standing by the open bed of his truck, chewing on a toothpick, not looking, while Daniel collected his stuff. Not that he cared, but it was all there, down to the last box of matches. He had stuffed it in the attic without telling anybody, but Leda must have discovered it, because most of it had been moved behind boxes of old books and clothes she had taken up there. She had even placed some of it in its own box, which she had labeled CAMPING EQUIPMENT, but she had never said anything to him about it. Daniel experienced a brief moment of guilt that he did not give her enough credit for having good sense.

He tossed the gear through the door one by one: sleeping bag, backpack, ground cover, canteens, water purifier, poncho, bungee cords, mess kit. He carried the camp stove with him when he crawled back out, and there was Andy, standing in the middle of the room, watching. Daniel straightened up. "What are you doing home from school?"

"What are you doing?"

"I thought I might go camping."

"Can I come?"

"No. Why aren't you in school?"

"I forgot my lunch."

"That's not a reason."

"I don't have lunch money either."

Daniel took out his wallet and handed Andy a ten-dollar bill, but Andy did not take it. "Lunch is over by now. Mrs. Reddick said if I forgot my lunch one more time, she was going to give me a detention."

"Why does she care?"

"She's a Nazi. Did you quit your job? Mom says you didn't."

"Well, I did. What do you think the Nazi's going to do when she finds out you've skipped school?"

"Does Mom know you're going camping?"

"No."

Daniel stuffed the gear into the backpack and slung it over his shoulder. Andy followed him downstairs to the kitchen. Daniel rummaged through the cabinets for food while he talked. "Maybe if you go back now, you'll be a hero. It was always the guys who got in trouble who were the popular ones when I was in school."

"The cool kids hate me. They're not going to quit hating me just because I get a detention."

Daniel stopped rummaging and looked at his son. He was surprised by a memory of taking him to Easter egg hunts at Tom and Elaine Fields's house. Andy would run around the yard with tears in his eyes, chasing the other children, who would be picking up eggs like crazy and putting them in their baskets. Every time they found a new egg, Andy would whimper and grow even more panicked, but no matter how much he and Leda and the rest of the grown-ups screamed encouragement from the edge of the lawn, Andy could not peel himself away from watching the other children long enough to *look at the ground.* Hannah also had been an unsuccessful Easter egg hunter, but her response was so different from her brother's. She would put down her basket, walk over to her parents, cross her arms, and declare the whole thing stupid. Daniel remembered being secretly gratified that his children were different, special. It did not matter, supersensitive or supercynical, at least they were not average lumpkins, good at Easter Egg Hunts and other activities dreamed up by dim-witted people. "Okay," he said. "Go get a backpack, your boots, and a change of clothes."

Andy went upstairs, then returned to the kitchen with the backpack and clothes.

"Where are your boots?"

"They're too small."

"Since when?"

"Since I grew."

"Shit. You got a knife?"

Andy shook his head.

"When I was your age, every boy had his own knife."

"Why?"

Daniel checked his watch. "I have no idea, but how about we get out of here before your mother gets home?"

But while Daniel was loading the car, Andy ran back inside. He told his dad he had to get one more thing, but when he reached the kitchen, he did not know what it might be. He looked around, determined to find something, and finally grabbed his baseball cap. Quickly, then, he wrote the note and left it on the kitchen table.

Dear Mom,

I'm with Dad, so don't worry. We've gone camping. I'll find out where and tell you later.

Love, Andy

P.S. You would have done the same thing

There were no grown men or school-aged boys at the mall. Daniel noticed this. He swore the lady at the shoe store looked at him funny when he asked for boots. She was thinking something was up; he just knew it, a grown man and a boy in the mall in the middle of a weekday morning? Daniel worried she might guess he was a criminal, kidnapping Andy, buying boots so he could take the boy to a hideout in the woods. He thought she was taking a long time in the back room, checking on Andy's size. What if she were calling the police?

But the woman was smiling when she returned with the boots, and Daniel made a point of saying things such as, "Walk around to make sure they fit, *son*," emphasizing the word, *son*, hoping the saleslady would notice.

Then he realized how silly he was being. Andy was *right there!* He could tell the police the truth. *That's my dad,* he would say.

But any competent kidnapper would think of this! Threaten the boy. Tell him he would die if he squealed.

Then Daniel began to worry about someone really taking Andy, and it took about a half a minute for the worry to accelerate to panic, and he felt weak and slightly nauseated. He reached out and touched Andy's small shoulder, knowing positively that he could not protect him, not from everything; there was and always would be another hole in the dike somewhere. And he knew in that instant that if something ever did happen to Andy, he would not be able to stand it. And Leda and Hannah, they, too, would be destroyed, but here was the crazy part. No one else would. This saleslady, for instance, would read about it in the newspaper and feel genuinely sorry for the family, but that's all, and he could see that his life was only as significant as, say, an anthill smashed by careless boys; devastating to the ants who lived there, but for the whole wide world of ants, nothing.

"And how will you be paying for these, sir?"

"What?"

Daniel took them to the highest point you can drive to in the Great Smoky Mountains National Park, before the road heads back down the mountain toward North Carolina. There was a parking lot up there. At the end of a paved trail to the right was the viewing tower on Clingmans Dome, but Daniel told Andy they weren't going there.

"Why not?"

"That's where everybody goes," he said. "I'm going to let you in on something, Andy. There are going to be people in your life who will tell you, if you can't do something right, don't do it, and those same people would accuse us of taking the easy way out by skipping Clingmans Dome, but I'm going to tell you something else. Life's too short not to take shortcuts. Those are the same people who dearly love to call your daddy by the two *M*'s, impatient and immature, but I have a name for them too. Boring."

"Impatient starts with an *I*."

"Right."

"Not an *M*."

"It was just a joke, Andy."

They finished stuffing the backpacks from the trunk of the car. Daniel was careful not to overpack Andy's. He remembered the loads he had carried back in high school on all those camping trips with Brian and Mr. Jameson and felt sure he could handle the bulk of it, but when he flung his backpack over his shoulder, he was stunned by the weight. It nearly knocked the breath out of him. He cinched the lap belt around his hips, but the weight still slammed down his legs like pile drivers. Already his knees hurt. He looked at Andy. "You okay?"

"Fine, Dad."

Once on the trail, he felt better. They lost sight of the rest of the people and soon could not even hear them anymore. Daniel made Andy stop to listen.

"I don't hear anything, Dad."

"Exactly. Listen to the silence."

"How do you . . ."

"Shhhhhhh."

Daniel closed his eyes. "You are listening to the sound of the world a thousand years ago." He stayed quiet for a few more minutes before walking again. "This is great. Isn't this great?" he shouted over his shoulder. "We should have done this a long time ago."

"Are there any bears?"

"Yes."

The trail was rocky and dipped down the side of the mountain before climbing again to the top. There were views through the trees, but not until they came to the first bald did they realize the extent. Layers of mountains spread out beneath them, deep into North Carolina on one side and past Gatlinburg on the other. Daniel took a drink of water. He was sweating all over the place. He handed the canteen to Andy, then pulled out a map.

"Do we know where we're going?" Andy asked.

"Sure, we do."

They crossed another bald before heading back into the woods, where the trail dropped straight down, and where Daniel decided the best thing to do with knee pain is ignore it. He found it helpful to turn sideways, allowing the less painful knee to take the weight as he inched downhill. Andy passed him, descending the hill like a hoofed creature, his light-as-air backpack bouncing behind him. At the bottom, Daniel took the map out again.

"What do we do if we see a bear?" Andy asked.

"We're not going to see any bears."

"How do you know?"

Daniel was studying the map and did not answer.

"Are you sure we know where we're going?"

"Did you bring a flashlight?" Daniel asked suddenly.

"No."

"Goddammit." He tore through both his backpack and Andy's, knowing there was no flashlight, because he had not packed a flashlight, but there was always a chance. Only a fool, he thought, would depend on memory alone.

But there was no flashlight. Daniel had planned to spend the first night in a designated campsite, but at this rate they would not make it there before the sun went down, and, without a flashlight, they could die if they tried to get anywhere in the dark. The trail would vanish under their feet, leaving them to wander around the woods, possibly to the edge of a cliff and over. He knew this, because he had been caught by darkness the night Fred grabbed him by the back of the neck and kissed him on the mouth, and he had swung, instinctively and with revulsion, swung and hit him in the jaw, without thinking, because he had no experience fighting. He did not know what he was doing. But Fred's practiced fists landed over and over and over until he was able to free himself enough to kick him in the stomach and run toward the trail without thinking once that he might need a flashlight. He would not have had time to grab one anyway. He found the trail and ran as fast as he could manage with his whole body hurting, certain that the sound of Fred's feet crashing on the ground behind him would follow soon, but he stopped once and heard nothing. He did not stop long. It had been dusk when he started running, and when it got dark, he tripped and fell, and that's when he broke his arm. And because his arm was screaming pain, and he could not see a thing, he sat where he was, sucking up tears. He thought he was doomed to sit there in pain in the dark all night long, but, like a miracle, the moon came up over the mountain, the glow from it first, burning upward, until it crested and shone like a floodlight on the trail. He got up and walked all the way down the mountain, holding his arm, looking over his shoulder, and feeling sick from his own stupid luck. Because if he had not tripped and fallen, if he had, instead, tried to find his way in the dark, he would have been lost. And what he had discovered in the moonlight was, about fifty yards from where he had stumbled and only a couple of feet from the trail, the mountain fell away a hundred feet.

So Daniel knew they had no choice but to camp in the middle of the trail, which was not allowed, but he had to assume the rule was not made to kill you, and at dusk they stopped and put up the tent. There was no water around, so they had to use what was left in the canteens, which was not a lot, but enough to cook a handful of noodles on the camp stove.

"You know what I should have been?" he said to Andy while they ate. "I should have been a field scientist. Something like a botanist. That'd be the life, you know, camping out, hiking through the woods all day. I could have done it, too. Easy. I don't know why I never thought of it. If I'd played my cards right, I could have landed one of those jobs you see on public TV or, you know, in *National Geographic,* where you get to go to some remote place like the tip of South America or an island off the coast of Africa or, you name it, the North Pole. You should think about a job like that."

But Andy was shaking his head. "I'm going to play center field for the Braves."

Daniel had to stop himself from stating the obvious (which went something along the lines of . . . *when pigs fly*). It must be written in some universal parent book, he thought, the impulse to squash such statements. To set children straight. To pull them off their high horses. What saved him (or Andy) was the bitter memory of sitting in Krystal, listening to Brian's dad tell Brian that, if he were really serious about wanting to play baseball, he'd be outside practicing four or five hours a day, and watching Brian (who was nine years old and dreamed only of being a Cincinnati Red) deflate as fast as a punctured balloon. Daniel took one deep breath and said instead, "I thought you wanted to be a pitcher."

"Pitchers don't hit home runs."

"And that's what you want to do?"

"Yes."

Daniel nodded. After a few minutes he said, "Me, too."

"I think the Braves have a good chance to win the World Series this year, don't you?"

"Sure," he said. "That's what's so great, you know, about baseball in the spring. There's always so much promise." Then to himself he silently finished the sentence. *And what is so sad.*

"Dad, how long are we going to stay out here?"

"I don't know."

"Do you think we should have told Mom where we were going?"

"Probably."

TWENTY-NINE

LEDA

Susan came over first. She and Leda decided there was no reason to call the police, not yet, anyway. Andy was with his father, for heaven's sake. They were camping. They would be home soon. "What do you want to bet they'll be home tomorrow?" Susan said.

"I don't want to bet," Leda said.

They decided to give Daniel twenty-four hours, then call the police.

Brian came next. He offered to go look for Daniel and Andy, but Leda convinced him he'd only get lost, too.

"We need you here," Susan said.

"How much you want to bet they'll call soon?" Brian said.

"I don't want to bet," Leda said.

The three of them were on the front porch that afternoon when a car, bringing Hannah home from track practice, pulled up in the driveway. Leda and Brian were up pacing. Susan was rocking in a rocking chair. Every now and then, one of them would stop and look off into the distance at the mountains where, they all had agreed, Daniel and Andy had probably gone. "Why did he take Andy?" Hannah asked, when they told her what happened.

"That's one of the things we don't know," Leda said.

"I would have gone," Hannah said.

All three stared at her.

"Why don't I go fix us something to eat?" Susan said.

"I'm not hungry," Hannah said. She reached down to pick up her backpack, then changed her mind and stood back up. She hooked her hands in the back pockets of her jeans. Embarrassed that everyone's eyes were on her, she looked down at the floor when she spoke. "They're making us say the Pledge of Allegiance at school, by the way. In case anybody cares."

Leda and Susan looked at each other. Brian asked, "Do you care?"

"Yes."

"Why?"

"Don't be a dolt," Susan told him, then turned to Hannah. "What's the problem, sweetie?"

"I'm not going to say it. They can't make me."

"That sounds reasonable," Susan said. Turning to Leda, she asked, "Doesn't that sound reasonable to you?" But Hannah had slung her backpack up onto her shoulder and was already walking away.

"Where are you going?" Leda called to her.

"I've got a paper due."

"You had a paper due yesterday."

"This is another one."

Leda and Susan looked at each other again. "She's too thin, isn't she?" Leda asked.

Susan nodded.

Leda looked across the hayfield and saw Arliss heading their way. "Shit," she said under her breath, feeling in no mood to watch Arliss's bad opinion of Daniel get worse. "Don't tell him anything," she whispered to the others. They watched Arliss cross the yard and come halfway up the porch steps and stop. Already his skin was as dark as it would get all summer, a sort of wood color that had hardened on him like paint. A map of wrinkles covered his neck and circled his eyes. He took off his hat and scratched his head. Two things, he said. First, Merle had sprained her ankle and needed to go to the hospital, and second, Lucille had come fresh but wasn't looking good.

"Who is Lucille?" Brian asked.

"A cow," Leda said. "He means she's about to give birth." Then no one spoke. This was as clear a deciding moment as Leda had seen in some time, because she knew what Arliss wanted. He wanted—no—he expected her to volunteer to take Merle to the hospital so he could stay with Lucille, but if she knew anything, she knew this: There were times she could deal with Merle, and other times she could not, and this was one of those other times. So she stood up straight and offered nothing. "How did she sprain her ankle?" she asked instead.

"She stepped in a hole. It may even be broken."

"Is it broken, Arliss?"

"Probably."

"Some hole," Brian said, but Arliss ignored him.

"Where's Daniel?" he asked.

"He'll be back," Leda said. "Okay, Arliss, I'll watch Lucille while you take Merle to the hospital."

Arliss scratched his head again. "If you're sure you can."

"I can help," Brian offered.

Arliss winced.

"This is the deal, Arliss," Leda said. "Merle needs you more than she needs me, so you go on. Lucille will be fine."

When Arliss left, Leda went upstairs to check on Hannah and found the door to her bedroom closed. She knocked, but there was no answer. "Hannah?" She cracked open the door and found her daughter sitting on the bed, crying. "What's wrong?"

"Nothing."

"Why are you crying?"

"I don't know."

Leda sat down next to Hannah, who moved away as if she could not stand to be touched. "Are you in some sort of trouble at school?" she asked. "Does this have something to do with the Pledge of Allegiance?"

"See? I knew you'd overreact. I shouldn't have told you anything." Hannah got off the bed, stomped over to her desk, and sat down. She opened a notebook and starting writing furiously.

Leda could see in the mirror on the wall the reflection of herself watching Hannah and was reminded of the time Susan had said she could spot the mothers of teenagers by the look on their faces. Controlled panic was how she described it. Susan believed it was because the world had become more treacherous. Used to be, the same kids who snuck behind the barn to smoke and drink grew up to be bank presidents, but these days, too many kids don't make it. Even the mothers whose kids are not in trouble today know they cannot count on tomorrow, she had said.

Leda was not sure the past was as innocent as Susan tried to make it sound, but she recognized the look. She spied it on the faces of friends who compared notes on simple things: How much allowance is right for a twelve-year-old? At what age are "R" movies okay? Whose house is safe for sleepovers? Which lyrics to which songs are appropriate? *Am I doing it right?* That was the real question. Watching Hannah was tricky, because, what kind of mother would try to stop her daughter from doing homework? All she knew was that something was uniquely unhappy about her daughter and that Hannah was determined not to tell her what it was. Leda was aware that a great deal of her time and energy these days was spent trying to think of just the thing to say to change that. "Dad and Andy are going to be fine, if that's what you're worried about," she said, quietly, but Hannah kept writing and did not look up.

After a while, Leda left and walked across the hall to Andy's room, where she stood, looking at the posters on the wall of Mark McGwire, Greg Maddux, Tom Glavine, Sammy Sosa, and Chipper Jones, until her eyes fell on the dresser and a coil pot he had made one summer at Susan's house. She picked it up and held it in her hand and found it to be heavier than it looked. Since coming home and finding his note on the kitchen table, her mind had not been far from the fear that she was wrong about what she had just told Hannah. Something could happen to Andy out there in the woods with Daniel. Specifically, he might die. What to say, then, about the coil pot, that he should not have bothered? Ah, but the coil pot would continue to claim its space in the world. It would insist upon its weight, would demand by its existence, *Where is the boy who made this coil pot?*

On an intellectual level, Leda understood that real children do die. Every day, all over the world. She closed her eyes, and whispered, "But not *this* child."

It took a few minutes, but Leda found out what was wrong with Lucille. The calf's two front hooves were headed straight, but its head was turned backwards over its shoulder, as if it were looking behind itself. In that position, it would not make it out of the birth canal without breaking its neck or killing Lucille or both. Leda did not want to take her out of the corner of the pasture, where she had gone to feel safe, but she did not see any way out of it. With Brian's help, and a bucket of corn, she led the cow to the barnlot and into a squeeze chute, then stuck a two-by-four through the bars behind her back legs so she could not kick. When she was certain enough that the cow could not move, Leda pulled on a pair of rubber gloves and greased her arms all the way up to her armpits with amber-colored Wesson oil that looked as if it had been sitting on the shelf for years. When she looked up, she saw Brian staring at her. "It's no big deal after you get used to it," she said.

Then she reached into the cow's vagina. What she wanted to do was take hold of the shoulders and push the calf back up the birth canal to give it room to bring its head around. She tried several times, but the calf kept slipping out of her hands, each time moving forward instead of backward, although it could only go so far without getting stuck on its own head. Lucille shuddered and tried to lurch forward. Leda motioned with her head toward the bucket of corn, and said to Brian, "See if you can't distract her with that. And talk to her."

"You've got to be kidding," he said.

She took her hands out of the vagina and straightened up, wanting to cry but forcing herself not to. "We can do this," she said.

Brian seemed startled by her words and picked up the bucket. "Okay."

She slipped her hands back in and braced herself. This time she put one hand on a shoulder and the other on what she hoped was the calf's jaw. She was up to her armpits in the birth canal, pushing hard with one hand, pulling gently with the other. She lost her grip a half dozen times, but after a certain point, the head stayed put, making it possible to resume where she'd left off until, finally, a fraction of an inch at a time, the head came forward. When it was facing straight, Leda attached chains to the front legs, and, working with the animal's contractions, pulled at a downward angle, first this way, then that. At the last minute before the calf shimmied free, Brian took the two-by-four away. Leda caught the calf, falling backwards onto the straw.

"I am not believing this," Brian whispered.

"We're not done," Leda said.

Because the calf was not breathing, she got Brian to pick it up by the hind legs and hold it upside down while she cleaned out its nasal passages and tickled its nose with a piece of hay until it made a choking sound and began to take in air. Then they rubbed its body all over with towels to stimulate circulation. After Leda released Lucille from the chute, Brian carried the calf to her and held it there until its fumbling lips found a teat. Sticky and bloody and soaking wet, Brian and Leda backed away.

"He's got twenty-four hours to get the colostrum or he will die," Leda said. "Look there, she's licking him already. That's a good mama. I think they'll be fine."

Brian shook his head. "I had no idea, Leda. Truly. None."

She shrugged. Then she turned and looked anxiously toward her house. "You think they've called?"

"Susan will let us know if they do."

"I know."

Leda led Brian to the spigot, where they washed their hands and arms and faces. Leda showed him where Arliss had killed the cow. It was not unheard of for a farmer to kill one of his cows in anger, and, in fact, Leda knew of at least two other instances when it had happened. One was Lloyd Pitt from across the road, who stuck a needle into the sore and swollen teat of a cow suffering from mastitis and got kicked for his efforts. He had killed his cow with a brick, which left him stuck with a calf and no mother. What was unusual to Leda was that, this time, it had been Arliss, who, as far as she could remember, had never even said an unkind word to his cows. But Brian only shrugged. "I always thought that old man would blow," he said.

"What do you mean, blow?"

"Who knew he'd go so far."

"What do you mean, go?"

"You never thought Arliss was a pot ready to boil?"

"Not in a million years."

"Well. I did."

As they walked back toward the house, Brian asked Leda what she was going to do when Arliss sold the farm.

"Why does everybody assume he's going to sell?"

"He's going to get too old to farm it here in a minute, don't you think?"

"Are you asking if I could run it by myself?"

They had reached the cemetery. It was a clear, moonless night, but not intensely dark. Lights poured out the windows from almost every room in Leda's house, yellow spotlights lit the construction site across the street, and the hazy glow from Glen Pike and the lighted steeple above the Raccoon Road Baptist Church shone upward into the night sky. Leda sat down in the grass with her back against the stone wall and shook her head. "The answer is no and yes. I mean, the cattle, no, but I'm resigned to that. We had to sell almost half the herd anyway, when Mr. Pitt sold the pasture out from under them, but, the truth is, I don't think I'll mind losing the cows. They aren't mine. They're Arliss's cows, and this is Arliss's farm. What I'd like to do is grow vegetables, maybe even some grapes, on a small part of it and let the rest grow back the way it used to be, whatever that was—I'll be curious to find out."

Brian sat down beside Leda. "Daniel's never acted as if he cared one way or another about this place."

Leda looked down. "I know, and I've never understood that." Through the window, they could see Susan in the kitchen, the phone on the table in front of her. "What's going on with him, Brian?"

"Honestly, I don't know."

"Tom is being patient with him, but it's like he does not care. It's almost as if he's throwing it up in Tom's face, all the years he's stood behind him; I don't know. Tom's given Daniel a lot of breaks, don't you think? I've been trying to remember, and it seems to me as if he's been protecting Daniel ever since that incident with Dr. Carmichael; you remember that? When he said some stupid thing to that girl from Iowa."

"You mean, ever since he put his hand up her skirt?"

Leda stared at him. She did not say anything.

"You didn't know?"

She shook her head.

"Shit, Leda. I'm sorry."

He apologized three more times. "Don't worry about it," Leda said each time.

Brian stood up and walked over to the other side of the cemetery and started throwing rocks at a tree. Leda listened to the rocks hitting the tree, a sound that should have been as irritating as a dripping faucet, but she did not care if he knocked the tree down with those rocks, so long as he wasn't sitting there staring at her. She needed a little room here, a little space, to take in what he had told her, because right now she was not sure she had not already known it. It felt like something she had forgotten, a memory she had somehow misplaced, and now that it had resurfaced, she almost found herself thinking, *Why of course. How could I have forgotten that?*

But she had not known, not until this minute, and she became aware that she should be furious. Yes, she felt strongly that furious was how she should feel, but she was already furious at Daniel for taking Andy to the mountains without telling her, so Brian's bit of news, his little bombshell out of the blue, was anticlimactic, wasn't it? It was like dealing in degrees of furious. She suspected that Brian over there throwing rocks was holding his breath, waiting for her to ask the next question, that being, how many times had Daniel cheated on her? But she did not care. Not at this moment, she didn't. Once or a thousand times, what difference did it make now?

When he tired of the rocks and sat back down, Brian started to say he was sorry again, but she would not let him finish the sentence. "It doesn't matter," she said, suddenly glad to have him here with her, close by, and they sat, side by side, both of them staring through the window at the phone on the kitchen table and at Susan sitting in front of it, reading a magazine.

"This is a lot to have to take, isn't it?" Leda said. "With Seth missing, too."

"Somebody needs to call the chickens the hell home."

They watched as Susan left the room, then came back with another magazine. In a little while, Hannah came downstairs and joined Susan at the table. Susan put down the magazine, and the two of them started talking. Rather, Hannah seemed to be the one talking; Susan mainly listened. Then Susan got up and found some cookies in a cabinet and poured two glasses of milk and sat back down. They ate the cookies, even Hannah, who ate five (Leda counted), and drank the milk and talked some more.

"You still love her, don't you?" Leda said.

"I've never loved anyone else," Brian said. Then he smiled. It was a feeble smile, a sad smile, and it reminded Leda of another night, a long time ago, when she had seen just such a smile on Brian's face. It was at the end of one of his parties, and she had walked into the room where all around him people were passed out on furniture and under furniture. Strange women, empty beer cans, half-empty glasses reeking of bourbon, open pizza boxes, spilled chips, puddles of ginger ale, ashes. Little Feat was on the stereo, Brian was playing some other tune on his guitar, and Daniel was asleep in a chair. She shook his shoulder, but he only groaned and turned over. Brian looked up. He looked around the room and seemed surprised to discover that the two of them were the only ones still up. He stopped playing his guitar. "You aren't leaving are you?"

"It's late, Brian," she had said.

"Don't go, Leda."

"We have to."

"Please don't go."

She shook Daniel again, and that's when she saw him smile. "Won't anybody stay up with me?"

THIRTY

DANIEL

Daniel was certain that, if he slept at all, it was not for long. He had been conscious of the whole night's passing, from the time of the deafening scritch-scratching of tree frogs, to when the forest settled into a deep-night silence, interrupted only by unidentifiable rustlings and the thumps of tree limbs falling to the ground. Even when he dozed, he remained conscious of where he was, alert to the noises outside the tent, aware that he was sleeping on the ground and that the ground was hard. Sharp pains in his shoulders or hips jolted him awake each time he drifted to sleep. He kept thinking about the people all through the centuries who had slept on the ground, and he worried over whether he should consider himself inadequate, not up to the task of simple survival, a casualty of an evolutionary downturn.

When he gave up actively trying to sleep, he studied the face of his son. Andy was sleeping like a person who had never contemplated horror, which, Daniel had just learned, was untrue. Truly, he had not been serious when, after dinner, he had asked Andy to think of the most horrible thing that could happen to a person. He had been thinking about returning to his novel and was considering, in a theoretical way only, the possibility of spicing it up with some more violence, and though he did not imagine Andy would come up with anything more serious than a brussels sprout pizza or farting in public, he had asked for Andy's opinion because they had run out of things to say. Andy had not hesitated. "Being skinned alive while hanging by your hands to the branch of a tree on one end and your feet staked to the ground on the other. Then, I guess, having boiling water poured on you."

"What?"

"You'd probably either be passed out or dead by the time they got to the boiling water, though."

"You've thought about this?"

"Not too much."

Then Andy had fallen into the sleep of the innocent, leaving Daniel to contend with an image he could have done without. So no one could have been happier when the birds started chirping, signaling that morning was near. He felt as if he had been holding his breath all night, and now he could let it out, and he breathed deeply and waited for the first sign of light. When it came, he was asleep, and Andy had to wake him up.

Daniel could hardly walk. He thought he could manage his stiff back and sore thigh muscles; what worried him were his knees, and he made a mental list of what to bring next time besides a flashlight: pain medicine and whiskey. And coffee. Just as with the flashlight, he knew without looking he had forgotten to pack any, but he searched through the backpacks anyway. No coffee, only instant oatmeal, but they could not spare the water to cook it, so for breakfast they tore off rubbery pieces of greasy cheese and ate them with broken crackers. Everything was damp. Daniel sat on a fallen log and felt the wetness seep through his pants.

"Chilly this morning," he said to Andy, who was sitting on the ground, shivering.

Andy nodded.

"But fun anyway, right? Are you having fun?"

"It's great, Dad."

"We should have done this a long time ago."

Andy nodded vigorously. Then he said, "Do you think we might ought to go home sometime today?"

"Do you want to go home?"

"If you do."

Daniel imagined himself explaining it later. *We were going to stay longer, but Andy wanted to go home. I had no choice; you know kids these days. They can't live more than a day without their PlayStations.* In no time, he believed it and was railing in his mind about how modern culture had corrupted his kids. It was true! He could fight all he wanted, but he could not defeat such a powerful adversary. He imagined himself standing on the stage of the Flying Dog, reading a poem about the youth of America being sucked into a self-destructive dream (a sticky-sweet, caramel dream, no doubt). He imagined the faces of the audience, forced to examine their lives by his words, stunned by his ability to nail truth. When he realized Andy was staring at him, he nodded and agreed that yes, maybe they should go on home.

Daniel studied the map. Clearly the fastest way home was the way they had come, but when he thought about climbing back up the mountain they had walked down, he doubted he could do it with a full pack on his back. He eyed the backpack. By now Andy had rolled up the tent; ditto for the sleeping bag; there was only the matter of tying them all together and moving out. Andy slipped his on and stood, bouncing up and down on his toes to keep warm. Daniel picked up a canteen and slung it over his shoulder. "You know, Andy, there's two kinds of people in the world, the kind that believe material possessions will make them happy and the kind who know there's more to life than what you own."

"Are you just going to leave it all here?"

Daniel started up the trail. "We can buy more."

"The tent? The sleeping bags? What about your pack?"

"It takes mental discipline to let go of things, Andy. I believe there's something about this in Buddhism. We should read more about it when we get home."

"But the camp stove. What about the camp stove?"

Daniel was wincing now with every step and could barely speak and walk at the same time. He stopped and wiped the sweat off his forehead. "You can carry it if you want."

He did.

It took them six hours to walk three miles. When they reached the car, Daniel threw himself across the backseat and closed his eyes. Andy ran to the public restrooms beside the parking lot and filled up the canteens and brought them back to his dad. Daniel reached out with a shaking hand and drank one of them empty.

"Do you want more?"

Daniel shook his head. "Let's go home."

They drove all the way to Pigeon Forge before Daniel thought to call Leda. He was expecting her to be mad, but not so mad she could not speak.

"Andy's fine, really, Leda. Better than me."

Leda did not answer.

"I can barely walk."

She still would not say anything.

"Okay, okay, we're coming home now."

He could hear her breathing.

"Don't be like this, Leda. I swear to God, I'll never do it again. We'll be home in an hour and a half."

Still nothing.

"Jesus. An hour, okay? I'll drive fast."

"Daniel."

"What?"

"Brian is dead."

THIRTY-ONE

DANIEL

In that last second, what did he know? What did he see? Did he see it coming? Did he know or see anything? The questions drove Daniel crazy.

Was the last second a slow plunge into darkness, or did the lights just snap off? Was there an instant to say, *No, wait*? Was there time to *do something*? To regret? Or was there simply driving on a road at night, then nothing? Driving on a road at night, then . . .

Did it hurt? For how long? Or was it quicker than that? Did he know he was dead?

Daniel felt like a child. I mean, come *on,* he told himself; the questions were old when Hamlet asked them. He believed, truly, that people had been dying for tens of thousands of years; they should be better at it by now.

But he wasn't. No, he was not good at it at all, and he wasn't going to be either. Hundreds of pictures of Brian flashed through his brain, and even when he tried, he could not make them stop. Brian with his catcher's glove, stealing home, striking out, Brian walking from the dugout with his helmet in his hands, Brian walking to the mound. Brian in high school holding hands with Susan, with a sketchpad on his knee, sliding a record album out of a sleeve, raising his hand in class, making a joke. Brian creek-hopping, shouting poetry from the top of a mountain, Brian walking through the tables at the

Flying Dog, flipping pizza, frying mushrooms, cooking peppers, making muffins, slicing cheesecake. Brian in a car, Brian grinning, Brian laughing, Brian drinking beer, drinking whiskey, drinking gin, Brian yelling at the umps, Brian playing guitar, playing guitar like nobody else. *Brian! Where the fuck are you, man?*

He screamed it as he walked around the house of Georgia the DJ, who had taken him home. Under the fleece blankets on Georgia's bed, he shouted Brian's name. It was while he was under there, he remembered Andy, stubborn little Andy who, at the age of four, had come up with a word for the end of numbers. Ananna, he had called it. Precocious counter that he was, he could make it all the way to three hundred, and when he finished counting, he would declare that the numbers went on in similar sequence until Ananna. But his equally stubborn and precocious sister, who understood the concept of infinity, would not leave him alone. *What's Ananna plus one?* she would ask. And, oh, Daniel could see it now, Andy crossing his arms, fixing his face in an unmovable glare, preparing himself to deny the evidence. It was a breathtaking thing to watch.

THIRTY-TWO

LEDA

The stupid thing about it, what Daniel would not quit talking about, was that Brian had been sober. It was something he never got over, the fact that Brian was hardly ever sober, that he had driven drunk a thousand times before and lived, that this time, *this one time,* it was the *other* guy who was drunk. The irony was unbearable. It was not, however, the only unbearable thing. What was left forever unsaid was that Brian would not have been driving home on Raccoon Road at that particular time in the middle of the night if Daniel had not run off to the woods with Andy without telling anybody. Leda counted hundreds of times she could have mentioned it, but she never did.

Seth came back in time for the funeral. Susan did not ask how he got the news about his father's death, but, clearly, there was at least one formerly clueless friend who suddenly remembered where he had gone. Austin, Texas. Brian had been right. He looked thin and scruffy, his chin spotted with uneven patches of orange hair, as if he were trying to grow a beard, but no beard would grow. To Susan's surprise, he did not return to Austin but stayed in Knoxville, moving into his dad's old apartment and taking over the running of the Flying Dog with some unexpected help from Georgia, who took it as her calling to make sure the Flying Dog restaurant, bar, and radio station lived on forever. Georgia arranged for Daniel to have a regular evening of poetry readings. They decided on Tuesdays. But that was later.

How is Daniel? How really? Whenever anyone asked Leda, she ran through the possibilities in her mind:

    A. Insane.
    B. One egg short of a carton.
    C. Out of his fucking mind.

   Daniel had gone from Brian's funeral to Georgia's house, and that was two days ago, and he had not come home yet. When Merle asked about him, Leda did not feel like telling her the truth.

   "He'll be fine," she said.

   She could tell Merle suspected something was amiss, but she got away with it because Merle operated on the premise that, if it's not been said, it's not been done. Merle's leg had turned out to be broken and not just sprained, and on this particular morning Leda had brought over some food. They had plenty. Susan had given her several days' worth left over from all the meals dropped off by members of her church, who were bypassing protocol (as if there could be such a thing) and treating her like a widow (which, Leda decided, she might as well be). Merle's cast started at her foot and went all the way up to the middle of her thigh. She was lying on the sofa with her leg propped up on pillows, flipping through new brochures of Florida.

   "You don't want to move to Florida," Leda told her.

   "It's warm down there."

   "It's hot down there."

   "That's why they have air-conditioning."

   "But Merle, you'd be a Gator. I can't believe you'd even consider it."

   "I would not be no Gator. I'd be a great big burr in a Gator's behind, is what I'd be."

   "All right, but I don't believe for one minute that Arliss would ever leave this place."

   "Better not blink then."

   Leda turned to the sacks she had placed on the kitchen counter and began taking out the food. Lemon chicken, pasta salad, and a marinated broccoli-and-cauliflower mixture; she had tried to select food items Merle might turn up her nose at, but would at least eat. Leda found herself too nauseated to eat. All she had been able to force down since the news of Brian's death was a handful of saltine crackers, but, oddly, she could not cry. Susan, who was generally stronger than she needed to be, had fallen apart, but Leda could not make herself cry, even when she wanted to, not at the funeral, not after the funeral, not a single tear. Her hands, however, shook. She made room for the food in the refrigerator and folded the sacks and stood for a moment, holding her arms over the sink, watching her hands shake. She looked up in time to see Merle shifting positions on the couch, her face wincing in pain.

"Where'd you put those pain pills the doctor gave you?"

"I ain't taking no pills."

"There's no reason for you to lie here in pain, Merle."

"I got a made-up mind."

"At least let me help you."

Merle was attempting to scoot down on the couch, but by the time Leda got over to help, she had already done it, so Leda fluffed up the pillows and repositioned them behind her head. Merle asked for the TV remote but did not turn it on. Instead, she closed her eyes. Leda sat down in a nearby chair. Soon she could not tell if Merle was asleep or awake. "I thought I'd walk up to the barn to check on that calf Brian and I delivered," she whispered. "Will you be all right here by yourself?"

Merle opened her eyes. "He's dead."

Leda sighed. "The calf, Merle. Not Brian."

"That's what I said. Starved to death. Arliss found him this morning. All's he could figure is, the poor thing's been sucking air this whole time, but with the commotion going on around here, he didn't catch it until it was too late."

Leda tried to remember, but she was almost positive she and Brian had stayed in the barnlot with the calf and his mother for a long time. Long enough anyway, and after that, hadn't they stayed outside by the cemetery for even longer? Surely they would have heard if something had been wrong. Before she could stop herself, she was sobbing.

"It weren't your calf," Merle said from her post on the sofa.

Leda shook her head. She was embarrassed and covered her face with her hands.

"It was Arliss's dime," Merle said.

Leda could not stop crying.

"You want a cookie?"

When still she did not stop, Merle muttered, "If you'd eat more of them, maybe you wouldn't be so tenderhearted."

Leda did not expect Arliss to say anything about the calf when she joined him later in the hayfield, but she wished he would. She guessed what he was thinking, that if *she* had taken Merle to the hospital, and *he* had stayed with Lucille, none of this would have happened; the calf would have lived, and Brian, too, more than likely. She vowed to argue with him if he said as much as one word, because she believed she had done everything Arliss would have done, and the calf would have died anyway. As for Brian? Well, you never know. You just don't.

But Arliss said nothing. There was hay to cut, and while he drove the big tractor pulling the haybine, she followed on the little tractor, fluffing it up with a rented tedder. Tomorrow they would come back over the field to rake then bale the hay in round bales, which they would leave sitting on the ground. They worked fast against the threat of an afternoon thunderstorm, the darkening skies reminding Leda of springtimes past when they had hurried against the weather. It felt good to hurry, because it's hard to think too much when you're in a hurry, and when, right in front of you, there's something real to worry about, like not getting the hay put up in time, or like lightning. But it was the familiarity that calmed her down more than anything else, the idea that she had seen these same dark skies and done this same work before, and both would be there for her again. She took comfort in the fact that, no matter who dies or whose husband leaves, certain things don't change. Children still need you, and hay needs cutting.

When they were done, she and Arliss parked the tractors in the driveway next to the barn to hose them off. Arliss went down to check on Merle, and when he got back, his face looked grim.

"She's still hurting, isn't she?" Leda said. "I think she ought to be taking those pain pills."

Arliss picked up a hose. "Well, she thinks you ought to go to church."

Leda stared at him. Anybody else, and she might have been aggravated, but this was Arliss, who kept his distance and expected other people to keep theirs, so she was puzzled but also surprised to find she was not sorry he said it. So many years she had spent avoiding the subject with Merle, who bombarded her with hints like religious spitballs, because, what could she say that Merle would hear? On the subject of religion, there was only one possibility in Merle's thinking, and a mind that closed cannot listen. Leda saw no reason to hurt her feelings, either, but it made her weary, thinking about all the times she had kept her mouth shut. The fact that Arliss kept his thoughts to himself signaled to Leda a person who was willing to consider other opinions, even if he did not agree with them, and the proof was in the way he treated his cows, changing his assumptions about this one or that one, depending on the evidence presented to him. Such, she believed, was not the behavior of a close-minded man, and more than once she had wondered if she could just be honest with him if ever the subject of religion came up, which, until now, it never had. For a minute, she even considered telling him what it had been like to be sixteen and to have her eyes opened to the ferocity with which so many different people, with so many different ideas, believed, absolutely, that they were the ones who were right. And how hard it had been, loving, as she did, the bells at Christmas, the way sunlight came through the stained glass, and the music (and, oh, what music!), to say, from some deep place in her heart, *I can't do this anymore.* Well, she thought, there was no need to go into all of that. But now that Arliss had given her the opportunity, she was determined not to stay silent, and she said something. "You know, Arliss, people can't just *decide* to believe something."

But Arliss was not listening to her. His attention was diverted by the sight of Bob's car coming up the driveway. Bob was alone, and he got out of the car and walked into the house.

Leda turned off the water. "You ever wonder what he's up to?" she asked. She said it offhandedly, not expecting a response.

"No."

Quick and emphatic was his answer, and it startled her. For one instant, his eyes met hers then he looked away. There was something there. She could not say it was anything so specific as a shadow that passed over his face, but something did. He was lying. And Leda had the odd sensation that she was with somebody she did not know nearly as well as she thought she did.

THIRTY-THREE

ARLISS

Arliss liked the young man. His granddaddy had grown up with Ted Minton over there in Clinton, and his mother was some relation to the Tennants, who had moved out of Loyston at the same time, and for the same reason, his family had left New Hope, but mostly he liked him because he was clean-cut and respectful, which can take you a long way. Farther than brains, in Arliss's opinion. He wore slacks and a yellow golf shirt. It had been a puzzle to Arliss why the young man seemed always to be wearing a yellow shirt, as if yellow were a uniform, and now, when he looked closely, he could see the name of the man's company, NEW HORIZONS, embroidered on the chest pocket, so, in a way, it was. On his feet he wore a kind of work boot, which said something to Arliss. It made a difference to him, if you knew what kind of footwear to wear on a farm.

Arliss had waited the entire summer before he let him come out again, and together they walked the whole place one more time. They walked out of the barn to the creek, then followed the south fence, passing the tin-roof shed where several heifers were keeping cool. They crossed the pasture and circled the pond. There had been a drought since the first of July, and the water was down, and the grass was dry and meager. He had been thinking about bringing in some round bales early just to keep the cows going, but maybe he would not have to do that now. They climbed to the top of the north ridge and followed the fence by the edge of the woods and stopped beside a bluebird box.

"You going to take down all the fences?" Arliss asked.

The young man nodded. "I don't see any other way to do it."

Arliss sighed. "It's something to see them come spring."

"Excuse me?"

"The bluebirds. In the spring." He studied the patient face of the young man in the yellow shirt. He could not decide if he were being indulged. "Nothing," he said.

When they got back to the house, Merle, who was cast-free but still walking with a limp, served them lemonade from a carton and Oreos with orange centers. When the young man commented that he had never seen orange Oreos, Merle explained that they were made for Halloween, but that Carr's kept a stock of them all year. "Now your true Vol fan will buy both the orange and the white and alternate them," she said. "Come see me over at Carr's Big Orange, and I'll give you a whole package."

"I'll do it," he said.

"On the house."

While Merle gave the young man directions to Carr's Big Orange, Arliss looked out the window and discovered that the brush against the stone wall between the graveyard and the dirt road had not been cut. He could not believe he had missed it! It was one of the places around the farm he could get to only with the small push-mower, and he had thought he had taken care of it the day before. He was tempted to go out there and mow it right now. He wondered if the young man had noticed. Probably. In contrast, the other three sides of the wall were trimmed nicely. It almost made him sick to think about how polite the young man had been not to mention it.

Behind him at the kitchen table, Merle was extracting information about the young man's parents, and where he went to church, and where he had gone to school, and if he had a girlfriend. Arliss excused himself and went outside and stood on the porch. It was cool for August, and in the sky an enormous white cloud had crested the ridge. There was rain in the air, he was sure of it. Over in the driveway next door he could see Leda and the kids packing the car to go down to Chattanooga for a few days to see her father. She waved when she saw him standing there, and he waved in answer, but his attention drifted back to the ridge. He did not do it often, but every now and then he indulged himself with a daydream. He imagined that he saw his sister Rosemary on fire and running down the hill. He saw himself running into the house and grabbing the quilt off his parents' bed and running back out to meet her. He ran fast and tackled her to the ground and rolled her in the quilt and squelched the flames. He saved her.

The cows were up there on the top of the ridge, searching for fresher grass, and the sight of them, looking tiny against the huge cloud that hung in the air above them, brought him out of his daydream. He wondered how long he had to mow that brush before it rained.

When he went back inside, the young man was asking, "You don't happen to carry those watermelon rind pickles down there, do you?"

"Only two dozen jars. We got pickled okra, too; you like that?"

"Yes, ma'am, I do, but I'm crazy about watermelon rind. I can't tell you how long I've been searching for them, down in Georgia, South Carolina, places like that. I don't know why I never thought to look for them around here. My grandma used to make them herself."

"Come get you some then."

"I sure will." He took a sip of the lemonade then turned to Arliss. "You don't have anybody who would want to keep the farm going, do you?"

"No."

THIRTY-FOUR

LEDA

Andy struck a sideways pose with his hands clasped around a bat high above his shoulder and one leg stuck out straight. "Who's this?"

"Andres Galleraga," Leda said.

He switched to a seated position, the bat still high. "Who's this?"

"Jeff Bagwell."

"Okay, how about this?" He straightened himself out and cocked his elbow three times.

"Ken Griffey, Jr."

They were in the side yard next to the driveway, where Brian had built Andy a pitching mound in the spring before he died. He had built the mound up with dirt and mulch and stacked a wall of square bales against the house for Andy to pitch into. On the ground, he had anchored a hub cap for home plate. Finally, he had spray-painted a red square on the hay, outlining the strike zone. From inside the house, you could hear the thwump, thwump, thwump, thwump of a ball hitting the hay until the bucket of baseballs was empty, then there would be a pause while Andy picked up the balls, before you would hear it start again. It was all Andy wanted to do anymore. All summer, Leda had tried to interest him in swimming, but he did not want to go swimming. She had tried to find him friends, but he did not want friends either. She would be glad when school started, so he would have something else to do.

That morning they had returned from Chattanooga, where Leda had gone to tell her father that Daniel had left. She had waited all summer to tell him, halfway hoping, if she waited long enough, she might not have to. But Daniel was still at Georgia's, and he was not coming home. She had not mentioned Georgia, exactly, when she explained the situation to her father. "He doesn't want to be married anymore" was the best rationale she could come up with, but her father seemed to understand that.

She had expected him to be surprised.

She had also expected him to suggest she move back to Chattanooga, and he did not disappoint her there, although *move home* was the way he put it.

The first thing Andy had wanted to do when he got out of the car was to show her his pitching. It was the last thing she felt like doing, but she had gone anyway. She sat on an old railroad tie step to watch, and now he was making her play this game.

"Who's this?"

"Chipper Jones."

"This?"

She sighed. "I don't know, Andy."

"Tony Batista."

Hannah was inside. Later she would go over to Carr's Big Orange, where Merle had given her a summer job, unpacking boxes and stacking shelves. At home she was reading the works of Aleksandr Solzhenitsyn and several books on the Cultural Revolution in China. (As she explained to her mother, "I'm taking notes on what happens when a state thinks it's okay to tell its people what to say.")

When Andy ran out of batters to imitate and resumed pitching, Leda rested her back against the step behind her. Something seemed odd. She had felt it since they'd been home, but could not put her finger on what it might be. Over the summer, many of the houses across the street had been finished, and, every day it seemed, new lawns were planted and mailboxes erected. Tricycles had appeared and swing sets, then the shouts of strange children and the barking of dogs. Maybe it was the sounds that were different, she thought. Maybe she was not used to the new way things sounded.

She stood and walked up the steps to the dirt road. She followed it all the way to the barn and looked around. She opened a gate and started through the pasture. By the time she got to the pond, she was running; all the way up the ridge she ran, to the top, where she craned her neck and looked everywhere. Then she looked again to make sure. The cows were gone.

THIRTY-FIVE

LEDA

"Okay," Leda said to Susan. "So what would you do if you knew you were going to die in twenty-four hours?"

"You mean a last meal kind of thing? I would have to think about it."

"I expected you would."

Leda had come along with Susan on a job to pull weeds out of a huge flower garden, established for a man who had wanted to reduce the size of his lawn so he would have less grass to cut. More weeds, less grass; Susan called it even. Leda was just glad to get away from the farm. It made no sense to work there when, just yesterday, she had discovered, first, the cows were gone, and, second, that Arliss and Merle had left for Florida. Florida! Bob had paid for them to fly down there to look over a new retirement community he had recently invested in. Leda knew for certain that Arliss had never in his life been on an airplane.

"My last day on Earth would have to involve running," Susan said.

"Of course."

"A long run. My last long run. How romantic."

"How exhausting."

"I would run to somewhere beautiful, like a mountaintop or alongside an ocean, and I think—I'm not absolutely sure of this—but I think, I would want to be alone."

"I wouldn't care so much where I was," Leda said. She had her camera with her, and she told Susan to hold still while she snapped a picture of some knotweed in the periwinkle. Then she put down the camera, and sighed. "That's not true. I'd want to be at home there on the farm. I would want Hannah and Andy with me, and I would hold them, all day if they would let me, and since it's my fantasy, they would have to let me, right? I would tell them to remember." She paused, as if to think about what she had just said. "I guess that's it, just remember."

"Well. You're a better woman than I am."

"I'm guessing Daniel would say he would spend his last day having sex, but I'm not sure it would be with me."

"Ha!"

"You know, Susan, I might could half stand it if she weren't named for a state."

"He's a jerk, Leda."

"You have no idea. And Georgia, oh my gosh, she had the nerve to tell Hannah she had prayed about all of this."

"If you say she got Daniel to pray with her, I'm throwing up."

Leda shook her head. "No, but listen to this; Hannah did not budge. Hannah stood there and asked, right to her face, if God had told her it was okay to sleep with a married man."

Susan smiled. "Hannah's going to be okay, you know that?"

"I'm working on it."

When Leda got home that afternoon, she found Bob's car in the driveway. She was not surprised. She had called him immediately after discovering the cows missing and demanded to know what was going on and where was Arliss? He had told her Arliss and Merle were in Florida, but about the rest, he would call her back. She did not take it as a good sign that he was here now, as if the news he carried needed to be delivered in person. Leda stood in the driveway for a minute. Whatever Bob was going to tell her, she did not want to hear, did not want to know, did not want to allow. That was it; she would not allow it! She needed something she could say no to right now. Needed to draw a line. Needed to put her foot down.

Instead, she panicked and ran up to the graveyard, then left toward the barn—*no, not that way!* The other way, toward the woods and halfway up the ridge, she ran until she fell down in the leaves and hugged her knees to her chest and breathed like a locomotive building steam, forcing her tears to stay put. When she was sure she was not going to cry, she eased up on the breathing.

The farm looked different now without the cows, and it smelled different, but she could not decide if it had really changed, or if her mind were making things up based, not on what she could see, smell, and hear, but on what she knew. All summer she had asked Arliss what he planned to do with the farm when he could not work it anymore, and all summer he had told her he did not know. Over and over she had promised; if only he would trust her, she would keep the developers away from it. Whatever it took, she would do. Because all around them, the land was going fast. She had seen vast tracts of it, cleared of all its trees, not just the scrap trees, the brush trees, the trees that could be replaced in a few years, but the dogwoods and red buds and even the big old oaks and poplars and hickory trees that had been there since before there was a Bearpen Lane. The only value that seemed to matter was money, not animal habitat, not where food might come from or how wholesome it might be, not oxygen, not community, not science, not balance, not beauty, not peace. People were ripping up the farms and forests like children on a sugar high, like ants working furiously on a venture they cannot see and do not understand. She knew smart people who could spit out good reasons for all this development, but as far as she could tell, most of them concerned an economy of the moment. When she closed her eyes she imagined herself a hundred years from now looking down on a ravaged earth with new people who would not quit asking, *Whose idea was this?*

But when she started digging into what it was going to take for her to keep her promise to Arliss, she ran into a stunning piece of information. She discovered that the county's zoning laws effectively encouraged development with no regard for conservation. Conservation was not even on the table. It had made her feel stupid and helpless, as if someone had snuck something past her. How had she not known the strength of the forces lined up against her? It reminded her of the morning the log cabin had burned, when she had gotten a glimpse of a reality bigger than she had known before, when she had seen that, all the while she was busy living, *other things were going on.* She believed she might never get over the fact that two people could look at the same piece of land and want something so very different for it. People like Bob, who were not bad people, but who seemed to want to turn every single piece of vacant land into a place for human structure. There was something about it that felt inevitable, like the one-directional arrow of entropy, only some people called it progress, and some people called it insane.

Assuming all this would be striking news to everyone, she had called the newspaper in town to see about running a series of articles on the disappearing farmland in east Tennessee, but no one there was interested. She had more luck with the alternative weekly newspaper, where Susan knew people. The editor there had told her, if she wrote it, he would print it. And she might. Someday. Right now she was too angry. It was old anger; she would concede that much, the rage of a child who has lost her mother and has to learn, too early, that life is not fair. But was rage going to make it fair, suddenly, once-and-for-all, a world blooming with fairness?

No. She remembered a long-ago night when Daniel had been railing against some injustice and Brian had stopped him. Anger only cancels your credibility, he had said, but Daniel had argued, "What if I'm right?" She knew what he felt like. And she realized that she did not know the answer to that question anymore.

Now what she wanted to know was how long before it would not be possible to drive along a narrow road and see round bales sitting in a field. To hear the echo of crows calling from a distant tree in a nearly empty landscape. To see the flash of a deer tail disappearing into the woods or a group of them grazing in a meadow at dusk. To look across a valley of uninterrupted trees or to see the veils of autumn sunlight streaming through their branches. To smell cut hay or fresh manure or animal hide or rotting logs or dusky woods. To listen to the wind. To listen to the songs from a hundred birds. She realized there was a great deal about her argument that was illogical, because her particular memory placed her in a car, for heaven's sake, and certainly there was a time, equally lamented, before there were roads, before there were even plows. She could not help it. All she could hope for was to put her finger on this page, and say, *Stop here.*

She walked back down the hill and entered the house through the screen door. Hannah was there, standing in the middle of the living room talking to Bob and his wife, Tina, who were both sitting on the couch. Daniel was there, too, standing by himself in a corner of the room. Leda did not see him when she first walked in, but felt her heart speed up the instant she did. She hardly saw him anymore, only when he came to pick up the kids, and he rarely got out of the car then. He showed up at random times to take them out to eat or to the movies or to the lake (Georgia had a boat!). After one such occasion, they brought back a box half full of Krispy Kreme doughnuts and laid it on the kitchen table without comment. Leda had stared at it for a while, then crumpled it up, doughnuts and all, and threw it in the garbage. Daniel looked thinner than he used to, but he'd had a recent haircut, and he had shaved, and his clothes were clean. He had lost the gaunt face of a person who's not eating, which had been his condition in the days and weeks right after Brian was killed. Friends had even remarked to Leda about how worried they had been about him, and how much better he looked now. (Not to worry, Georgia was nursing him back to his old self, and who was going to say she didn't have her hands full! Leda was tempted to call her on the telephone. *Good luck, sweetheart!*)

As soon as Leda walked in, Hannah turned and stomped past her out the door. Tina almost stood up, but Bob rose first, and something in a glance from him made her sit back down. She smiled at Leda and said, "I was just telling her she ought not to make such a big deal out of this Pledge of Allegiance business. As I tried to explain, she needs to think of her future. She'll be up for National Honor Society this year, and before she knows it, she'll be deciding on a college. Think of the teacher recommendations she will need!

Believe me, Leda; I've been here with my girls, and I know what I'm talking about. She does not want to get on the wrong side of her teachers. This little tiff of hers is simply not worth it. I tried to tell her, but she is so stubborn."

Bob was smiling and shaking his head. "She is her daddy's daughter."

"No," Leda said, deliberately avoiding Daniel's eyes. "She's her mother's." She crossed her arms. "Okay, Bob, tell me. He's already sold the farm, hasn't he?"

Bob did not flinch or duck or hide his eyes, but held her steady stare, and she appreciated that. "They haven't closed the deal, but yes," he said. "For all practical purposes."

"I don't know why he couldn't have told me himself."

"Sit down."

"I don't want to sit down."

He put his hands in his pockets. "I could tell you he's a mean old bastard. I could say that he is incapable of thinking about anybody but himself, or that he has the communication skills of a fence post, or that he's trying to swindle you in some way, and some of it might be true, and some of it might not. The real answer is, I don't know. But I can tell you what I think. I think he might have been afraid that you would talk him out of it. And of all the people in the world, you maybe could have. That's why I didn't tell you. Besides the fact that, you know, it isn't your farm."

She sat down. "So what's going to happen to it?"

"Well, I think you will be pleased by the result, Leda, because, as you may know, the real enemy here would be a trailer park. These plans call for a very nice subdivision, and not like the one across the street on the Pitts' property, either. Tasteful. Acre lots. Strict building restrictions so nobody can go berserk on us. The models are all done in a clapboard farmhouse style, modernized, of course, but in such a way as to keep your house from sticking out. I can show you pictures if you'd like. I've told the developer to go ahead and bulldoze Mom and Dad's house because, hey, there's nothing there worth saving. But a couple of coats of paint, and Belle's House will blend right in."

"It hasn't been Belle's for fifty years, Bob. It's our house."

"I really hope, Leda, you will not judge it before you see it."

"I would have left it alone. I would have let it grow back the way it was."

"That is the one thing he would never have let you do."

"You don't know."

Bob looked at Daniel, who looked at the floor. "The thing you have to remember about Dad," he said, "is that he single-handedly wrestled this sorry piece of land into the farm you see around you. It took a lot out of him. Even I don't know how much, but I know he lost his sister."

"I know that."

"And his father. And some uncle who supposedly hung himself rather than move away from New Hope."

"Exactly. Don't you see? Arliss was forced off of one farm already; I cannot believe you would do it to him again."

"Be careful you don't romanticize the past, Leda. There was nothing romantic about New Hope. Those people were starving; they were barely making it, some of them weren't making it. TVA was the best thing that ever happened to them, I'd bet my life on it."

"You're on."

"And you don't know what you're talking about."

"I'm telling you, Arliss won't stand for his land being torn up, especially not for a subdivision, even if he does lose his mind entirely and move to Florida."

"Better developed than fallow; that's how he feels about it. It would kill him to think all his work had been for nothing. All those deaths. Put some houses on it, move some families in there, at least it will continue to be of some use, and that means something to Dad. If it's not useful, it's not worth anything."

Leda noticed that Daniel was nodding in agreement. She said, "Use? Are you crazy? If you want to talk about use, I know a fox who might have something to say."

"I don't think you understand my father, Leda."

"She never has," Daniel said.

Leda looked at him. "Now all of a sudden you're agreeing with him?"

Daniel for once seemed unable to think of something to say. "I told Andy I'd meet him outside," he whispered.

They watched him leave. His absence had the effect of making them lose track of where they were in the conversation, and for a few minutes, neither Bob nor Leda said anything. Leda looked at the floor. Bob looked out the window. Then Leda started to say something, but Bob, whose spectacular patience was slipping like a mask, interrupted her. "It's hard for me to believe you didn't see this coming, Leda. I mean, what did you think was going on out here, everywhere, all around you, for years? Haven't you noticed? This place is booming. It's a happening part of town. Did you think you'd be able to keep this tiny piece of land exactly like it is forever, all to yourself, like some island out here in the middle of a growing community?"

"Yes."

She said it just like that, and Bob stopped talking. He looked as if he had more to say, but didn't. Leda continued. "I could keep on growing hay, if I had to. If they want to see farm income, I could do it. We've already got an acre of timothy for the horse people, and I've been working on the figures to expand that operation. I've also looked into growing grapes. How does your own stash of homemade wine sound? There are other options, Bob, if you would just give me a chance."

There was in the room an uncomfortable shift. Leda felt it. She saw when Bob and Tina looked at each other. Then Bob cleared his throat and said, "Dad's going to give the house to Daniel, Leda."

She stared at him, then at Tina, who was smoothing her skirt over her knees and looking at the floor. It took a few minutes for her to understand what he was saying, but before she could respond, he said, "Of course, you guys might not split up after all; I mean, we all know Daniel. He's about as grounded as a dog on wheels. As far as I know, the two of you could stay right here forever. Anything can happen."

———

Leda did not get up when Bob and Tina left. She sat listening to the sounds of Andy throwing the baseball and Daniel talking to him. She found herself hoping that Daniel was liking what he saw in Andy's pitching ability. Andy had been working hard over the summer, but she did not know how to judge. In her mind, everything Andy did was terrific, but she had said it so often that Andy got irritated when he heard it. He did not necessarily believe her.

After a while, Leda stood up. She walked out the back door, up to the dirt road, and over to the barn. It was cool in there and quiet. Dust was thick in the ribbons of sunlight crisscrossing the barn. She went over to the little tractor and climbed up. All the times she had worried about the danger of thrown rocks, would she miss that? She remembered how much she hated having to cover her mouth and nose with a bandanna to keep out the clouds of dust and insects that would envelop her head, but it did not make her feel any better. She bounced up and down on the seat. She loved scooting over the pasture on this little tractor, the sun on her skin, the wind in her face. What she would say to Arliss when she got hold of him! She had gone over and over it in her mind, listing the crimes he had committed, selling the farm without telling her first. She had practiced it so many times, it was starting to sound like a speech.

She was startled out of her thoughts by the sound of someone pulling into the driveway, and, when she looked, saw it was Arliss and Merle. She got down off the tractor and walked out of the barn, where she stood at the top of the hill to watch them. Merle shimmied herself out of the truck then stood in the driveway tugging at her dress. Arliss carefully shut the door and walked around to the back of the truck, where he began untying the ropes that held their suitcases. When Leda started down the hill, Merle saw her first and waved. Then Arliss looked up.

"There's not enough room in them itty-bitty seats to fit a squirrel," Merle was saying, as Leda came closer. Her hairdo, which showed the marks of having worn tiny curlers the night before, had not survived the trip. It was sticking out on one side, but the back was mashed flat. "On top of that, they make you wear them silly seat belts! I say, if you want to take your chances, it's none of their business. I told that girl, 'What are you trying to do, choke me to death?' but she wouldn't listen to a word I said. I asked her, 'What's a seat belt going to help if the plane falls out of the sky?' And you know what she had the nerve to say to me? 'We're not taking off until you buckle it.' Shitfire and a cat's ass, she didn't have to be so snippy about it, did she, Arliss?"

Arliss had not moved. He was standing behind the truck with a suitcase in each hand. His wrinkled neck was too small for his shirt collar, and his sleeves nearly covered his hands, which made him look like a comic book character who had shrunk in his own clothes. His face was pale, but that could have been the result of breathing stale airplane air. Arliss had never been the kind of man who spent any length of time indoors; it was bound to have an effect on him.

Merle was saying, "When I told that girl his ears was a'hurting, she had the nerve to tell him to chew gum. What kind of fool did she think I was? Chew gum, my foot. 'We don't have no gum,' I told her, but I think she was a Yankee. Them people are raised mean. But we ain't doing that again, right, Arliss? We're getting in our truck and we're driving down to Florida on our own four wheels, and, I'll tell you one thing right now. We ain't never coming back."

Arliss looked frozen, as if he did not know whether to put the suitcases back on the truck, or set them on the ground, or carry them into the house, and because he could not decide, he just stood there.

"Y'all are going to have to come down and see us, now," Merle was saying. "There's an orange tree right outside our patio. I'll be able to reach up and pick me an orange right off the branch without getting out of my chair. They got oranges and grapefruit both down there, don't they, Arliss?"

Arliss had set his eyes on some unidentifiable point in the truck bed and did not take them off.

"We met a lady down there from Kingsport, who's going to be living right down the hall from us; now if that ain't a small world, I don't know what is. Vols fans, don't you know. She and her husband play bridge, and the two of them promised to teach me and Arliss as soon as we get settled in."

Leda tried to imagine Arliss playing bridge. She had not forgotten a single word of the speech she had practiced, but the man in front of her right this minute looked like somebody who'd been through a hurricane and lost everything he ever owned, and, instead of the speech, she was remembering a list. *Don't look them in the eye. Don't hurry them. Try to see what they might be seeing. Watch for signs of illness. Remember that a cow fears anything it does not understand.* She decided she would not know where to begin. "It sounds nice, Merle," was all she said. Then she turned around and walked back up the hill.

THIRTY-SIX

LEDA

Leda put the photograph albums in a box. She did not think he would notice they were gone, but her books were different. Daniel assumed all the books in the house were his, but she had books of her own, and she put every single one in boxes. Of the photographs that hung on the wall, she took the ones of the farm she had taken over the years, plus the family portraits, mostly school pictures of Hannah and Andy that, when placed side by side, memorialized the history of their teeth. She left only one. It was a picture of her and Daniel and the kids one summer at the beach. She felt certain that Georgia would take it down, but she wanted her to have to.

Next she packed the dinnerware. Plates, bowls, glasses, and silverware, her grandmother's china, her grandmother's silver. If Daniel missed the patterns, the blue and green leaf design that circled the plates they ate on every day, for instance, he would have to keep it to himself. Georgia would bring her own dishes. As for the glasses, there was a motley collection, three or four of one style, two or three of another, and one or two of still others, representing the survivors of nearly two decades of accidents, but she doubted he would miss them. Georgia probably had a matching set.

She carried the boxes to her car. Some of the men who worked for Susan would bring a truck for the big things, furniture, beds, even the refrigerator; Daniel was being remarkably unpicky about what she took with her. Her father had offered her the house she had grown up in, her grandmother's house, which was too big for one man by himself anyway, if she would move home, but Chattanooga was not her home anymore, and it never had been her children's home. So he bought her a house instead, a small one she had found in Susan's neighborhood near the end of a dead-end street lined with thick old trees, and even though it was not far from downtown, it was quieter than the farm. Bearpen Lane was getting to be a busy place now, with new subdivisions breaking ground down the entire length of it, and all the activity over on Glen Pike, the fast-food restaurants and sit-down restaurants with clever names and gas stations and movie theaters and home improvement stores and home furnishing stores and office supply stores and real estate offices and bank branches and copying stores and eyeglasses stores and shoe stores and dry cleaners and newly-widened roads already jammed with traffic. Even the horse farm with the white fences and the house you could not see from the road was a strip mall now. Downtown was practically a refuge by comparison.

When she could fit no more boxes in her car and was ready to leave, she spied Crazy Fish's bowl sitting on the floor in the corner of the living room. She smiled, thinking first about his tricks, then remembering how she had cared for him, and what a survivor he had been. The glass bowl was cloudy with a sticky film of dust, and she took it to the sink and washed it with soap and warm water until it was clear again and squeaked when she rubbed her fingers against it. She took it outside and placed it on the front seat of her car, remembering the last time it had ridden on the front seat of her car, next to Crazy Fish himself in his locked-tight Tupperware container filled with water, the day they had moved to Belle's House. What a terrible day that had been, but she was not thinking about all that now. She was remembering her neighbor Mrs. Grable. Leda thought about how she had watched for the old woman that whole day as they loaded the U-haul, expecting her to emerge any minute, to get in the way and bombard her with gruesome stories of her family's health problems. She had readied an arsenal of excuses for why she could not stand there and listen, but Mrs. Grable never came out. More than once Leda had been sure she saw the lace curtains part, then quickly close. Standing in the driveway after Daniel and the kids had driven away, Leda could not decide if she should say good-bye. She remembered thinking how much easier it would be if Mrs. Grable would just come on out. *Follow the script, for heaven's sake,* she had thought. *Play the pesky neighbor one last time!* She walked toward the front door of the old lady's house and rang the bell but heard nothing, no hint of movement from inside the house. She knocked on the door, thinking the bell might be broken, but still nothing. Twice more she tried, then she and Crazy Fish drove away. It was one of those things in her past that had always bothered her, that she had not shown more kindness to Mrs. Grable.

Then again, she did not know why she had to dredge up every little stupid thing she'd ever done. She changed her mind. She picked the fishbowl back up from the seat and shut the car door.

She was supposed to drive straight from the house to the ballpark where Andy was playing, but his game did not start for another twenty minutes, so she started walking up the ridge. Just as she reached the top, she saw the fox. It ran out of the woods and headed away from her across the field, so most of what she saw was its tail, but it had to be a fox. It did not run like a dog, and it did not run exactly like a cat either, and there was nothing else it could be. Then, just before it reached the woods on the other side of the field, it stopped, and she knew. Leda could not believe it, but there it was, stopping and turning to look at her. She had already frozen still, but it froze, too, and sat down on his haunches the way a dog would, but she could see even better now how very much it was, clearly, not a dog. It was skinnier than she would have imagined, skinny like a weasel, and it gave her chills to see it looking right at her. She did not know if she should be frightened. She knew that the time she and the fox stared at each other was no more than a few seconds, but it seemed longer, like an impossibly long time, really, and when it darted away into the woods, she was sorry but knew she had no right to be. After all, who else got even a few seconds?

There were people who would not believe her, who would tell her foxes don't behave that way; she knew it, and that was fine. She would not claim to know much about foxes, so it was hard to know one way or another. She could not swear she would believe her either.

She turned around and walked back to the edge of the woods where the fox had come from and, there, she found what she was looking for. A tiny cedar tree. Using a trowel she had retrieved from the screened porch, she dug around it, careful not to cut its roots, then lifted the whole thing from the ground and placed it in the fishbowl. She would take the sapling to her new house and plant it in the backyard and see what happened. She looked down at the dirt on her hands. She wiped her hands on her shorts and picked up the fishbowl and walked to the edge of the ridge, where she sat down in the grass one last time.

So, how was she? People kept asking. Not that good, really. She was not good at all. *How the hell should I be?* was what she wanted to say, and yet.

And yet. The truth was, there were times when she was, really, okay. She would look around and realize she did not feel sad or even angry. She could not say she was happy, but she was not unhappy either. She was working a little for Susan, and the series of articles she had written on land development had gotten her a job writing part-time for the alternative newspaper as well, so she had work to do. She liked the little house her father had bought her and did not mind that he had spent the money. Moving had meant that Hannah was enrolled at another high school, which seemed to be having a positive effect. She would not claim that Hannah was happy, exactly, but happier, maybe? As for the farm on Bearpen Lane, well . . .

She looked around. Bulldozers had already carved a road straight up the middle of the field where hay had grown every year for as long as she could remember. Soon it would be the entrance to Bearpen Place, and she would not recognize it anymore. Arliss and Merle's house was leveled and gone, and there was nothing left of the barn but a stack of old sun-bleached lumber. Leda figured the graveyard was next. Plans had been made for the remains to be moved to the

Baptist church, but with Arliss and Merle down in Florida, who was going to visit them there? The bluebird boxes were still on the fence, but not for long. Even the fences would be gone soon, and the woods behind them, cleared. Trails that had crossed them since Daniel and Brian were children would be buried under new lawns. She could not imagine what it was going to look like, but for certain, nothing like the place she knew. Daniel had quit his job at the university and was going to keep the house, and with Georgia's money, the two of them could stay there forever if they wanted. But, surrounded by other houses, it would not be the same house, would not have the same feel, the same play of light through the windows, the same sounds or smells. It was true that she would miss the farm, but what she missed did not exist anymore.

But there was no way she could sit there and pretend there weren't plenty of people who, simply, were not all that torn up about what was happening to the farmland on Bearpen Lane. Just the other day at Kroger she had run into Lloyd Pitt's wife, who had talked about how good it made her feel to see all the families enjoying their new homes on her old farm. She told Leda she had been sorry her own children had not grown up in a neighborhood with other children, and when Leda mentioned that, Yes, well, maybe, but it sure wasn't as pretty anymore, Mrs. Pitt had said, "Well, you can't blame the farmers. That land's all we got for our retirement." So it was complicated. That did not mean it was right or that she had to like it, but she would not deny the complexity. Then Mrs. Pitt had reached out and touched her sleeve.

"You remember the cherry trees that used to line our driveway?"

"Yes," Leda had said. "I do."

But was memory enough? She thought about all the photographs she had taken of the farm and wanted to laugh. The answer was no. But it was something. She closed her eyes and rested a hand on the fishbowl beside her, remembering the summer Crazy Fish died, when she had lost her house, her job, even her dignity. Days followed summer days with no hope, then hope appeared. Arliss came to the door, *(Can you help me for a minute?)* and changed her life.

It was times like this, when she was not happy but not unhappy either, that she felt sorry for Daniel. Because he had come so close to finding a way to make sense of his life. Then he balked.

Susan was sitting in the bleachers when Leda got to the ballpark. Andy was on a new team this spring, and Leda saw that the opposing team that afternoon was the one he'd played on in the spring. She recognized the coach, Con's dad. In the short time she had been there, she'd heard him yell at his third baseman, his first baseman, his catcher, the umpire, and Andy's coach, even though his team was up six to two in the third inning. "Does that guy always yell?" Susan asked, when Leda sat down.

"Yes. Has Andy pitched yet?"

"Not yet."

But halfway through the next inning, with the score now eight to two, the bases loaded, and no outs, they saw him run to the mound. Leda's elation held while he threw his practice pitches, but it disappeared when she turned and saw who was waiting in the batter's box. Con, who, if he had not grown three inches over the summer, was clearly wearing heels.

So nobody was surprised, least of all Leda, when Con murdered the first pitch, a solid hit that soared over the left fielder then landed foul. Leda could hear the people in the stands.

From the parents on her side: *If that ball stays fair . . .*

From the parents on the opposing bleachers: *Do it again, Con; straighten it out next time.*

The confidence that her son would mess up was overwhelming, but Leda watched Andy, who did not look where the ball went. He never took his eyes off Con. The next pitch was low, and the next, inside (although Leda would like to know by how much), but the fourth flew fast and dead center over the plate, and Con did not move. Con's dad was on his feet, yelling something about eyeglasses, but it was too late. Strike two.

Con fouled off the next two pitches, until Andy threw another ball, this one low again, and the count moved to three and two. His teammates were cheering for him, but not hysterically. This was not a game-winning moment (and in fact, his team would go on to lose the game nine to six), although they could have used this out right now. No one but Leda knew what this moment might mean to Andy. She held her breath. Another foul. Then Andy threw a fastball, once again across the plate, but this time a little to the inside corner, and Con swung hard, and his hips turned, and his arms straightened, and when the bat came around, it turned his body with it and knocked him off his footing, and there was the sound of the ball hitting the catcher's mitt. Strike three.

Andy did not pump his fist in the air. He did not shout or cheer or taunt. He did not point with his thumbs up to his cheering team-mates. He did not search the stands for his mother. He did not grin at his coach, who was shouting, "Attaboy!" He reached up and adjusted the bill of his cap a quarter inch, no more, which could have been an acknowledgment to the crowd, but just as well could have been, sim-ply, the adjusting of a hat. Then he came set to face the next batter.

No one scored on him that inning. He struck out the next batter for two outs then forced a pop-up for the third, and while he was running to the dugout, Leda turned to Susan. "Do you remember when Crazy Fish died?" she asked.

"No."

"You don't remember?"

"I really don't."

"But you do remember Crazy Fish, don't you."

Susan shook her head no.

"Well," she said. "I do."

ACKNOWLEDGMENTS

Harvest would not have been written if not for Gay Morton, teacher, poet, naturalist, farmer, and friend, who fought a good fight. It would not have been completed without the help, advice, and expertise of Jane Pearce, also farmer, writer, and friend. I am especially indebted to Ted Nelson, of the Tennessee Valley Authority, who generously gave me his time and access to original reports from 1930's era TVA relocation workers. Similarly am I grateful to Kirsten Benson, of the University of Tennessee, for her time and willingness to open her classroom to me. Thank you, Anne Bridges, also of UT, for Sut Lovingood and for assisting me with the cover photograph. Thanks to her cohort, Rod Jones, for his disc-wizardry. For the photograph itself, I thank TVA's Pat Ezzell for her help and for her beautiful book *TVA Photography: Thirty Years of Life in the Tennessee Valley,* and Mrs. Gail Wilson Knoll for giving me permission to use the work of her father, Marshall Wilson. For bleacher banter (and all those laughs), I thank the "Smoke Moms," especially Susan McLemore. For his hard-to-believe-but-true stories, I thank my uncle Raymond (Rangfoo) Walker. For their wisdom and critical eyes, I am indebted especially to my über-editor and mom, Charlotte, and to Brenda Rasch, Pat Hudson, and Mary Smith. For support beyond the call, I thank Duff Bruce.

I am most grateful to my agent, Henry Dunow, for his diligence, expertise, honesty, and steadfast belief in me and this book.

Many good people at St. Martin's Press have worked hard for *Harvest* and for me, especially my editor, Carin Siegfried, who skillfully guided the process with encouragement, good sense, humor, and patience. I am beholden also to George Witte, Thomas Dunne, Sara Schwager, Kevin Sweeney, Shea Kornblum, and Stephen Lee.

More than words I owe my family, especially my father, Charles Francis Landis, Jr., for the depth of his love and because he is, and has always been, my moral compass. Charlotte Walker Landis, my mother, my soul mate. My big-hearted brother, Charles. Bruce Jr. and Charlie, my sons, my heroes. My husband, Bruce, for everything and for always.

Sources I read in preparation for writing *Harvest*:

TVA and the Dispossessed, by Michael J. McDonald and John Muldowny, The University of Tennessee Press, Knoxville, TN, 1982

Tennessee Valley Authority: Reservoir Family Removal Section, Norris area, Knoxville, TVA, September 1, 1937

Valley of Vision: The TVA Years, by Martha E. Munzer, Alfred A. Knopf, 1969

Sut Lovingood's Nat'ral Born Yarnspinner: Essays on George Washington Harris, edited by James C. Caron and M. Thomas Inge, University of Alabama Press, Tuscaloosa, Alabama, 1996

Sut Lovingood's Yarns, edited for the modern reader by M. Thomas Inge, College and University Press, New Haven, 1966

The Story of a Farm Boy's Life, by Buford Smith, New Hope Press, Dothan, Alabama, 1991